I can't imagine Mum's face when I tell her.
When I start to explain what I've done . . .
and why I had to do it.

My phone starts to flash with a silent incoming call.
The S.O.S. I was desperate for.

'What's happened?' he asks. I thought there'd be
comfort in his voice but no, it makes it real,
makes it terrifying.

'He's at my flat,' I whisper.

'I think I killed him.'

Also by

DOROTHY
KOOMSON

DOROTHY KOOMSON

all my lies are true

REVIEW

First published in 2020 by Headline Review
An imprint of HEADLINE PUBLISHING GROUP

First published in paperback in 2021 by Headline Review
An imprint of HEADLINE PUBLISHING GROUP

1

Cataloguing in Publication Data is available from the British Library

ISBN 978 1 4722 6042 0

Typeset in Times LT Std 10.25/15pt by Jouve (UK), Milton Keynes

Printed and bound in Great Britain by Clays Ltd, Elcograf S.p.A.

MIX
Paper from
responsible sources
FSC® C104740

Headline's policy is to use papers that are natural, renewable and recyclable
products and made from wood grown in well-managed forests and other
controlled sources. The logging and manufacturing processes are expected
to conform to the environmental regulations of the country of origin.

HEADLINE PUBLISHING GROUP
An Hachette UK Company
Carmelite House
50 Victoria Embankment
London EC4Y 0DZ

www.headline.co.uk
www.hachette.co.uk

Dear Lovely Readers

When I finished writing *All My Lies Are True*, my sixteenth novel, it was November 2019. The world wasn't in a brilliant state to be honest, but most of us were muddling through and hoping for something better in 2020.

Who knew that 2020 would turn out to be the year that threw us the biggest curveball in my living memory? Certainly not me, which is why *All My Lies Are True* unfolds ten years after we said goodbye to Ice Cream Girls Poppy and Serena in 2010. When I was typing those words, I really wasn't expecting for us to spend a portion of the year confined to our homes, for A-Levels to be cancelled, for spending time together to be considered a highly dangerous activity.

So, I'm writing you this note to say: when you read about Serena and Poppy, and their friends and families doing 'normal' stuff like going to work, revising for exams, living it up at parties or turning up at a hospital, please bear in mind that it was created at a time when the social physicality of the world was as we'd always known it to be. All the situations, emotions and crimes I write about are rooted in reality and are based on real people's experiences, but they play out on a made-up background. And this book's background is a little bit more made up than my previous novels.

I sincerely hope that *All My Lies Are True* brings a welcome reminder of what our lives were like before a pandemic altered everything; and I really and truly hope you enjoy the book.

With the best of wishes

Dorothy Koomson
April 2020

For G & E

Part 1

Part 1

The Ice Cream Girls?!
What happened next?!

Posted by: Nia Burkinshaw   3 Comments
Last updated: 12 January

Does anyone remember the so-called Ice Cream Girls? They were accused of killing their teacher? They were having an affair with him? Does anyone remember that?! My mum has been asking me for ages if I can find out about them on the internet and ask you all on here.

Most of you would have been too young, like me, but Mum really remembers them and thinks about them all the time. Apparently they treated him really badly and then they killed him at his house. Their names were Serena Gorringe and Poppy Carlisle. They were in London and this was in the eighties. Do you remember this picture of them? The one in the polka-dot bikini is Serena, the one in the blue one-piece is Poppy.

Mum says the trial seemed to go on for ever but only Poppy went to prison. Serena got away with it. They both kind of ghosted everyone until a few years ago when Poppy came out of prison (I was only six!! then). Mum says she thinks she heard that Poppy might have ended up in Brighton because that's where the other Carlisles had moved to.

Mum also says that everyone at the time thought Serena changed her name? I've had a look and I think the Gorringes all still live in London but there's no mention of Serena anywhere.

Mum would be really interested to hear if anyone knows what happened to them?? She was really, really fascinated by the story, because they were like the evil superstars of her time and it kind of just ended when Poppy went to prison. Mum also says she thought when Poppy got out again that she might find Serena and they'd go on a murderous hunt together again, but nothing. (BTW – Mum said that, not me!!)

If you could ask your mums and dads about it on the off-chance that someone might have heard or seen anything, that'd be well cool. DM me, or drop me a line or leave a comment below. Kisses.

#TheIceCreamGirls #PoppyCarlisle #SerenaGorringe #London #Brighton #murder #teacher

Share **Like** **Repost**

<Previous Post Next Post>

Leave a comment
3 comments

Kat Allen 14 January at 09.45 a.m.
I think I'm probably your mum's age because I remember them! Every now and again I wonder what happened and where they ended up. Be fascinating to find out.

Lucie Craft 15 January at 11.45 p.m.

Just read up on this story! I'm in between your age and your mum's but I think I remember this. It is brilliant. Love to find out more.

Elenee G 16 January at 10.38 p.m.

I'm your mum's age, also. One of them looks so much like a woman whose daughter used to go to my son's school. The Serena Ice Cream Girl. Her daughter was called something like Variety or Verity, something like that. She had a son, too – I can't remember his name. Wouldn't it be a mad coincidence if it was her? I'm sure she was called Serena or something beginning with S. Her surname definitely began with a G because ours does and they were near each other on the register. I'll ask my son when I speak to him next if he remembers them. Will keep you updated.

verity

Now

'Well, look and see who is here,' he says right beside me.

Frowning because I'm not sure how it's possible for him to be here right now, I turn towards the sound of his voice. I can't believe it! 'What are you doing here?' I ask, unable to hide my delight.

Automatically, I look around to check there's no one to see us together. Then I glance down at my phone in my hand, check its screen is black and it hasn't accidentally dialled anyone or isn't live-streaming this chance meeting. Just to be sure, I press the side button and wait for my phone to ask if I'm sure I want to turn it off. *Yes, yes, I'm sure,* I think. *I don't want you telling on me.*

'What are you doing here?' I ask him again.

'I've come to visit my freaky toys,' he replies.

We're standing in the entrance of the Hove Museum. On the first floor of this historic building in the posh part of Hove, there is a toy museum full of the creepiest things I've ever seen. Porcelain dolls with chipped and peeling faces sit in glass cabinets with threadbare, faded teddy bears resting beside them, all of them staring out at us humans as though begging to be released. Along a narrow corridor, which is flanked on each side with cases of other old, spooky toys that I'm still convinced come to life when you're not looking, is a slightly larger area with dilapidated games and odd books that you're allowed to touch. As if to add to the creep factor, from a speaker that sounds like it's attached to an ancient wind-up gramophone, a story is read over and over about someone who doesn't want to go to school. I love this place. Since I was tiny this and Hove Library were the two places I always begged my mum to bring me to visit.

'Are you really here to visit the freaky toys?' I ask him.

'Yeah, of course! They're like my best friends. When I was little, I would go on and on at my mother until she brought me here. What about you?'

'Same. I used to pretend they were actually my toys that were being stored in this attic in a haunted house—'

'—where time's stood still,' he finishes with a laugh. 'I can't believe there's another person on Earth who understands the true beauty of this place.'

'Me, too! How come we've never talked about this?'

'Yeah, not the sort of thing I tell people, to be honest.' He glances around, checking again there is no one watching us, no one who would recognise us and tell the wrong person they've seen us together. 'I can honestly say until this moment I've never met anyone who has understood it. Until you. And speaking honestly now, I've always been a bit dubious about you cos you're a bit on the dodgy side, but this discovery has shown me that you have real potential, little one, real potential.'

'I can't believe the amount of cheek that just came out of your mouth. I'm not sure I'll be able to forgive it.'

'Oh, shush. Come on, are you going up? We can do the tour properly. I've never been around with someone who appreciates it before.'

'Me neither.'

Without saying anything, I hold up my phone, double-check he's turned his off, too. He fishes his out of his back pocket and shows me that, yes, it's off and no one will be finding out about us that way.

'Freaky dolls first?' he asks as we walk single file down the narrow corridor to the clunky old lift.

'No, ghost mirror first.'

'Ghost mirror it is.'

The moment the lift doors shut we're all over each other, kissing as though we haven't seen each other in years, necking like we're not going to see each other in just a few hours. We step apart the moment the lift bumps itself onto the first floor, then fix our faces and straighten our clothing as the doors clunk open.

'I love you, Verity Gillmare,' he whispers into my hair before I step out into the corridor.

'And I love you, Logan Carlisle.'

verity

'Don't forget the popcorn, Vee!' my brother, Conrad, called from his place in front of the television. He was getting ready for his friends to come over and I was obliging by grabbing him some supplies while I nipped to the shops. 'Giant bags of it, OK?'

Our parents had driven up to London to visit my grandma and I was staying over to look after Con. He was sixteen and loved the fact that I slept over to 'look after' him. Mainly because he got to stay at home in Brighton when Mum and Dad went away, and because he knew he could do whatever he liked except hurt anyone, get arrested or get anyone pregnant. There were other things on the list, sure, but those were the three biggies.

I slept in my old room which the 'rentals had kindly redecorated so it was a proper grown-up spare room that I loved to chill out in. I was convinced Mum did it so I'd move back in, but Dad had been clear when they'd helped me with my flat deposit – no takey-backsies. In other words, once you've left, you stay left. Visits are fine, nice, encouraged – but two nights were all he'd put up with.

I shouted 'OK' to my brother then shut the front door behind me, just as a man with dark-blond hair opened the creaky metal gate and stepped onto the black-and-white tiles of the garden path. He was at least ten years older than me and wasn't dressed like a postie or a delivery driver; he also wasn't carrying a clipboard or wearing a lanyard. He had a physique and way of holding himself that made his tan-coloured chinos, cream shirt and black jacket look extra expensive and ultra delicious.

'Hello,' he began, sounding pleasant enough.

'Hi,' I replied cautiously. Just because he didn't have a clipboard on display didn't mean he wasn't someone intending to sweet-talk me into signing up for a home-cooking box that I'd never properly use or giving more to charity when a significant portion of my wages went that way already. 'Can't stop, just on my way out.' I had never sounded so *breezy*. I high-fived myself in my head for managing to be so detached and cool and busy.

'No worries,' he replied. 'I was looking for Serena Gorringe.' His eyes raked over me in a quick, efficient fashion. 'From your age, I'd say you're not her.'

That stopped me in my tracks. No one used Mum's maiden name any more. Obviously Grandma was still a Gorringe, as was Aunty Faye, but not Mum.

'I'll just knock,' he said.

'She's not in,' I said, giving him my full attention and stepping into his path so he didn't have easy access to the front door. 'Neither's her husband, my dad,' I added for good measure. I wanted him to know that Mum was married.

'Typical me,' he said, sounding dejected. 'It took me so long to work up the courage to come here and now she's not in. Great.' He flopped his arms up and down in frustration. 'I'm not sure I'll get the courage up again.'

'You sound like you're going to propose to my mum or something,' I told him. 'Like she's the great love of your life and this is all you've lived for.'

He didn't say anything to that. And his silence ignited a series of sick feelings all along the bottom of my stomach. I looked him over again. He was far too young for Mum but nine years earlier, she'd left us for nearly two weeks. She and Dad pretended like it never happened, but it was long enough for eight-year-old Conrad to notice, so obviously I knew. Was it for him? No, surely not. He was a good ten years younger than her. But what if he *was* the reason? What if she was involved with him and Dad found out and that was why he made her leave?

None of us ever talked about why Mum left. She was just gone – coming back daily to give us breakfast; then after school she was there to give us dinner and say goodnight. And then, after what seemed like a forever, she was back. And Mum and Dad were mostly fine and then they were overly fine and loved up, and we all acted as if it hadn't happened. Was he the culprit?

The man in front of me said nothing. And if he wasn't going to propose or something, wouldn't he say so? Wouldn't he be denying it?

'How do you know my mother?' I asked him with an edge to my voice. He'd hardly tell me on her doorstep if they had been sleeping together, but it was worth a try.

'I don't know her,' he said.

'What do you mean? In a "I never really knew her cos you never really know anyone" kind of way, or a "she's a complete stranger who I have a freaky connection to" kind of way?'

'Somewhere in between the two, I guess,' he said.

I glanced at the house, wondering when Conrad would see us

standing there and come out to find out what was going on. 'Too cryptic for me, sorry,' I said, an even bigger edge to my voice. 'Can you just speak your speak. Tell me what you want with my mum.'

The stranger seemed to grow very tall in those moments – he stood up in his frame and suddenly he was towering over me, his arms fastened across his chest in a tight hold and his face set so much like dried cement it was as if he'd never speak again. When he did eventually push words out of his pursed mouth, it was to say: 'I want to ask her to confess to murder.'

'What?' I replied. I couldn't have heard that right. 'What are you saying to me?'

'You heard me . . . I want her to confess to murdering a man called Marcus Halnsley so that my sister, Poppy, can finally clear her name.'

verity

Now

'I can't do this any more,' he says quietly. 'You know I love you, and it feels like I've been in love with you since for ever, but I can't do this secrecy stuff any more.'

We're lying flat on our backs on my bed staring at the ceiling. We've been like this for a while. I'd lain down here like this to hide from him while he dragged my vacuum cleaner around my flat like a recalcitrant donkey, violently fluffed every single cushion, and passive-aggressively wiped or dusted surfaces until they noisily squeaked their cleanliness. When he'd finished tidying up, he'd come in here to say something, changed his mind and lain down next to me, not speaking. We've been like this for twenty minutes, I think. And now he's speaking, he's saying this, even though it's impossible what he's asking.

'It used to be quite nice before, but now it's not working for me. We need to stop living like this and tell people about us. Our families, our friends. We're not doing anything wrong. I want to be able to hold your hand in public, go out wherever we want without worrying who'll see us. Hell, I want to invite you over for some shockingly bad food at Sunday lunch with my parents. I just want us to be a normal couple.'

I want that, too. Of course I do, but it's not that simple, is it? 'Logan—'

'I was thinking, just hear me out, I was thinking, if you casually invite me to your father's fiftieth birthday party in a few weeks, we can tell them in a low-key way then.'

'No, Logan. I can't do that. It's my dad's party. I can't hijack them like that. I'm sorry, no.'

'Just admit it, you don't want to tell anyone, do you? You just want me to stay your dirty little secret for ever.'

I imagine for a moment what it would be like if we step out of these shadows of secrecy into the bright, bright world of other people's scrutiny. Their faces, their reactions . . . 'Logan, just think of the fallout, how hurt everyone will be. I – we – really can't do that to them.'

'So you plan on us staying secret for ever?'

'Not for ever, just until . . . I don't know, I just need more time.'

'It's been a year!'

'It hasn't. Nowhere near. We've known each other a year but we haven't been together a year.'

'It's never going to be more than this, is it?' he says sadly. 'It's never going to be more than this undercover crap.' He's looking at me; I can feel his eyes on me, but I can't face him.

'That's not true,' I reply.

'I want more, Verity. I love you, and I want an end to this secrecy.'

'And if I don't want that just yet?'

'Well, that's it, then, isn't it?' he says with quiet finality. 'It's over.'

I turn to him then, and he is still staring at me.

'I don't want it to be over,' I declare. In my head it *is* a declaration, and the words sound brave and bold and decisive. But uttered into the air between us they sound scared and flimsy and pathetic.

This is how we end. I know it. Because I can't give him what he so desperately wants, this is how we end.

I'm not sure who moves first, who does it first, but we're suddenly kissing, crushing our lips together, attempting to make it not true. We're undressing each other, we're trying to hold on to each other tight enough to make it permanent, close enough to not let anything come in between. By the end we're both crying, both clinging, both trying to keep ourselves together. And afterwards, immediately afterwards, he is off the bed, angrily snatching up his clothes, furiously pulling them on. This is how we end but he let himself forget and indulge, and he is raging because of it.

'Are you going to tell?' I ask as I watch him get dressed. 'About us? Are you going to tell people?'

'So you can hate me for ever? Yeah, right. Properly screwed myself over there, didn't I?'

I sit up, desperate to stop him leaving like this. 'Look, let's just take a break. Give each other some space. Once my dad's party is out of the way, let's sit down and talk about it properly. In the meantime, let's give ourselves the chance to see that our lives don't work without the other one in it.'

He pauses in getting dressed and stands very still while he listens.

'All we need is a bit of space. Spend time apart, meet up to talk things through. Just not crowd each other. And then we'll try to sort it out.'

'You really want to do that?'

I nod vigorously. 'And in that time, too, we can think about how we tell everyone, if that's what we decide to do.'

'You'll really think about telling people?'

'Yes, I really will.'

I watch his shoulders fall; see him physically relax as the anger drains away. He returns to the bed, a happy, hopeful smile on his face.

I tip my face up to receive his kiss. I close my eyes as he presses his lips on my nose, my forehead, my cheeks.

'And can you think again about your dad's party? It really would be the perfect time to tell them.'

'Log—'

'Just think about it. Please? Please?'

'All right. I'll think about it.' Yes, I'll think about it. I'll also have to think about making sure the party doesn't happen, either; just in case Logan decides to turn up anyway.

verity

Now

Mum pulls back the light-blue curtain and steps out of her dressing room. I click the button on the side of my phone to make the screen black and hide the message I'd been halfway through typing and, just to be sure, I turn the phone face down on my lap.

Mum notices and her eyes linger a fraction too long on my phone, curious, as she's always been, about what I'm up to, but she doesn't say anything. Mum has always kept her eye on me, tried to find out what I'm doing without actually spying or snooping. Everything my mother has ever done has technically been upfront – she'll try to snatch a look at my phone rather than pick it up, she'll ask me who I was emailing or talking to rather than read behind my back or lurk around eavesdropping. She wants to know, but doesn't want to do what's necessary to find out.

She's odd like that. When I was younger it used to drive me crazy, not knowing when she'd finally cross the line – as far as I know, she never did – but knowing she wanted to. She was always watching me, noticing little things – I could almost see her mentally filing something away for later, asking in roundabout ways about snatched parts of my conversations that were almost always innocent. My brother, Con, didn't get it

18

anywhere near as bad, but to be fair to her she did it to him, too. Does it to him, too, probably. Cos he, poor kid, still lives at home. *Urgh, that wasn't very nice, was it, Verity?* When did I start getting so snarky about my mother?

Face down in my lap, my phone has the answer: bleep, bleep. Since him, of course. Since he told me the truth about her.

'What do you think?' Mum asks. She runs the palms of her hands down the front of the royal-blue dress, trying to smooth out the soft, silky creases that are created by the way the garment flows down over her body to her ankles.

'It's nice . . .' I say in what I hope is a diplomatic voice. She's looked better. The dress is nice and it clings to her curves in all the right places, it shimmers in the light and it looks expensive and stylish, but . . .

'But . . .?' she says. 'There is a "but", isn't there?'

How do I answer that without getting into trouble? 'Thing is, Mum . . .' I begin.

'Oh, don't worry, I know you hate it. I can tell by the look on your face. This was the best one.' She flops her arms up and down. 'I just want to look nice for once.'

'You always look nice,' I reply automatically.

'Wow, my daughter, you almost sounded like you meant that. Not!' she laughs as she returns to the dressing room, not giving me a chance to argue.

'Is that it with the dresses now?' I call hopefully.

The shop, cosseted right in the heart of The Lanes, is deserted on this Sunday lunchtime. The assistant stands at the other end of the shop, leaning against the counter, examining her rather impressive rainbow-painted nails. She should really be chewing gum and checking her mobile to complete her 'disinterested, bored and was meant for better things' look.

'No, there's one more,' Mum replies.

I get up and edge nearer to the changing room. 'Why are you doing this, Mum?' I ask. 'You know Dad's going to hate it.' That isn't just me trying to kill the party, Dad will hate it.

'He won't,' is her muffled reply. I'm guessing she's taking some clothes off or putting clothes on.

'Have you actually met Dad?' I say to her.

'I've known him longer than you,' she states, her voice much more clear now that she obviously has the dress on.

'Well, Con and I might have a theory that would explain how that's not actually true because I've known him all of my life – you know, twenty-four years – which is actually one hundred per cent of my existence; while you've known him what, twenty-nine years? And that works out to be about . . . umm . . . sixty per cent of your life? One hundred outweighs sixty.'

Mum's reply is a big sigh. 'OK, you win. You've known him longer, but he will still want this. I promise you.'

Because it's what you want, I want to say to her. *Dad will say he wants it because you want it. And what you want, you get, no matter what, right?*

My body floods with red-hot shame. That was awful. Truly awful. I look around in case the shop assistant has approached and heard what I said inside my head, or anyone else with telepathic powers has wandered into the shop and is now disgusted at the awful thing I just thought about my mother.

Thankfully, the shop is still empty, the music pulsating from the speaker by the door thrumming out a constant, half-hearted beat.

I hang my head. *This can't go on*, I tell myself sternly. *You're going to have to tell her that you know. You're going to have to talk about it. Because if you keep thinking things like that . . . they're eventually going to come out of your mouth. Then it'll be too—*

Mum suddenly whips back the curtain, making me jump, step back and nearly trip over my feet. For a moment, from the look on her face it's clear she knows. She knows what I was thinking, she knows what I've been doing, and she knows that I'm probably the worst daughter a woman could possibly have.

'Are you all right?' she asks, watching me struggle to right myself.

'Erm, yeah, yeah,' I say. 'I mean, of . . .' My voice drains away when I properly see her. 'Wow, Mum,' I state. 'That dress looks amazing on you.'

She looks down at herself. 'Do you really think so?'

'Absolutely.'

She puts her arms around her waist, hiding the main part of the dress. It's elegant, a demure scooped neck, fitted bodice that eases down into a full skirt.

'I'm not sure,' she says.

I step aside to let her have full access to the looking glass behind me. She takes a tiny step forward so she is framed by the full-length, brass-edged mirror.

She does look incredibly beautiful in this dress. In this *yellow* dress.

She stares and stares at herself, and with every passing second I can see the anxiety, the fear, the spectre of yesteryear growing in her eyes.

I don't know why she picked it up. It's not like she's ever worn anything yellow over the years. We didn't have yellow clothes growing up, and we certainly never had anything yellow in the house. It's the sort of thing you only notice when you know.

She takes a step back as the horror starts to stain her face and sharpen her breathing. Maybe she thought she was ready. Maybe she thought she could handle it. Maybe this is something she's done many, many times over the years, only to realise when she's actually got it on that she can't be wearing a yellow dress.

'Are you OK?' I ask her.

She shakes her head, trying to release the past's hold on her, I guess. At the same time she says, 'Yeah, yes. I'm fine. I'm fine.' She steps back again, still fixed on her reflection. 'I, erm, would you be a love and see if there are any other colours of this, please, love?' she says without looking at me.

'Yeah, sure. Any particular colour?'

'I don't mind. I don't mind. Any.'

'Cool,' I say, and pocket my phone.

'But not pink,' she adds, just as I'm about to move away.

'Not pink,' I repeat. 'Got it.'

Like a lot of things with my mother, you only really understand why she does the things she does and avoids the things she does when you know the other thing about her.

You only really understand my mother when you know that she was once an Ice Cream Girl and on trial for murder.

March, 2019

This guy ordered double espresso in a teeny-tiny cup. He actually drank it, too. He didn't do what I usually did, which was order a drink and then let it sit there while it slowly went cold and end up remonstrating with myself for the waste of money.

The café I'd persuaded him to come to was small and wannabe

intimate. Unfortunately, there was something so dispassionate about its design – its wooden benches had just the right amount of cracks and whorls and uneven areas; the industrial, metal-topped stools and chairs were on the wrong side of comfortable; their crockery was faux vintage and, to be painfully cool, they mixed up the patterns and designs so your order was often served in a mishmash of styles – that it ended up coming across as clinical and cynical. The staff, who could probably have made the place welcoming despite its austere feel, could not look more disengaged with the whole process of serving coffee and dry, stale-tasting pastries.

'Can you start at the beginning?' I asked. I picked at a flake of almond that sat like a burnt fingernail on top of the miniature croissant I had paid £3.50 for. If Con were here, he'd have been calculating how much each bite cost and sniggering at my craziness in paying that much. I don't know why I bothered to buy it when my whole body was clenched so tight that swallowing saliva was difficult, let alone food. 'I mean, what you said is a whole universe of info to process and that was just two lines. So could you start at the beginning and tell me why you think my mother was involved in a murder and who this Poppy person is, besides your sister, and how she connects to my mum and, yeah . . . can you start at the beginning?'

He sighed heavily. 'What's your name, *Serena's* daughter?' he asked instead of starting at the beginning. His words were shot through with a snide, sinister venom that was like a snake's bite and it chased a smattering of goosebumps across my forearms and down the centre of my spine.

'Verity,' I replied. 'What's your name, Poppy's brother?' I didn't have the same poison in my voice, but there was enough of a tinge of it that would tell him how he sounded, and how unnecessary it was. It wasn't

23

like I'd called him a liar. In fact, I'd done the opposite by bringing him here and buying him expensive coffee and pastry.

He heard and understood what he'd done because his whole demeanour softened a fraction. 'Logan, my name is Logan Carlisle. Poppy is my sister. My big sister. And over thirty years ago, she went to prison for a crime that your mother committed. And I need your mother to confess to that so my sister can finally get on with her life as an innocent woman.'

I accidentally snapped the almond flake I had been playing with in half. 'You're very good at the big, dramatic statements, Mr Carlisle,' I said. 'I'm surprised there isn't a big, dramatic "duh-duh-duhhhhhhh" every time you open your mouth.' That wasn't fair, but it was true. Because come on. *Murder? My mother?*

'How much do you know about your mother's history?' he asked.

'She met my dad, she got pregnant, they got married. Had another child. Yes, they've tried to pass off my conception as a honeymoon thing, but come on, no one is that naïve.'

'Before that. Before she met your father.'

'Was there a before she met my father?' I wasn't being as facetious as I sounded – Mum and Dad acted as though nothing existed before they got together. And I never questioned that. Other people might internet search their parents, but I wasn't someone who needed to know that. I mean, I'd already partially worked out that Mum might have left nine years ago because of an affair. If that was the case, I didn't want to know because that would mean I'd have to judge her, and judge her pretty hard.

'Awww, I see you've had all the luxuries and privileges of ignorance. I couldn't ever get away from the fact that my sister was in prison and wasn't there when I grew up. She's still on licence so she can't even commit the pettiest of crimes because she'll be sent back to prison and forced to serve the rest of her life sentence. And I have to watch her tear herself apart every day because what happened to her in prison lives with her constantly.'

I had often contemplated things like that. What happened to the people who went to prison and came out? Not even the ones who claimed to be innocent, just those who walked out of the gates determined to never go back. Did they get on with their lives? Because how would that be possible? Everything you do would have your conviction history running through it like words through a stick of rock. Every official thing needed you to declare where you were, what you'd done, who you once were. How did you get on with your life when that history was always following you around? It was just a thought I had, though. Nothing I dwelt on. Nothing like this man was telling me; he had to more than dwell on it because his sister was living it.

And what about the long-lasting effect of his sibling's jail time on Logan Carlisle? Con and I used to fight all the time. I mean, it was practically expected that we would irritate each other so much it could take the plaque clean off the other's teeth, but what would he be like if I hadn't been around when he was growing up? Would he be doing what this man was doing and confronting the person he blamed for my predicament?

'You know, all of this would be so much easier if you started at the beginning,' I said, trying to be patient.

Ever so slightly he scrunched up his lips and the ripples of his jaw showed he was grinding his teeth together. Angry. He was angry. I wondered briefly what he would have done if he had spoken to Mum. Would he be behaving like this? Less angry? More righteous? Softer and more coaxing? I couldn't work out what this man's gameplay

25

would have been if he'd got his intended prey. And Mum would have been prey. The look in his eyes, the barely concealed contempt, the hint of a snarl around his mouth suggested she was someone he was desperate to get his hands on and rip apart.

'From what I know, it started in 1986. For Poppy, anyway. For Serena, your mother, it started before that. Marcus Halnsley was their teacher. He'd taught them history in separate schools and they both had an affair with him. It went on for a couple of years. And then the night they tried to leave him, he was killed. Stabbed.'

He was talking, saying words and I was listening to them. But my mind was also doing that multi-tasking thing and doing basic maths: 1986 would have meant my mum was fifteen or sixteen when she was . . . But if, as he said, it was earlier, that would mean fourteen. My mum was fourteen and she was sleeping with her teacher? My mum? This man, this Logan Carlisle, had clearly, obviously never met my mother. I was still partially convinced my parents had only had sex twice in their lives and those were the times my brother and I were conceived. There was no way . . . *No way.*

'Stabbed. He was stabbed through the heart. They both went on trial but my sister went to prison. Your mother got away with what she did.'

'Whoa there,' I said. He was older than me, but he felt very much like my age or even slightly younger. Definitely more naïve than me. How else would anyone say all that and expect the person they were saying it to to just accept it? 'I'm not saying what you've said isn't true, but could we slow down with the accusations and conclusions? I mean, if any of this happened, wouldn't I have heard about it? Any of it? Some of it?' I placed my hands palm down on the fake-vintage table. 'Like I said, I'm not saying it's not true. But at the moment, I literally only have your word for any of this. And you could be a complete fantasist, you could have the wrong Serena, you could be someone sent to wind me up.'

He glared at me, his nostrils flaring slightly as his gaze slid down his nose and slapped me. That's what it felt like, a slap from someone who felt nothing but contempt for the person in front of them. 'I was meant to be talking to your mother, and she'd obviously know that this is all true.' He sat back in his seat, the look on his face solidifying rather than dissipating after my challenge on his lack of proof. 'When I picked this up, I didn't think I'd need to do this, but you know, if I'd been allowed to be a Boy Scout, I'd have been pleased that I heeded the "be prepared" advice.'

He reached into the inside pocket of his jacket and pulled out his mobile phone. It had a large screen, the latest model. Shiny, new-looking. 'I've got the original at home. Obviously I don't carry it around. But I thought, you know what, let me take a photo of this, just in case.' As he spoke, he was working on the phone screen. 'Just in case I meet someone who doesn't believe me.' He practically slapped the phone down in front of me with an 'argue with that!' flourish.

It was a photo of a newspaper clipping.

And yeah, it could be doctored, altered, edited, but I knew it wasn't.

As small and blurred as that image was; as unremarkable as it looked in terms of high definition and pixel resolution on this shiny screen, I'd know her face anywhere.

She held an ice cream that made her look coy and coquettish, she had a tiny two-piece swimsuit that showed she had a body she was proud of, and she had the words, 'AS COLD AS ICE CREAM' above her photo, labelling her as what she really was.

My mother was an Ice Cream Girl, like he said. Did that mean he was right, too, about her being a killer?

poppy

Now

The sky isn't one type of blue. It never is. It is blue overlaid with blue, overlaid with azure and sapphire and teal and lapis. It is blue upon blue upon blue.

The sky is never simple, never one thing, never easy to define. The sky is there as a reflection of my life, something that at first looks clear and simple, but when you move closer, look a little bit deeper, there's always so much more.

'MumMumMumMum,' comes from the backseat.

'Yes, sweetheart?'

'Is Dad late, again . . . *again*?'

'Yes,' I reply through my teeth. I don't mean to grit them, but I can't help it. It's all right for him, he won't get the little digs and sideways looks about lunch being delayed because we're a nanosecond late; he'll get the red carpet treatment as usual. He can do no wrong since he's almost made a respectable woman out of me, so my parents won't care that he's – I look at the car clock and grit my teeth harder to stop the seethe – twenty minutes late. 'If he's much later, we'll have to go in without him.'

'But won't Grandma ask you why you can't support your husband for once and won't Grandpa nod in the background because he doesn't understand why you can't support your husband for once?' One thing my daughter is not, is unobservant. She picks up on everything, even the stuff I think no one has noticed or I believe has gone over her head, she'll bring up at a later date with her almost near-perfect recall and analysis of the situation. She has just described exactly what our Sunday lunches turn into. We could walk to my parents' house from our place, but we always drive because we need somewhere to hang around while we wait for Alain. I can't remember a time when he was on time for Sunday lunch.

'Yes, sweetheart, that's what will happen, but I don't want us to be sitting in the car for much longer.'

'It's fine, Mum, honestly,' my seven-year-old says. 'It's giving me a chance to catch up on my reading.'

I lower my head to hide the smile that takes over my face. She is so grown-up sometimes, her words so definitive, that I have to remind myself that she isn't even double digits in age yet.

A loud rapping at the window causes me to almost leap out of my seat, hands up ready for battle. I still jump at loud, sudden noises – more than the average person, I think. Alain opens the passenger-side door and gets in. 'How are my two favourite girls?' he says.

Once he's in place, I continue to stare out of the windscreen so I don't scowl at him. I'm aware of him, though. His hair is damp and freshly washed, I can smell the lavender and mint from his shampoo; his body is recently showered and towel-dried – he still has notes of the Dead Sea sulphur soap he uses wafting around him. And I can feel the heat radiating from him from where he's run to get here.

'Dad, you're late. It's not very polite to be late. At least that's what Grandma is going to say to Mum later.'

'Yeah, sorry about that,' Alain replies to our child while looking at me. 'I can't help it if her parents find me adorable.'

'You're not being very fair, you know, Dad,' our daughter continues to admonish. 'Mum gets us here on time, but she gets into trouble for you being late. That's not very fair.'

I know he is looking at me so I continue staring out of the windscreen. I have to stop myself glowering or giving any indication of the insurmountable rage that is building up inside. He always does this and it always winds me up and I always have to stop myself from letting out my frustrations because, more often than not, Betina is around.

'You're right, pumpkin, that's not very fair.' Alain loses the cheeky-chappy tone to his voice and sounds somewhere near regretful. He reaches out, slips his hand onto the back of my neck, carefully caressing away the tension. 'I'm sorry,' he says softly. 'I'm really sorry.'

I almost fall for it, almost allow my eyes to slip shut and my body to lean towards him while his hand works on releasing all the knots lined up in my neck and shoulders like the first row of a knitting project. *Almost* fall for it. I remind myself that this has never been the problem with us. The physical contact between us has never been an issue or something that isn't smooth and easy and every kind of pleasurable.

'Uh-huh,' I reply to his apology, leaning away from him and causing his hand to slip away. I've heard it all before. Just last Sunday, in fact.

'Come on, Small Stuff, grab your things,' I say. 'Let's go before we're even more late.'

June, 2012

'Poppy, what are you doing awake?' Alain asked.

I was sitting downstairs in his living room, wearing his dressing gown, with my legs pulled up in the armchair. The lights were out and I had been listening to the hum of various appliances thrumming through the house. I loved this place; it was big enough for a family, but cosy and intimate, too. I always felt as though the house liked having me here, that it relaxed when I was around, just like I felt able to breathe out in its four walls.

'Just thinking,' I whispered to him.

'Thinking about what? And can't it wait till morning?'

'Not sure I can stop thinking about something once it's in my head,' I replied.

'What is it you're thinking about?'

'I'm thinking . . . I'm thinking we've been together nearly two years. And I'm going to have to make a choice soon.'

'A choice about what?'

'I missed out on so much. When I was younger, before I met Marcus, I had plans. I wanted to travel. Go interrailing, maybe visit Australia.'

'You can still do that. We can do it together, if you want.'

'In theory, yes, but the reality is I have no cash and absolutely no will to do all the planning that it would take. But that wasn't the only thing I wanted to do. I wanted to . . . I wanted to get married and have a child. Or two. I keep thinking about Serena and how she's got it all sorted. She married a handsome doctor and she's got two kids. That could have been me. And I'm wondering if I need to start thinking about that now.'

I chanced a look at him then. I wasn't sure how he'd take this revelation. I was effectively saying we'd have to commit to each other or I'd move on.

Alain sat back on his haunches and stared at me very hard in the darkness of his living room. 'That sounds like an ultimatum,' he eventually said. His voice was subdued and his face seemed disappointed more than anything. 'We seem to have skipped from a discussion about the future to an ultimatum without actually having the initial conversation.'

'Fucking hell, Al! You know I don't dress things up. I don't do hinting. You know when I say something it's full on, unadorned. And you came down here and asked me what I was thinking, and I told you. Actually, I only told you a fraction of it.

'What I was thinking was: do I talk to you about having a baby or do I just leave? Do I even truly want a baby? Babies grow up and they become children. What if they turn out like me? What will I do? And then, I think, there's nothing wrong with me. Except I'm hugely gullible. As evidenced by the fact I let someone abuse me for years, and then, when I should have known better, I was essentially tricked by another man who I fell in love with and whose house I'm in.

'I met my best friend in the world when I was in prison and she isn't here any more because her burdens were too huge and the world wouldn't give her a chance. And sometimes I measure time by the last time I cut up, the last time I wanted to cut up, and occasionally even the last time I had the urge to cut up but managed to resist it. So, is having a child a good idea when that is my background, those are the broad and fine strokes of who I am?

'That's what I was thinking, *Alain*. I didn't invite you into my thoughts, you basically barged your way in and now you're feeling under siege because my unvarnished, unrefined feelings and mindscape are unpalatable.' I was getting more and more angry with each word. 'Do me a favour next time, Al, don't ask a question you're not ready to hear the answer to.'

Once the dust storm from the tornado of my angry words had

settled, and the room had returned to its dark peacefulness, Alain felt safe enough to speak. 'Sorry,' he said. 'Sorry. I panicked. No one has ever said that they're thinking of having a baby with me before.'

'You were married before.'

'Yes, and we, hand on heart, never once talked about having children. That should probably have been the first clue that we weren't going to last. My initial panic notwithstanding, do you really want a baby?'

'I don't know. I think so. But do women like me get to have babies?'

'Women like you?'

'Women who've been to prison.'

'I bet there are loads of prisoners with children. You must have met dozens of them inside.'

'Yes, but they had children before they went inside. They had life experience. I've kissed two men my entire life – and you're number two. Do women like me come out and then find a man who loves them and then go on to have children? I don't know. I've never seen it. Do women like that exist?'

'I'm sure they do.'

'And are they fucking up their children while they're doing it?'

'You won't fuck up our child.' Alain stopped moving and an awe-struck expression rapidly took over his face. 'That sounded pretty amazing. Our child. Wow.'

He stood up suddenly, took my hands in his and pulled me to my feet. 'Do you want to have a baby with me, Poppy?'

'I don't know,' I replied. 'It was just a thought.'

'Do you want to have a baby with me, Poppy?' he asked again.

'Maybe,' I replied.

'All right, I'm really hoping third time will be the charm . . . Do you want to have a baby with me, Poppy?'

I held my breath. Did I? With all the things that plagued this thought, all the worries that nibbled away at my peace of mind, did I really want to risk it all by doing this? I felt the house shift; it seemed to be holding its breath, waiting to find out what was going to happen next, too.

'Yes,' I replied. 'Yes, yes I do.'

Alain grinned, the house relaxed and I waited and waited for a flurry of panic to rise up and overtake me; I waited and waited and waited, but it didn't come.

Now

Mum opens the door and 'Betina!' she exclaims when she sees her granddaughter. The creases that give away my mother's years, the hardships and sorrows she's endured, *always* melt away when she sees my child. She seems to glow in her presence and I sometimes wonder if she ceases to exist when Betina isn't around because of how animated she becomes when we arrive.

I'm ninety-nine per cent certain that the only reason they put up with me is because of her. That extra one per cent is me clinging onto the idea that my parents do actually like me being around. I mean, it's because of me that Logan and Bella moved back to Brighton so they regularly see them, so I like to think the other one per cent is the credit they've given me for that.

'GRANDMA!' Betina shouts and throws herself at my mother, wrapping her arms around her and squeezing. The love and unrestrained admiration is mutual. Betina has no boundaries when it comes to sharing love with her family, she is open and giving all the time. After squeezing my mother to pieces, my daughter releases her and goes tearing into the house looking for Bella, Logan and my dad.

'Hi, Mum,' I say quietly. I can already feel the disapproval as it ripples itself onto her face like the tide as it washes over the pebbles at the very edge of the beach.

'Hello, Poppy.' *Twenty-five minutes, Poppy. Twenty-five minutes you've held us up for. Have you no respect for anyone but yourself?* That's what she's actually thinking while she says those two words.

'Mrs Carlisle,' begins Alain, Mr Charm himself. 'I must apologise. I was held up at my rugby game and I've made these two late. I'm so sorry, it's incredibly rude of me. I will endeavour to be on time next time.'

'Oh, A-Lun, what have I told you? It's been ten years now, you must call me "Ethnie" or "Mum". Either is fine. None of that "Mrs Carlisle" business any more, do you hear?'

'Yes, of course, sorry. And apologies, again, for my tardiness.'

'It really is no issue,' Mum tells him. 'We're starting a bit later today, anyway. This has given us the chance to have a little *a-pair-of-teeth*.'

Aperitif, Mum means, of course.

'Oh, good. But I am sorry.'

After Mum has led the way into the house, Alain leans in and whispers against my ear, 'See, that wasn't so bad.'

'OK,' I say, because I despair. Honestly, for how observant our daughter is, he is spectacularly clueless. 'You didn't see that look she gave me, did you? And you didn't notice how she emphasised *aperitif* because they never have them. She's majorly pissed off, but I'm the one who'll get the snark, not you. So, no, I suppose for you, it's not that bad,' I reply and follow my mum down the corridor.

July, 2012

Couldn't quite believe it. Not really. It must have happened right away. *Literally* right away. I held out the stick and Alain's pale, nimble fingers took it from me, his eyes fixed on my face. One of us was shaking, but I wasn't sure who. We'd bought the test as a bit of a joke since we'd only just officially started trying. We both knew it wouldn't happen straight away. Not given my age and my body only just getting itself back to normal after so many years of poor nutrition and minimal exercise. I'd thought about taking folic acid, but didn't want to tempt fate. Since it would take ages and everything.

And look.

LOOK.

Alain looked at the test and frowned as though the result was changing right before his eyes.

'I guess that's it, then,' he said.

'Have you changed your mind? Cos it's totally fine if you have,' I told him in a voice that was clearly saying it was not fine, even though I had changed my mind. I wasn't sure whose idea this was, but it was obviously a stupid one. Me, a mother?

And what was I going to tell my parents? How were they going to feel about this? I was essentially a thirty-something teenager in their eyes. This would be confirmation of everything they thought about me. Yes, we'd sorted some stuff out and our relationship was better, but this would not be the good news it would have been if I was married and settled and respectable.

Alain dropped the test and immediately took me in his arms. 'Why would I have changed my mind? I want nothing more than this.'

I relaxed, relief bubbling through me. 'OK,' I said.

'Why? Have you changed your mind?' he asked, obviously unsettled by my less than emphatic response to his reply.

I shook my head. Of course I'd changed my mind. I didn't need to tell him that, though. It only needed one of us to still want to do this for it to work. Yes, it would have been better if it was me who was all in and certain, and who wanted this, but for now, while I worked out what it was going to do to my life, Alain had to be the happy, certain one about going through with this pregnancy.

Now

Alain walks us to the car after we take our leave. Every Sunday I'm reminded how bad my mother's cooking is, and every Sunday I swear I'm going to get there early so I can help. My sister, Bella, was there and she did what she could to make the roasties edible, but Mum, tears in her eyes, had only put the chicken back in the oven to properly cook after Dad had intervened and said that no, chicken wasn't like beef and lamb, and that if it was difficult to carve and still had red bits, then it wasn't cooked and it would most likely poison us all. After that we were all cool with the gravy being lumpy and the Yorkshire puddings still being frozen. All of us collude in this, in allowing Mum to serve us terrible food and not saying a word unless absolutely forced to. Even Betina eats what she's given without complaint.

'How many Sunday lunches has Logan missed now?' Alain asks as we round the corner to where I've parked the car. There was a time when I'd just park up outside their house and bound in, expecting him to join us a little later. And then when he wouldn't get there for sometimes up to an hour and Mum and Dad would be looking at me like it was my fault, I decided to wait in the car. When they made it clear they'd seen me in the car and disapproved of that even more than sitting on the sofa waiting for him to appear, I started to park two streets away.

'I don't know. He hasn't been for at least three months,' I reply to Alain's question.

'Wow, he must be completely smitten with this new woman of his.'

'I guess so.'

'No hints about who she is?'

I shake my head. 'No, none at all. Which is odd because after him and Henrietta broke up all those years ago, it was like he didn't get to four dates with a girl before he was dragging her over to meet the future in-laws. This one, though, nothing, nada. He hasn't even told us her name. Not even Bella who he tells everything to.'

We arrive at the car and he hugs and kisses me, then kisses and hugs Betina, before helping her climb into her seat in the back.

Once she is in and shut away so she can't easily hear the rest of the conversation, he turns to me. 'I really am sorry about being late again. I could try to excuse it but I suppose it all boils down to me being unbelievably crap. I'm sorry. I'm going to make sure I'm on time next week.'

'OK,' I reply, because what else am I going to say that will make a difference?

He sighs. 'Same time next week?'

'Actually, can you have Betina an extra night this week?'

'Oh, any particular reason?'

'What do you mean?'

'Any particular reason you want me to have her?'

'Don't you want to spend more time with your daughter?'

'Of course I do, I absolutely do. I was just curious.'

'Curious about if I'm sleeping with someone else?'

Alain glances over my shoulder as crimson shame creeps up his cheeks from his neck. 'Yes, basically.' He refocuses on me. 'Are you?'

'I have to work late. Not that it's any of your business.'

'It's not my business but I do still love you so it kind of feels like my business when it totally isn't.'

'OK,' I say.

We stand in the awkward silence of people who don't know what to say to each other to end their meeting. 'I'll see you, then,' I say and begin to move to the other side of the car.

He reaches out and stills me by putting his hand on my forearm.

'I'm serious, you know, Pops. Nothing's changed for me. You're still the love of my life. Always will be. Just say the word, and I'll do whatever it takes to come home.'

'My flat isn't your home, Alain.'

'But where you and Betina are is my home, which is what I meant. And you know that's what I meant.'

It'd be so much easier, simpler, if he'd cheated on me, or if he'd battered me emotionally, raised a hand to me physically; everything would be clear-cut and sorted then. We'd have set pick-up times for our daughter, we'd be able to tell our families we weren't together and we'd be able to move on without a second thought for the other person's plans. Joint Sunday lunches would be a distant memory because I wouldn't be a forty-eight-year-old woman pretending to my parents that I can keep a relationship going.

When has anything been simple and easy in my life?

'I'll let you know when you can pick up Betina,' I reply and quickly head for the driver's side of the car before 'I love you, too' slips out of my lips. I do not want to say it. Feel it? Yes, of course. I love every part of Alain. But I don't want to admit to it.

verity

Now

'Do you remember that dress shop we went to in Uckfield when we were looking at wedding dresses?' Mum asks. She's driving me home despite me saying I'd get the bus down. She'd insisted because she wanted to spend more time with me. We'd spent most of the morning traipsing round shops and sitting having stupid coffee and cake, how much more time did she want to spend with me?

'Yes, I remember that shop,' I say to her.

I stare out of my window, the shapes and colours of Brighton moving past. I try to focus on them – the smudges of humanity, the sketches of nature, rather than the irritation that is clambering up through my whole being at being here with her a minute longer than necessary. I stare out of the window, also, so I don't remind her that we were stopped by the police that day we went to that shop and the police officer was vile to us. Absolutely vile and she had laughed it off when I'd asked her. She'd laughed it off instead of confessing that it was because of her past.

'I'm wondering if I should try over there for a dress,' she says.

I roll my eyes while still staring out of the window.

'What?' Mum says.

'Pardon?'

'You just sighed, probably rolled your eyes. You don't think that's a good idea?'

I shrug. 'Sure, yes, why not.'

'Oh for . . . could you sound any less interested, Verity? Hmmm? I truly doubt it.'

'I just think, *Mum*, that you should check with Dad first if he wants a party. And before you say, "you only turn fifty once", just because something means something to you, doesn't mean it'll be as important to the other person. It's just basic good manners.'

'It's meant to be a surprise party,' she says, sounding utterly deflated.

Shards of guilt flutter like butterflies in my stomach. I shouldn't be like this with her. And if I can't stop it, I shouldn't be around her. 'Look, you know, it's up to you what you do. You just asked my opinion and I gave it.'

'You certainly did that,' she replies. 'You certainly did that.'

My mother lays a gentle hand on my forearm before I can open the door to escape. 'Have I done something to hurt or upset you, Vee?' she asks.

Yes, I want to say. *Yes, you have. Your life is a lie. Our life is a lie. Everything I know about you is a lie.*

'What could you have possibly done to upset me?' I ask.

She smiles to hide her smirk. 'Ah well, if I didn't realise I'd upset you before, I'm certain of it now,' she says. 'I'm sorry. For whatever it is. I'm sorry.'

Whenever I stare at my mother, I know I am seeing a mirror to my future; watching her features as the barometer for how I'll look in the coming years. Right now, I'm looking in the mirror to how I will look if I keep things from my family for years and years and years; how I would look if I was a murderer. 'I won't ask to come up,' she says. 'I'll just see you soon.'

Embarrassed suddenly at my mother's grace and patience in the face of my hideous behaviour – and it has been hideous – I want to say something. Anything that will let her know I'm sorry. That I love her. And that I wish she'd told me all that stuff before I found it out.

'Yes,' I eventually say. 'I'll see you soon.' And I exit the car before I get an attack of conscience and decide to confess all.

serena

Now

'Evan Gillmare, I love you.'

I'm down on one knee beside Evan's favourite chair in our living room. He has a beer in his hand and is watching a match on TV. I'm not sure which match it is, although I'm sure he told me earlier and asked me if I was going to join him. I love that about him – his unending optimism that after twenty-nine years of knowing me, twenty-five of them together, I may still say yes and watch the footy with him. Even when he and Conrad would spend most of the day chatting about the match, planning their snacks and drinks and what they'll do during half-time, he'll still ask me if I am up for watching the match with him. Sometimes I'll join him for athletics, and the Olympics or global events, but never football.

My husband's dark eyes study me for a moment, probably remembering the time ten years ago when he got down on one knee and began a conversation with very similar words. Neither of us realised then that it would be the start of our lives imploding, because the next day, Poppy Carlisle was released from prison and everything kicked off. Evan's gaze darts back to the television screen, watching his team run around the pitch as they battle for a place in some championship or league or something. I haven't quite got his complete attention. Maybe I should have waited, but what Verity was saying earlier today – no, not just what she was saying earlier, the way she looked at me – made me think I'd better check. Better make sure I'm not imposing my will on him.

I've been pretending for quite a while that my grown-up daughter hasn't been looking at me in that way. It's a sort of disdain, like I have done something to her that she can't forgive. When she couples it with her clipped words and obviously bitten tongue, it makes me feel awful.

I haven't asked her about it to any real degree because I'm too scared of the answer I'll get. What it is that I've done wrong that has made my firstborn turn on me. Apart from a few incidents, Verity was the model teenager. She didn't act out, she didn't start huge rows, she was mostly pleasant to her brother. This has all been a shock, that she can be like this, that our relationship can feel like it is hanging on by a fast-thinning thread. I also don't confront it because I don't want to push her further away.

Easiest thing to do is to ask Evan about the party. Find out what he wants.

'Evan Gillmare, I love you,' I repeat to get his attention again. 'And I know we've spent most of our lives together, but I want to celebrate you. I want to let every one of our friends know that I constantly celebrate you being in our lives, so for your birthday, your fiftieth birthday, I'd like to have a huge' – I use my hands to emphasise the word HUGE – 'party. You're only going to be fifty once in your life, so I'd like to have a party. Well, to be fair, I've been organising said HUGE party but it was going to be a surprise and then it wasn't going to be a surprise and then I've been wondering if there should be a party at all because Verity said you'd hate it.

'And, technically, she has known you longer so she may well be right.'

'How has she known me longer?' Evan asks, eyeing me up like I'm out on the edge of a very high ledge and he's wondering what he'll have to do to coax me back in. 'I have to have known you longer to have actually made her with you.'

'Well, talk to our children and they'll explain that, proportionally, Verity has known you all her life, that's one hundred per cent, and I've known you something like sixty per cent of my life, so she wins. In the knowing-you-for-longer stakes.'

Evan abandons the football and stares at me hard and long, his forehead a concertina from his deep, confused frown. He's still handsome, my husband. More handsome than the day I first spoke to him, I think. That was the time he threw his drink in my face and I thought he'd done it on purpose. From that moment on, when it turned out he hadn't thrown his drink at me and he had no idea who I was, he had set me free. I thought he was good-looking then, but he has grown into his features now. His smooth skin and dark, brooding eyes, his wonderfully full lips, and his broad nose, are so him – so *handsome* – I find myself staring at him sometimes, amazed that he liked me in return, and perplexed that he's stuck with me for so long. There are many women who would love to take dishy Dr Evan off my hands but he rarely looks twice at them.

Right this minute, though, he's looking at me like I am a bit unstable. And like he's trying to work out what to do about it. Does he deal with the crazy, or does he ignore it in the hope it'll go away when I find something else to worry about. 'So, this party, then?' he says by way of telling me he's going to ignore my comments about my daughter knowing him longer. 'When is it?'

'In three weeks, if you want it. You absolutely do not have to feel pressured into it. We can go out for a meal, just the two of us, we can drag the kids along, we can get my mum and my sisters down, your family down, have a big family meal. Whatever you want.'

'I want what you want,' he says.

'Oh, please! You say that now, but when I start getting the bunting out and ordering the photo booth and making it fancy dress, suddenly there'll be no "I want what you want." It'll be all "How old do you think I am, Sez?" So better you just tell me the truth about whether you want a party or not now.'

'Yeah, no photo booth or bunting and definitely no fancy dress.'

'See?'

I can see his attention is drifting, heading back to Football Land, so my window for getting this sorted is shrinking fast. 'A party would be good,' he states.

'Only if you're sure you want one.'

'I didn't know I wanted one until you asked me. Now I'd be offended if I didn't get one.'

The relief. It's so sweet it brings a sudden rush of tears to my face. I wasn't imposing my will on Evan. I wasn't being controlling. My husband notices the sudden emotion crowding its way into my eyes and turns away from the football again. 'What's going on with you and Vee?' he asks.

'What do you mean?' I ask, knowing exactly what he means.

'You wouldn't normally be bothered by something like this. But you seem to have taken this completely to heart. What's going on?'

I shrug, flop my arms up and down hopelessly. 'I don't know, Evan. We're not connecting any more, if that's the word to use. I thought going shopping together today would make things better, you know, bridge the gap that's grown since she's stopped coming over as much, but if anything, spending time with her has made it worse. She was categorical that you'd hate the idea of a party, let alone a surprise one.'

'Do you want me to have a word with her?'

I shake my head and get to my feet, my knees creaking and complaining as I do. 'No, no, it'll just make it worse. She'll think I've been complaining to you about her.' I have to accept that it's me she has the issue with. Not Evan and Con; me. I don't know what I've done, but it has hurt her and she hates me because of it. 'I suppose things seem worse, I guess, because my years of smugness have had to come to an end. I mean, I always thought I'd got it so right because she didn't really rebel, she mostly talked to me or you, and we had no real dramas. I actually had the arrogance to think that was somehow down to me. Not, you know, just plain old luck. Trust me to end up with the twenty-four-year-old teenager.'

Evan swaps his beer into the other hand so he can take mine and rub it reassuringly. 'It'll work out fine,' he says. He has a way of doing that. Even when it's a disaster and you know it won't be fine because it can't be fine, the way he speaks is so soothing, he makes you think it will be.

'Right.' I rub my hands together. 'Now that I've tricked you by getting you to veto the outrageous things, I can go off and do the other things I really wanted to do and you'll accept them because they're not as bad as the photo booth, bunting or fancy dress.'

My husband is lost to me. He's glued to the screen, his features twitching with every touch and pass of the ball. 'I literally have no idea what you've just said, but I know you do, so go enjoy yourself planning my party. Just let me know the date and what time I need to be there.'

I drop a kiss on Evan's head of black, curly hair; he seems to be edging back to growing the Afro he had in college. 'I will,' I say happily before I leave the room.

The moment I'm out of sight, I have to stop and lean against a wall, using it to keep me upright. The swirl of worry and fear that I'm losing my daughter whips itself up inside like a hurricane building up speed to begin its destructive path where nothing will be left standing. I have to take a breath, then another then another. I know what a panic attack is now, and I know when one is approaching. I know what I have to do to stay safe, to head it off or see it through.

This is bad, I think as the panic whisks itself up even more. I push myself harder against the wall, trying to force breath into my lungs.

If Evan has brought up the problem with Vee without me even mentioning it to him, then things with my daughter are not only as bad as I thought, they're actually a lot worse.

verity

'In my dreams, I would sneak and sit next to her on the sofa, because if I was next to her, then she wouldn't be able to leave. They wouldn't be able to take her away. I wouldn't have to watch them put on handcuffs and speak to her like she was lower than dirt,' Logan Carlisle said to me.

This was the second time I'd met Logan Carlisle. The last meeting had ended not long after he had shown me the newspaper cutting on his phone. I'd been so shocked I'd told him I needed to go away and have a proper look around on the internet for information. That Mum and Dad were away so he couldn't talk to her even if he wanted to right then, and could we meet up to talk about it again?

This time we went to a café just off London Road. It was not too far from where I lived and I was reasonably confident no one would see us together. We sat down with our orders and he had started talking – unbidden, unasked.

He continued: 'In real life, I would sit as close to her as possible, sharing her body heat, enjoying the time when we were just together. I remember never wanting to leave her side because somehow I, this six-year-old kid, could keep her there.

'And I remember how cold it was in the corridor, when I sat on the steps for days and days and days, even after Bella stopped doing it because Poppy told us she'd be back. We believed her. *I* believed her. I needed her back and thought she'd be back, so I sat there and waited for her. Every day was a fight to get me to eat, to go to the toilet, to go to bed, to go to school. Every day I didn't want to leave the step because I knew more than anything she was going to come back. My parents tried to tell me without telling me at first. They'd say to give it a rest, to wait for her elsewhere, to remember that she hadn't meant for me to sit there *literally* until she came back. But I knew better. I can still remember the taste in my mouth, the way I would get so cold sitting there, the way my stomach would churn and dip and rise as I sat there waiting for her.'

He looked at me then. Fixed me with his gaze as though he had suddenly remembered he was talking to another person rather than just wandering the maze-like alleys of his memory, losing himself in the paths and recollections of yesteryear. 'Do you have anything like that in your past, Verity? Memories so vivid and real that it feels as though you've somehow jumped back into your body from that particular time and experienced it again, which is why you now remember it so totally – physically, mentally, emotionally?'

I shook my head. 'Not for a sustained period.' Understanding flitted across his face, a small smile wafted onto his lips as he lowered his gaze and swirled his coffee around its boat-like cup. *You had a happy childhood*, I could almost see him thinking. *No one and nothing made you feel like I did. No one stole your childhood and replaced it with nothing. Not even with something awful, just having the person you loved removed and in their place was a nothingness no one even tried to fill. Because she was not dead, she was not here, she was just nowhere. And no one wanted to acknowledge nowhere. No one wanted to dress up or fill that void, so they just left you to it. You have no idea, what it's like to live with your loved one in limbo. You have no idea what it's like to have a childhood that was full of love and care and attention and still hollow and sad and empty. You have no idea because you had a happy childhood.*

I was almost submerged by a wave of guilt from the way he was looking at me because yes, I had been happy. There were bad times, there were arguments and pain and misery sometimes, but all in the context, the cocoon, of things being good; life being so much more than fine. My parents were happy together and they made their whole lives about Conrad and me. I felt wretched, sitting in front of this man, because he went through that, and my mother could have been the cause of it.

She was there. That was the worst part. The articles told me she was there. The way she lived her life told me she was there. Even now, Mum would not eat ice cream. Would not buy ice cream. Would pretend it was not happening if we had ice cream. I remembered when we were pulled over nearly ten years earlier, how the police officer spoke to her. 'It's almost like he knew you, Mum,' I'd said to her at the time and she'd dismissed it. Not denied it, or asked how he could possibly know her; she'd brushed it away like something that needed to be hidden under the rug of our lives. And I'd thought nothing of it. I'd thought nothing at all of it beyond being upset that we'd been stopped by the police when I didn't think we'd done anything wrong.

And now I realised that I had accepted my mum's dismissal because we'd been so happy. So settled and sorted that I wouldn't have had any reason to question what my mother did as a teenager, whether she was a murderer and whether she'd let someone else go to prison for her crimes. Because only a monster would do that, surely. Only a monster would let someone else take their place in being punished. And my mum wasn't a monster. She just wasn't. That was what was so awful about this. About meeting Logan Carlisle, about reading those stories – they were none of them the person I knew.

People said you could never really know anyone, but could the woman who'd dedicated her life to me and Con and Dad really be the smiling, sexy siren who'd killed her teacher?

Maybe Poppy, Logan's sister, had been like that, but not Mum. How could she have made us all so happy if she was really like that? But then, how could I listen to Logan talk and *not* doubt her? Because he was not making this up. He knew his sister and she wasn't like that. I knew my mum and she wasn't like that.

'Look, I think I should talk to your mother as soon as possible,' he said suddenly.

My face – my whole body – contracted with the fear of this.

He saw and, sighing, said, 'Look, Verity, I just need to talk to her. It won't be awful, I'll just ask her about that time and ask her to consider going to the police, admitting what she did.'

'But how do you know she did anything?' I said.

I was talking like this was all reasonable and normal, like it was something I could just bring up with my mum. I'd wanted to, several times since I'd met Logan Carlisle last week, but seriously, how was I going to say, *'Mum, were you screwing your teacher? Did you kill him? Cos some guy wants to have a word with you about it.'*

There was no scenario where I could say something like this and it would end well. But I had to do it because it'd be so much worse if Logan Carlisle marched up to her and laid it all down.

'How do I know?' he spat. 'You don't think any of it is true, do you? You don't think she did anything, right?'

Logan Carlisle was angry all the time. Not just a bit grumpy or cross, he had a deep, unremitting rage that gushed through his veins. It tensed up every muscle in his body, tautened the skin around his lips and his eyes. And the fury flashed in his eyes whenever he wasn't looking directly at me. I couldn't let him rock up to my parents' house and confront Mum when he was like that. It was bad enough to be around it, imagine being the focus of it?

'Do you have any idea what he did to them?' he snapped when I didn't immediately reply.

Of course I didn't. From what it said in the papers, it was bad, though. They both suffered, or so we were supposed to believe. I never believed what was written in the papers, I always, *always* questioned articles, checking for things that didn't add up. For example, they said he was abusive, but the people the reporters spoke to about Marcus Halnsley had nothing but good things to say about him. They weren't all the same people, either. They were from the various schools he'd taught at, the different pupils he'd worked with, the neighbours who knew him well. No one had a bad word to say about him apart from the two people accused of his murder. Either the papers were missing something, or all the people who knew him were colluding in presenting a false image of him, or Mum was lying . . . But Mum wouldn't lie about that, and I got the impression that Logan Carlisle didn't believe his sister had made it up, either. I shook my head at my coffee companion, clamping my lips together to stop myself running off my mouth.

'The papers weren't even close to revealing what he did to them. He completely *brutalised* them. From what my sister hinted at and has said a couple of times, Serena had it worse. He was with her longer so he had time to refine what he did to her.'

My eyes widened at the thought of it.

53

'She's not that forthcoming, but if I press her, she will tell me things. Except about that day of the picture, the day when they got the name "The Ice Cream Girls". No matter what I ask her, Poppy won't talk about it at all. At all. I think it was awful. The worst of it . . .' For the first time since we'd met, the anger dissipated a little. 'I'm not going to retraumatise your mother. I wouldn't do that. I know she's as much a victim as my sister was. I just want to talk to her, I want to say I understand, that Poppy went through the same hell. And that I understand why she did it, but can she just come forward now, tell them it was an accident or something. Clear Poppy's name.'

Logan Carlisle picked up his coffee cup, clearing the cappuccino-foamed sides by swirling its contents around, then returned the cup to its saucer. 'I can imagine that after everything that happened, she went back. She probably still loved him because I'm pretty sure Poppy did, even after everything he put her through. But I can imagine she went back to help him and then he probably started on her again and she grabbed the knife to protect herself and accidentally killed him. She probably knew that no one would believe her so she ran.

'I can understand that. Poppy would probably understand that, too. I just need your mum to admit to it. The police will understand. They understand abuse and its effects so much more now than they did then. I bet she won't even get jail time, and Poppy will be free. We can tell our parents it was a misunderstanding. Our family can start to heal again.'

I was sure it wasn't that simple. Pretty sure Logan Carlisle knew it wasn't that simple as well. He was just telling himself – and therefore me – that it was that straightforward. And I had to do something to stop him crashing into my parents' lives and ruining things again.

Con and I never talked about it, but we hadn't forgotten the time

Mum moved out. None of us ever talked about it, but it was there. A rut in the road of our family's story, a pothole that almost derailed everything. I couldn't imagine what having this man rock up into their lives would do to my parents' relationship.

'We don't know what happened, though, Logan, do we?' I began, trying to be placatory while heading him away from going directly to Mum. 'Everything you've just said could be as equally true of Poppy, couldn't it? *She* might have gone back to help, *she* might have been in danger from him, *she* might have been the one who accidentally killed him in self-defence but couldn't say that because she knew how it would seem.'

Angry Man Logan Carlisle was back, but he'd brought some add-ons – indignation and utter disgust – with him.

'What I'm saying is,' I rushed on before he unleashed his temper on me. 'We don't know anything beyond what your sister has told you – which you admit is not very much – and the stuff in the papers, which we don't know how much was embellished.' I had no clue where I was headed with this, all I knew was I had to keep talking, had to stop him from going to Mum with this. I probably wouldn't be able to put him off for ever, but I had to stall him. Stall him until I could work out what the best thing to do was. 'What would be helpful would be having a time machine so we could go back and see what happened for ourselves.'

'Really? You think that might be helpful? I'll get right on it.'

'If you had any knowledge of quantum science, you'd know time travel isn't as unlikely a proposition as you might think. It's just not currently possible, or so people want you to think.'

'You're not going to distract me with this kooky science-geek thing you're trying to pull,' Logan Carlisle snarled. 'I. Need. To. Speak. To. Your. Mother.'

Time travel. I was being silly, but it had sparked off something in my head. What if we *could* time travel? 'I wasn't trying to distract you, I was actually working up to an idea. Look, I'm a solicitor – well, training to be one – and I've just realised: what if you – and I – *could* actually talk to my mum and your sister from back then? Find out from them what they say happened, piece together their story from what we know and what we can find out? That would be better, wouldn't it? If nothing else, it'll put you on a much better footing when you talk to my mother, rather than using fading newspaper clippings and half-told stories from someone who has been traumatised her whole adult life?'

'What are you talking about?'

'Time travel,' I replied. 'Not literally us physically travelling through time, but getting the court transcripts and reading them.'

'Can we do that?'

'Yes. The case is over thirty years old so it might be a bit trickier, but I'm sure we can get them if we pool together all the information we have about the trial at that time.'

He frowned slightly, twisted his lips fractionally as he thought about it.

'I don't know what job you do, Logan, but I'm sure you never do your work without getting as much information as possible.'

Time travel was going to help me: delay. I just needed a delay to work out a way to bring it up with Mum and/or convince him not to. Because once he saw the court records, I was sure he'd realise that if it could have been Mum, then it was just as likely to have been his sister. And if it wasn't either of them, then it must have been someone else. Or, if he saw the court records, he might understand that it *was* his sister after all, and maybe she wouldn't talk about it because she knew, deep down, that she went to prison for the crime she *did* commit.

'If I did go along with this, how long would it take?'

This was where the time came into it, too. It would literally buy me time. 'Potentially a few weeks,' I said.

He rolled his eyes as though he could see right through me. 'Of course.'

'No, don't look like that,' I said quickly, desperate to keep him on side. 'It might take time but then it might not. It totally depends on which transcription service compiled the records. But in that time, we'll keep in touch with each other, we can even meet up regularly so you can see that I'm not trying to blow you off. I mean, you can sit with me while I fill in the correct forms, help me send them off so that you can see I actually do it and I'm not playing you. Hey, we could even set up a joint email address for the correspondence so you can see if anything comes in and you're not sitting worrying about whether I'm scamming you.'

'You really think this would help?'

'Well, it can't hurt, can it? I mean, who doesn't want to go into any situation better armed with information? I seriously think it could help give us both a proper understanding of what was happening at the time. I mean, memories get blurred and we remember things differently to how they actually happened. The court transcripts will help put everything in a clearer context.'

'That might work,' he said.

'But . . .' I said, bringing it up now.

'But?'

'Seeing as we're not applying under the Freedom of Information Act because we're not involved, it's going to cost.'

'How much?'

'I don't know exactly, but they usually charge per day of sitting if you want the full day's transcripts.'

'How much?'

'Like I said, I don't know. I can find out. But it can run into the hundreds . . . per day.'

'I don't have any money.'

'Neither do I.'

'Well, we can't do it, then.'

'We could save up?' I suggested. 'But anyway, let me find out potentially how much it'll cost and then we can decide if we need everything from every day or not and what we'll do.'

Logan Carlisle looked down at the cup in front of him, his eyes seemed to be trying to burn a hole in the ceramic. 'You had better not be trying to play me, Verity,' he said with enough menace to let me know he would do me serious harm if I crossed him. 'This isn't a game to me. At all.'

'It's not a game to me, either. And I don't know why you're threatening me. I haven't done anything to you. If anything, I'm trying to help you.'

He said nothing for a few more minutes. 'All right, we'll do it your way. As long as you're really trying to help and not stall.'

'I'm really trying to help.' I really was. I was trying to help everyone involved, especially my mum.

poppy

Now

'Where've you been, oh brother of mine?'

I've ambushed Logan outside his work because that seems the only way I get to see him nowadays. He works down near Old Steine in one of the big office buildings that have been erected and filled in recent years. He's a financial adviser or something . . . He regularly tells us he's got a new job/been promoted and we all kind of cheer/clap/make excited noises because none of us really know what it means.

'Ahh, my biggest of sisters.' My brother smiles and envelopes me in a bear hug. I love that he is so free with his emotions. I was worried, when I first saw them again, that there'd be a barrier created by the time apart, but there wasn't. It was like we'd always been friends, always been close.

'It's pretty out of order leaving us to the parentals,' I tell him as I come out of his hold. 'You know they always behave better when you're around.'

'Nonsense,' he says. 'The 'rentals love all of us the same.'

We both know that's not true and we both know this is a conversation we've been having for more than ten years. Basically, our parents favour Logan because, ten years ago, after I left prison and when I was finally allowed by my parents to make contact with him and Bella, he discovered how much they had kept me away from them over the years. And that discovery made him lose the plot with them.

I'd never seen anyone as angry as he was; he screamed at them, and refused to speak to them for weeks. Mum and Dad were desperate by the time I got him to calm down and engage with them. I'd negotiated us all around the kitchen table – thankfully Mum was too upset to cook – and I explained to Logan that they were doing what they thought was best. That they hadn't meant to hurt any of us. And they'd only held off on giving my number to him when I was released from prison because they weren't sure I was going to stick around. I didn't mention them lying about Dad's birthday, or them not telling me where they'd moved to. After that, when Mum and Dad had grovelled and apologised, their relationship was constantly on rocky ground. Obviously I felt responsible, it was another element of the fallout from me being in prison, but I had made peace with the fact that they would always believe I was guilty. I had to do everything I could to not cause damage to the relationships around me by returning to their lives.

Ever since, Mum and Dad behave much better when Logan is around. They don't want him to think that they're horrible to me or that they are anything other than loving, kind parents.

'So, who is this lady who has caught your attention so much you've abandoned your family?' I ask him.

Logan smiles and his face lights up in such a unique way, I know that she's special, whoever she is. He is totally in love. 'Just someone,' he says.

'Just someone, huh? How long has it been going on with this "just someone"?'

'A while.'

'Oh, please, Logan. Can you just give me something! You're always introducing girls within minutes of getting their phone number, why won't you open up about this one?'

We're walking towards a local bar on the other side of The Lanes, I realise. Neither of us has suggested going there, but that's the direction we've started to head in. When he first moved to Brighton eight years ago and it was all fresh and new, he and Bella and I would go there after work. We'd sit and talk and talk and talk. There seemed to be so many words out there that needed to be released in our stories and observations and chats. It was so easy. So simple. But the years, they pile things on and they take things away and you have to leave certain things behind when the clock strikes midnight to end that time period in favour of another era. There was a golden era when they moved here, and that lasted a while and then went away. Now we have had to find new ways to be together.

'Look, it's complicated and I want things to work out on all levels so I'm keeping things quiet for now.'

I sigh. Complicated is a euphemism for so many things, usually, 'married'. 'So she's married, then?'

'No, I wouldn't do that.'

'Yes you would, yes you have. Who do you think you're talking to here?'

'All right, I wouldn't do that *now*. And no, she's not married or otherwise attached. She was officially classed as single before we got together. She has no kids, she has a job, she has her own flat and she's a good person.'

'Oh yeah, overburdened with complications there.'

'Sister Pops, how's Alain? Still got that great job? And fantastic house? And still making sure his world basically revolves around his daughter?'

Wow, that was a low blow. 'Yes, he's still going for citizen of the year.'

'And you're still split up from him, why?'

'We haven't split up,' I state. Not officially. Not outside of anyone but him, me and Betina.

'Could have fooled me.'

'You know nothing about it, Logan. So leave it, all right?'

'Fair enough.' We get to the bar, a dark and brooding pub that sits right in the middle of the parade of shops in this street like the gap of a missing tooth in an otherwise bright, healthy smile. 'Truce, Pops?' He points to the doorway. 'Once we go in, no more aggro, all right?'

'All right, baby bro.'

'And no "baby bro" nonsense, either.'

September, 2012

'What you doing?' Alain asked. He came into the bedroom where I had a holdall open on the bed and was carefully adding folded clothes to it.

'Packing.'

'Going somewhere?' he asked gently.

'I've rented a flat down near Hove seafront. I'm moving.'

'I see,' he said calmly. He sat down on the bed and said nothing for a few seconds. 'Any particular reason why?' He was confused and I didn't really blame him. I'd done all this on the quiet because I knew he'd be upset and wouldn't understand.

Carefully, I placed the top I had in my hands into the bag and sat down next to him. 'I need space, I guess.'

'Space?'

'I've never lived on my own, Al. I went from my parents' house to prison to my parents' new house to living here. I've never had to look after myself in the sense of living by myself and making my own decisions.'

'And you have to do this now?'

'Yes.'

'You're three months pregnant, in case you hadn't noticed.'

'I've noticed. It's why I'm doing it. I need to know I can take care of myself so I can take care of this little one.'

'I think that's bullshit. I think you're scared that you're happy and you want to sabotage things before they go wrong in a way that's out of your control.'

'If you say so.'

'You don't think you can have the baby and the guy, so you're leaving me before I leave you.'

'I want to be on my own for a bit, Al. Just for a bit. I didn't think we were spitting up. I just want to be by myself when it hasn't been imposed on me by someone else.'

'And I don't get a say in it?'

'Not if you understand what I'm talking about.'

'Do you love me?' he asked quietly. And then held his breath, as though he couldn't be sure of the answer.

'What kind of a question is that?' I replied.

'One you're not going to answer, clearly.'

I turned my whole body towards him. 'Of course I love you. I don't know how you could ever doubt that.'

'Apart from the fact you're leaving me, you've never actually said it. Not in two years of being together.'

'OK,' I replied. He sounded so sure of that, so certain, that I didn't want to argue. 'I love you.' I said it again in case he was right and in case I needed to prove I did by being emphatic about it. 'And I'm not leaving you, I'm going to me.'

'I have no choice in the matter,' he said sadly. 'No choice whatsoever.'

'It's not going to be for ever. Just for this next little while so I can find out who I am.'

'Fine,' he said. And left the room without another word.

By the time I moved into the tired but beautiful mansion flat not far from Hove seafront, he had come round. He realised that I meant it, that I really was going to me and not leaving him. He helped me move, he was on twenty-four-hour call. By the time I moved, Alain had come to realise us living apart was probably the best thing for us to stay together.

March, 2013

Her body was so very tiny, her teeny veins were visible under her mottled beige-pink skin. Her white nappy seemed far too big for her, it was actually almost the same size as she was. She had swathes of shiny, curly black hair, and her blue-hazel eyes were closed. I was grateful for that, because she wouldn't see that she was in an incubator instead of in my arms. My daughter.

My. Daughter.

She was so beautiful. Everyone says that, I know that. Everyone looks down at their progeny and thinks no one could be more perfect, but it was true. My baby was something I could not describe without using words like 'beautiful' and 'gorgeous' and 'angelic'. I wanted to hold her close, kiss her newborn head, inhale her fresh scent, stroke every contour of her face, count out those toes and fingers. But I couldn't. She'd been rushed here straight from the delivery room and she was being protected and kept alive in this clear plastic box, while connected by tubes to various machines. I wanted to hold her close, revel in the different type of nearness we were going to share. It was painful, actually, physically painful listening to the doctors talk about her condition and know that it was keeping us apart that bit longer.

I put my head to one side so I could look at her from the same angle she was lying in.

Alain had gone to get us some food. Probably from outside the hospital, possibly from one of the cafés downstairs. I didn't know. I didn't much care. I couldn't even think about eating, had told him as much, but everyone – the nurses, the doctors, Alain – had kept repeating: you need to eat to keep your strength up, you need to eat to encourage your body to make milk for when she comes out of her little plastic prison.

'I love you, baby Betina,' I whispered, edging as close to her as I could get. There'd never been any question she'd be named after the woman who had saved my life when I was banged up.

Looking at her, I couldn't understand how my parents could do that to me. How they could just walk away from me just because I'd gone to prison. I'd had her two days and I knew there was nowhere else on Earth I would rather be than by her side. 'I love you and I am never going to let anyone hurt you,' I promised this tiny being who I was charged to take care of. 'I am going to protect you from everyone and everything. I am going to love you and love you and love you. I am going to make sure you have everything you ever want and that the world is kind to you.'

I know you will, a voice said in my head. I looked up and saw her standing there – a shimmering, shining figure. This wasn't like when Marcus used to come to me, this was nice. This was my best friend smiling at me, radiant and ethereal, as she should have been, could have been if the world hadn't spent so much time beating her down.

'Is it really you?' I asked, my voice a whisper, my hope teetering on the edge of despair.

Course, she replied. *Had to see the little one, didn't I? Had to see you in all your glory.*

'I've called her Betina,' I said, accepting that this was Tina and she was here to see me. She'd found a way to come to me when I needed her.

Good name, Ice Cream Girl. Good name.

'I wish you were here to see her properly,' I sobbed suddenly, the big, fat, gloopy tears coming from nowhere and drizzling down my face. 'I wish it had worked out for us.'

I'm here now, and that's all that matters.

I nodded. 'I suppose so.'

'Who are you talking to?' Alain asked, suddenly appearing beside me, all gowned up to keep the area as sterile as possible.

I glanced briefly at Tina, she waved a little goodbye, before she disappeared.

'Betina, of course,' I replied to Alain. 'Who else would I be talking to?'

March, 2013

'Do you want to come home with us?' I asked him.

Betina was spending her third day in an incubator and I wanted

66

something to be normal. Settled. I loved living alone, had taken to it in a way I didn't realise was possible. Being in charge of me and having Alain come over whenever was the ideal situation. But when we eventually left the hospital with our daughter, it'd be perfect if he came home with us.

'Of course I'm coming home with you.'

'I mean, do you want to come home and stay with us for good? Move in and be a family at the flat?'

'Really?'

'I keep looking at her and I keep thinking what if I don't get to bring her home? What do I do? And then I think, what if I do get to bring her home? What do I do? And then I realised that with either scenario, you being there would be ideal.'

He slipped his arm around my shoulders and pulled me close. He was so good at that, so casually loving. He was going to be a great father. 'I would absolutely love to move in with you two.' He kissed the top of my head. 'And we're going to take her home. Of course we're going to take her home.'

Now

'Don't be a stranger,' I tell my brother as we stand outside the train station. I'm going to jump on the train back to Hove and he's going off to wherever his girlfriend lives. He's pretending he's going to his flat in Rottingdean but he's absolutely not.

'She's younger than me,' he says suddenly. 'That's one complication. Another complication is that her parents would not approve so we're keeping things quiet for now. Actually, I kind of gave her an ultimatum about coming clean, going public, and it went the wrong way. So we're taking some time. Which makes it all the more difficult to talk about her.'

A few drinks and talking about other things have released these revelations.

'I'm really sorry. I had no idea. What are you going to do?'

'Wait until she changes her mind, I suppose. Nothing else I can do, really. I love her so much, Pops. She is everything, and I suppose I'm having a hard time believing she doesn't feel the same way.'

'She probably does, but if you say her parents wouldn't approve, then that's probably a big thing for her. Especially if she's . . . you know, "young" like you say.'

'Whoa there, Poppy, she's not *that* young. Only ten, twelve years younger. Not like it was with you. I'm not *him*. Not all men are like *him*.'

'I know that,' I reply. I hate that Marcus gets brought up at all, but I especially hate that someone like Logan has to say that. That Logan has to put himself in the same frame as Marcus because I was once-upon-a-time involved with him and he knows what happened.

I know not all men are like Marcus, not all men will let you down like Alain, and I hate that my brother sometimes feels that he has to remind me there are good men out there.

'I wasn't suggesting that. I mean, early twenties and if she's close enough to her family to be worried what they think, then that's still young. That's still being torn between you and what her family will say. She's probably going through the agonies right now, wondering what the best thing to do is.'

'Maybe you're right.'

'Of course I'm right. It'll work out, I promise.'

'Right, I'd better go. Give my love to Alain.'

'I will. Try not to worry, Loges, it'll work out, I just know it will.'

My brother gives me a wan smile and goes towards the taxi rank at the back of the station, while I find my platform to get back to Hove. I'm sure it'll work out for him, even if it didn't work out for Alain and me.

September, 2017

Although we'd lived together in my flat for nearly five years, I still knocked whenever I went to Alain's house in Poet's Corner. He'd taken to going there to work because our four-year-old was into everything. She would run around, she would climb, she would ask questions, she would demand we play with her . . . she would basically make working from home impossible. It was joyous, but not helpful for him.

We were in between tenants at his house, so he was staying there to work for longer and longer periods.

'Coming!' the voice on the other side of the door called. I frowned, looked up at the door number, to double-check I was in the right place. The voice on the other side of the door was—

Obviously she was wearing a towel. One of the blue-and-white ones Bella bought us when I officially moved in with Alain. It wasn't one of the bigger-sized towels, so it barely concealed her very shapely form. Her blonde hair was 'casually' piled up on her head, and droplets of water glistened on her shoulders. It was three o'clock in the afternoon, Betina was with my parents, and a naked woman had just answered the door to my partner's house.

I curled my fingers into the palms of my hands, took a couple of deep breaths. Prison Poppy would be considering whether to hit first and ask questions later or not. I was wondering if that numb feeling I was experiencing was a heart attack or not. 'Is, erm, is Alain here?' I asked calmly.

'Oh, yes, he's upstairs. Taking a nap. He's pretending to work but I know he'll have dozed off. Do you want me to get him for you?'

I stood stock-still and listened to her speak. I remembered . . . I remembered when Marcus made me meet Serena for the first time. How I convinced myself it would work out. He'd told me so much about her, but despite what he repeatedly said, she didn't look vulnerable, she didn't look like she would harm herself if he left, she didn't seem to need him to be with her while he was with me.

A lot of me knew it was nonsense, that he was using me, manipulating me, setting me up to tolerate anything. I was young enough to ignore the sensible part of myself. I was naïve enough to stay. Right then, I wasn't young, I wasn't naïve. Even from the doorstep I could smell the place, I could feel how much she had infused the house with her presence. Once upon a time it'd been like that with me, it'd felt like my place because everything about it was touched and loved and adored by me. The place was hers. *Theirs* now. I had no business here.

'No, no thank you.' I stepped back onto the elaborately tiled path. 'No, no, I'll call him. Thanks, thanks so much.'

She frowned like I was a bit crazy. 'I didn't do anything,' she said with a smile so sweet and gentle and 'pretty' I knew instantly what had drawn him to her. Apart from the figure, the breasts, the hair, the smooth skin, it was her smile. Her sweet, sweet smile. I had a smile like that once. I'm sure we all did. We could all smile in such a way that made us pretty.

'You've done more than you know,' I replied before I walked away.

September, 2017

His stuff was packed by the time he made it over.

Mum had been overjoyed at the idea of keeping Betina a bit longer. 'Take all the time you need,' she'd cooed down the phone before hanging up so fast I was sure there would be scorch marks on the hall table.

I didn't realise how quick a packer I was until it was necessary to work fast. All his clothes, books and CDs. His computers and electronic devices, his shoes, and incidentals like his toolbox, cables and magnets were all collected together as well. What didn't fit into his suitcases and holdalls were piled up next to them on the floor of the corridor.

While I was doing it, collecting bits of Alain to remove from my life, I hadn't felt anything. I was completely numb to it. I wasn't angry, I wasn't crying, I was moving on with my life, putting these pieces into the jigsaw of removing Alain from my world.

'It wasn't what it looked like,' he said as soon as he came through the door. 'It honestly wasn't what it looked like. She's just staying there for a few d—' His voice snagged when he saw his world, his life, laid out in the corridor, waiting for him to remove it. 'Poppy, no.' He came further into the flat, flattening himself slightly against the wall to edge past his belongings. 'Just give me a chance to explain.'

'Explain what?'

'She's just staying there for a while. Nothing happened between us. She's an old friend—'

'Old girlfriend,' I corrected.

'Not in many, many years.'

'Do you know, I really wish I cared about that. It is not the fact you had a half-naked woman at your house that's the problem. It's not that

71

you used to sleep with her. It's the fact that I can't trust you, Alain. We never dealt with how we met, what it meant about you and, I suppose, about me because I ignored what you did.'

'We've got a child together, Poppy. Don't you think we've moved on from that now?'

'Alain, we could have a million children together and what difference would it make if I can't trust you? I thought I could rely on you. When . . . I couldn't at all. Our relationship is built on dodgy beginnings. You lying to me and trying to use me to make a name for yourself. Me coming back to you because I needed help. Me moving in with you without being asked to. Me pretty much talking you into having a child. And then asking you to move in because I was scared of being alone with or without a child. Our relationship is built on trash. And no matter how much you try to pretty it up, trash is trash is trash and it'll always collapse under the weight of its shaky, insubstantial foundations.'

I could tell by the way he looked, the set of his expression, the way he held his body, that Alain wanted to seize my arms, shake some sense into me. 'We are not built on trash,' he said sternly.

'OK, we're not built on trash. Can you get your stuff out of here before I have to go and collect Betina? I'd rather she wasn't here for any drama.'

'I love you, Poppy. I'm not giving up without a fight.'

'Fight yourself, Alain. I'm too tired. I shouldn't have had a child with you. This would be so much easier if I hadn't.'

'Popp—'

'I'm tired, Alain. Everything that's happened, even how we met, has led to Betina. So I can't wish any of it away. But, you know what, I thought we were going to be honest going forward. I have brought so much to you, I have been so vulnerable in front of you, and you could still hide a woman living in your house from me. It's the pointlessness of that lie when you're not even sleeping with her that's mind-blowing. And it's something you don't come back from. *We* don't come back from.'

'I wasn't sure how you'd take it,' he explained. 'She needed somewhere to crash, and you've seen her, she's not exactly unattractive. I wasn't sure how you'd feel about me going over there to work when she was there all the time. It was a stupid thing to omit, but it wasn't malicious.'

'Do you want a hand taking your stuff to the car?'

He closed his eyes in regret. I remembered, quite clearly, when we were here last time. When I had to get dressed so he could tell me the truth. I shouted at him then. I was still Prison Poppy ninety-nine per cent of the time. Every little thing used to enrage or scare me. And when I was scared that made me angrier. I felt trapped all the time and being with Alain back then had been an escape from all those feelings. When he told me the truth about how and why he came to be in my life . . . I remembered the horror of it, the anger that drove me into the bathroom, ransacking the cupboard until I found that blade. I hated myself for falling back into that as much as I hated him. I hated that, after that, after I was forced to do that, I started again.

Even after I got back with Alain. Even when I was meant to be happy and everything was sorted because my brother and sister were back in my life after our parents had tried to keep us apart, sometimes the blade was the only way to cope. I didn't want to go back there. Having Betina to focus on, having a job, having a normal life that wasn't defined by my sleeping with a teacher and going to prison for it (even though I was still living under the threat of being for ever on licence) were the most important things in my life. I didn't want to be reliant on a blade, to wonder when I'd need that type of release again.

'Do you still love me?' Alain asked after he had crammed most of his stuff into the back of his car with the seats folded down.

'I'll never stop,' I replied. 'But love isn't the issue. Trust is. And believe me, if I don't trust you, I can love you all I want but it's never ever going to work.'

verity

Now

This is the first proper day without him.

I've been trying to distract myself all day, and I've stayed extra, extra late at work, trying not to think about going back to the flat and him not being there. About the end. I let myself in and feel for a moment, just the briefest of moments, relief. He isn't there. He isn't cleaning and he isn't waiting to tell me something that I've done wrong.

That relief, that momentary sense of freedom from what being with Logan is sometimes like, is quashed by the other feeling: the counterpart to the relief side of the coin – horror at the thought of having to be without him. The slam of the door makes me jump when I shut it behind me.

I stand in the corridor for a moment, not sure what to do. Should I text him? Should I leave it? I've lived here perfectly happily on my own for years, why am I now fretting about someone who moved in without being asked to not being here?

My mobile is in my hand anyway so I check the screen. Check the text messages. Check the messaging apps. All silent, all empty of new contact, all a reminder that it has ended.

Yes, we talked a good game: we were just giving each other space, we were going to talk about what next, but those are just the pauses you make on the way to the end. No one does 'space' and then gets back together.

What you doing?

It's one text. It won't. Of course it won't hurt.
The reply is almost instant:

I was out with my sister, now I'm waiting for you.

I reply:

????

Suddenly he's in the corridor. I can tell from here he's been drinking and I can tell he hasn't accepted that the end has come for us. We don't speak. We don't need to, not really. I drop my computer bag, which I'm still holding, I let go of my bag and I shed my jacket. In that time he comes to me, and I reach out my hands to place them on each side of his face as he bends his head and kisses me.

May, 2019

It cost us nearly ten thousand pounds to get everything – opening remarks to judge's closing comments.

When I'd originally told Logan Carlisle how much it was going to cost to get everything, I had expected him to go off on one – for him to accuse me of stalling and trying to delay things. But he didn't. He said he'd find the money somewhere and hung up without another word. *Rude*, I'd thought as I put down the phone. *Rude and deluded*. Where was he going to get that much money from? He must have got it from somewhere, though, since the documents were emailed to us three weeks later. Without being asked to, I spent a few days printing them out so it would be easier for us to process and then we arranged a time to meet.

'Come in,' I said to him on the day.

I'd told him to come over to my flat because it would mean we could work on the stuff a bit later into the night and, more importantly, there was less chance of us being seen together.

The last thing we needed – I needed – was anyone seeing me and him sitting in a café together and mentioning it to Mum and Dad. And that would totally happen. Someone would randomly bust us without realising that was what they were doing. Dad used to get Mum to buy him his 'treats' from the supermarket because he knew if he did it, he'd most likely run into someone who he'd been extolling the virtues of healthy eating to hours earlier. Brighton was a city, but not like London – there were lots of people living here, and they were dispersed, their lives seeming to barely touch, but at the same time, everything seemed interconnected, overlapping and smothering. You met people all the time who were linked to you or would become linked to you in a way you didn't even realise was possible.

I was already technically lying to my parents by not telling them I had waylaid this man on his trip to confront my mother, I didn't want to have to outright lie about it, too.

Logan Carlisle hesitated for a moment on my doorstep, and for the first time since I'd met him, he seemed unsure of himself, uncertain about what he was about to do. Gathering up his courage, he stepped into my blue-carpeted hallway and stood there making the place look untidy and *small*. I suppose Dad and Con, both taller than Logan Carlisle, never really lingered in the corridor when they came over so they didn't have this shrinking effect on the place. Or maybe it was seeing the place through his eyes for the first time. I couldn't imagine anyone who could rustle up ten thousand pounds at the drop of a hat would live in place like mine – a one-bedroom conversion just down from The Level in Brighton.

'Shoes off?' he asked, looking at my feet in their monster slippers.

'Yes, please,' I replied.

He kicked off his pristine trainers revealing odd socks – one was a green-and-black paisley pattern, the other was a green-and-purple stripe arrangement. The socks made me feel a lot less silly about my big monster slippers – especially when, noticing my look, he explained, 'I can't wear matching socks.'

'You can't wear them? What, you're allergic or you'll get in trouble?'

'Both. I don't feel completely dressed if my socks match. I think it's something that started when I was little. My parents were so controlling after . . . you know, with Poppy, so things like wearing odd socks to school were my only rebellion. Kind of stuck. Years later I still do it.'

'OK.'

'I had a girlfriend once who tried to cure me of it by buying me only black socks. Do you know how I got around that one?'

I dread to think, I thought as I shook my head.

'I coloured in the brand name on the soles of the socks different colours so they didn't match any more.

'Oh. OK. That seems very . . . *committed* of you.'

Logan Carlisle, for the first time, laughed. Loud and long, he laughed. That one action, that simple act of raising his lips and crinkling up his eyes erased years from him, dissolved for the briefest of moments the burden on his shoulders, and freed him from the cage he carried with him. 'That's a very diplomatic way of putting it.'

If he laughed more, scowled less, Logan Carlisle could be a very attractive man. If you liked his sort of looks.

'Don't worry, that's my only quirk – apart from the sixty million other things, I suppose.'

In the living room, I'd arranged the papers I'd printed off into piles on the floor. I had put each day's court proceedings in order in a line in front of the sofa. From the sofa I'd placed my two largest, squishiest cushions on the floor for us to sit on. I had highlighters, sticky notes and paper clips; Blu-Tack, felt-tips and erasable biros. Everything we should need to get through the papers.

'Welcome to the archive,' I said. 'Do you fancy a cup of tea before we start or would you like to get straight to it?'

He shed his brown leather blazer as though he meant business and tossed it onto the back of the sofa. 'Let's get to it. Tea can always come later. I'm hoping you've got lapsang souchong. Organic no less.'

'Yeah. Yeah, that's what I've got. Only I've got a special one that tastes like ordinary tea. It's a special organic flavour they're trialling.'

He did it again: laughed. Creased up his face and allowed mirth to escape his lips, to dance on his features. It was almost embarrassing how much that suited him compared to how he normally was.

'Do you want to read first?' he said, shy now that he had shown – twice – that he wasn't all anger, all business, all threat to my family's very existence.

'Yeah, cool.' I took my seat on the purple fluffy cushion to the left of the sofa and nearer the television, Logan Carlisle took the other one.

Five hours later we knew three things:

1. He *was* joking about lapsang souchong tea – he drank coffee.
2. Reading court documents was tiring and we'd both worked up a huge appetite.
3. Poppy Carlisle and Serena Gorringe had both been absolutely screwed during the court process.

'Is this as bad as it seems?' Logan Carlisle asked me. He sat back, leant against the sofa and then proceeded to stretch his long, solid arms up and his legs out, carefully avoiding my neat piles and the heavily high-lighted pages. 'As a lawyer, are you reading this and thinking that everything was going against them when they walked into that court-room? That the very real possibility that they both *wouldn't* end up in jail hadn't even occurred to anyone involved?'

'Yes, it's as bad as it seems,' I replied, frowning as my eyes wan-dered over the highlighted pages. 'They never had a chance,' I reiterate. 'Their briefs . . . what were they thinking? They didn't call any wit-nesses to show what sort of man Marcus Halnsley was. They didn't call the ex-wife to talk about if there'd been abuse allegations against him in the past. And I bet you there were loads.

'They didn't look for any of the other pupils he'd groomed – because what he did to Poppy and Mum was too slick to be something he just fell into. They didn't bring in medical records, even though both girls would have needed medical attention.

'It's like they almost literally phoned that defence in. And this is only halfway through day two!' I sat back and recapped my high-lighter. 'I'm sure Grandma and Grandpa will have paid Mum's legal team a lot of money but they wouldn't have known that they weren't doing their job properly.'

We sighed dramatically, hopelessly, in unison.

'I wasn't expecting these to be a cheery read,' Logan Carlisle said. 'I mean, I don't know what I was expecting, but this is depressing the living daylights out of me.'

'And me. And I look at these types of documents day in and day out . . . what a mess.'

'I could use a drink,' he stated.

'One coffee coming up.'

'No, a real drink.'

Minutes later I handed him a condensation-covered beer that I kept in the fridge for when Conrad came over and settled down with a large glass of white wine for myself. 'I already feel completely demoralised,' Logan admitted.

'We can't let it get us down. I mean, we know your sister went to prison so it must have been bad.'

'No, you're right. It'd explain why your mother didn't tell, though. With all this' – he tapped the top of the nearest pile – 'if I were her, I would have kept my mouth shut, too.'

I pressed my finger on the black screen of my phone to bring it back to life: 20:32. 'Shall we call it a day?' I said to him. 'Start afresh again . . . I don't know, when do you want to come back?'

'Tomorrow?'

'*Tomorrow?*'

'Yes, I want to get all of this done as soon as possible.'

'I have Sunday lunch with my family tomorrow. It's the one time we get together and have a chance to . . .' My voice dried up like a drop of water in a hot pan when I saw his face. 'I'll see if I can move it.' I could not move it. Mum insisted on Sundays together at least once a month. She wanted us to connect, never forget how much we mean to each other.

81

'No, no, I don't want to take you away from them. What sort of a git would I be if I did that? Let's just get back to it after these drinks.'

'OK,' I said miserably. I was so hungry. So hungry. Saturday nights on the sofa with a takeaway and my next favourite binge-watch was what I looked forward to all week. Sometimes Zeph would persuade me to go out, sometimes my mate Howie would ask to drop by, but Saturday nights were made for me to be alone and chill.

'You have other plans?' he asked.

'Not really. Just food and TV.'

'Don't let me stop you.' He started to stand up.

'No, no, look, you must be hungry. Do you fancy getting a take-away, pausing for a bit to eat it and then getting back into it?'

'If you don't mind losing your Saturday night to this.'

Of course I minded. But I had to show willing, which in turn would keep him onside and away from my mother. 'Not at all. Tonight it's pizza. You fancy pizza?'

'Yes, I could eat a pizza. I could definitely eat pizza.'

Now

My knickers are urgently tugged down and then off . . . his fly is practically ripped open . . .

June, 2019

Over the days and days we spent together poring over and over the papers, Logan grew quieter and quieter. His brows knitted themselves together so often he was just one big frown, his eyes darting over the highlighted pages as if searching for the words that he'd missed the first time round that would confirm what he thought, what he *knew* to be true. As time went on and the days became more days became weeks, became a month of working almost every evening and most weekends on the papers, he became almost mute. Because, I realised, he had come to understand that Poppy could have done it. That while Mum walking free might have been a mistake, the only evidence about who did it pointed clearly to Poppy.

I kept suggesting we re-examine the papers, thereby drawing out, elongating, basically delaying the moment we had to admit that neither of us were sure about our loved ones and their involvement in this crime. It could have been Poppy. It might have been Serena.

'Are we just going to do this indefinitely, then?' Logan finally asked just over a month after we'd started. I'd known him nearly two months now and he was actually quite good company. He was respectful of my space, always clearing up after himself, asking before he did anything, conscious of imposing himself on my time.

'I don't know,' I replied as I rubbed my hands over my eyes to hide from the truth. 'Maybe. Hopefully. Probably.'

I felt Logan stretch forward to put down the paper in his hands on the top of its relevant pile and then straighten the stack before he sat back. He reached out and gently took my hand away from my face. He was half smiling at me, as though he knew what I was doing and why, and wanted to do the same himself.

'This didn't work out the way I thought it would,' he admitted.

'Me neither.'

'I thought I'd find the back-up I needed to prove my sister was innocent and then I would have that vital bit of evidence everyone missed to take to your mother and force her to confess.' He grimaced at his own naïvety. 'I seriously thought I'd be able to say to her that she needed to come clean to the authorities before I went to them and they launched a reinvestigation. I had visions of there being a big retrial and Poppy having her conviction overturned and walking away with the apologies of the court. I could even see my dad's face as he had to apologise to her for not believing in her all those years.

'And now, I'm just sitting here petrified because I can see why Dad believes she did it. Why Mum doesn't want to think about whether she did it or not. And how I might have been wrong all these years.'

Logan was still holding on to my hand, and he was staring intently into my eyes as he talked. 'Do you think she did it?' he asked.

Against my skin, his hand was warm and so gentle, and normal. It felt normal for him to be holding my hand like this.

'I think her legal people let her down. That what happened during the trial was a complete character assassination of her. That she wasn't necessarily convicted on the evidence but on what people wanted to believe about her as this vixen who was now dressing up in smart clothes for court when she was always ready to jump into bed with anyone and ruin the lives of "good" men. I hope that things have got better since and if she was on trial today she'd get a much fairer hearing and better defence.'

'Please answer my question,' he begged quietly. Ever so slightly, ever so gently, his hand tightened around mine, as though holding me, reassuring me that I could say what needed to be said. 'Do you think she did it?'

'Yes, she might have,' I said, feeling wretched. 'And so might Mum.'

We both stared at each other, a beat of silence pulsing between us as we had to acknowledge what both of us didn't want to: either of them might have done it; both of them might have done it.

Logan carefully let my hand go. 'Now we're stuck, aren't we?'

'Yes, and I blame you, Logan Carlisle. I absolutely blame you,' I said trying to make light of it.

He snatched up the chance to step out of the moment immediately. 'Don't be blaming me, whose idea was it to get the court papers?'

'Yours!'

When he burst out laughing, incredulous at my cheek, I laughed, too. It was so freeing suddenly. We'd been so serious, so sombre during the whole process. We'd chatted and joked and had some nice moments, but the overarching feeling had been oppressive, and laughing now seemed to clap away those feelings that had shrouded us, like you clapped and banged to clear old, scary spirits from a haunted house.

'Watch it you, or I won't give you this present I got you.'

'You got me a present? Gimme, gimme, gimme.'

'Well, present might be overstating it. Actually, it's not really a present at all.'

'Who are you? Take-back Boy? Either you've got a present or you haven't. Which is it?'

'One of the guys I work with—'

'Not hearing "present" in this conversation,' I interrupted.

'—had these two tickets that he bought months ago. And now he can't make the show—'

'Here, present, present; here, boy, here, boy.'

'—and I said I'd have them because I knew a girl who liked all that space stuff and thought she might want to go instead.'

'Back up, what space stuff?'

'At the Brighton Centre, that science guy is doing a show about space and quantum realms and all that jazz and I know you're into all that stuff so I said I'd take the tickets off his hands and see if you wanted to go. It's this weekend. He's proper gutted he can't make it, but I assured him if you weren't busy, they would go to a good home.'

'Are you saying you've got tickets to the Prof's show in Brighton this weekend?'

'Yeah.'

'The show that sold out when I was on holiday and I haven't been able to get tickets for since?'

'Yep.'

'The one I was seriously considering travelling up to Manchester to see?'

'The very one.'

'Oh my God, Logan!' I threw myself across the gap and flung my arms around him, trapped him in the hugest of hugs. 'That's amazing! I can't believe—' I let him go and sat up. 'Wait a minute, how did you know I like "all that space stuff"?' We had never talked about it, except that time I mentioned time travel.

Logan used his finger to circle the room. 'I have never been to a house before where the owner has a framed picture of a periodic table where most people have a nice bit of modern art or those dogs playing polka.' He pointed to the image on the wall above the television. It was such a part of my life, my backdrop – having been the one I'd had in my bedroom growing up – that I didn't even notice it was there. 'I've never seen so many books on quantum physics in one place in my entire life, it's like a one-for-one ratio to the novels on your shelves.' He pointed out of the door. 'You have an atomic clock in your kitchen as well as all the tea towels with elements and your fridge magnets spell out various formulae—'

'All right, all right. I know when I've been rumbled. I love all that science stuff.'

'Why didn't you become a scientist?' he asked. 'I mean, I've been dying to ask. You obviously have a passion for it, and understanding of it, so why didn't you do it?'

'Because I wanted to be a solicitor.'

Logan waited for me to say more. When no more was forthcoming, he frowned at me. But not like he had been frowning for all the past weeks, just puzzled. 'That's it? You wanted to become a solicitor?'

'Yes.'

'And not a scientist?'

'No.'

'Why not?'

'Because I wanted to be a solicitor.' I said it slower so maybe he'd understand.

'That doesn't make sense.'

'Yes, it does.'

'It doesn't.'

'It does. In the multi-worlds theory of quantum science, there is a Verity Gillmare that is a scientist, I'm sure. But in *this* world, *this* Verity wanted to be a solicitor. So *this one* is training to be one.'

'Fair enough, I suppose.' He shrugged but still looked baffled. 'So are you going to come with me to see this science guy?'

'Oh, I have to go with you?' I said, disgusted.

Logan did a double-take, shocked at my horror. His light-brown eyes searched my face, wondering why I was suddenly so averse to spending time with him. When he saw the slight twitch of my mouth, caused by the excitement of going to see the Prof talk about science, and absolutely not because I'd get to spend more time with Logan away from all this heavy stuff, he started laughing. 'You had me going there,' he said. 'You really got me going.'

I laughed along with him, ignoring the swirl that was happening inside; the shift and move of my heart, the re-centring of my emotions was absolutely nothing to do with wanting nothing more than to spend more and more time with Logan Carlisle.

Now

My legs are pushed apart . . . his erection is free . . .

June, 2019

I could hear his heart beating.

In the dark, surrounded by over a thousand people, all of us listening, focusing, thinking, opening up our minds to the possibilities 'out there', I could hear his heart beating. It drummed out the unique pattern of a man I'd developed feelings for.

His arm was lightly touching mine on the armrest our seats shared and his warmth flowed straight into me. Where we touched lit me up – the electrons dancing where they met, causing me to want to dance, too. It'd started a while back, of course. Me noticing him, wondering about him, thinking about him. He'd become a regular fixture, a conundrum that walked into my home almost every day and didn't really seem to want to be solved.

And tonight, when I'd seen him standing outside the Brighton Centre, handsomely dressed in an open-necked white shirt, tight blue jeans and black jacket, my heart had started to triple beat. I'd admitted it then. Accepted that I had crossed the line in my head, and I was desperate enough to want to move those feelings into another realm – into reality.

He'd smiled and said hi, and I was lost. Absolutely set adrift in the space of my life. How could this ever happen? Me and Logan Carlisle? My mother would . . . I couldn't even imagine what my mum would do. And his sister. What would she do? Think? Say?

I'd returned my hello with a swallow of my longing and stopped a bit further away than normal, out of reach. Out of reach, I might have been, but he still leant in for a kiss on the cheek and I kind of stepped even further away to stop him, stop it all, and we ended up with him awkwardly kissing the air and me kind of patting him patronisingly on the shoulder. *Good start*, I thought to myself.

I'd dressed up. Put on my favourite red minidress with a zip down the front that I usually wore with boots. I'd made a fresh batch of flax and marshmallow gel, and slicked my hair down. I'd applied make-up with Stormzy living it up in the background. I was going out and I was going to have fun. And then I stopped and looked at myself. My dress, my hair, my make-up, my black suede boots waiting for me in the hall. I was going out on a Saturday and I was looking ready.

Ready for what, exactly? I asked myself, sounding like my mum's mum with her Ghanaian accent and African disdain in my head. *Ready for what?* What foolishness was this? Dressing up for Logan Carlisle! *And what would you be doing with him?* Grandma's voice was asking: *What are you going there for?*

Grandma's voice was in my head while I took off the dress and stripped myself of the lacy underwire bra and matching lace knickers I'd put on. I had absolutely worn them for me – because I wanted to feel nice, sexy, *sexual*, while I was with him.

When we'd had that awkward moment in the street, I was back in jeans, T-shirt, trainers and sensible, everyday underwear.

But still, I could hear his heart beating. I was craving and becoming a little intoxicated by the warmth from where we touched. I was so aware of him. Of how physically close he was to me – an orbiting body that was pulling me closer and closer to him. I was listening to what was going on in front of me, I was hearing my favourite theories about space and time and the loop that they formed around our reality, our possible realities, and I was failing to pull myself away from the event horizon: the black hole of being attracted to the man beside me.

I'd had – a few – crushes before; one or two I'd even kissed and got close to sleeping with, but none of them felt like this. None felt as— I felt my heart stop as I realised he was watching me. He was staring at me and I was staring back at him, listening to his heart beating. Wondering if he was listening to mine.

The night was black. A beautiful, comforting, enriching darkness that slipped itself around me as soon as we left the Centre and stood on the pavement outside. The sea shooshed beyond the aquamarine railings in front of us, its waves rubbing noisily over the pebbles. The stars seemed to sit low in the sky, as though they knew we'd been talking and thinking about them and they'd come closer to give us a proper look. The world was a chaos, a madness of voices and excitement and Saturday night and life and sea and night creatures and expectation.

Suddenly Logan grabbed my hand, pulled me back through the crowds pouring out of the Centre behind us and tugged me with him to where the grey-sandstone building curved towards a gap in the buildings between it and the cinema. He ignored the people tutting and cursing and sighing, he kept moving, taking me with him, until we reached his destination down the side of the Centre.

He pushed me back against the wall and then didn't hesitate before his lips covered mine. My arms went up and wrapped themselves around his neck, his body pushed itself closer to mine, his knee slipped between my legs as his tongue moved into my mouth. I eagerly kissed him back, delighted and shocked at the same time. I'd wanted this to happen, I'd known it shouldn't happen, but I'd craved this. I'd been desperate for this.

He pushed closer, his body wanting to extinguish any type of gap between us. I pulled him as near as possible, as desperate as he was to bring us together.

Kissing under the stars.

Embracing under the cosmos.

Where everything begins and ends, we were kissing and kissing and kissing.

The start of something perfect and complete; the end of something immaculate and whole.

Now

We become one in an instant . . . our groans swallowed by the kisses of the other . . .

June, 2019

His side of the bed was empty when I woke up.

Foolishness. I instantly heard Grandma say in my head. Grandma was so lovely. She loved her grandchildren and she took so much pride in us. So much so that sometimes I'd see Mum side-eyeing her as she brazenly took credit for our accomplishments, but she was always there for us. And sometimes, being an African grandma meant telling you in a quite unvarnished fashion how foolish you had been. I swallowed and rolled onto my back, stared at the ceiling.

There was a mark on the ceiling, from what, I did not know. I suspected it was a water stain from the flat above, but it'd been there from shortly after I moved in and was shaped like a pair of hands reaching out to each other. It hadn't changed in shape or size so I knew it wasn't growing. How I longed to curl up in that stain right now. Hide from my foolishness.

Last night had been incredible. Unexpected and incredible. And now I was going to be cringing the whole day, wondering if I should tell Mum about Logan Carlisle before he told her. If I should confess to everything, right up to last night, and give her the chance to prepare herself for what he might do next.

Urgh. I did not relish that conversation. Even the thought gave me the heebie-jeebies.

I shuddered.

Shower.

I'll have a shower and formulate what I'll do, I decided.

I rolled over on my side, stared out of the window. The gardens at the back of my flat were still. Sunday mornings were always like this. Peaceful and quiet, people respecting the day of rest for many hours.

Slam! The front door went and every nerve in my body stood on end. This was it. The only thing I worried about living on my own – a serial killer breaking in and doing away with me while I was minding my own business.

And I'd left everything that could possibly be a weapon back in the main part of my flat. The bedroom, at the turn at the end of a long corridor and next to the bathroom, thankfully wasn't the first place you'd head to, but you'd get there. And there weren't that many places to hide here.

Footsteps and then Logan's head popped around the door, just as I was reaching for my phone to call 999.

'You're awake, sleepyhead,' he said.

'I'm awake,' I stated.

'I went out for breakfast. Found a nice café not far from here. Got big breakfast sandwiches, juice and cappuccinos. I also went to the newsagents and got my usual selection of Sunday papers. I don't know what you read so I got you a science magazine or two.'

'I thought you'd . . . Never mind.'

'You thought I'd ghosted you?'

I nodded.

He shook his head. 'Never. Just didn't want you to think I was expecting what happened last night or that it's ever been about that.' He held up the breakfast bags. 'Hopefully this shows you I'm sticking around?'

'What flavour of science magazine?' I replied.

'Only the best for you, my darling,' he said before he disappeared back down the corridor.

My darling. I liked the sound of that. I really did.

Now

We finish together, focused only on each other, and eventually we pull ourselves apart.

'I'm sorry,' he pants, frantically tidying himself up. 'That won't happen again. I'm sorry, I'm sorry, I'm sorry.' And then he's gone. Left. Departed. Without me having uttered a single, solitary word.

Part 2

Part 2

serena

Now

Someone is following me again.

Twice before in my life I've felt the chill of someone's attention, their gaze being focused on me at different times of the day, during different parts of my day. First of all it was the press as part of their need for dirt on an Ice Cream Girl, and then it was *her*. Poppy.

The press aren't interested in me any more. That's a plain and simple fact. So is it Poppy? Would she bother? The last time I saw her, she seemed certain and genuine that she wouldn't follow me again. That she had left all of that behind and was laying that part of her life to rest. I was doing the same. I have done the same. Mostly.

'Oh, hello, Serena,' calls Sarah Sherwood, when I enter the office. She has come in early and her two children – Max and Millie – stand by her desk, hunched over her phone playing a game.

Our large insurance broker's company's office, Doyle & Co. is empty now, but in about half an hour, this place will be buzzing: young people, older people, every people will flood in and take up their seats and the phones will start, the emails will ping, the noise of people working will rise up and hover over the office like a low-hanging canopy of sound until everyone starts to leave again.

'Have you got the kettle on?' I ask Sarah as I try to shake off the awful, unsettling feeling of being under scrutiny.

'Yep,' she calls.

Who could be watching me? And why? Is it Poppy? But why wait till now? Ten years have passed since she resurfaced. Maybe something has gone wrong in her life that she blames me for and she wants . . . what? Revenge? If that was the case, wouldn't she just turn up? What would be the point of cat-and-mousing it when I know of her existence? I know she knows where I live and work, but I have nothing more to give her.

Unless she's planning on telling Verity and Conrad? But again, why now?

She wouldn't. Would she? It would explain Verity's definite and increasing aversion to me. What if Poppy's already told her and Verity is disgusted. What if she's already told her and Verity hates me for being that person? But surely, *surely*, if Poppy was going to do that, she would have told me what she'd done already. What would be the point of telling Vee without letting me know what she'd done?

I'm being ridiculous, of course; no one is watching me. No one is following me. No one has any reason to do that. No one.

'You two are here early,' I say to Millie and Max once I've made myself a herbal tea. Their mother is blonde but Max and Millie are both tall redheads with cute freckles, although I'm not sure how they'd feel about me describing them like that. Although her brother is tall – probably the same height as a lot of women – Millie is about the same height as Verity, so she is tall, too. I remember Verity at eleven, she was quiet and taciturn like I was. She used to listen to everything that was said to her then decide whether she was going to comment or not. She hasn't changed that much, but in many ways she's a million miles from that girl, too.

'Andy had a work emergency,' Sarah explains, 'so he had to drop them off here on the way. I'm just waiting for Miles to come and take them to school.' Miles is Sarah's much older son who lives on the other side of Brighton.

'Oh, you should have done it,' I tell her. 'I would have covered for you.'

'I know, but—' Mid-sentence the phone the two children are playing with starts to ring. 'Oh, that will be him now. Come on, you two, grab your things, I'll take you down to your brother.'

As Sarah helps them to gather their school rucksacks, sports bags and laptops, my mind wanders back to what I was thinking about before – who could be following me?

'Oh,' Sarah says, tucking a blonde lock behind her ear and adjusting her glasses, 'before I forget. There was a man asking about you earlier.'

My entire being grows still. 'What man?'

'Well, I don't know. He was outside, and he seemed nice enough. Young, quite good-looking, suit. He just asked if you were still working here. I asked him who wanted to know and he said he was an old friend.'

'Right. But you didn't get his name?'

'No, no name. I said to him if he was that good a friend, then he'd know whether you worked here or not. And he laughed and said fair enough. Then he said he was wanting the details of Evan's party because he knew the venue had changed.'

'What did you tell him?'

'Nothing! I wasn't going to tell some random anything about you. He could have been anyone. He didn't seem dangerous or anything, but he was very interested in you and you can never tell these days.'

'No, you can't,' I reply. 'Well, thanks for keeping me mysterious.' I'm trying to sound nonchalant and carefree about this, but now I am scared. Terrified. I was not imagining it. I am being followed. And this person is bold. It's a man and he has no worries about approaching the people I work with. And how he knows that Sarah is a work colleague is even more terrifying.

'See you soon, you two,' I call to Max and Millie.

'Bye,' Max says before he disappears out of the door. 'Bye-bye,' Millie calls before she follows her brother out of sight.

Alone in the office, I sit in my seat and stare at my computer.

Someone is following me. It'll be about the past. It's always about my past. I can't shake it off, no matter how hard I try. Things will be calm, quiet, comfortingly boring and then something will happen to shatter the peace. And it's never just one thing, either.

One thing starts it and several things follow it.

Someone is following me. And I have no idea who or why.

poppy

Now

I feel sick. Absolutely sick to my stomach.

I've been called in to the school to talk to the head teacher and Betina's form tutor and I know it can't be anything good. Alain is away but it can't wait for his return, apparently. Which means I'm expected to go on my own – which is not going to happen. A swirl of anxiety whips itself up inside me at the very thought of it. I am still on licence – will be for the rest of my life. The slightest thing I do wrong, and I could be sent back to prison.

'Hey,' Logan says, arriving beside the school gates. We're early, only by ten minutes, but it's enough to show we're both a bit nervous.

'Hey!' I exclaim and throw my arms around my brother. Thank goodness he could come.

'It's not that big a deal,' my brother tells me.

He doesn't realise how much of a big deal it is.

'You know I can't do this sort of thing. I get too wound up; I hear even the smallest criticism as an attack and I go into defence mode. It would not be good for Betina if I was arrested.'

Logan smiles, his expression comfortingly patronising as he dismisses my concerns. 'That won't happen, silly,' he says. He slings his arm around my shoulders. 'You're so hard on yourself.'

'I'm not, you know,' I state. It's hard to explain to someone who hasn't been there what it feels like in these situations. No matter how long ago it is, these situations bring out the prisoner in me.

'Let's see what they have to say before you try to get yourself locked up again, all right? It might be nothing.'

'It might be,' I mumble as we go towards the silver intercom box that will allow us to enter the school. Logan is not a parent, he does not know that you're never called in for 'nothing'. It's always something and it's almost always your fault. Not your child's, yours. Or at least that's how it feels. Whenever I get a line or two about behaviour in her reports or on the reading record, whenever a teacher calls me over for a 'chat' at the end of the day, whenever she comes out brandishing a yellow (warning) or red (unacceptable) behaviour card, I see me in her. I see that my worries before she was born were absolutely justified: I am going to mess her up, *damage* her, in ways that will be impossible to undo.

Sitting here with those two women on the other side of the desk unnerves me.

They look so comfortable and secure in their roles. I've always thought that about them. The one in charge wears a black suit with a blue shirt, the other one, the form tutor, has on a furry pink jumper and brown suede skirt with knee-high boots. They wear twin expressions of concerned condescension and it's this that will be my undoing. Whether they realise it or not, they are looking down on me and it's that sort of thing that sets me off.

I am not the teenager who was driven into prison thirty years ago.

I am not the woman who walked out of prison ten years ago.

I am so much more than that. Sure, they're a part of me, but I am better than that. No, 'better' sounds like I think there was something wrong with me before. I have moved on to the next stage of who I'm supposed to be. I have a job running the cleaning company that I worked for when I first came out of prison – Raymond found his dislike of me waned the more I worked for him and eventually, when he wanted to take a step back, asked me if I would step in for him. I did that. I became enough to take over someone's business. I became enough to become someone's mother. I don't need to feel small, to think I'm going to drown in unworthiness.

'Your partner couldn't join us today, Miss Carlisle?' the head teacher asks.

I resist the urge to say 'obviously not' and smile instead. Not every question needs answering. I found this out a long, long time ago.

'You'll have to put up with me instead,' Logan says, charm itself. 'I'm Logan Carlisle, Betina's uncle.'

The pair on the powerful side of the desk are in confusion. Is he my brother or my ex-husband? Family friend or sperm donor? 'Uncle' has become such a vague, nebulous term that neither of them knows how to react to this.

'I'm Poppy's brother,' Logan helpfully supplies. 'Alain is away on business and Poppy thought she might need a little support.'

'Oh, not at all,' the head teacher, Mrs Long, states. 'We just wanted to touch base about Betina and how you think she is getting on.'

'Isn't it more about how *you* think she's getting on?' Logan says for me. I was going to say that, but I know how it would have come out. Aggressive. Angry. Defensive. I remember Tina, friend Tina, would say all the time that no matter how she said things, people would take it the wrong way. They would paint her as aggressive, and dismiss everything that came out of her mouth because of it. I didn't get what she meant until I had been out of prison for a while and realised that prison face, convict voice got you nowhere. Tina said this happened to her *before* she went to prison, simply because she was speaking up while Black, and the thought of that, how just being normal was criminalised, made me depressed.

Mrs Long doesn't like being challenged, even in the mildest way, so blatantly ignores Logan, and focuses on me. 'Miss Carlisle, are things difficult at home for Betina at the moment?'

'I'm not sure what you mean by "difficult",' I say, careful to modulate my tone, to suppress Prison Poppy.

'Betina often talks about her father,' says Miss Glasbern, Betina's form teacher. 'She says he doesn't live at home any more? Whenever we have discussions or do work about families, Betina brings up how her father isn't at home.'

'And that's a problem?' Logan asks.

'Only because we think it might be contributing to her "acting out".'

'I don't know what "acting out" means,' I state. Euphemisms irritate me. Just say what you mean or don't say it at all. Stop dressing it up and sending it out there – how is a person expected to understand when you won't be clear in what you mean.

'Betina is disruptive in class,' Miss Glasbern says. 'She calls out rather than waiting her turn, she won't sit still, she's often talking when she should be getting on with her work. She has progressed to fighting the other children who she perceives have crossed her.'

I bet my prison reports said that about me. I did call out, speak up. I frequently wouldn't sit still if something was happening. I was often talking when I should have been working. And yeah, when other people crossed me I would absolutely fight them if I had to. I didn't like it, but

I wasn't a fool. If someone came for me, I always made sure they didn't do it again. All of this is fine in prison, but unacceptable in school when you're seven.

'This is all news to me,' I offer. 'No one has said anything before.'

'We only really call the parents in when the problem becomes unmanageable and we're starting to look at our options.'

They're going to ghost my daughter. They're going to get rid of her, make her some other institution's problem.

'Have you thought about changing her class?' Logan interjects before I can say any more.

'Miss Glasbern is an excellent teacher; if Betina struggles in this environment, I'm not sure what moving to the other class will do.'

'I'm sure Miss Glasbern is brilliant, and she clearly cares about my niece, but I'm talking about moving her up a year. I'm assuming, since you haven't mentioned it, this situation isn't a result of frustration that she can't keep up with her classmates. I'm thinking it's frustration that everything is too easy for her and she's bored out of her mind.'

Both teachers stare at Logan as though he's simultaneously spoken a different language and solved the hardest equation in the world while insulting their authority.

'I only say this because I remember being exactly the same way when I was her age. *Exactly* the same way. I think my parents were called in and told that they would have to move me if I didn't stop the behaviour – they didn't call it "acting out" then – and because the class below was full, they had to move me into the year above. Technically, they weren't allowed to do that because it was a state school but they tried it and it worked. I had been bored and being properly challenged transformed my time at school.'

Logan and Bella never tell me things like this. What growing up was like. We kind of act like we've only known each other as adults. They both ask me questions about prison but not about before. They talk about their university years and beyond, but never before. If I ask, they change the subject. I didn't know Logan got into trouble at school. And there was stuff going on at home when he was Betina's age. There were arrests, a trial, their sister disappearing from their lives because she was in prison. It'd be a miracle if that trauma didn't come out in behaviour at school.

'That's a very interesting point but—' Mrs Long begins.

'But you're going to dismiss it out of hand?' I say. Again, calm citizen, not Prison Poppy. 'My brother may have a point. It might be the answer to the problem and you're not going to even explore it?'

'We wanted to know how she was feeling emotionally, if the disruption at home was behind the recent troubles. We would be remiss in our safeguarding duties if we didn't start this conversation.'

'"Safeguarding"?' Every single one of my hackles is raised. Every. Single. One. What is she talking about that for? What is she implying? Does she think I harm my child? 'I haven't done anything to hurt my child. What are you saying?'

'No one is accusing you of—'

'That's what it sounds like. You're saying I'm harming my child. I haven't done anything to her. Me and her dad aren't together right now, no, but they see each other almost every day. Every day. That's more than most children who have two parents that work outside of the home. She loves her dad and the days she doesn't see him she talks to him on the phone or video call. There's never a time when she wants to see or speak to him that she doesn't. I'm not harming her at all.'

'No one is—'

'Do you know how difficult it is to get by without feeling like a failure? Do either of you have children? Especially ones who are constantly asking you questions and wanting you to explain things to them? Things that you haven't a hope of understanding, let alone explaining, without spending a lot of time in the library or on the internet? I mean, the World Wide Web. Because they're two separate things, did you know that? Betina told me. She said someone created the World Wide Web and built it on top of the internet, which already existed. Did you know that? I didn't. Not until my seven-year-old told me. And every time I use those words interchangeably, she picks me up on it. That's how bright she is.

'And she wouldn't be telling me things like that if she felt scared or unsafe. She's full of those kinds of facts. You know, when she was four – *four*, so not even at school yet – she told me all about this creature called a Uviss. It was scaly like an armadillo but had a long nose like an anteater and ears like a cat. But it was a vegetarian and despite its short legs, it was always trying to climb trees. She told me all these details about this creature and I was so impressed that I told all the people I worked with. Described it exactly like she did. And I can see by the looks on your faces that you've never heard of a Uviss. Well, guess what? She made it all up. All that detail, and it was a creature from her imagination. That's what I'm dealing with. Someone who is always a million steps ahead. And you've had her for years. You should have noticed how bright she is and you should have been thinking about putting her up a year. Why is it up to my brother to teach you your job? Why haven't you even considered she might be bored instead of trying to criminalise her and make her the victim of a bad single mother? Huh?'

Alarmed faces greet me when I stop talking.

Logan leans over and puts his hand on my arm. 'That'll do, Pops, that'll do,' he says carefully.

From my head to my toes a wave of embarrassment crashes over me, leaving me a hot, red, glowing mess. *What an idiot. What an absolute idiot.* I shouldn't have been worried about being arrested, I should have thought about being a complete fool in public.

'I think we're agreed that we should try Betina in a new class before we decide if there are other, deeper issues we should be concerned about or investigating,' Logan says. 'Yes?'

'Yes,' Mrs Long readily agrees. Her green eyes keep darting towards me then snatching themselves away in case they stay on me too long and cause another outburst. 'I think that might be a good idea.'

I want to make Miss Glasbern feel OK about Betina moving, I want to say that Betina loves being in her class, she adores her as a form teacher, but, overall, I think it's best that I keep my mouth shut.

Mrs Long shakes our hands at the door to her office. I smile and don't speak, Logan thanks them for their time and says he looks forward to hearing good things about the upcoming move.

Logan does well to keep it together until we're on the pavement, heading quickly away from the school before he cracks up. He stops and bends double, his hands resting on his thighs while his laughter spills out of him like a flood. The happy sound lights up everything around him. It wasn't that funny. Behind him, the light shimmers and I can see Tina doing exactly the same thing, clutching her middle, giggling her head off. I wish she was really here. She would have come with me, she would have been as good as Logan at standing up for me and Betina. Or would she have done what she was always trying to do: make me stand up for myself? Rescue myself. And I suppose I did do that in the end. When pushed, I did step up and step in.

I watch my brother and my dead best friend laugh at my outburst, my going the Complete Carlisle. I watch and my horror melts, dissolves into light titters, then fuller-bodied giggles and finally into full-on laughs.

'I am ridiculous,' I say between laughs.

'Yeah, you are!' Logan and Tina say at the same time between gaps in their mirth. 'Yeah, you are!'

While Logan eventually straightens up, composes himself, Tina keeps on laughing. Her laughter elongates my giggles. 'Come on,' Logan says, 'let's swing by Bella's and grab her up. She needs a break. We can all go for a long lunch.'

'No, no, I need to get to work.'

'Nonsense,' he replies. 'A few hours off won't hurt any of us and I have to do your face and your hands when I tell her about this. It won't work without the face and hands.'

I still hesitate. I really do have so much work to do. I still always want to do my very best to prove that I can do this job and I can continue to make a success of this business. Raymond's business was solid, but under me it's thriving. I have expanded it, extended it, made it a business that people know and trust. I can't ever slack off from that.

'Life is short,' Logan proclaims. 'And as you know, it isn't actually that short. We want to spend as much time together as we can, don't we?'

Tina has finished laughing and she's nodding at what he's saying. *Go on*, she whispers directly into my head. *Go on and have fun with your family. What's all this time for if you can't enjoy it?*

'All right, I'll call Nicole on the way to pick Bella up, ask her to divert the phones when she leaves the office.'

'That's the spirit,' Logan replies. 'I wonder if a Uviss has that much spirit.' And he dissolves into laughter again.

*

'Next time, you have got to take me with you,' Bella says. We're two bottles of white and six bottles of beer down and the story has grown and expanded with every retelling, even I've joined in because it feels so ridiculous I can't quite believe I reacted like that.

'Oh, right, so you can sit there with us, a line of Carlisles terrifying the teaching staff? Pretty sure they're the ones who're meant to scare us.' I shake my head and then down a mouthful of too-tart, too-chilled wine. 'Bet she wished she'd waited for Alain now and hadn't insisted I come in without him,' I smirked loudly as Mrs Long's face wafts across my mind again. 'That will teach her! Literally teach-*er*!'

Bella sprays wine all over table. 'You are out of order,' she admonishes and wipes a sleeve over her mouth. 'So, you and Alain . . .' My sister always pronounces his name phonetically – A-Lane, 'You do school and stuff together?'

'Yeah, course.'

'Sounds like you've got the most civilised break-up on Earth.'

I snarl at Logan from the corner of my mouth. 'Who said we'd broken up? *Logan?*'

'You think that pitiful show you put on every Sunday works on anyone except Mum and Dad? And not even on them; they just pretend it works on them because if they pretend hard enough they think it'll be true.'

'Don't know what you're talking about,' I say. More wine. I need more wine. I down what's in my glass and then pour myself another from the dregs left in the bottle.

'For the record, I think he's a really nice guy. Decent, good-looking, clever, good dresser, adores the bones of you and Betina. I just wish you'd allow yourself to be loved. And loved by a man as decent as A-Lane.'

Away from our parents, Bella is a different person. Almost literally. Away from our parents she lives in a nice yellow-bricked house two streets over from Mum and Dad. She runs a publicity business from the office she's created in her converted attic. She has client meetings, she runs campaigns and she gives definitive advice you'd be downright silly to ignore. Around our folks, Bella barely speaks and when she does, she stutters with nerves, and she keeps dropping things. If Logan has a position of strength with the Carlisles, then she has one of no agency.

'You really need to listen to her,' Logan says. 'I was saying the same to her the other day. She really needs to listen to you.'

Bella turns a look on him that is worthy of one of Betina's disdainful expressions. 'Like you're one to talk. You've been going out with someone for nearly a year and you're still too chicken to tell us her name, let alone let us meet her.'

It's Logan's turn to turn on me. '*Poppy,*' he hisses.

'Like I need Poppy to tell me you're completely in love with someone but won't allow yourself to admit it because it'd be too weak? You'd be too happy?'

Logan meekly takes a long pull on his beer and shuts up. It's almost worth being told off to see that look on his face.

'What a mess we Carlisles are when it comes to love,' I say with a smile.

'What? No. Don't put me in with you two freak-show screw-ups. My love life is perfectly fine, thank you. I have a man who loves me and who I love and our life is on our planned trajectory.'

'Those men who live on the telly aren't really your boyfriends, Bels,' Logan patronises. 'They're make-believe.'

'Erm, I know?' she replies with such sarcastic scorn, we both stare at her. 'Myron is very real.'

'But you broke up with Myron when you moved down here,' Logan says.

'Says who?'

'Erm, you just never talk about him. Never bring him up. Never see him. Nothing.'

My sister wrinkles her nose. 'I see him every Thursday to Sunday. Where do you think I go? Why do you think I'm there a bit later for Sunday lunch every other week? I'm on my way back from London. And on the alternate week he comes here.'

'But you don't bring him to Sunday lunch,' I say.

'You think I'm inflicting *that* on him? Unlike you two messed-up dudes, I know how to love and to be loved. I like my partner and I won't put him in rubbish situations.'

'Wow,' Logan says.

'Yeah, wow. In eight months we'll have saved enough money to pay off the mortgage on the house and we can afford for him to move here permanently.'

'What? Just how?' I ask.

'"How" is that when I see a decent person and he offers me love, I go with it. I accept his love and I give love back and I enjoy myself around him. Love is not complicated for me. It doesn't have to be for you two, either. Just get over yourselves.'

With our sister's words ringing in our ears, we spend the rest of the afternoon getting very, very drunk.

verity

July, 2019

'It's been three weeks and neither of us has mentioned the elephant in the room,' Logan stated.

I was reading one of the science magazines he'd bought me that morning on the breakfast run, and he was interspersing his reading with long pauses to kiss lines of desire up and down my skin.

'I don't see an elephant,' I replied.

He moved to snuggling into the crook of my neck. 'Be serious. This is serious. What are we doing here, babe?'

'We're doing something that allows you to call me "babe" without a hint of irony.'

'Are you going to tell your parents?'

'Are you going to tell your sister?'

'I was meant to be getting your mother to confess. I got waylaid.'

'Waylaid, huh?'

'In the best way possible, but still waylaid. I don't know what to do now. Because I do not want this to end. But I suspect it will if I march in and tell your mother I think she got away with murder.'

I placed my hand on his forehead and moved him smartly away from my body. 'Excuse me?'

'I wouldn't put it like that,' he said, trying to come back to where he was.

'But you still think she did it.'

'And you still think Poppy did it.'

Deadlock, I thought. 'Deadlock,' I said.

Logan sat back. Slowly he ran his hand through his hair as he let out a long sigh. 'Deadlock.'

'Can we just not tell anyone? No one really needs to know, do they?'

'No, I suppose they don't if we're going to just let my sister continue with this half-life she's living. You know, seeing as I started all this for her.'

'I don't know the answer, Logan,' I snapped. He had raised every single hackle, had destroyed our Sunday-morning buzz. 'If I ever meet anyone who tells me how to deal with this sort of thing, I'll pass on those life lessons to you quick smart.'

'Is this what it's going to be like? If we try to make a go of this, we're going to be sniping at each other?'

'Probably,' I replied. 'So let's just call it all off now. You go back to your plan to confront "Serena" now that you know there is no evidence to suggest she did do it and your sister didn't. And I'll go back to pretending I don't know way too much about my mother.'

Prosecution: Miss Gorringe, what was your favourite sexual position with Mr Halnsley?

Serena Gorringe: Pardon?

PR: What was your favourite sexual position with Mr Halnsley?

SG: I don't remember.

PR: You don't remember?

SG: No.

PR: Are you saying you have had so much sex that intercourse with Mr Halnsley became nothing remarkable or different and you had to find ways to make it interesting? Like through sex games or torture?

SG: No. I never did anything like that.

PR: But you can't remember your favourite position? How are we to know that you didn't participate in sex games or torture?

SG: I didn't. I just didn't.

PR: Did you enjoy the sex you had with Mr Halnsley?

SG:

PR: Please can you reply verbally, Miss Gorringe. For the record. The record can't see you shrugging as though you don't have a care in the world. I'll ask again: did you enjoy the sex you had with Mr Halnsley?

SG: Sometimes.

PR: Sometimes. Sometimes. It wasn't boring and humdrum?

SG: No.

PR: You didn't find yourself needing to become more and more extreme to make it interesting?

SG: Nothing like that. He was my first.

PR: But you've just told the court how you couldn't remember how much sex you had, so much so, you couldn't remember what your favourite position was.

SG: He was my first.

PR: I put it to you, Miss Gorringe, that those times you didn't enjoy sexual intercourse with him were the times Mr Halnsley couldn't satisfy your voracious sexual appetites and threatened to walk away.

SG: No.

PR: I put it to you, Miss Gorringe, that you knew Mr Halnsley
was growing tired of the sexual games you and your
co-defendant, Miss Carlisle, were playing with him and
you couldn't stand the thought of someone else deciding
when your relationship was over, that your often
uncooperative victim was gathering the strength to
walk away, so you conspired with Miss Carlisle, to
murder him.

SG: No, no, it wasn't like that. It honestly wasn't like that.

Some of the things I had found out were life-altering, core-shaking, and not the sort of thing you could pretend away. Not like my relationship with Logan. Relationship, hah! We'd slept together a few times: he'd stayed over three Saturday nights and bought me breakfast, which we ate in bed while we read the newspapers. We'd kind of skipped many, many stages of what you would call relationship-building and were acting like we'd been together for years. I suppose learning all about the criminal, potentially murderous, past of your loved ones would do that.

'I don't want to call it off,' Logan stated quite firmly. 'I . . . I think I'm falling in love with you—'

'Well don't. This issue we're having isn't you leaving wet towels on the floor or me closing the blinds in the wrong direction, it isn't something that's going to go away, so don't fall in love with me.' I was being snippy, snarky and a bit of a bitch. But hearing Mum in my head, her voice replying, '*Yes. Sometimes he forced me*' to the question: '*Do you mean to tell the court, Miss Gorringe, that Mr Halnsley sexually assaulted you?*' was still messing with my head.

PR: Do you mean to tell the court, Miss Gorringe, that Mr Halnsley sexually assaulted you?

SG: Yes. Sometimes he forced me.

PR: How many times?

SG: I don't understand what you mean.

PR: How many times did Mr Halnsley, who I would beg the court to remember isn't here to defend himself, "force you"?

SG: I . . . I don't know.

PR: You don't know how many times you claim to have been raped? I find that hard to believe. Was it once, twice, ten times, a hundred? How many, Miss Gorringe?

SG: I was just . . . He just . . . Like when we'd have an argument, he'd . . . afterwards . . . to . . . he'd say . . . Sometimes . . .

PR: You're not making much sense, Miss Gorringe. Is that because you hadn't thought through your lie—?

Defence Barrister: Your honour—

PR: I'm sorry, I'll rephrase. You seem very distressed, Miss Gorringe, would you like a few moments to compose yourself?

SG: No. No, thank you.

PR: If you're sure? I'll continue. You said that after an argument, Mr Halnsley would sometimes force you to have sexual intercourse with him.

SG: Yes.

PR: Was this all the time?

SG: No. Just sometimes.

PR: But always after an argument?

SG: Usually.

PR: A lot of couples in healthy relationships often talk about 'make-up sex' after a quarrel being the best type of sex they have. It literally is part of the making-up process. Something they do as part of their healthy relationship. Which sounds very much like what you are describing.

SG: It wasn't like that. I didn't want to.

PR: You didn't want to make up? You wanted to keep the argument going?

SG: No, I mean I didn't want to have sex sometimes.

PR: So you used the withholding of affection to control Mr Halnsley?

SG: No, I just didn't want to have sex after an argument.

PR: Let's focus on that for a moment, shall we? You say that after an argument Mr Halnsley would sometimes force you to have sex?

SG: Yes.

PR: But didn't you earlier testify, Miss Gorringe, that you were so scared of Mr Halnsley that you didn't dare to . . . what, was it . . . oh yes, here we are: 'I always did as I was told and didn't dare to answer back'? You said those words earlier.

SG: Yes.

PR: Which is it, Miss Gorringe? Either you were too scared to answer back or you had arguments that led to make-up sex that he 'forced' you into.

SG: They weren't normal arguments. It was after he said I'd done something wrong. After he'd hit me or something. He'd say he was sorry and I had to say I was sorry too—

PR: And were you? Were you sorry?

SG: No.

PR: *You weren't sorry for upsetting him?*

SG: *No, I was. I mean, I hadn't done anything to be sorry for.*

PR: *I'm not sure I understand. You, by your own admission, were often the cause of the arguments with Mr Halnsley; these arguments, again by your own admission, sometimes turned physical but you weren't sorry for causing them and don't see why you had to be sorry, much less say it. Did you feel blameless in what happened in your relationship, Miss Gorringe?*

SG: *I don't know what you mean.*

PR: *Did you feel like you were perfect and Mr Halnsley was always in the wrong and that his need for love and affection from you was wearing and somehow weak?*

SG: *No.*

PR: *Did his need to put any unpleasantness that arose between the two of you behind you as soon as possible and get back to normal, which included sexual relations, irritate you?*

SG: *No. It wasn't like that.*

PR: *I put it to you, Miss Gorringe, that you have fabricated this whole idea that Mr Halnsley sexually assaulted you by twisting the very normal elements of your relationship into something nefarious to elicit the sympathy of this court.*

SG: *No, I didn't do that.*

PR: *I further put it to you, Miss Gorringe, that you often did things that you knew 'wound up' Mr Halnsley in order to get a reaction from him because that is all a girl with your type of background knows.*

SG: *No, that's not true.*

*

The way the prosecution painted Mum still gets to me. The fact they hinted that Mum was from an unstable background when her parents were sitting right there, probably hand in hand, terrified for their girl. The fact that even if she did come from an unstable background the implication had been that justified what he did to her. The fact that Mum's barrister allowed all those things to be said about her, didn't stop every little thing being twisted so at every turn it sounded like she was in control and she was aggressive and she caused all of it.

I was mad about how she was portrayed and not properly defended.

And I was angry with her, too. Yes, I know she was young. But how could she let herself get into that situation? Why didn't she just walk away the first time he hit her? The first time he raped her? Hell, the first time he raised his voice to her? And he was bedding someone else. Right in her face. He basically had her in a hideous, forced sister-wife situation and she put up with it. Or rather, she put up with it until he wound up dead.

Logan took the magazine from my lap and slung it off the bed. Then carefully he climbed on top of me and looked into my face in the most open, honest gesture he'd made since I met him. He stared into my eyes, while I stared back, deep into his hazel-brown eyes. He had eyes like glass whirlpools: on those rare times he allowed me to look into them, they drew me in, swept me up, kept me hostage.

'I don't want to stop falling in love with you,' Logan stated. 'Being with you is the best thing to come out of this. All these years, all that hurt and pain and horror, all the tears and absences and confusion, have all been made bearable because of you. Because of being with you. I don't want to stop falling in love with you.'

PR: Miss Gorringe, you say that your arguments with Mr Halnsley, a highly regarded father of a young son, often became physical. And that you often came off the worst in these altercations. Did you need medical attention on any of these occasions?

SG: Yes.

PR: Didn't the hospital flag you up as being a regular visitor?

SG: I went to different hospitals.

PR: You deliberately went to different hospitals so your secret would remain intact?

SG: He said it was better to do that so people didn't know.

PR: Mr Halnsley said that?

SG: Yes.

PR: You just did as he told you?

SG: I always did what he told me to do.

PR: Even if it meant lying to the authorities?

SG: Yes.

PR: So under the right circumstances you're willing to lie to those in authority.

SG: He told me to.

PR: Did you realise that lying was wrong?

SG: Yes.

PR: But you did it anyway?

SG: He made me.

PR: How exactly? How did he make you? Did he stand next to you and force you to?

SG: No.

PR: Did he threaten you with what would happen if you didn't do what he wanted?

SG: It wasn't like that. He just said I had to.

PR: And you did it, no questions?

SG: I couldn't argue with him.

PR: I could examine why you claim not to be able to argue with him, but we'll move on. Miss Gorringe, if we're to believe how terrorised you were by him, why didn't you walk away? What kept you there with him if he was so terrible?

SG: I don't know.

PR: I'm sorry, can you speak up? I couldn't quite hear that. Why didn't you leave if everything was so dangerous for you?

SG: I don't know.

PR: I put it to you, Miss Gorringe, that you do know. You know because you have fabricated the idea that Mr Halnsley was abusive towards you. I further put it to you that it was you, in fact, who had Mr Halnsley in your thrall, and it was he who spent a lot of time capitulating to your will, who had to come up with ways to keep your relationship a secret as you became more and more dissatisfied with what he could offer you. I put it to you, Miss Gorringe, that far from being the victim you are trying to paint yourself as, you, in fact, were the aggressor: a violent, manipulative young woman with a voracious sexual appetite who grew bored of the game she was playing with a dedicated father and continually upped the stakes to keep herself entertained.

SG: It wasn't like that. Really it wasn't.

PR: Of course it wasn't, Miss Gorringe. Because you say it, you expect everyone to believe it.

SG: It's the truth.

PR: If it's the truth then why can't you tell me why you didn't walk away? Why, Miss Gorringe, why?

Logan's hands were on my hips and he pulled me towards him, moving me further down the bed. 'I don't want to stop falling in love with you,' he repeated. 'This is incredible. Us is incredible. I don't want to stop falling in love with you.'

He pushed my black sleep vest up to my chest, then over my head until he took it off.

'I want to keep falling in love with you,' he said passionately. He lowered his head and covered one of my nipples with his mouth. I couldn't stop myself gasping.

'Do you want me to keep falling in love with you?' he asked as he raised his head and moved to the other breast. Another gasp, another arch of my back as my body ached for him. This was the easy part of it, of course. It had been since we first did this three weeks ago. 'Do you?' he asked again when he had made me weak with desire.

'Do you?' he asked as he pulled down my stripy black-and-red sleep shorts. 'Do you want me to keep falling in love with you?'

He stripped himself of his pyjama trousers and reached under his pillow for a condom. 'Do you want me to keep falling in love with you?' he asked me again, sounding ever more desperate; ever more scared about why I wouldn't answer.

I didn't answer because my head was full of Mum. Ever since we'd stopped reading the court records, they'd been playing over and over in my head. I didn't understand. Why she couldn't leave. Why she didn't leave. The only reason, I could think, was that she loved him. And that terrified me. The things that love could make you do, make you put up with.

DOROTHY KOOMSON

Did I want any part of it when that was where it could lead? I liked sex when I had it. I liked sex when it was with Logan, but now he was bandying around the word 'love' not long after saying he thought my mother was a murderer. Love shouldn't be that confusing, should it? Love shouldn't be about those things, should it? Or was I being naïve? Love is part of life and life is messy; is love just about messiness? Is love about being caught up in the general melee of the confusing mass of mess that is life?

Logan lowered his face to mine, stared into my eyes again. He looked terrified. Absolutely terrified of what I might say. 'Do you want me to keep falling in love with you?' he asked yet again.

I nodded my messed-up, messy head. 'Yes,' I whispered. 'Yes, I do.'

He entered me with a smile of relief and a sigh of desire mixed in with happiness that I did want him to fall for me. That maybe I was going to fall for him, too. I grabbed his shoulders, pulled him closer, deeper; wrapped my legs around him so we were nearer still.

'Logan,' I breathed as he thrust hard into me. 'Logan.'

'Verity,' he breathed back. 'Verity, Verity, Verity.' Over and over. 'Verity, Verity, Verity.' I closed my eyes and allowed his voice to caress me. 'Verity, Verity, Verity.'

Part 3

serena

Now

'It's your party day!' I cry to my husband.

Yes, by the way he grabs the nearest pillow and places it over his head, he is mostly asleep, but who can sleep when there is so much excitement to be had? 'Evan, Evan, Evan,' I say close to my husband's ear. 'Evan, Evan, Evan. Party day, party day, party day.'

He mumbles something under his pillow and it's only with a bit of a struggle and a tussle that I can get it off him to hear what he has to say. 'What did you say?' I ask.

'I said, if you've ever loved me, please let me go back to sleep.'

'But it's your PARTY DAY!' I reply. I wish, every time I say 'party day', something exciting would happen like fifty dancers would appear, or fireworks would explode, or something. I tell Evan this. Explain I feel remiss in my birthday duties.

'Sleep. Just let me sleep,' he replies, pulling the duvet up over his head.

'Fine, then!' I say in exasperation. 'I'll go downstairs and make your special birthday-party-day breakfast. See if I can get the children to do a dance every time I say "party day".'

I meet Verity in the corridor. She looks like she's slept for once.

Since she moved in nearly three weeks ago, I've noticed how little she sleeps, how much she works, how tired and fretful she seems. She'd confessed that she'd come back to stay with us because she'd broken up with someone and being at home alone was too much for her.

And maybe now she's emerging from the relationship fog, since she looks like eight hours of slumber have passed over and through her body. 'Morning!' I say to her.

She raises a smile in return.

'Your father's not really inhabited the whole "party day" thing yet, so I'm making him banana-and-chocolate pancakes for breakfast to see if I can change that. Can I interest you in a couple?'

'Yeah, sure, why not?' she replies. She's still avoiding eye contact, but this is progress. Maybe a little bit longer here will bring my daughter back to me.

Conrad emerges from his bedroom and I'm reminded again how much of a man he is. Every day I'm reminded because, in my head, he'll always be eight. The golden age where he didn't mind being hugged by me, where he still came and sat down next to me and started conversations about nothing, and when I was convincingly taller than him.

He is bare-chested above his tracksuit bottoms and he stands in the corridor stretching himself out, making himself seem even bigger.

'Aww, my second child. As I was just telling my firstborn, I am about to make banana-and-chocolate pancakes to see if I can get your father into the "party day" mood. Would you like some?'

'Safe, Mum, safe,' he says. 'Black coffee as well.' *My eight-year-old should not be drinking black coffee*, I think.

'Of course, sweet second child of mine,' I say to him. 'Coffee for you, too?' I say to my daughter.

She nods and then does the old Verity trick of darting down the corridor, skirting around her brother and getting into the bathroom before him. She grins at him, waggles her eyebrows and then slams and locks the door.

Conrad, still half asleep, stands and stares at the bathroom door in shock.

'What the . . .?' He turns to me and raises his hands, looking for some kind of help. 'Mum!' he says, exasperated.

She must be feeling better if she's up for things like that.

I'm definitely feeling better. Definitely more relaxed because he's gone. Whoever it is who's been watching me, stalking me, has gone. I'm assuming it was the man who was asking Sarah from work about me. He hasn't been spotted again and no one at work has reported being asked about me. The weight of scrutiny has gone, too.

It's been one full week without it. I'd been worried they'd be hanging around trying to find out the new venue for Evan's party, but nope, I can tell they've gone. Long may it continue.

'You snooze, you lose,' I tell my son. 'Use the one downstairs.'

'This is out of order!' he says through the door. 'Really out of order.'

'Tell it to the judge,' my daughter calls back. I grin to myself because she is definitely feeling better.

And I grin to myself as I skip down the stairs because it feels like old times, better times, that period that wasn't so long ago when my daughter didn't hate me and I didn't have a sense of impending doom.

verity

Now

Logan: Let me come to the party.

Logan: Everyone will be there, we can tell them all in one go.

Logan: Please don't ignore me, Verity, let me come to the party.

Logan: If we tell everyone now, we can relax and enjoy the party.

Logan: I won't ask her about it on the night.

Logan: Let me come to the party, please.

Logan: Verity, I just want to be with you.

Logan: You're killing me here.

He's relentless. *Relentless*. I can't let him come to the party. And he knows that. I came back to live with my parents because the flat was too empty without him in it. And I needed a way to stop myself screwing him again like I did the night after we broke up.

And these last couple of weeks of living back with my parents, which have meant Logan and I have been forced to properly go low-contact, have been fortifying, too. Hard, difficult, but what we agreed. He knows that.

The messages started earlier today. All along the same lines, all along the same theme. The centre of my chest is a tight ball of anxiety. That ball of anxiety has been sitting there for weeks – months, if I'm honest.

When we paused it, took a break to find some space, it had loosened itself. I hadn't wanted to admit that to myself; I'd acknowledged it briefly, then focused on the missing him, the wanting him, the how was I going to cope without him. When I moved back in here and had been forced to stop thinking about it twenty-four seven, that ball had all but dissolved. I'd actually managed to forget about it for a while. I'd actually managed to laugh, think, *breathe*, without the ball of anxiety reigning me in.

I know it's my own fault, that if I'd told the truth, this wouldn't be happening.

But no matter what, he can't come to the party. He can't. I won't let him ruin this for Dad. And Mum. Being around her has reminded me how much I like her. Respect her. Love her. It's reminded me why I got to know Logan in the first place.

I sit on the edge of the bed. I have to do something. I can't let him come here, which is what I'm scared he'll do if I keep ignoring him. I have to talk to him, reason with him.

Verity: Where are you?

Logan: At home.

Verity: I'll meet you at my flat so we can talk.

Logan: I don't want to talk.

Verity: Please? Let's just meet and talk.

Logan: All right.

I've got one shot at getting this right. One shot.

verity

Now

'Come on, Vee, man, you don't even live here and you're hogging the bathroom,' Conrad calls from outside the door.

'I'll be a minute,' I reply, trying to control my breathing.

'I don't see why you're not in your own yard,' he calls.

'And I don't see why you speak as if you grew up in South London, but here we are,' I retort.

That sounds normal, I hope. That sounds stinky enough to be as normal as the rows we usually have over the bathroom. I need to sound as though nothing remarkable has happened. As if everything is OK and I didn't—

I feel like retching again. I've already been sick two times. I've already emptied the contents of my stomach because of what happened. I throw myself onto my knees and lift the toilet-seat lid. But nothing comes out. There's nothing left.

'Damn, Vee, can you just get a move on!'

'Use the shower room downstairs!' I call to him.

'I don't want to. I like this bathroom. And seeing as I LIVE HERE, I think I should be allowed to use it when I want.'

Deep breath, deep breath, deep breath.

'I'll be out in a minute!' I reply to my brother.

Calm, calm, I need to be calm. My hands are shaking, trembling out my terror. I need to calm down. I need to not do this now. We're going to the party soon. I need to keep calm. Act normal. Pretend none of this happened. My hands. They have scrapes along the knuckles, and my nails are chipped and split. I'll have to paint them. Hide them. But that means . . . I run to the sink, snatch up the soap and run it over my fingers, my hands, my wrists. I need to clean my hands because they'll have *evidence* on them.

Unexpectedly, bile hits the back of my throat again, and I have to abandon washing my hands to throw myself back in front of the toilet to empty my already empty stomach.

'VEE!' Conrad hammers on the door. 'Come on! I gotta get ready. What's wrong with you, man?'

I drop back to sit on my bottom, shaking and quivering. *What am I going to do? What am I going to do?*

'VEE—' My brother is cut short by my mother's voice. I don't hear what she says to him, but I do hear him tut, tut again and sigh, then stomp away.

'Vee?' Mum calls through the door. 'Vee, can you open the door?' Her voice is calm and measured. Exactly what I need right now. Exactly what I need to latch onto right now. I need to get myself there. To that place where I am calm. And behaving normally.

'Verity?' she asks again.

I push myself up until I'm on my feet. I reach for the flush and then push down, filling the room with the same sound that is whooshing through my brain.

'Are you all right, Verity?' Mum's voice is the motivator I need. I wash my hands. Stare at my reflection for a moment, see my eyes are wide and bloodshot, my skin is clammy and dull.

'I'm fine,' I say to my mother as I try to wipe the fear from my face. 'I'll be out in a minute.' I breathe deeply through the O of my mouth, try to ease my racing mind, my burning, quaking body.

'OK,' she replies.

Breathe, calm, chill. Chill. Chill. Chill.

I wipe my eyes again, swallow and swallow to get rid of the lump of fear that sits like a mountain at the back of my throat. *You can do this*, I tell myself. *You can do this.*

When I unlock the bathroom door and leave, I find Mum leaning against the wall by the door. I jump and have to grab the doorframe to stop myself falling over in fright.

Mum stares at me from behind her half-made-up face. Her hair is a mass of long, spiral-shaped, pink-and-yellow rollers. She has a pale-brown concealer pressed into the skin under her eyes and her eyebrows have been filled in and shaped to perfection. She was right in the middle of getting herself ready for the big party when she had to stop to come and sort out the commotion caused by her two children. She probably thought all that shit was over when we grew, but no such luck for Mum. I bet she didn't even hesitate, I bet Dad would have pretended he couldn't hear it – like he used to all the time.

I'm desperate to throw my arms around her and tell her everything. *Everything.* Because I know she'd help me. She'd know what to do right now. It was probably like that for her that night. She was probably scared and desperate to tell someone so they could help her. I should throw my arms around her and let her be the mother I know she is. I know I've been angry with her this little while because of all her lies, but that doesn't matter. Not right now. Right now, all that matters is—

'What's happened?' she asks.

I shake my head. 'What do you mean?'

'You don't look very well. What's happened?'

I shake my head. 'Nothing.'

'Nothing?' Mum asks, clearly not believing me. Obviously not understanding the truth in what I was saying. Nothing has happened because everything has happened. Everything possibly bad that could happen has happened, so it's cancelled itself out and become nothing.

'Just tired, Mum. I thought going out for a walk would help but it's done the exact opposite of helping.' How easy it is to lie. How plain it is that my mother doesn't believe me.

'Verity,' Mum says with a finality that suggests she's about to tell me off. 'If you are in some sort of trouble, tell me. I will help you. I will do everything I can to help you.'

I manage to twist my face into something like the shock and horror and disgust I would normally feel at being asked that question. No one can help me now. No one. 'What trouble would I be in?'

My mother sighs and lowers her head while she composes herself. I know she wants to force me to tell her what's going on and I know she won't. Not when she's organised this party and it's for Dad. She'd do almost anything for Dad.

'Look, Mum, there really is nothing to worry about,' I state. Again, not a lie. There is nothing to worry about because there is *everything* in the world to worry about. 'And I had better get on or I won't be ready in time. Looking good doesn't happen all by itself.' I'm curling my fingers into the palm of my hand to hide my scuffed knuckles and chipped, battered nails.

'It certainly doesn't,' she agrees. 'The taxi's booked for five thirty. You know Dad will leave whether any of us are ready or not.'

I nod eagerly. 'Better get on with it, hadn't I?'

'Yes, you probably should.'

I hide my slight limp as I walk down the corridor to my room, aware that Mum is watching me. Mum stays where she is until I have opened the door, stepped inside and shut it behind me.

Maybe it's the pretending, the trying to inhabit the calmness in her voice, but I don't collapse when I seal myself into my bedroom. I stand behind the door, listening, waiting for Mum to walk away. By the time she does, by the time she has returned to applying her make-up and fixing her hair, I know what I have to do.

I take out my mobile, call up the number of the person I know will help me and type:.

S.O.S

I press send.

Everything is normal in my room, everything is ready for tonight. My dress is laid out on the bed in front of me. My make-up is laid out on my desk, my hair scarf is hanging on the silver ball of the bed end, waiting for me to put it on so I can start the getting-ready process for real. I need to get going, get moving, act as though everything is normal. Mum wasn't kidding about Dad leaving people behind if they weren't ready on time. That's what he does. I need to get going.

I can't though. Nothing is normal. Nothing is ever going to be normal again.

I look at the mobile in my hands. Silent. Flaccid. No help is coming.

I'm going to have to open this door, go and tell Mum everything. Ruin Dad's party, ruin Mum's life. Destroy everything.

I can't imagine Mum's face when I tell her. When I start to explain what I've done . . . and what I had to do. Why I had to do it.

My mobile flashes up with a message. The response I was desperate for:

What's going on?
S.O.S

Seconds later, my phone starts to flash with a silent incoming call.

'What's happened?' I thought there'd be comfort in his voice like there had been in Mum's before, but no. Just hearing his voice makes it real, makes it terrifying.

'He's at my flat,' I whisper. 'I think I killed him.'

verity

Now

The music is too loud.

Yes, it's a party, and yes there is a lot of space to fill with people and music, but it's all relative. They don't need the music to be this loud. Music is like air, it expands to fill the space it is in. I bet I could write down on one of the glass walls that looks out over the sea a formula that would explain that, that would convince the DJ to *please* turn this racket down.

Every beat is scraping itself over my raw nerves, each bar is scoring itself into those nerves and every note is drilling down into my mind. They're playing golden oldies, music from Dad's youth that we grew up on. I know every word to every Tupac choon, Run DMC can't get by me without me noticing something new, Public Enemy are old friends of mine. They're the sounds of my childhood because they were what Dad would listen to around us, but tonight they're torturing me. Everything is tormenting me because I don't know what is going on.

He said he'd call me when he'd sorted it, or he'd show up at the party like he was meant to and we'd be able to talk without anyone being suspicious. But it's been hours and nothing. Maybe Logan wasn't dead. Maybe he's at the hospital now, being taken care of and telling the police what happened. What I did. How he came to be hurt. I didn't know what Howie, my other best friend, was going to do. He'd said he'd sort it for me, and when I'd asked how, he'd said he'd tell me afterwards. 'He's probably not dead,' Howie had whispered. 'I'll go make sure. It'll be all right, Vee, it'll be fine.'

It is not going to be fine.

'Drink?' Zeph asks, stepping in between me and the view of the sea that I have from standing by this pillar. The Sea Maiden, this place Mum's chosen for Dad's 'surprise' party, is a mass of contradictions. It is right on the seafront, literally step outside the floor-to-ceiling glass doors and you're on the promenade; a few more steps and you're on the top of the shingle leading down to the water. It's a beautiful curved building, 1930s art deco in shape, modernistic glass and white and wood in design, and just completely soulless.

No matter what the incarnation – and it's been through a few over the years – no one seems to have been able to configure it so the building has warmth, personality or draw to it. Sure, it's the people who come here that make it 'happen' but even these partygoers, gathered together to celebrate one of the best people they know, can't make it do anything but surface sparkle. The happiness, atmosphere and general good humour exist only in the vacuum that the building creates, they don't seep into the walls, the windows, the attitude of the staff. When we leave, the good times are going with us.

My best friend since I was five holds out a flute of fizz and I want to snatch it out of her hands and down it in one. I want to climb over the bar, grab all the bottles of all the drinks and down all of them, too. I want to drink myself into oblivion and forget the last year as well as today ever happened. But I have to keep a clear head, I have to act normal.

'Thanks, Zeph,' I say and accept the glass.

'I love your parents, Vee, you know I do. They are the coolest and I'll fight anyone who tries to chat shit about them, but God can they stop calling me "Zephie"? Even your brother, who loves to wind me up about the way I breathe sometimes, doesn't call me that any more.'

I laugh. The days of me correcting them about her name are well gone. 'They can't help themselves,' I remind her. 'You know I've told them a million times that you dropped the "i" and "e" but they forget. It's like they've got a blind spot about it.' I grin at her. This is cool. This is normal. This is what it's like to be OK with the world and not carrying secrets, not feeling as though your whole life is a lie. 'Where are your folks?'

'Mum's over there somewhere' – she points behind her to the buffet area – 'smouldering because I'm drinking and in her mind I'm still six so I shouldn't be. And Dad's over there –' she points in the direction of the dance floor – 'trying to dance away the fact that they came to pick me up earlier and he saw condoms in the bathroom cupboard.'

'Oh.'

'Do you know how well those things were hidden? For exactly this reason. It's not like I've got any use for them so I stashed them really well. The man comes to my house, hunts out my birth control and then starts to have a reaction.'

'I bet the drive over was fun.' I shudder at the thought of it. My parents are mostly cool, but that, I could not handle.

'Super fun,' she laughs. 'So much fun I think I'm going to do it again every Saturday night for the foreseeable.'

I laugh again and the anxiety that has been weighing down my chest lightens.

'Where's your man?' Zeph asks. She's pretending to scan the room, but I can see her eyes, made up in a spectrum of silver colours to match her silver, thigh-length dress and silver platforms, are watching me, ready to detect any lies.

'Who said I have a man?' I'd so love to down this drink right now. I know one drink can't hurt, would probably be good for me and calm me down, but one would lead to another and until I hear, I can't.

'The out-of-office you've put on our friendship says you've got a man,' she replies.

I lower my glass and turn completely to her. 'Do you really think I've ducked out on our friendship?' I ask her.

She shrugs in that way that says yes. 'It's no more than I deserve, the amount of times I've done it to you, but yeah, you've not been there.' She shrugs again. 'Good for you, I guess.'

My frown deepens. 'I'm sorry,' I state.

Zeph shakes her head. 'Don't say sorry. My ass needed you to do it. At the very least it's made me get up and go out there and find more friends; at the very most it's made me realise all I did was take, take, take.'

'That's not true.'

'It is. I'm not saying I wasn't there for you, or I don't love you like the awesome dudette that you are, but yeah, I was selfish in our friendship. I wasn't always present, supportive, able to put you first.'

'This is a bit too heavy for my dad's party, you know?' I say to her and take a sip of my drink. One sip can't hurt, surely. 'And you're a great friend. Always have been. I could not love you any more than I do. And I'm sorry I haven't been around as much. I'll change that. I'll absolutely change that.'

'He's not here, then?' she asks. She's looking directly at me. And I wish she'd stop it. What do I say? I don't want to lie, but I don't want to talk about it. If I say, no, he's not here, she'll ask about him and want to talk about him, and after we've just admitted that our friendship has suffered, I can't not tell her stuff. If I say we've split up, it'll still be the same conversation, but I'll have to tell her why we split up. The other alternative is to lie. And I am sick of lies.

I turn away slightly as I give myself up to the conversation we need to have and say, 'No, he's not—'

Logan.

I almost drop my glass in terror.

Logan is standing outside the Sea Maiden.

Logan is standing right there, staring in at me.

It's him, he's there, standing there in the clothes he was wearing earlier, a big lump of congealed blood mixed in with his brown hair. His face is drained of colour, his eyes are hollow shadows of themselves.

He is a ghoul, his ghost come to haunt me. He stares at me through the glass wall of the Sea Maiden, damning me, telling me that he is coming to drag me to hell. I step back, throw my hand over my mouth and start to shake.

'Vee?' Zeph asks. I can hear her, but everything else is slowing down. The too-loud music is becoming echoey and distant in my ears, the people around me start to move as though someone has pressed a slow-mo button, my heart, my body are stuck by a fast-setting glue. But I can hear Zeph. I can hear her saying, 'Vee, what's wrong? What's happened?'

Logan's eyes, hollowed out by rage and anger and pure, unadulterated hate, continue to glare at me. *I've come for you*, he's telling me. *I've come for you.*

'Vee, what—Whoa! Who's that?'

I turn to Zeph, who is looking out of the window at the ghost of Logan. 'You can see him?' I ask.

'Man with his head caved in?' she replies. 'Yes. Everyone can see him. That dude needs some serious medical attention.'

He's not a ghost. He's not a ghost. I'm not going mad. He hasn't come to haunt me. And, he's not dead. Best of all, he's not dead.

People outside the party are starting to notice him, a couple of men are approaching him. But he ignores everyone, everything, he just stares at me. Glares at me. Promises me.

'Do you know him?' Zeph asks.

I don't have the chance to answer because Logan crumples and collapses. A couple of people leapfrog over the barrier separating the Sea Maiden from the general promenade and go to him. 'Call an ambulance!' someone shouts.

These words trigger about a third of the room into action, including my father. I spot him on the dance floor, his arms around Mum, and suddenly he's speeding towards the door like the other medics in the room, seeing what he can do to help.

'Do you know him?' Zeph asks me again.

I manage a nod, not sure if I should go out there or if I should leave it. Leave here and run away.

'Come on, then, if you know him.' Zeph takes the decision out of my hands. She removes the flute from my hand, probably a good thing because my whole body is so numb I'm likely to drop it, and then after she's dumped it somewhere, she drags me outside.

At the door, I come back to myself and realise I can't go out there. I'll give myself away. I'll probably confess. I try to pull away, but too late, Zeph has us outside and out beyond the barrier and is pushing through the crowd.

Dad is on the floor beside Logan. He has his wrist raised while the fingers of the other hand rest on Logan's neck as he checks the unconscious man's pulse. 'Finding it hard to get a steady pulse,' Dad tells Dr Joiner, someone he has worked with for years, who is also on the floor beside Logan. She nods and starts the CPR again. A couple of people are on their phones, saying medical words. The whole place is frantic with people trying to help Logan.

'Verity knows who he is,' Zeph declares.

I turn to her, horrified. Why would she say that? And so loudly most of the crowd turn to look at me.

'Do you, Verity?' Dad asks, still working on Logan.

I don't reply. How is this the moment I tell him that I've got a boyfriend? *Had* a boyfriend.

'Verity,' Dad says sternly in his no-nonsense 'doctor voice'. It only ever comes out when things are serious. I guess this is serious. Very serious. And I want to run away. I want to run as far, far away from here as possible. 'Verity, do you know this man?'

I nod. 'Yes.'

'Who is he? Does he have any other medical conditions? Do you know who would have attacked him?'

'I . . . I—' I can't speak. Because to speak is to answer those questions. And to answer those questions, especially the last one, is to condemn myself with the truth or to protect myself with a lie.

In the crowd, I can feel Mum's eyes on me. I don't know where she is, but I know she is looking at me. And I know she is telling herself she should have pushed me earlier. She should have got me to open up to her.

'Verity.' Dad's doctor voice again. 'Who is he? What is his name?'

Suddenly, I know where Mum is. I look up and to the right and she is there. In her blue dress that she bought without me, with her fancy hair and perfect make-up. I stare at her and she stares at me. If she knows what's coming she doesn't show it. She looks like she knows this is because of me, this is because of earlier. And as I knew she would, she looks as though she wishes she'd pushed me to tell her what happened. But if she knows what I'm about to say, then she doesn't give any indication whatsoever.

She simply stares at me as I stare at her.

'He's my boyfriend,' I say to Dad as I look at Mum. 'And his name . . . his name is Logan Carlisle.'

poppy

Now

'Mum, can you teach me how to multiply with decimals?' Betina is trying to drag out the bedtime process, as usual.

We've had a discussion about whether the toothpaste I buy is good enough when she has teeth coming through, we've had her reading and 'just one more page'ing while sitting on the toilet. I've sat through several changes of pyjamas while she tries to find the perfect warmth-coolness-softness combination. And now that I've managed to get her into bed, tucked up and supposedly ready for sleep, we're on to maths. Like I have a clue about maths.

'I can't do that, sweetheart. I am not the maths parent.'

'Can you call Dad, then, and ask him?'

My daughter's face peeks out from the duvet. She looks like her father, of course she does. She has his blue-hazel eyes, fringed with dark lashes, and his pink, rosebud lips. She has her grandmother's hair texture – a slight Afro wave that comes from Betina being one-eighth Black on Alain's side.

She looks like her father, but behind her eyes there's always something being thought through, calculated, worked out before she decides to ask me about it. This conversation may seem to be about maths, it may be designed to extend the bedtime process, but really it's a way to get me to call her dad. She misses him and spends a lot of time working out complicated plans to compel me to get him to come over.

'You know what, sweetheart, I'm not going to call your dad right now. It's Saturday night, you spent most of this morning with him when he took you to dance club, and then for lunch, he's done his weekend bit.'

'But I forgot to ask him about it then.'

'Well, you can ask him tomorrow.'

'But, Mum, *seriously*, if you want me to do well at school and in my exams, I need to know how to multiply with decimals. It's the same with you giving me the Wi-Fi code – I might as well have it now since I'm going to be living here when I grow up.'

I curl my body forward and scoop up my girl in my arms. 'Goodnight, Betina. I love you. Sleep well.' There are times when there is no point in entering into a discussion-cum-argument with this child. It will only result in me giving in to something undoable.

'Night, Mum,' she replies, receiving my hug and returning it a hundredfold. When I pull away, she pushes her forefinger onto the centre of my nose while whispering 'Boop' like she has just pressed a magic button. I've stopped asking her why she does it because the answer is always the same: *I like booping your nose.* Why? *Because you've got a boopable nose.* Said with an air of exasperation that I don't know something so obvious.

In the living room, everything is neat and tidy. While Betina was out at her class with Alain, I had managed to spruce the place up. I drop onto the sofa and pick up the house phone. I stare at the sleek black receiver, a present from Alain when I first moved in all those years ago. Never mind Betina wanting to call him, I do.

These past few years, time hasn't just been marked out by when

I last picked up a blade, it's been measured by when the last time I wanted to call Alain was. When was the last time I called Alain? When was the last time I let him come over and woke up next to him in the morning?

I've been doing well of late. It's been six months. Six months, two weeks, four days. It's been that long since I gave in to myself and slept with him. Which is probably why the Sunday lunch thing irritates me more. I'm not feeling as kindly towards him because we're moving further and further away from being a couple.

My mobile buzzing and ringing on the other side of the room makes me jump. Then I leap up, because it's that kind of noise that wakes Betina and then she's awake for hours as the ten-minute nap she's had will work like a booster.

'Bella' is flashing up on the screen.

Huh? I think as I lift the phone to my ear, while clicking the call answer button. *She never calls. She always texts.*

'What?' I whisper into the phone when she speaks. No hello. No preamble. Just straight into what has happened.

She continues to talk, pausing to calm herself every few words to stop herself spiralling off into hysteria.

'I'll meet you there,' I tell her. 'I'll get Alain to come and stay with Betina and I'll meet you at the hospital.' I'm about to let her go when I say desperately into the phone. 'Bella? Bella? Don't tell Mum and Dad. Not yet. Not until we know what's happening. If we have to wake them up, I want to be able to tell them something concrete.'

She agrees and then rings off.

I have to sit down. Take a moment before I can call my ex.

Logan has been attacked. He's at the hospital and they don't think he's going to survive the night.

verity

Now

Mum is silent on the drive over to the hospital.

Dad went with Logan in the back of the ambulance, which seemed to take for ever to arrive. They didn't send a first responder because there were several trillion doctors at the event, and when the paramedics arrived Dad and Dr Joiner had already done as much as anyone could.

Mum sits beside me in the back of the taxi in her finery, her large black-and-red scarf wrapped around her like a pashmina she wants to hide behind. I can see she feels uncomfortable, exposed in the dress. She's only dressed like that because it's Dad's party, normally she is covered up and casual. Not boring, but not willing to draw attention to herself.

We'd left before the police arrived, even though they'd asked everyone to stay where they were. We'd said we were going to be at the hospital and the police could find us there, and then we called a taxi so we could follow Dad.

'Are you going to say something?' I ask my mother quietly when the taxi pauses at the roundabout by the Palace Pier, having just left the West Pier. I love the two piers in Brighton mainly because of how different they are: one gaudy and overdressed, the other tired and decrepit, standing proud despite the way time and the elements have ravaged it.

When we pause at the entrance to the Palace Pier, the hum of the engine seems to count out the time it will take for her to say something.

'I don't know what there is to say, Verity,' Mum states.

'Just say something. *Anything*.'

'All right. What I keep thinking about is how your dad reacted when he found out about . . . well, you obviously know all about my past. I keep thinking about how he reacted to finding that out about me. I remember how terrified I was by his response and I don't want to do that right now. I don't want to scare you. I don't want to shout at you and call you a liar. I don't . . . I don't want any of it, so I think it's best I don't say anything at all.'

Mum refocuses on the outside world again. I've got the sea side of the car, she has the street side. On her side the buildings have different combinations of lights, people unintentionally hide themselves by stepping into the shadows. I have the better deal, I can see the sooth-ing, comforting blackness of the water, I can feel the rise and fall, push and pull of the world in motion. I can send my mind out there as a way for me to not be where I am right now.

I want to tell her that I'm sorry. That I didn't mean for any of it to happen. That we were never meant to get involved in that way. That today was not meant to happen like this. But it's better I just sit here and do nothing. Say nothing. Nothing I say will make it any better. Nothing I say will unhurt my mother.

July, 2019

'So, tell me, who was your last bay?'

'My last what?' I asked.

'Your last boo, your last bay. Who were you last involved with?'

'Oh, you mean, my last bae? My last "before anyone else"?'

'Ohhhh, is that what it means?'

I shook my head and curled my lips into my mouth to stop myself laughing out loud. 'Maybe you shouldn't be using words you don't understand?'

'Hey,' he laughed, and tickled me in the side. Giggling, I twisted away and tried to shift away from him on the sofa.

'I thought it was . . . Anyway, who was your last "before anything else"?'

'That's even worse!' I squealed. 'Just ask me who my last boyfriend was, if you want to know. Stop trying to be down with the kids when you're so obviously not!'

He laughed again and I paused to relish the sound. It was lovely when Logan laughed, it made my heart dance and my stomach skip. I liked, too, that when he laughed it was because of me. He shuffled up the sofa and lay his head on my shoulder. 'All right, sweetness, who was your last boyfriend?'

'I've not really had that many people you could call boyfriends,' I said. 'I had a few flings in college, like most of us did. I had a friends-with-benefits-type thing going on for a while. Actually, it's technically still going on because we never really ended it. We just call each other and if we don't answer, it's cos we're with someone else.'

'Has he called you recently?'

'Nope. And I wouldn't answer if he did.'

'Anyone else?'

'A few dates here and there. And, urgh, there was the very unwise kiss in a hotel with one of my bosses.'

'You had a fling with your boss?'

'No, I kissed one of the bosses.'

'One of your current bosses?'

'Yes, he still works there but he wasn't my direct boss, I was just training in his department at the time.'

'So what happened?'

'Nothing. Had a crush, kissed him, both regretted it, never mentioned it again. Total non-event. What about you, who was your last relationship with?'

Logan sighed and sat away from me then and my heart sank. I'd somehow stumbled into that area again. Since the day when he asked me over and over if I wanted him to fall in love with me, we'd done our best to avoid subjects that would take us anywhere near where The Ice Cream Girls resided. We just didn't talk about it any more. I'd packed away the papers, hidden them in the storage cupboard in the bathroom, behind the spare fan, extra bucket and boxes I couldn't bring myself to throw out. We just pretended away that part of our lives and, for me, that included not seeing my parents as much. Because when I did I'd be reminded that I wasn't telling them about Logan and I'd replay bits of Mum's testimony and be either tearful or furious. I didn't know how much Logan saw his sister or family because we didn't talk about it.

And, by asking this question, I'd obviously thrust us back into that arena and we'd have to slog it out or pretend I hadn't asked. 'I was with someone for quite a while,' he said, staring at the fireplace, trying to be somewhere else – that much was obvious from his rigid body, the clenched jaw, the scrunched-up brow. 'We were talking about marriage when Poppy came out of prison. That was meant to be a good thing, you know? I finally had my sister back. After twenty years she was in my life again and what I wanted more than anything was to spend all my time with her. And Bella. The three of us back together.

And it didn't matter she'd been away, she was back and we could pick up again. Be brother and sisters again.'

'And your fiancée-to-be had a problem with that?'

'More the fact that I hadn't mentioned having a sister in prison. Let alone one who went to prison for murder. As far as she was concerned, she couldn't trust me. I'd hidden this huge thing from her, I could be hiding another family as far as she knew.'

'Really?'

'I can understand it, to be fair. It came from nowhere, this sister of mine. She was quite close to Bella, too, so it was like a double betrayal. She didn't realise, though, we didn't talk about Poppy – at all. My parents acted as though she was dead for so many years and, after a while, Bella and I did, too. I mean, sometimes we'd talk about her, but not for any length of time. We just made ourselves forget. It was easier that way. And I feel bad about it. Especially when we found out that she'd been writing to us and sending birthday cards and Christmas cards and our parents never even passed them on.

'If you found out that this situation had been playing itself out right in front of your nose, in the heart of your relationship, wouldn't you be a bit peeved?'

'I suppose so.'

'We limped on for many, many months after she told me how she didn't trust me. I did everything I could to please her. I didn't want to lose her. I was totally in love with her. But it was not going to work out.'

'That's really sad.' I clambered over the sofa and cuddled up to him. He slipped his arms around me and held me as though he never wanted to let me go. 'Really sad.'

'No more sad than . . . than a sad thing.'

'Quite true.'

'So, your boss you had a thing with—'

'Let me stop you there. I didn't have a thing with him. It was nothing and we're not going to talk about it because there's absolutely nothing to talk about.'

'All right, all right. Point taken. But what about your friend Howie you're always getting messages from? Nothing happened there?'

'Nooooo, no, no, no. Howie is one of my best friends from college, nothing more.'

'How come?'

'We're just better off as friends. I met him in college and we discovered we were both from Brighton so we instantly bonded. Well, he's over in Southwick, but you know what I mean. But it's all platonic.'

Logan tipped my chin up to look at him. 'I'm glad.'

'Oh? Why are you glad?'

'Because I get you all to myself, don't I?' He dropped a kiss on my mouth. 'I get you all to myself.'

Now

'He slipped into a coma just before we got here,' Dad says when he exits the bowels of the hospital where I assume they were working on Logan. I think Mum texted him to tell him we'd arrived and he came out of 'the back' carrying his tuxedo jacket and not seeming to notice the amount of blood staining the front of his white dress shirt.

Honestly, he had looked so handsome. When he and Mum posed (ironically) for pictures in front of the fireplace, I'd got a lump in my throat. They looked so incredible together, the perfect couple. And now Dad is covered in blood, and Mum is covered in horror. She looks close to broken.

I don't know how drunk Dad was before. But when Mum was giving the speech about him, he seemed pretty sober. But then, I'm never quite certain if Dad can get drunk. He has a few beers but I've never seen him slurring his words or stumbling around or talking shit because too much booze has loosened his tongue.

'A coma,' Mum repeats. 'Will he come out of it?'

Dad sits next to me on this bank of chairs, so I am a Verity Gillmare filling between the bread of Mum and Dad. 'No one knows. He had bleeding on the brain as well as significant swelling. It looks like it happened quite a few hours ago so no one is sure how he managed to get himself to the beach.'

Dad presses his fingers over his eyes; he looks exhausted. Really very tired. He looks like he has aged a lifetime in the hour it's taken to get from the Sea Maiden to here. Mum wraps her scarf tighter around herself and she looks just as exhausted, just as aged.

'Is he . . . Is he related to . . . ?' Dad asks.

'He's her brother,' I explain.

I'm sure Mum knows that, has worked that out, but I don't think she can speak about this.

'The police said they were on their way here to talk to me,' Dad states as though I haven't enlightened him about who the man whose life he was trying to save was. 'They'll be here soon, I expect.'

I thought, I genuinely thought, that when Mum and Dad found out there'd be a lot of shouting. And recriminations. Tears. A lot of snot. And many, many, many words of explanation needed. I didn't expect silence and more silence.

Conrad has been left behind to sort everything out, to coordinate what happens with the police interviewing people, and overseeing everyone who wants to stay and say goodbye to those who are leaving.

It's a big responsibility, but Con can do it. He and his mates – the Brain's Trust I affectionately call them because they are all intelligent but clueless – will charm the remaining partygoers and make sure everything is settled properly.

It is a normal Saturday night in an A&E department: the whole of the human experience seen through the damage people do to themselves outside of 'business' hours. We watch them arrive, the people from nights out who can't hold their alcohol or keep themselves upright; the parents cradling young children who've come to the wrong department and are directed elsewhere; the ones who've been stoic and hung on and hung on but can't take it any longer and have had to seek help; the accidents that have left huge gashes and broken bones and bruised spirits. They arrive and arrive and arrive, wave after wave after wave of humanity hurt, people pained. They are seen, they are triaged, they take their seats around us. And wait. Like us, they wait. I suspect we might be waiting all night, since none of us is saying anything about leaving.

After what feels like a forever, the doors swoosh open and another blast of night air is swept in, bringing *her* with it. *Them.*

I know who she is straight away. She is aged, like my mother is aged, but she looks the same as she did in the original photo.

Poppy Carlisle.

Behind her is a younger version of her, a feminine version of Logan. Poppy dashes to the reception desk with protective ceiling-to-waist-height glass, the gaps strategically positioned so you can speak but no one can reach in and grab the person on the other side.

The moment she appears, Mum stiffens, her body suddenly ramrod straight, as though a huge current has been sent through her body.

Poppy Carlisle can barely get the words out she is so upset. Her sister stands behind her, biting her bottom lip and clenching her own hands.

Eventually, Poppy Carlisle stops questioning the woman behind the counter when the receptionist points in our direction as the people who came in with her brother. I watch her whole body inflate with a breath, deflate with an out breath. She's desperate to do something.

It takes a moment for me to realise Mum is getting to her feet. That she is stepping forward, towards the Carlisle sisters.

Poppy Carlisle is already turning towards her as she looks for the person who can possibly tell her what happened to her sibling.

Her face and whole body recoil when she realises who is standing in front of her.

serena

Now

From the moment I found out who he was, I knew this was coming.

It was that moment, racing towards me at speed, that I couldn't avoid, couldn't duck out on and had to face with my whole being.

While Verity and Evan have been sitting there in their own little worlds, not talking and thinking, I have been counting. Counting up the seconds and turning them into minutes and turning them into hours before I am back there. Back in the world of The Ice Cream Girls with Poppy Carlisle.

She's older.

Her face is fuller, her hair is neater and shinier and, if I'm not mistaken, a few strands of grey have found their way into her brown locks. Under the harsh strip lighting, which bleaches everything a shade or two brighter and paler, she looks ready to collapse. Shock. I've had nearly two hours to get used to this. I've had over an hour of counting to brace myself for this and I'm still not there. I'm still floored.

My daughter has been having sex. Not something I really thought about or wanted to think about. Once she went to university, once she left home, it was one of those things she was most likely to do and I would never have to think about until she told me she was pregnant.

When/if she ever told me she was pregnant, I'd have confirmation that she was sexually active. But until then, it was not my problem. But now I know. Now I know she has been having sex and the person who she was last doing that with was a Carlisle.

Poppy Carlisle's brother.

Poppy's hazel-brown eyes move over my face, my hair, my body. Scrutinising every element on display with the horror of someone who cannot believe what is happening to them. She takes me in and I can see she is wondering why I look like I do. How can someone who was quite dowdy the last time she saw them suddenly be so gaudy and showy with fancy hair and make-up and an outfit designed to flatter her body in every way? I'm embarrassed to look like this. Ashamed that I was obviously out having a good time when something like this was happening to someone in her family.

When I can't stand it any longer. When the staring and assessment and shock have gone on for long enough, I have to speak. I have to say something to bring us both into the present, into this unexpected moment.

I open my mouth, ready to say a few words about what has happened, what we know, how Evan knows a little more than they probably told her at the reception desk. I open my mouth, reaching for the words that are efficient and necessary and informative.

And out comes, 'Hello, Poppy,' instead. There is nothing more I can say. Nothing more I can utter that would feel appropriate or even possible right now because my mind is confusion, my tongue is tied.

She silently but visibly deflates, her whole body giving in to the action.

'Hello, Serena,' she replies.

poppy

Now

Once Alain arrived at my flat, I called a taxi because even if I had been able to drive, parking would have been a nightmare and I didn't want to spend precious minutes driving around and around looking for somewhere to dump the car.

Ten years ago it would have seemed impossible that I could drive a car let alone own one, but lots has changed since I came out. Mobile phones weren't little boxes of witchcraft to me any longer. Having keys to my own place was normal. And owning a car was vital to my life running smoothly.

Bella was a wreck, standing outside the wide glass doors when I got out of the taxi. She was wringing her hands and she was shaking, her clothes were dishevelled and her hair was escaping its haphazardly formed ponytail. I threw my arms around her, trying to calm her down. Her heart was racing and her whole body was trembling as I held her against me. 'What if he dies?' she kept saying. 'What if he dies?'

'What happened?' I asked.

'I don't . . . They said he was on the seafront. They found my number on his phone. I was the last person he called. They said he was at the hospital. What if he dies?'

I didn't want to think about that. Not even in abstract. 'Come on,' I said. 'Let's go in.'

She hesitated, refused to move from the spot. 'This is like when you went to prison, isn't it?' she said. 'It's meant to turn out all right but it doesn't. It goes horribly wrong and our family is never going to be the same again.'

'No,' I said sternly. 'No, it's not like that at all. Come on, let's go and see him.' I don't add, *before it's too late*, which is exactly what it felt like.

I remember coming here with Serena that time. That time is seared into my memory like the scorch lines in a steak. The terror I felt then that she was going to die is nothing like this terror now. If Logan is taken from me now, like this, I don't know what I'll do. I really don't know what I'll do.

'Hello,' I say, my voice is calm and normal, not high and hysterical like it wants to be. 'My brother was brought in earlier. Logan Carlisle. He was found on the seafront.'

The woman seems to be in no rush to get the information up. The whole area is filling up with people suffering from the usual misadventures that seem to befall them on Saturday night more than any other night of the week. The woman behind the counter takes an age to look at me, to get the right screen up in front of her. 'Date of birth?' she asks.

I tell her and she types some more into the keyboard, then looks up at me. Her manner has slightly shifted, now she looks concerned. Now she confirms how awful it is. 'He's in surgery right now,' she says. 'If you could take a seat, when the surgeon finishes, someone will come and talk to you.'

'That's it? I – we – just have to wait until someone comes to talk to us?'

'Yes, I'm afraid so.'

'But I need to know what happened.'

'I'm sorry, I don't have that information. Those people came in with him. One of them is a doctor, he may have more information. But other than that, I'm sorry, all I can advise is for you to wait.'

'Who did you say came in with him?'

The woman behind the glass partition points behind me and I spin in that direction.

She's standing right behind me. Not too close, but close enough for my whole being to have a reaction when I see her. Near enough for my body to entirely freeze, then unfreeze to allow me to take a step back.

This can't be happening.

It really can't be happening.

We stare at each other for a forever.

This forever has been stretched out over the last ten years, over the last thirty years. I have not seen her in ten years. I've often thought I might, living and working in Brighton like we both do, but no. I think Fate has intervened, keeping us apart, allowing us to live in peace.

I have not seen her in ten years.

Now I am staring at her and she is staring at me.

And all that history, all that stuff we left at Marcus's grave all those years ago, is rushing back in like grains of sand falling back into the empty end of a large hourglass. The particles of time, those feelings, emotions, moments, actions, memories gush in. All that stuff, all that everything that made up the connections of our lives is pouring back between us.

We stand staring at each other and wait for the sands of time to smother us.

'Hello, Poppy,' she eventually says.

'Hello, Serena,' I reply.

serena

Now

'What happened to my brother?' she asks in the moments after we've reacquainted ourselves with each other. 'The woman said you came in with him. Why?'

'We don't know what happened to him. He was outside where we were having a party on the seafront. No one knows why he was there or how he got there. Or what happened to him.' I point vaguely to my left, at Evan. 'There were a few doctors there and they helped him. Evan was one of them. He came in the ambulance with him.'

Her gaze flitters over Evan and a little shimmer of shame crosses her eyes as she remembers what she did, how she tricked him to get to talk to him so she could get at me. 'It was just coincidence that he just happened to be near you?' she says, as though I am making up outlandish things and she is not going to fall for a word of it.

I shrug. 'I don't know. Probably not.' I take a deep breath. Once I say this. Once I verbally admit this to another person, let alone her, I am setting our lives off on a trajectory that none of us will be able to control. 'He and . . . he and my daughter, Verity, were involved.' I point vaguely to my right, where my daughter is sitting. The area is almost entirely full now, with more and more people gushing in as if through an open wound that is going to be difficult to seal and heal, but Poppy knows immediately who I mean.

'Involved?' Her shock raises her voice and causes her eyes to run over and over my daughter's form. 'What do you mean, "involved"?'

What do you think I mean? I want to snap. *Has the shock made you thick or something?* 'They were together,' I say quietly. 'Dating.' *Screwing. Fucking. Making love. They were together.*

'*Dating?*' Her distressed gaze keeps darting between my rapidly wilting eldest child and me. 'How? Why? *How?*'

I don't have answers for her. My questions are many and detailed and I cannot ask them because I do not want to shout at Verity. I do not want to give her any idea that I might be as furious and hurt and *scared* as I am. I am scared because you do not mess with another person's past in the way Verity and her boyfriend have been doing and not create consequences that are felt by everyone involved.

'Is this some kind of sick joke?' Poppy asks me.

I wish, I think. I wish because once the punchline is delivered, we can all walk away, we can all go back to our normal lives. But this is not a joke. And any punchline that does come with this will leave us all with bloodied noses. Marcus only ever punched me in the face once. He didn't break my nose, but he did bloody it. And he did realise his mistake because it was a very visible representation of what he was doing. He did not want other people to notice, to talk, to possibly be motivated enough to try to help. Once was probably enough, though. I'm sure I never did whatever it was that set him off ever again.

'No, this isn't a joke.' I indicate to Evan, ask him to come over so he can tell her what he knows.

In his presence, Poppy stands up straighter, her scowl drops away, and she seems meek almost. Is she scared of Evan? Embarrassed by what she did? Or is it more? Is it something that will put us at odds again? Because I will tolerate almost any woman looking twice at my husband but not her. *Never* her.

She nods and stares at him with big doe eyes while he tells her what he knows. About Logan's injuries, what he and the other doctors did to make him comfortable until the ambulance arrived, how he was unconscious but stable when they got to the hospital. The reason why they needed to operate to relieve the pressure on his brain.

'Is he going to die?' she asks when Evan has finished talking.

'Everyone is doing all they can for him,' my husband replies. Which feels as close to 'probably' that Evan can say without actually saying the word. 'Try not to worry,' he adds, placing a comforting hand on her shoulder. 'He's in the best place, receiving the best care.'

I can't believe he's touching her. Comforting her. And I can't believe it's bothering me. Of all the things that are happening right now, this is what is causing the most unpleasant feelings to rise in me.

Evan seems to suddenly remember himself and takes his hand away. He needs to not do that again. He needs to not touch Poppy Carlisle again. Ever.

My husband returns to his seat, while Poppy reaches out and takes the hand of the woman next to her. She looks a bit like Poppy, not so much a younger version, but a slimmer, different version. Her sister, I am guessing.

'Once the police have been to take our statements we'll leave,' I say to Poppy. She nods in response, but has, to all intents and purposes, forgotten I'm there.

Verity doesn't seem to have moved during all of this. She has basically been pretending she isn't there. And right now, I wish she – and we – weren't here, either.

verity

Now

Still no one is talking.

Still everyone is silent unless they absolutely have to be. The police didn't show up at the hospital. They said to go home, that it had been an exceptionally busy Saturday night, so they'd come over tomorrow. They'd got details from Conrad about who Logan was and how I knew him. They said they'd definitely need to speak to me and they would do that at some point tomorrow.

I have no idea what I'm going to say.

I have no idea what has happened to Howie as I haven't heard from him since he said he'd go check up on Logan.

I have no idea if I should go to my flat and try to tidy up in case the police want to look around.

I have no idea about anything and I keep checking my phone, keep hoping Howie will call or text or anything to let me know that he is all right and tell me what happened to make Logan end up on the seafront. The fact Logan was there and the fact I haven't heard from Howie is scaring me.

The way Logan had been . . . I can't stop my hands going to my throat, feeling for the echoes of where his hand had been earlier; had he held on long enough and hard enough for bruises to develop?

I'm scared to call Howie, though, in case the police ask me why. I could lie and say I wanted to ask why he wasn't at the party, but I have enough lies to contend with, I don't need any more. It's probably best to stick as close to the truth as possible. If they ask, I will tell them . . . I will tell them that I went to the flat, that Logan attacked me, that we fought, that I defended myself and then I left him there. Then I called my friend to go and check if he was dead or not.

How am I telling the police that? How am I telling anyone that when it sounds like a monumental lie?

On top of all that, on top of trying to get my story straight for the police in the morning, there is the silence from my parents. They say a few words to each other, but that is it. Even Dad, who is usually every taxi driver's best mate, is silent on the way home. Silent and still and disappointed, I guess.

Is the silence worse than shouted words? It feels like it.

Mum doesn't want to shout at me so she's saying nothing. But I suspect it's more than that. It's the horror of seeing Poppy again. It's probably rendered her mute and fragile.

The silence, though, it's not good. It's not good for my mind, it's not great for my stability. What is she thinking? Feeling? Going to do?

'Goodnight,' Mum mumbles the second we cross the threshold. She doesn't wait for me or Dad to answer, she simply goes up the stairs and straight into her bedroom. She didn't even look at either of us.

Dad towers over me in the corridor. We're a tall family, but Dad has his persona to go with his height, so in the darkness of the corridor, he stands beside me, staring at me, and it is imposing.

I've seen him looking at me like this before. The last time I did something so awful he couldn't quite believe what was playing out in front of him. I made him do something that could have lost him his job. I'm still not sure how much of it he told Mum, but I remember how he looked at me at one point. The way he'd seemed so disheartened.

Despite his current very obvious upset, Dad slips an arm around my shoulders and pulls me towards him. Slowly he presses a kiss onto the top of my head. 'Try to get some sleep,' he says, 'doctor's orders. Goodnight.'

And then he's gone. Slipping back into silence, leaving me all alone with the memory of what happened earlier that day. What made me fight my boyfriend. Wondering what could possibly happen to him now. The thing is, I don't think I did that to him. I don't think I hit him enough to cave his head in like that. Which means . . . What did I unleash when I asked Howie to go over to check on him? What did I trigger?

The number for the emergency services in Ghana is 18555. When we were younger Mum and Dad said to text that to them at any time and they would come for us. I've had cause to use it twice in my life and both times Dad came for me. Rescued me, solved the problem and, like I said, put his job on the line to save Zeph and me. I don't think Con has ever used it; if he's got a problem he usually calls me first because I can't technically tell him off.

I take my phone out for the millionth time and stare at it.

No word from Howie to explain what happened when he went to my flat. Obviously no word from the hospital about whether Logan will survive.

And obviously no way I can type 18555 and have either of my parents come and rescue me.

poppy

Now

My flat is in darkness by the time I slip the key into the lock.

The sun is probably going to begin its ascent into the sky soon, bringing with it light and Sunday and the coming twenty-four hours that I'm going to have to tell Mum and Dad that because I was stupid enough to be seduced and manipulated and abused by my teacher when I was barely fifteen, their son . . .

I thought I was being quiet as I opened the door, but Alain is standing halfway up the wide corridor by the time I step through and shut out the world.

'How is he?' Alain asks. Despite the very dim lighting, I can see the concern that has taken over my ex's face. And that breaks me. Causes the tears that have been lining my throat and stinging my eyes since I climbed into the taxi to the hospital to finally triumph. I've held them back, held myself strong, held Bella together and now I can't do it any more. Now, I have to cover my face with my hands and give in. Collapse. Allow the crying to consume me.

'Oh no,' Alain whispers, then comes towards me, envelopes me in the type of hug he is expert at delivering. 'Oh no.'

We stand in the corridor for long minutes, me sobbing and Alain holding me. I'd tried to insist that Bella came in with me, or at least let me come home with her, but she wasn't having it. She wanted to go home and be on her own. Actually, I think she wants to be away from me, from my past and how it has brought this to our door – *again*. My past, their pain.

'I'm so sorry,' Alain whispers against my hair, and kisses me. 'I'm so sorry.'

I shake my head. It's not what he thinks. Through my shaky, tear-filled voice, I tell him: surgery was a success, the swelling is likely to go down now the pressure on his brain has been reduced, everything is looking positive. Except, they're not sure when he'll wake up. If he'll wake up. Nothing is certain with his type of injuries. Nothing can be predicted for after he wakes up, either. He could have perman-ent brain damage, he might have no problems at all. We won't know until he wakes up. But the crucial thing is this: he might not wake up. And from the way the doctor spoke, the way all the medical people spoke, they do not think he will wake up. They think they've just saved his life so he can spend the rest of it sleeping it away in a hos-pital bed.

'I'm so sorry,' Alain soothes in a soft voice at the end of my words. 'I'm so sorry.'

In the dark kitchen, Alain pours me a drink from the bottle of liqueur he brought me back from a work trip to Portugal last year. I've not had a chance to try it – and it looks like it will be sickly sweet, claggy and cloying over my teeth and at the back of my throat.

It is all that and more, but it also warms a path from my mouth to my stomach and reminds me that I can feel; that my body is sentient and capable of feeling. Alain knocks a drink back as he sits beside me at the table. He takes my hand between both of his and focuses on my face as he says, 'What can I do to help?'

Nothing.

There's nothing any of us can do. That's what's so frustrating.

'I haven't even told you the worst part,' I say. I remove my hand from his and pour more sticky dark-brown liquid into the large Baileys glass I've been drinking from. I keep pouring until the liquid is right near the top. Telling Mum and Dad in a few hours will be so much easier with a hangover. Even if it isn't, the headache will act as a filter for their wrath; will dull the harm that I experience as a result of it.

'What could be worse?' Alain asks, putting his hand over his glass to stop me pouring more into it.

I smirk at him. As I would have smirked at myself a few hours ago when I didn't know. '*She* was there. Serena.'

'Serena? *The* Serena?'

'Yes, *the* Serena. She was there at the hospital for Logan.'

'What? Wait? *What?*'

'His girlfriend. The one he's given up everything and everyone for? The one who he is obsessed with and has been breaking his heart over and is "complicated"? It turns out, she's Serena's daughter.'

'Wait. *What?!*'

'Isn't that just peachy?' I take another huge mouthful of the thick, brown liquid, and it slimes over my teeth, my already furry-feeling tongue and tear-constricted throat before sliding down my oesophagus. 'For the past year my brother has been screwing the offspring of the woman who ruined my life.' Another gulp. 'And there was me giving him advice to stick with it. And Bella was telling him to allow himself to be loved.' Another gulp. 'And all the while. All the while . . . *Complicated*. Fucking *complicated*, that's what he called it.' Huge gulp.

' "Complicated" is married . . . kids . . . lives on the other side of the world, not . . .' Gulp, gulp, gulp. 'I keep cycling between being destroyed that he's in a coma and being glad the fucker isn't awake because I'd fucking kill him. Serena's daughter!' If I drink any more of this liqueur I am going to throw up, but I can't stop. I need something to take the edge off. To take all the edges off. I'm only now starting to process this, and each thing that goes through the processing part of my mind comes out with razor-sharp edges that cut me to the quick. I am so hurt. Devastated that he would do this.

He's seen first-hand what being involved with Serena did to me, how it ruined all of our lives, and he's still done this. He's still got involved with her, gone to bed with her. *Fallen in love* with her, from what he was saying.

'How am I supposed to deal with this?' I ask Alain. 'I mean, he's an adult, he can do whatever the hell he wants. But this feels like . . . a betrayal. A huge betrayal.' Another one. Another one to add to all the others I've had in my life.

'To be honest, Pops, I'm still back at the stage of him sleeping with Serena's daughter. Isn't she like fourteen or something?'

'No, she was ten years ago. She's probably twenty-four now. She was sitting there. And my God she's pretty. *Beautiful.* I mean, Serena was always beautiful and sophisticated, her daughter is even more stunning, if that's possible. And I bet you she's clever like Serena was.'

'You're clever.'

'Not like her. Marcus was always telling me how bright Serena was. How that was what attracted him to her in the first place. She had this incredible mind as well as being beautiful and having the perfect body. She was the complete package. He just liked me because he could see potential in me. Potential to be a bit thinner, to talk a bit better, learn a few more things, find out how to please him in bed. Serena was all of those things without him putting in any work. She was complete. I was just a mess.'

'That's what he told you?'

'Most of it; some of it I just got from the things he said and the way he said them. The way he treated me. The things he told me after he had to hurt me.'

'What do you think he told her about you?'

'I don't know. It's not like we asked each other what was said when we weren't together. I didn't have to, though. I always knew I could never match up to her.'

That's the final straw for Alain, apparently, and he wrestles the glass out of my hand. He probably thinks the drink has addled my brain and let out a stream of stuff with my freed tongue. When really the booze has just made things clearer, brought the memories back into sharper focus. I can see the past a lot better right now. I can see how and why everything ended up the way it did.

'Point is, Alain, I can see why Logan fell for Serena's daughter; she's probably the better version of someone who was already damn near perfect.'

'What are you saying?' Alain is aghast. 'Serena wasn't perfect. Far from it. And I bet he said the exact same things to her as he said to you. It was the simplest way to control you both by talking up the other while simultaneously putting you down. It kept you both doing whatever he wanted and stopped you from coming together and realising you were too good for him.'

'I wasn't too good for Marcus. I wasn't anywhere near good enough for him. Don't you see? Marcus knew everything. He was right about everything, too. He was . . .' I feel the tears returning. Rushing back to sit behind my eyes, to seal over my throat, to cloud up my mind. 'He was everything. I loved him so much. I just . . . it felt impossible to be without him, you know? Without him, the world was horrible. Nothing worked. I was . . . I remember being so happy when I was with him. I remember feeling like I could do anything, be anything.

'And I hated her. Serena. I hated her, not just because she was so perfect in a way that I could never be, but also because she took that part of him away from me. He was rarely ever focused on me a hundred per cent because there was always *her*. And she was already perfect. And I had to try so hard to be even partway good enough for him. And I tried so hard. *So hard*. I can't believe . . .' I cover my mouth – my treacherous, confessing mouth – with my hand, and immediately the tears that have been flooding out of my eyes run over my fingers as they cascade down my face.

I can't believe he's dead.

I can't believe he's gone and I didn't get another chance to make it right with him.

I can't believe that after all this time . . .

I keep my hand clamped over my mouth so I don't say it out loud.

So I don't let anyone know this devastating secret.

I can't believe after all this time, after all he did, all I've been through, I still love Marcus.

Part 4

poppy

Now

The sun has finally arrived, making herself felt by edging up into the sky, lighting up the path in front of her so she can see where she is going on her journey, while brightening up the world for us, too.

Alain has put me to bed as a way of calming my hysteria.

He's taken off my clothes and put a glass of water on the bedside table and tucked me up. He's told me he'll take care of Betina when she wakes up, and I need to rest. I'm in shock, he's said. That's why I broke down like that. That's why I am saying things that aren't true. *You're in shock*, he repeats, *so you are misremembering things and amplifying untruths*. He says I am breaking myself up because the shock of seeing Serena and the shock of knowing Logan might die is too much for me.

He sits in the hollow the crescent my body makes now that I am curled up, and he strokes my cheek, telling me to go to sleep. Telling me that things will be better after a sleep.

Nothing's going to change if I go to sleep now, I want to reply. *Nothing's going to be different. I'm still going to wake up and feel like I do.*

'Please can you get in with me?' I ask him.

He hasn't been in this bed in months. Well over six months. Once

179

upon a time, if he came over to see Betina and we stayed up late talking afterwards, he'd just fall asleep in it with me. No big deal. But recently, he has been sleeping on the sofa. Neither of us suggested it, it just felt like the right thing to do.

'Are you sure that's a good idea?' he asks.

'You really know how to make a girl feel wanted,' I say weakly, a reminder of what I said to him ten years ago just before he confessed to me about how we really met, how he engineered those meetings and had planned on using me.

Without another word, he strips off his T-shirt, he unbuttons his jeans and takes them off, he pulls down his tight, white underpants, and pushes off his socks. I shift along the bed to let him in, noting that he's hard before his body has touched the mattress. He still wants me. Still desires me, which is good to know right now.

Within seconds of the duvet covering us both up, we're kissing. We've kissed these last six months. We've kissed quite a few times, probably once or twice a week, but not like this. Not without clothes, not with our hands running over each other's body, not with our bare skin pressed close, not with our breath panting out desire.

Alain breaks away for a moment. 'Do you have a rubber johnny?' he asks. Since I asked him that ten years ago, he always calls them that because not enough people use that name for them any more, apparently.

I shake my head against the pillow as I gaze up at him. He's amazing looking. Really. In a decade he's aged into his looks. More happy wrinkles around his eyes, a few strands of grey in his black hair, his lips as full and kissable as they ever were. I still sometimes wonder why he chose me, why he's stuck with me. Even when we haven't been together, haven't kissed, he's been clear about caring for me, loving me. Betina aside, he still adores me.

'Are you back on the Pill?'

I shake my head again.

'You could get pregnant,' he states, like I don't know that.

'I don't care,' I confess. 'I just want to be with you.' *I just want to forget about everything by being with you.*

Alain looks at me like I am a puzzle, a quandary to solve. He gazes at me as though he knows what I'm doing, and he's not sure if he should go along with it. He stares at me as though he wants to do this but he's not sure how either of us will cope with the potential consequences.

'I'll pull out,' he finally says. 'I'll pull out.'

I arch my body towards him, telling him what I want, begging him to become a part of me. *Please*, my body whispers to his. *Please. Now. Please.*

That's it, I say in my head as he enters me. *Yes, that's it. That's what I need. That's what will make all the confusion, all the thoughts, all the Marcus disappear.*

I pull Alain closer, bring him deeper, move him harder. I want him to fill me, to complete me. When he's with me like this, there's no room for anything else. No space for betrayal, or regrets or inadequacy. There is nothing but the pureness of a man moving inside me, looking down at me with love, and my body being slowly but decisively brought to the very edge of desire, of pleasure, of ecstasy and then being tipped over in the blissful abyss of orgasm . . .

Alain is kissing my cheeks, my neck, my forehead. He's running his fingers through my hair. He's acting like he won't get the chance to do this again so is indulging himself in me as much as he possibly can.

Sex had been good. Special. He'd been about to pull out, like he promised, but I'd asked him not to. I'd wanted him to stay with me, be with me all the way. And I felt better. Much better than I had when I was sitting at the kitchen table.

Through the fuzz, the calm and hush of afterwards, *I've got to tell my parents*, flitters across my mind. *I've got to go and tell my parents about Logan and about Serena and about everything.*

'I'll come with you,' Alain says.

'Pardon?' Has he read my mind?

'You were all calm and blissed-out and then suddenly your face has changed and you're clearly worrying about going to tell your parents about Logan, so I'll come with you.'

'Who's going to look after Betina?' I ask.

'I'm sure Carolyn won't mind if we drop her off at Prince's Crescent for a few hours.'

'OK, I'll text her.' I go to reach for my phone and Alain gently pushes me back against the bed.

'Not right now. Right now, I need you to please get some sleep. The next few days are going to be hectic. You need to rest.'

He's right. After today, I'm going to stay at the hospital as much as I can so I can be there when Logan wakes up. So for now, I'd better get some rest.

Alain is taken aback when I don't argue, but instead cuddle up to him and close my eyes. Logan's going to need me to be strong for him so I need to sleep.

It starts just as I'm drifting off, as my last hold on wakefulness slips away. *Do you think I like doing these things, Poppy?* Marcus says in my head. *Do you think I like having to teach you these lessons?* I can't fight it. I can't get rid of it. All I can do is allow myself to fall asleep with the sound of Marcus's voice swirling through my mind.

serena

Now

The shed, *my* shed, is a mishmash of things I can't do in the house.

It started when I wanted to revamp our bedroom but didn't want to buy more 'stuff'. Evan, who had known me since I was eighteen, who had been married to me for twenty-five years, did his usual thing of listening to me talk about it for a while with interest and then tuned out. I'd never been very creative, artistic or good with my hands in that way. But I'd seen enough TV makeover shows to think I could try my hand at painting the drawers in our bedroom an interesting, vibrant colour.

After a fashion (tears, recriminations, arguments, frustrations and upsets – all from me to me) I managed to create something that was 'different' to what had been there before. 'It's really good,' Evan said in the neutral tone of a man who knew his future sex life could be in the balance. It wasn't too bad. The paint wasn't blobby and uneven in *that* many places; the dust from where I'd sanded it down hadn't stuck in rash-like little clumps too often; the new handles weren't too small for the size of the drawer. Buoyed by this success, I decided to turn my hand to 'upcycling' more things around the house.

Verity had mostly left home for college so pretended not to notice anything that didn't turn out quite right, Conrad just side-eyed me whenever I asked his opinion on my creations and Evan . . . my darling Evan, put up with so much until he declared that he couldn't stand to be surrounded by my half-finished 'projects' any longer and either I took it outside or I stopped.

We erected a smaller bike store for their bikes and accessories and I emptied out as much as I could get away with from the weatherboard brown shed that stood at the end of our long, narrow garden, and it became my workshop for when I worked on my projects.

I would have loved all new tools and benches and paint palettes, but instead my 'place' was a collection of the tools and paints and varnishes and DIY debris people accumulate over the course of their lives. I had very few specialist tools, most of them were old and had seen better days but still worked, so I still used them.

This morning, after we have all risen and avoided each other by grabbing toast and retreating to our rooms for breakfast, I escape to the shed, having mumbled to Evan something about working on the book stool.

I'd found a load of books dumped in a skip recently. They looked so forlorn and unloved sitting there, and at the same time the air was burgeoning with rain and I knew these books, these pages and pages of knowledge, needed me to rescue them. They weren't suitable for my house – most of them were damaged and repairing them would be impossible – so I'd prevailed upon my son to help gather them up, put them in my car and take them home to the safety of my shed. Once there, the piles had taken up a huge amount of floor space and I didn't really know what to do with them.

I'd finally settled on making a stool out of them. This meant, of course, faffing around trying to find the right combination. Finding books to slot in next to each other that would create a solid, tightly packed structure. It was a puzzle that I needed right now, to try to take my mind off the last few hours.

I shouldn't have had that party, I realise as I unlock and then enter the honey-wood structure. I usually leave the door open, but today I push it shut behind me. I heft over a couple of large paint tins and push them behind the door to make sure no one can creep up on me. I need to think and I need people to announce their presence, because this type of thinking won't take kindly to being interrupted.

I unfold a badly rusted outside chair that I'm determined to clean and restore *at some point* and sit myself down. I'm wearing my up-cycling clothes of jeans, top and jumper with my hair hidden under a blue-and-red scarf.

What is unravelling around me is a nightmare I never even dreamed possible. I've often wondered, sure, if I should tell the children about what happened, about my history, but there seemed no point. It was a long time ago and things had resolved themselves after Poppy re-appeared in our lives and I was forced to tell Evan *everything*.

I ended up with a more solid, honest marriage as a result of that time and in return, rather than being vigilant and protective of my family and my marriage, I got complacent, I got lazy, I got arrogant. I thought all the bad things were over. I thought *that* part of the past had been *finally* laid to rest and I could, for even a moment, let alone the rest of my life, forget about it.

I want to take care of you for ever. His voice echoes in my ears. *I want to take care of you for ever.*

I cover my mouth with my hands.

Remember, this is our little secret.

Lower my head.

Just relax, I'll show you what to do.

Close my eyes.

You're special to me, I hope you realise that. This was very special to me.

Good girl. Good, good girl.

My hand goes to my cheek as the echo of a pain remembered reverberates.

Don't ever tell me you don't want to do something again, OK?

Air leaves my body in a gush.

I only went with Poppy because she's a virgin and you weren't, the first time . . . a complete virgin? No one had ever kissed you or anything like that? Real or not, a kiss is a kiss is a kiss, baby. And Poppy had never been kissed before. She isn't damaged goods.

More air leaves my body.

Poppy, she's nothing. I can't get rid of her just yet – me being her first means she's really attached to me.

My chest burns with emptiness, with the vacuum of airlessness.

God, Serena, you know I love you. Why do you make me do these things?

I drag air into my lungs.

You shouldn't have worn her dress. And you shouldn't have got ice cream on it.

That small amount of oxygen is knocked out of me almost immediately.

It's over now, baby, OK? Let's make up.

I press my hands over my chest.

You can make it up to me.

Try to hold in air.

You can show me how much you love me.

Try to breathe through this pain.

Stop saying no, you owe it to me, Serena.

Curl forward.

You owe me. You owe me this.

Try to breathe.

Please stop crying, baby, we're only making up.

Breathe. Breathe. Breathe.

I can't breathe. It's too much. The memories are too much, too violent and too fast. It's too much. I can't process them. I can't stop them knocking air out of me. I can't stop them consuming me.

I can't breathe. I can't cope and I can't breathe.

I don't want this to be in my life again.

My knees thud loudly as they hit the floor and I push my hands harder against my chest. I'm having a panic attack. I usually know what to do, how to get through them, but I can't stop this. My heart is bolting, galloping, the sound uncontrolled and loud in my ears.

I rock forward. Breathe, breathe, breathe, brea—

Bam! Bam! On the door.

It shocks my body out of its panic, brings me back to the here and now.

'Mum?' Conrad calls.

'Yes?' I manage, despite the burning in my chest, despite the shaking of every part of my body.

'The . . . the police are here. They want to talk to Verity and search the house for anything related to what happened to that guy.'

poppy

Now

Carolyn's house is very Sunday when we arrive.

The smell of a Full Carolyn breakfast lingers in the air as we make our way to the kitchen at the back of the house. A Full Carolyn is basically what people call a full English but with mushrooms, pancakes, black pudding, melon, mango, pineapple, and homemade smoothies. Every Sunday she does this. And every Sunday she has a virtually open house so the friends of her kids who stay over are welcome to join them, as are their friends, like us.

We walk through her large, circular hallway, from which all the rooms and stairs lead off. This house is just divine. It sits at the top end of one of the roads that leads down to the sea. From some of the upper rooms you can get an oblique view of the sea.

I love her kitchen, which runs the full width of the back of her house and has glass doors all along the back that look out onto the garden. We've spent many a night sitting here, drinking, talking, putting the world to rights. She is so not the sort of person I would meet in every-day life, except, I suppose, as a cleaner, which is why it makes sense that she was actually a friend of Alain's originally.

He used to work in London on the newspapers and through that he met a designer called Sam Bailey. He and Sam and her husband, Matt, had been thick as thieves, apparently, so when Alain said he might move to Brighton, she'd said he should look up her old friend Carolyn. She set up a blind friendship date and the pair instantly fell in love. I often teased him that they had literally swapped Sam and Matt and their two children, Dot and Seth, for Carolyn and her husband, Phil, and their children, Maia and Megan. 'It's literally like for like,' I used to joke. Alain used to protest then tried to defend himself by saying things like, 'Sam's got brown hair and Carolyn's blonde.' Then he just accepted what I was saying because it was bloody true.

Carolyn was significant in my life, though, because she represented normality. If she did know about my past – as an Ice Cream Girl and/or a former convict – she never let on. She treated me like a human being and like a friend and that made all the difference in my life. She was another piece in the puzzle that made me feel normal; that made the nonsense with my parents not so awful.

Carolyn welcomes Betina with open arms. 'So, pumpkin, you're going to hang out with your Aunty Carolyn for a bit while Mum and Dad go off and do stuff, huh?' she says.

'Yes, I am,' Betina replies. Despite what the head teacher implied the other day, my daughter loves most people and is always up for spending time with them. She runs into Carolyn's arms, who effortlessly scoops her up.

The pair of them seem to be staring each other out while simultaneously checking out each other's features in case they've changed since they were last together. 'Well, there are several things we can do,' Carolyn says seriously. 'I'd love to take the wakeboard out for a bit, but I think your mother might have some kind of breakdown if I attempted to do that with you. So, we can do some baking or we can give Maia a makeover. She's been looking far too ordinary pretty recently. I'm thinking me and you could put some pink in that blonde hair, a new orange eyeshadow, I'm sure I've got blue mascara somewhere. How does that sound?'

'Excellent,' Betina replies.

'Great. Obviously, we'll have to trick her into it, but I'm sure it'll be fine.'

'It'll be fine,' Betina echoes.

'But in the meantime' – Carolyn puts her down – 'I'd like you to do me a favour. Megan didn't make it down to breakfast this morning. As you know, that's not allowed in this house – Sunday morning breakfasts are everything. So could you go and wake her up? You know where it is, don't you? A good old-fashioned piley-on should do it. Are you up for that?'

'Oh yeah!' Betina squeals then darts out of the room. None of us move or speak we just leave it three . . . two . . . one . . . and she's back in the room, hurtling towards her father. She throws her arms around him. 'See you later, Dad!' she says. Then she moves on to me before her dad has a chance to speak or even ruffle her hair. 'See you later, Mum,' she says to me. She does linger with me, allows me to fold my arms around her, kiss the top of her head, squeeze her extra close. And then she's gone, desperate to carry out her mission to the best of her abilities.

'How are you?' Carolyn asks the second Betina's footsteps clatter at the top of the stairs. 'How's Logan?'

'I called earlier, they said he had a comfortable night but there's no real change, he's still in a coma.'

Carolyn shakes her head. 'And they don't know what happened?'

'The police are on it, apparently. They've taken statements from a few people, and they're going to his flat later. But no one really knows anything.'

'I'm sorry, sweetheart, this is so rough. If you need Betina to stay over, or anything, just let me know.'

I'm about to thank her when a wail, from someone who has been dragged from the depths of comfort to a world of hell, sounds throughout the house. The sound is swiftly followed by Betina's giggling.

'Oh, that's my girl, Betina,' Carolyn says with a delighted chuckle. 'That's my girl.' She grabs her phone from the middle of the table she was in the middle of clearing and in a swish of blonde hair dashes out, throwing 'I'll see you later' over her shoulder.

Rather than leave, I pull out a chair and sit down. 'I don't want to do this.'

This confession isn't a surprise, especially not to Alain. He says nothing and I pick forlornly at a piece of watermelon that looks perfect to sink my teeth into. I would have loved to have had my breakfast here this morning before trekking the short distance to my parents' for whichever version of badly cooked Sunday lunch we'd be getting. I would have loved to just have a normal Sunday. 'Don't suppose there's any way out of it, is there?'

Alain takes my hand. 'I'll be with you. It'll be fine.' He rubs the back of my hand reassuringly. 'Remember when you went to tell them you were pregnant? You thought they'd freak out. They didn't. It was the first time your mum hugged you in years, you said. And your dad spoke directly to you. Properly.'

'This isn't a baby, Alain.'

'I know, but it might not be as bad as you think. And you don't have to tell them about Serena. Not yet. Not until you know if it's relevant.'

Just when I think Alain has got it together. Just when I think I can trust him, he suggests something like this. 'I'm not going to *lie* to them, Alain. Not even by omission. It's bad enough I didn't tell them straight away because I wanted to have something concrete to tell them, imagine what they'll feel like if they find out about Serena being involved later? They'll wonder why I didn't tell them. They'll have their faith in me, as tenuous and tiny as it is, shaken, and I don't want that.'

He looks embarrassed, as he should. We split up because of his lying and here he is, trying to get me to lie my way out of a bad situation. 'You're right. You're right.' He hauls me to my feet. 'Come on, then, the sooner you tell them, the sooner you get to see Logan.'

serena

Now

There are so many of them.

They stand on the doorstep, they stand on the path, like uniformed clockwork toys waiting to be wound up and let loose on our house.

Evan stands at the door with a woman who is a good head-and-a-half shorter than him, but what she lacks in height she more than makes up for in confidence and self-crowned authority. Evan is reading through the papers in his hand and will clearly not let them in until he's finished.

This is like 1988.

This is like watching my life repeat itself on a digitally remastered video film. This is 1988 and any moment now my father is going to finish reading the paper in his hands and the police officers will push past him into the house. They will spread out. They will each take a room and they will start to look. They will turn things over, pull things out, snap things apart, push things aside and accidentally knock things down, smash things into pieces, rip things into shreds. I will stand and watch. I will see everything in slow motion, I will want to scream at them to stop. I will try to tell them I'll confess to anything if they will stop this wilful, sanctioned destruction of my home; if they will stop the violation that will make me never feel safe again.

Conrad is in the corridor by the kitchen. I want to whisk him out of here; he does not belong in 1988 after all. Evan has stepped aside and his back is against the wall by the front door, and he is staring at the coat rack opposite. Verity is on the stairs, standing aside to let officer after officer after officer climb up the stairs to begin their violation of our bedrooms, our bathrooms.

I stare at her, but she is staring at her father. She is focused on him so she doesn't have to look at me.

I don't want to whisk her out of here. She does belong in 1988, because, after all, she put herself there when she started sleeping with Poppy Carlisle's brother. My eyes continue to bore into her, glaring and staring until it's too much for her – she has to give in and turn to face me.

I hope you hid the clothes you were wearing well, I tell her with my look. *Because this isn't 1988 and no matter how many times you wash them, you'll never, ever get the blood of your victim out enough for the police* not *to find a trace.*

poppy

Now

'What's happened?' is Mum's greeting when she opens the door to us.

Alain and I both look at each other and then at my mother.

'I was about to call you. Bella has been here for about an hour and she hasn't stopped crying. We can't get anything out of her. What's happened? Do you know?'

'Can we come in?' I ask. Bella. I knew I should have stayed with her. By the time we left the hospital yesterday she was barely keeping it together. The only thing she was definitive about was the fact that she didn't want me anywhere near her.

In the kitchen, Bella is sitting at the head of the table, her face in her hands, sobbing and sobbing. My father, my big, strong father, is sitting beside her, his hand on her shoulder, his head near hers, asking her, begging her, to talk to him. To tell him what is wrong.

'I've tried your brother, but his phone is off. We were about to call you.'

Bella raises her head, running her hands down her face to dry her tears. She glares at me, her expression one of pure, unadulterated hatred. I've never seen Bella look at me like that before. I've never seen anyone who claims to love me look at me like that. I didn't think it was possible.

'What's going on, Pepper, love?' Dad asks me this. For the first time in more than thirty years he has used that nickname for me. For the first time in more years than I care to mention, he has deliberately and intentionally spoken several words to me.

I'm momentarily floored; halted in my tracks. Has Bella's distress really done this to him? He hasn't been able to talk to me in ten years, thirty years, if I think about it properly, and he decides to start now? When I'm about to destroy them all again?

'Logan's in hospital,' I state. I was going to preamble, say I was sorry, explain how it was probably going to be all right and for them to try not to worry, but the look on Bella's face, the affection in Dad's voice have thrown me. I need things to flip back to normal as soon as possible. 'He was attacked last night.'

'Last night?' Our parents exclaim together. 'Why didn't you call us?'

'Everything happened really fast. And you couldn't have done anything.'

'He's our child,' Mum says. 'How can you think to keep something like this from us?'

'Because . . . if either of us had called you, you would have wanted to come to the hospital and there was nothing you could have done. We saw him for thirty seconds and waiting at the hospital was horrible. All those people. We wanted to spare you all of that.

'And . . . and Serena Gorringe was at the hospital.' I lower my eyes when I say this so I do not see the expressions that take over their faces. I keep my eyes down as I plough on: 'She was there because . . . because Logan has been going out with her daughter for the last year.'

A loud fump as Mum drops into the nearest chair, a protracted sob as Bella begins to cry again, an audible gasp as Dad inhales sharply.

Alain is beside me, he takes my hand, slips his fingers through mine, holds me close. 'I'm sorry. I had no idea. I had no idea he was dating her. I didn't think she'd ever be back into our lives. And I don't know if any of this is connected to what happened to Logan, but we'll find out. We'll find out. The police were there. They're going to be talking to all the people who were near where he was found to try to see if they can find out what happened to him.' I shake my head to stop the tears. 'I'm sorry,' I say again. 'I'm so, so sorry.'

My partner/ex/whatever he is squeezes my hand, tells me to stop. Stop apologising, stop talking, stop being the bad guy in this scenario. I didn't do this to him so I should stop apologising for it.

'I'll drive you to the hospital,' Alain says. His voice is commanding and calming at the same time. 'Poppy and I rang them earlier and there's been no change, so let's get ourselves together and I'll take us over there.' When no one moves or does anything, Alain raises his voice a notch. 'Come on, we're all keen to get to the hospital. See him. If you want to come you need to start getting yourselves together now.' It's only a notch that his voice has been raised, but it is enough to get them moving. They stand up, and in a drugged, zombie-like state, they all move towards the door to get themselves ready to go and see Logan.

'They all hate me,' I tell Alain.

'They're just in shock. Like you were last night. It'll be fine.'

'I love that you still have the ability to be bright and sunny about this.'

'I get it from our daughter,' he says and tugs me into a hug.

serena

Now

They've decided to speak to me first.

They made a big show of putting us all in separate rooms, each of us 'accompanied' by a police officer, so we don't forget ourselves and try to speak to one another. In other words, we don't have a chance to get our stories straight – although what they think we would have been doing last night if we were that way inclined, I don't know.

I've pushed the sofa cushions back into place to sit down and DI Brosnin and her partner, whose name I didn't catch or didn't absorb (can't remember which), sit in the armchair and Evan's favourite chair.

'This is quite a turn-up for the books, isn't it, Miss Gorringe?' DI Brosnin states. She's putting it out there straight away that she knows who I am.

'It's Gillmare,' I state calmly. 'I go by Mrs Gillmare now.'

'Oh, sorry,' she says with a fake smile. 'I didn't realise. Most women have no reason to change their names nowadays. But like I say, this is quite a turn-up for the books. How long has your daughter been dating your old partner's brother?' she asks.

This is hell.

First we had a tour of 1988 and now we're visiting hell. That one sentence, that one question, needs to be completely unpicked. And in the unpicking, I will make myself seem like I have so much to hide. But if I don't unpick it, I am admitting to something they couldn't make us confess to all those years ago.

'Poppy wasn't my partner. She was a girl who was dating the man I was dating at the time. And I don't know how long my daughter has been seeing Logan Carlisle.'

'You know him well enough to know his first name?'

'Verity told me it yesterday.'

'But she didn't tell you she'd been seeing him?'

'No.'

'Odd that she didn't mention it when they've been together for the best part of a year, according to the text messages on his phone.'

A year. This has been going on for a year. Verity has been lying to us for nearly a year. This is why she has taken against me so much. This is why she has been distant and low-level rude and disengaged from family life. Sure, she shows up for Sunday lunch, yes, she comes and hangs out here sometimes, but she is almost always distracted. Constantly 'not there'; vacant.

'Where were you yesterday afternoon?' DI Brosnin asks me.

'I was here.'

'You didn't go out at all?'

'Well, I went out in the morning to pick up the cake for the party, but other than that, no.'

'What about your husband?'

'Why are you asking?'

'Because we believe that Mr Carlisle, Logan, received his injuries sometime between two and four p.m. yesterday. His text messages show he was in contact with your daughter until she asked him to meet her at her flat. Just after those messages he spoke to his sister, Bella Carlisle. After that, no one spoke to or had any kind of interaction with Mr Carlisle, as far as we can tell, until he showed up on the seafront.

'So, again, where was your husband yesterday afternoon?'

'Here.'

'The whole time?'

I know what she's thinking and no, it's not possible. Evan wouldn't. He just wouldn't. I'm more likely to than him. 'He went out for a little bit.'

'What time?'

'I genuinely don't know. It was in the afternoon at some point.'

'How long was he out for?'

'I don't know.'

From the pocket of the other officer, whose name I didn't properly register, a jolly musical ringtone trills into the space after my answer. He takes out his phone, looks at the screen and then decides to walk into the corridor to take the call.

DI Brosnin doesn't even acknowledge him leaving. 'And your son?'

'What about him?'

'Was he here all yesterday afternoon?'

'Not exactly.'

'Did he go out at an unspecified time for an unspecified length of time, too?'

If it was silly to think that of Evan, it is completely and utterly ludicrous to think that about Conrad. He is the most gentle boy in the world. His build and height – like his dad's – plays into every stereotype we're bombarded with about Black men, but, like the stereotype, it's wrong. My boy would not harm anyone unless in self-defence.

I'm about to tell her how ridiculous she is being with these questions when the nameless officer returns. He leans in and whispers into

DI Brosnin's ear. By the time he's finished speaking, she is grinning, her pink-coloured lips drawn back over her smoker's teeth. She flips shut her notebook and stands.

'Thank you for your help, Mrs Gillmare. I will need you, your husband and your son to come down to the station at some point for questioning, but for now, I need to speak to your daughter.'

She leads the way out of my living room and down the corridor to the kitchen, moving with the entitlement of someone who lives here or believes everything is theirs for the taking. Verity has been sitting on one of the kitchen chairs, staring at the tabletop, while a police officer stands by the sink watching her do nothing. She looks up when we arrive in the kitchen.

DI Brosnin doesn't break stride as she marches towards my daughter. Verity is, thankfully, dressed. She is wearing jeans, a long-sleeved T-shirt and a long, long cardigan that has seen better days. 'Verity Gillmare, I am arresting you on suspicion of attempted murder,' states the police officer.

'What?' I hear myself say, even though I was expecting this. I knew DI Brosnin was going to be leaving with one of us in chains, but I thought it would be me. I really thought 1988 would play itself out to the degree that I would be the one falsely accused. 'Why are you arresting her?'

DI Brosnin finishes telling Verity she does not have to say anything but anything that she does say may be used in evidence against her. Then she turns to me. 'Last night, after we found out her connection to the victim and her address, we conducted a search of Miss Gillmare's flat and found a significant amount of blood as well as signs of a struggle. In two rooms.'

'That could be blood from anywhere,' I say.

'Yes, Mrs Gillmare, we know that. There were also two different sets of fingerprints found in the blood. We don't have the DNA tests back yet, but along with having what we believe to be the weapon used, I would be remiss if I didn't arrest Miss Gillmare,' she cuts in. Dismissing me, she spins on her heels and tells her officer, 'Take her away.'

Again Verity avoids my gaze. Again she pretends I'm not there. She can't face me, she can't look me in the eye, not until she has handcuffs around her wrists and she is level with me as they lead her out. Then she looks, then she acknowledges what is going on by acknowledging me.

And in that acknowledgement, she looks so little. So young. She looks like a little girl lost who is being taken away at her most vulnerable moment.

When she looks at me like that, it's then that I want to move, it's *then* that I want to snatch her up and whisk her out of here because it is 1988 and she doesn't belong here.

But by then, of course, there's nothing I can do to save her.

poppy

Now

In a couple of days they're going to move Logan from this room. Bella and I were here, briefly, last night. The room is slightly bigger than a two-person cell but it seems smaller because of all of the machines surrounding his bed. Some are large with a computer screen at the top, others are wide, blocky columns that have lights that bleep, others still are mounted on arms that hang down from above and can be readjusted at will. The room is filled with bleeps and beeps, sounds and noises that are, I'm assuming, good. Constant short sounds are a sign that everything is stable, everything is fine – Logan is doing all right as long as that sound is still punctuating the air at regular intervals. Alain is outside with Mum and Dad, who have been in on their own already. Two visitors at a time. They're very strict about that. We'd tried to argue, to say that we are a family and need to go in together but the senior nurse, with a smile that could melt rock and eyes that could probably shoot laser beams, kept looking at us with an expression that basically said, 'Tell me again and again how so very important you are that you get to break the rules' until we got the message and stopped.

It was better for Mum and Dad to be on their own, anyway. They could talk to him, hush him, love him without feeling they had to temper anything for mine and Bella's ears.

'I didn't mean for this to happen,' I whisper to Bella. She has been avoiding me, ignoring me, pretending that I don't exist since I walked into the kitchen at 34 Surry Hills Street. In the hours since I last saw her, she's obviously gone away, done a load of thinking and decided this is all my fault. I've been thinking the same thing, of course I have. She is behaving – as are Mum and Dad – as though I don't feel culpable; as though I have shrugged off all responsibility when it comes to Serena and her brood and the impact they have on my life.

'I know you didn't,' she whispers back.

'I didn't know,' I say. 'I had no idea what he was doing. Who he was doing it with.'

'That's not what I'm angry about,' she replies.

'Well, what, then?' I ask her. I stare at her across our brother's hospital bed. 'Why do you barely look at me and when you do, you look like you want to murder me?'

'Because . . . because he was doing this for you.'

'Doing what for me?'

'Over the years he's been talking about clearing your name. It was like an obsession with him. I told him to leave it, but he was convinced there was a way to prove you were innocent. I thought I'd got through to him, I thought he'd left it. But, no, he went ahead. He made contact with the Gorringes and now . . . And *now* look at him.'

'I had no idea,' I reply. 'No idea at all. I would have told him to stop if I'd known. All of that was over as far as I was concerned. I spoke to Serena ten years ago, we settled things. I moved on. *We* moved on. My life is perfect as it is. The very last thing I would want is to drag that all up again. Do you or he think I'd want any of that around Betina?

You think I ever want her to hear the stories, read all that stuff about me and Serena in the papers? I thought if I just left it, I could pretend it hadn't happened. And now look at this.'

Bella is staring at me, and she doesn't look like she wants to glass me. 'I'm not angry at you. I'm pissed off with him and with myself. For not seeing sooner what was happening, for not . . .'

'For not what?'

She flushes, lowers her head and hides behind her veil of long, brown locks. But I can see she's shaking, trembling again like she did last night. And I suddenly understand what she's really annoyed about, what has truly ignited her anger.

'You're pissed off for not asking if I did it,' I supply. 'You think if you'd asked, and I'd told you the truth, Logan wouldn't have gone off on his wild goose chase in the first place.'

Even behind her mask of hair I can see her cheeks glowing with embarrassment.

'You know what, Bella, I wouldn't have told you even if you'd asked. I decided, after the last time I spoke to Serena, that I was going to move on from every last scrap of my past. I had you and Logan back. You two were the only ones I cared about having back in my life. The only people I'd be trying to prove my innocence to would be Mum and Dad. And whether I did it or not, as far as they're concerned, I am guilty. I fucked my teacher, and I got caught out. Not by getting pregnant, but by going to prison. When I realised that, I just let it go. And now Logan has dragged it back into my life.

'I'm not going to spend the next however many years trying to prove I'm innocent. I am not going to start living half a life to make you or Mum and Dad or even Logan feel any better. I have a daughter and she deserves the best of me. And even if I didn't have Betina, I deserve to live my life without trying to prove anything to anyone. Innocent or guilty, I was punished; I spent twenty years in prison. I don't have to answer to anyone.'

Bella has stopped looking so indignant and furious now. She seems mortified, that red glow growing stronger and more virulent with every passing second.

'You know what, Bella,' I say suddenly, her blushing, her embarrassment in this situation irritating every single nerve in my body, 'screw you.' This is why my beloved Tina died, this is why I still had to cut up. It was never enough. When you are a prisoner, a convict like me or Tina, you are lowly. And even if you go back to 'real life' you are still lowly, you are always that number. You are never completely human again. Innocent or not, people always expect a piece of you whenever they demand it. They always expect an answer. They always expect you to want to prove yourself worthy of being around them. It probably isn't conscious, it rarely is malicious, but it is there. It is always there at the back of their minds. It is always there as something they wonder about and feel entitled to ask about. And I might expect it from others, from potential employers, from banks, credit card companies, even my supermarket loyalty scheme, but from Bella? Logan? No. Not from them. Not when they are all I've wanted these last thirty years.

'Screw you,' I say again. 'Screw you for making me feel like this. My brother's in a coma and instead of processing and dealing with that, you're acting like I'm meant to be sneaking around feeling guilty for something I didn't do. And you know what, screw Logan for doing this, for detonating this in our lives. And, actually, screw Mum and Dad for making me feel terrible all these years.' They need to hear that, I decide. It'll do no one any good if they *don't* hear me say that to them.

I spin on my heels, the rubber on the bottom of my trainers squeaking on the floor. Bella says nothing, she just watches me leave.

In the corridor, waiting on the bank of uncomfortable plastic chairs, are my parents and my lover. I march towards them. I want to swear at them. I want to unleash the full Prison Poppy on them so we will all know that I'm done now. I'm not going to play this game any more. I'm not going to pander to their sensibilities when it's clear from earlier that Dad can call me Pepper when he needs to, he can be affectionate and remember how much he loved me when it's convenient to him. I'm not going to play any more when it's been clear all this time that Mum is capable of overt displays of affection because of the way she is with my child.

Like I just said to Bella: screw them.

Alain is on his feet and in front of me in an instant. He's obviously seen from my face what I'm about to do, what I'm about to say, and he's decided to intervene.

He slips one arm around my waist, the other goes on my bicep, as he yanks me towards his body so he can stop me moving. 'Don't,' he murmurs into my ear. He tries to take a step back, to push distance between my parents and me. 'Don't. Their son is in a coma. This isn't the time.' He holds me closer, blocks me from moving towards the couple holding hands, a swirl of sadness and worry shutting them off from the outside world. 'It needs to be said, it does,' he continues to murmur, 'but not right now, Poppy. Not right now.'

I'm about to push him off, tell him to do one because I'm done with the scrabbling around for scraps of affection. I'm done with using my daughter as the only reason for them to tolerate me. And they need to hear it. They need to hear it all and they need to hear it right now. Before I can free myself, though, there is a flash of black over his shoulder. A black uniform. Following a person in normal clothes. Immediately my breath snags in my chest, my heart skips up to beat in triple time.

'Mr and Mrs Carlisle?' the plain-clothes officer asks my parents.

'Yes,' my parents reply and stand up. 'That's us,' Dad adds.

They keep holding hands as they stare at the person in front of them. 'Logan Carlisle has you down as his next of kin,' the officer says. 'I'm going to be your family liaison officer, so I'll be with you throughout this investigation.'

'OK,' Dad replies. He looks at the officer suspiciously. I guess he hasn't got over what happened, either.

'We've been conducting an investigation since last night when your son was brought into the hospital. We're very surprised but pleased to say that we've made an arrest.'

'You've made an arrest? Already?' I say.

The officer turns to me. 'And you are?' she asks.

I sigh, and then say, 'I'm their daughter Poppy.'

The officer nods, while her eyebrows do a tiny dance of recognition. She knows who I am and she was expecting me. 'Yes, Miss Carlisle, we've made an arrest. I believe you may know her. She's called Verity Gillmare. She's the daughter of your former accomplice, sorry, partner, Serena Gorringe.'

serena

Now

I didn't actually expect them to send someone so senior.

After the police left, taking Verity with them, Evan had been floored. He'd not known what to do for several minutes, which must have been a strange place for him as he always knows what to do in any given situation. Conrad had stood on the first step, eyes wide with shock, wondering what to do as well. I was the only one who moved.

I dashed past both of them, up the stairs and into my bedroom. I'd had to stop for a moment at the absolute bloody state of the place. They hadn't searched, they had excavated. Everything, *everything*, had been overturned and it turned my stomach. They had been into everything, had touched and probed every single thing in my bedroom.

Another flashback to 1988 hit me and nearly felled me, because I knew now that this was something approximating how Mum and Dad had felt. I'd only ever focused on the awfulness of what I was going through. It never occurred to me how the whole thing must have horrified my parents. How powerless they must have felt to watch their home be violated, have their daughter accused of murder and then have to stand there and watch her be taken away.

At the time, I could only think of the shame I'd brought on them, now

I realise I changed the course of their whole lives. I made them feel like this – insignificant, vulnerable, scared.

I shook aside those thoughts, forced myself to find my phone amongst the mess and focus on 2020, on getting Verity the help she needed. Once in my hand, I called up the internet and found the law firm Verity worked at. I probably shouldn't have called them since she works there but they'd find out anyway and I thought they were more likely to care since she was one of theirs.

The woman I'd spoken to on the emergency number said someone would meet me at the police station, but she wasn't sure who yet. Once that was sorted, I could run back downstairs and hug Conrad. Take him in my arms and reassure him that no matter what, I was there – *we* were there. We were all still reeling, having been sucker-punched by the police arrival and then how suddenly everything seemed to shift to a faster, scarier gear.

I realised as I was holding Con that they hadn't been that desperate to search our house. They were just making sure that Vee didn't abscond, that we didn't help her escape. That's why they didn't mention that they'd already searched her flat, that they'd found something, that they were just waiting on tests so they could slap on the cuffs. They were just going through the motions until they could confirm there was something for her to answer to.

While I held Con, I willed Evan to come out of it, to reanimate himself from his stupor so he could help me, could come with me to the station in the hopes of seeing our daughter.

It took a bit longer to get him together enough for him to move. We had to delay our departure because I was dressed in upcycling clothes and looking a mess wouldn't make anyone feel better about the situation. By the time I had pulled on hole-free, clean clothes, Evan was back. He was present and he was ready to go and do whatever was necessary to get our child back.

The man who walks into the police station not long after we have arrived introduces himself as Darryl Palmer. He is tall, smartly dressed in a suit even though it is Sunday and he looks like the type of person who would normally be settling down to a big family meal. His black-and-white hair has been cut in a way that emphasises his cheekbones and the flattering way life has pressed creases into his smooth skin.

Once upon a time and not so long ago, I would have thought this man was a lot older than me, possibly older than Evan. I would have looked at his suit, his sensible, high-powered job and creased skin and I would have thought he knew everything about everything because he was older than me. Nowadays I come to realise quite quickly that people like him are usually the same age as me, they are just more confident in who they are and what they do.

'I'm one of the partners at Frost, Palmer, Cummings, Quarry and Carter,' he tells us as he shakes my hand and then Evan's hand. 'I'll ask to see Verity and will go and talk to her. Try not to worry, we will have this sorted out as quickly as possible. Try not to worry.'

'Thank you,' I hear myself say. This police station is very different to the one I first walked into thirty-two years ago to confess about being at Marcus's house the night he died, but it still gives me the jitters, makes me feel unsafe. Like the upended rooms, this is a flashback to a time when my life was out of control and heading for disaster.

Darryl Palmer is about to approach the front desk when I call him back. 'Tell her I love her,' I say to him urgently. 'We love her and we're going to wait right here until they let her go.'

He looks at me, then at Evan, sizing us up. Wondering what sort of people he's dealing with here, how he is going to disseminate information to us. 'I'll tell her you love her,' he states. Obviously, clearly he's not going to add the part where letting her go is brought up. Because he clearly, obviously, thinks that's not going to happen any time soon.

Part 5

verity

Now

Time is ticking down for the police to question me. At the most they will have ninety-six hours. At the very most. At seventy-two hours they will have to go back to the courts for an additional twenty-four hours, and in the absence of evidence and/or a statement from me, they really will have no choice but to let me go.

That is why I have decided to stay silent. If I don't say anything, they won't be able to get anything to charge me with. I should request a solicitor, but that would mean speaking and I need to stay consistent in my silence. They need to know that no matter what, I am not speaking, not engaging.

And, if I don't speak, I can't be forced to lie.

Because there is no way I can explain things without lying right now. I have to stay silent, and I have to stay calm.

In my silence I have had to undress. I have had to undress and remove all of my clothes. Every last thing. I don't remember feeling humiliation before, but I have certainly experienced it now. I had to stand in the presence of two female officers and hand one of them my cardigan, my T-shirt, my jeans, my black knickers, my black under-wired bra. Everything I removed was taken between two plastic-gloved fingers and bagged and tagged. I had to wait there, my nakedness – breasts, pubic hair, tummy rolls – on display while they took their own sweet time to hand me the clothes I am now wearing: a grey tracksuit and plimsolls.

In my quiet, I have had my fingerprints scanned. No more ink that won't rub off easily, now it is a computer that takes the unique lines, marks and whorls of my hands and locks them safely away.

In my noiselessness, I have had my photo taken without smiles, without finding the best angle, without trying to show my best side. Just front, left, right, straight ahead each time.

In my quiescence, I have had a giant cotton bud (buccal swab) run around my cheek to capture my DNA. Process it, file it. Keep it near to match against evidence, file it away to keep track of any further crimes.

In my enforced hush, swabs have been taken of my hands, my nails have been clipped, a sample of hair has been yanked from my head. Blood will be drawn in the very near future.

And now, in the peace of an interview room, I sit and wait to extend my silence to the interview. I cannot, will not, speak.

The door opens and I immediately sit up straight, brace myself to not react no matter what they throw at me.

My entire body feels like it is lifted up and then thrown down when I see who is actually there. Mr Palmer.

Mr Palmer. Great. Just great. He is one of the partners where I work. So, not only do my work know, they've sent me him. When I thought this couldn't get any worse, when I thought I couldn't be any more embarrassed, they had to send Mr Palmer to make my humiliation complete.

June, 2018

'So, trainee, you do realise you're on Felicia duty, yes?'

I'd been told this several times by various people I worked with tonight, at the end of the first day of the strategy and planning conference the big wigs and senior solicitors were attending in Leeds. I had been picked as the only trainee allowed to attend so I was not drinking too much and was showing them they were right to choose me.

We were all staying at a large hotel in the city centre, and as one of the newest and most junior staff members, I wasn't in on the joke. It was centred around our ferocious office manager, Lorna, but I couldn't quite work out why they were calling her 'Felicia' and what it had to do with me.

As the evening wore on, though, I began to understand. At night, neat, low-bunned, skirt-suited, tortoiseshell-glasses-wearing office manager Lorna transformed into her alter-ego 'Felicia' who wore sprayed-on jeans and a see-through chiffon top without a bra. 'Felicia duty' involved watching while she started with Prosecco, moved on to white wine, raced through port and then downed tequilas like there was something chasing her, patiently waiting for her to drink herself under the table, and then taking her up to her room. Apparently you just had to put her on her bed, preferably in the recovery position with a sick bowl beside her just in case, and then 'Felicia duty' was done.

Once I'd worked out what 'Felicia duty' involved, I'd decided to make my excuses quite early because there was no way I was putting a woman old enough to be my mother to bed. What sort of nonsense was that? Stupid me decided to go to the bar, though, and when I returned, everyone had gone. Everyone except Mr Palmer, one of the newer partners, whose department I was currently working in.

'Yeah, that's why they were all being so nice to you earlier,' he said when I retook my seat, looking around incredulously at all the empty chairs. 'Never turn your back on them because this is what they do. They'll be partying in someone's room.'

He'd arrived just over eighteen months ago, apparently . . . and everyone had a crush on him. *Everyone.* It wasn't hard to see why. He was cool, confident, calm. Decent enough not to leave me alone with 'Felicia'.

'You can go to bed, if you want,' I said.

'No, couldn't do that to you.' He sipped his drink then smiled, checked his black runners' watch – the same one that Con had been trying to convince Mum and Dad to buy him for ages – and visibly worked something out. 'Anyway, she's been drinking a lot faster tonight, so I reckon she's got about two more minutes before—' Mid-sentence, Lorna/'Felicia' wobbled in her seat like a spinning top finding its centre and then fell forward, her forehead landing loudly on the table. Thankfully there were no glasses in the way. '—the end.'

He stood up and I could not help but notice him all over again. When everyone had disappeared off to change earlier, he'd got rid of his charcoal-grey suit with yellow tie and had returned in black jeans, black shirt and black high-top trainers. Everything he wore emphasised the lithe fluidity of his body.

'Why do they call her "Felicia"?' I asked as he gently picked her up.

'I don't know. She calls herself it, from what I gather. Something to do with it being her alternate persona for when she's away from home.'

'But there's the whole, "Bye, Fel—"'

'Yes,' he cut in. 'But beyond this, I tend not to get too involved with the stuff people who work for me do. It makes everything much simpler.'

I nodded. Of course it did. Of course. I felt more than a teensy bit foolish. I really thought . . . I cringed inside. I had entertained for a few minutes the idea that he wasn't simply waiting around to help with Lorna, but that he might have been very slightly interested in spending time with me. *Stupid, Verity.* How very cringey of you. Zeph was going to laugh her head off when she found out that one.

'This is the part where you say, "Bye, Felicia",' Lorna mumbled as she lay sprawled on her hotel bed. We'd put on the sidelights and I took off her shoes. She smirked at her joke. She clearly had nooooo idea what it really meant. She'd probably just read it on socials, on a meme, and had decided to grab it for her own purposes. Cos there was no way that lady was using those words if she properly knew where it came from and why people used it.

'So we just leave her like this?' I asked Mr Palmer as I watched her shift and wriggle and move herself up the bed, far more easily than someone who had drunk as much as she had should be able to.

'Yep.' Mr Palmer shrugged his shoulders. 'She'll be fine in the morning as well. It's like she stores up all this energy to be the most efficient mother and worker and then when she's away, she lets it all out.' He turned to leave, an indication that I should do the same. 'Watch her turn up at breakfast like she went to bed at eight with a good book and a face pack.'

In the corridor, Mr Palmer and I paused outside her room. I felt like we were at the end of a date and that this was the moment I should tell him my flatmates were out as a way of inviting him over . . .

As if he had come to a decision, Mr Palmer started down the corridor towards the turn at the end that led to the bank of lifts, walking slowly with his hands in his pockets and his face set in a grim expression. I walked beside him, my hands nervously fidgeting with themselves.

'My wife was actually called Felicia,' he said as we walked.

'No way!' I exclaimed. 'You're lying.'

'Yes, way,' he replied, a small smile on his lips. 'She was surprisingly fine about it. Sanguine, you could say. She said at least it was something you only heard now and then, not like, "sure, Jan" or being called a "Karen" for every bad thing a woman did. As I'm sure you know, there are a million memes and gifs dissing the Jans and Karens of this world.'

'Dissing' coming out of Mr Palmer's delicious mouth gave me all sorts of conflicted feelings. On the one hand, it was like my dad saying it – a total no-no; on the other hand it was as if he was breakfast, lunch *and* dinner made man, so anything he said or did was fine with me.

'You get a hundred Karen disses for one "bye, Felicia" so she reasoned she got off lightly.'

We seemed to be walking slower the nearer we got to the lifts. When we eventually arrived, we stopped in front of the bank of large grey doors with the red display reading 'o' for all three lifts. They were waiting to whisk us away to our separate floors, and the words to invite him to my room were teetering dangerously on the tip of my tongue. I wanted to say them, to see what would happen, how he would react. He could only say no, or he could pretend he didn't hear or he could report me to HR for sexual solicitation. I quickly clamped down my teeth and pressed my mouth closed. Imagine coming away with a STD – Sexually Transmitted Dismissal – without any actual sex taking place.

'At one point she joked that she should have that on her gravestone. Gallows humour at its best.' As those words left his mouth, he physically sagged where he stood. He was staring at the small up and down buttons in the space between the first and second lift and he was slowly disintegrating. The memory of his wife was obviously ravaging him, dragging him back to the recent past when he'd lost her, throwing him forward to all the days he would have to spend without her, drilling him down into the present where nothing much made sense.

Slowly he breathed out. 'Turns out drinking and talking about your late wife are not a winning combination,' he said.

Still not quite trusting myself to speak, especially now when he was so in need of a hug, I reached out and rested my hand on his bicep. Just a comforting gesture so he knew he was not alone. I hadn't been through anything like that, hadn't lost anyone like that, had barely had a proper relationship, so I didn't completely understand. But I could be there. I knew from other times in my life, with other people, that sometimes all you needed to be was there.

After a few seconds of us standing like that, Mr Palmer reached up and encompassed my hand with his. After a few more of those seconds, I looked up and my gaze collided with his. My dark eyes were studying his face, his equally dark eyes took in my face, pausing dramatically on my lips.

This was one of those moments where I could choose. I could take my hand away, shift my gaze to a safer space, move away. Or I could shiver slightly as he took his warming hand away from its place on mine, and I could take a step forward and lift my face to his as he pulled me towards his body and kissed me in one smooth move. Yeah, I could do that. I could definitely do that – so that, of course, was what I did.

When we crossed the threshold of room 612, our hands greedily reached for each other, hungrily pulling the other towards us, desperately finding our lips so they could be together again. He pressed me back against the wall, not bothering to slot the card into its place so the lights could come on. His lips crushed mine under his, his hands roamed my body as though trying to take in the whole experience of suddenly being allowed to touch me. Just as frantically, I explored his cool skin with the tips of my fingers, trying to read him through every line and wrinkle and imperfection I could reach. He broke away momentarily and then his lips were on my neck and I sighed, pleasure turning the sigh into a soft, throaty groan. His hands found their way inside my clothes, mine slid over the erection straining in his trousers. I reached for the buttons and suddenly it was gone. He was gone. He was stepping away and leaving me panting as the wall held me up.

'What am I doing?' he asked himself, horrified. Even in the dark of his hotel room, the shapes of furniture barely visible from the street-light that threw a little light our way, I could make out the shock on his face, in the rictus of his body's muscles. 'What am I doing?' He covered his mouth with his hands. Pulled his hands away again. 'You're young enough to be my daughter. What am I doing?' He balled his fists against his temples. 'I can't believe I did this. I'm sorry. I'm so sorry.'

I straightened up and tried to sort myself out. Tried to slick down flyaway strands of hair, pulled my top down and tugged my skirt back into place. I felt so foolish. Because, come on, girl, what was I doing? The man was literally old enough to be my father. Not even a teenage dad, my full-on-adult-when-he-had-me father. What was I thinking? Clearly I wasn't thinking, I was fantasising.

'This is so terrible,' he said. I didn't move as he scrabbled around with the key card and the slot beside where I was standing, but I cringed, screwed up my face and put my hand to my eyes, when the lights came on.

Oh, but things were better in the dark. So many things are. In the light, this was a man who was very clearly older than me, who was more senior than me, with whom I was participating with in potentially screwing over my career.

He took another step back. 'I'm sorry,' he said, calmer, more like the Mr Palmer I knew. How messed up was *this* situation? He was still Mr Palmer in my head even though he'd had his tongue in my mouth and I'd had my hand on his cock.

'You don't have to say sorry,' I replied.

'Oh, I do. This should never have happened. You're a junior member of staff, this is sexual harassment.'

'No, it's not, because I wanted this as much as you did. I didn't feel any pressure.'

'And there was none, but it's not good. Because you might have felt pressured but had no real confidence to tell me no. This is what they mean about sexual harassment. How do I know that when I kissed you, you weren't too terrified for your job and your reputation to tell me no and walk away?'

'I was fine. And I kissed you back. I've had a crush on you for ages.'

'I shouldn't have done this.' He massaged his eyes with his forefinger and thumb. 'I'm going to have think about what to do next. I'll have to tell HR, of course.'

'Nooooo,' I said, eyes wide with horror. 'Nooooo. You can't. That'll go down on my record. And if I ever am sexually harassed, even if it's elsewhere, no one will believe me. They'll just think this is what I do.' I knew that was how those things worked. No one gave women the benefit of the doubt. They always brought up your past as an example of why they shouldn't believe you.

'That's not—' Mr Palmer couldn't even pretend that wasn't the case. He lowered his hand and looked at me. He sighed eventually and then asked, 'What do you want to do?' Like I'd know! He was the grown one, the one with the big age in this situation, shouldn't he be the one saying what should happen?

'I think I'd better go,' I stated, to myself more than anything. I had better go and pretend this never happened.

'Again, I'm sorry. I don't know what came over me. Well, I do, it was talking about Felicia and you being kind to me and being incredibly flattered by the attention from someone so beautiful.'

I didn't know what to say to that, how to respond without getting myself into even more trouble.

'Any other situation, I would have asked you out, properly. Dinner and movie or gig. This would come at the end of a very nice time together.'

Now why did he have to say that? It just made it more difficult. 'I'm finding it hard to leave,' I confessed, facing him full on. I wanted to see his reaction, to find out if what I suspected about men was true. They just needed the opportunity . . . the green light to do what they wanted. They could be restrained and noble; considered and considerate until they saw a little 'in', a hint that they could get away with something they really wanted to do, so they twisted that 'in' to be permission to do whatever they liked with a defence handy if challenged.

His face, as handsome as it still was in the bright light of his hotel room, creased into a smile as he lowered his gaze momentarily before it was focused on me again. Focused on me and quite openly undressing me. 'I'm finding it hard to keep my hands off you,' he replied. 'But this can't happen. It just can't happen. *Ever*. For both our sakes, I think it best you leave.'

At the door, as I moved my hand to the handle, I felt him come up behind me, press himself against me, nuzzle my neck, run his hand down the length of my body, move it between my legs and rest it on my bare thigh. 'I don't want you to go,' he whispered, his voice heavy with longing. 'You have to go, but the last thing I want is for you to go. I want you to stay. I want to make love to you so much it's almost painful. You need to know that. I want you to stay, but this can't happen because of everything else, not because I have no desire for you.'

All right. That felt better. I didn't realise I needed to hear that, but now that I had, I could go without wondering if he'd just changed his mind because of how I looked or something I'd unintentionally done.

I nodded and felt momentarily adrift and lost when he stepped away, almost as though for those microseconds his lust, the curl of his body around mine was all that had been holding me up.

'I'll see you in the morning,' he said in his Mr Palmer voice. 'Bright and early for breakfast before the day's sessions.'

'Yes, sir,' I couldn't help myself saying. 'See you in the morning.'

And we both knew that would be the last time we talked about this moment of craziness.

Now

Obviously, now that I'm in this situation, it's him who has to appear.

Mr Palmer places his briefcase on the table and doesn't move towards it. Instead, he pulls out the seat opposite me, sits down and stares at me. He's waiting for me to speak. To say something.

It's been nearly two years since our encounter at the conference. He has been nothing but professional ever since. No one would ever guess what happened and almost happened between us in that room. He's waiting for me to speak, but I'm not going to speak to Mr Palmer. Or anyone. I am staying silent, no matter what.

'When I heard what happened, I offered to come down to see you and represent you, Verity,' Mr Palmer eventually says. He's obviously guessed I am not speaking. He pushes his tan, soft leather briefcase to the side and sits back in his seat. 'I'm not going to take any notes right now because I want nothing on record.'

I remain silent, wary.

'You're in a lot of trouble,' he states as though I don't know. 'I'm going to do my best to help you. But you have to tell me everything. And when I say that, I mean *everything*.'

I must shake my head because he says sternly, 'Yes, Verity, everything. Staying silent with the police is one thing. Staying silent with me is another. The only way I am going to be able to get you out of this is if you tell me everything. *Everything*.' He opens his hands again, to reiterate he's taking no notes but we have the solicitor and client bond in place, so he won't repeat what I tell him.

As recently as two months ago, when things were dire with Logan, I wondered what my life would have been like if I had fucked Mr Palmer in that hotel room. I wondered if my life would have been less complicated when, at the time, he seemed to be the complicated option.

'I don't know where to begin,' I say.

'Anywhere. Just tell me, Verity. Just talk to me.'

serena

Now

'I've advised Verity to not say anything in any of the interviews,' Mr Palmer says to us when he exits the police station. I couldn't stay in there so we've been waiting outside. 'I'll be with her for every one of them, but I've told her to remain silent.'

'But doesn't that make her look guilty?' Evan asks. My husband has no idea. He has no idea that, innocent or guilty, once you're in there, everyone thinks you're guilty. Everyone treats you like you're guilty. You start to believe you're guilty. Innocent until proven guilty is just a nice thing to trot out for the people who are unlikely to find out the actual truth of being arrested and accused.

Mr Palmer's impassive face sags a little for a moment, just a moment, but it's enough. It's enough to tell me that he knows something – lots of things – that we don't know. It's enough to tell me that he thinks she's going to go down for this and he's desperately trying to work out how to help her.

When he pulls himself together again, he keeps his focus on Evan. Even though I am the one standing directly in front of him, even though I was the one he was offering comfort to before he went to speak to her, it is Evan he feels comfortable looking at.

'It simply means that, for now, while the police are still gathering evidence, every time they speak to her, she needs to keep her thoughts and reactions to herself. What they are doing when they initially speak to you is trying to get you to lay down your main story. What will form part of your defence. They want you to tell them something that they can prove is a lie. From there, they can cast doubt on everything you say so when it gets to court, they can point to your story and say, "this is a lie, this is a lie and this is a lie". And believe me, they can find the lie in every single word, no matter how innocent or "true" it might seem. Verity needs to keep quiet because whatever you say the first time around is usually what they can use to convict you. It's the best way forward right now.

'I'm going back in now; I need to speak to her again before the interviews start. Try not to worry.'

Mr Palmer is avoiding looking at me. For the whole time he talks to us up until he leaves, he does not look in my direction. And I know why: it's because he thinks she's in this situation because of me.

verity

Now

'Do you understand that no matter what the police officers say, no matter what they dredge up, you are not to say a word?'

I nod.

'It's late, Verity, they're going to keep going at it as late as possible because they think it will make you trip up. Stay silent and try not to react too much to whatever they say.'

I nod again.

He has his yellow, lined legal pad in front of him and stares at it for long seconds. Then he gets to his feet and paces the room for a few seconds. 'I should have done something,' he suddenly declares. He's agitated, openly upset. 'I saw what was going on, but I kept telling myself it was none of my business because of what happened between us.'

'What do you mean?' I reply.

'I've watched you disintegrate over the last year. You've changed from a vibrant, happy young woman with time for a kind word for everyone around to someone who seems so burdened, isolated and very much broken.'

I can't quite believe he has said that. About me of all people. I'm no party animal, never have been, but 'burdened', 'isolated', 'very much broken'. Those are strong things to level at someone. Especially me. 'Me? Have you met me?'

'Of course I've met you, Verity. Which is why I can quite confidently say that. I've kept an eye on you from a distance because I know you're capable of great things. But I saw the change in you. It was slow, but definite,' he replies. 'I'm sure all of your family have seen it, too. And your friends, those that you have left. But no one wants to interfere in these situations. I certainly didn't because of the Leeds incident. I kept convincing myself that I was paying too much attention to you because of those few moments of madness. I can't speak for your parents, but they probably don't see you enough so don't want to upset you by asking leading questions. Or asking you why you've changed so much.'

'Are you saying it was because of my being with Logan?'

He stays silent, but his expression is one hundred per cent saying: 'Obviously.'

'But I love Logan; I was happy with him.'

'I know you were. Women in your situation always are.'

Women in your situation. How patronising and demeaning! Darryl (because that's who he's become now he's my solicitor) makes it sound like Logan was mistreating me. *Abusing* me. *Beating* me. I fold my arms across my chest and sit back. I'm probably glaring at him with my mother's face. Actually, my grandmother's face. No one could withstand Grandma's glower.

'That sounded wrong,' Darryl says. 'I'm sorry. I'm just . . . very frustrated with myself and effectively making this all about me. I should stop. Do you need anything?'

Yup: proper clothes, proper shoes, proper food, proper way out of here. I shake my head.

'Before they arrive to speak to you, I need to advise you, after everything you have told me, that you need to speak to your mother.'

I shake my head. What is there to say to her? How do I explain this stuff to her? I saw her face when she realised who Logan was. I watched her do everything in her power not to break down when she found out I'd been dating him, sleeping with him, starting to build a life with him. What good is telling her the rest of it going to do?

'You need to talk to her,' Darryl states with a firmness that says he means it. 'She's going to form an important part of your defence.'

Mum is? '*How?*'

He stares at me as though I am being deliberately obtuse. When I don't buckle under his gaze, he sighs. Deeply. As though he wants that sigh to reach the bottom of the ocean with the depth of his frustration. 'She went through an abusive relationship. No one believed her or Poppy Carlisle at the time, but things have moved on since then. People see things a lot more clearly now. Her experiences will help to put into context a lot of what you went through.'

'What are you talking about?' I ask. Because, you know, what is he talking about?

'She was in an abusive relationship and, as a result of that, it looks like you've ended up in a very similar situation with Logan Carlisle.'

I wish he'd stop with this. 'I wasn't in an abusive relationship. Logan wasn't abusive. We just had times that weren't great but all couples do. He wasn't abusive. I know what abuse looks like and it wasn't that.'

Darryl says nothing for a time. He looks me over with an expression I can't quite work out. I *think* he thinks I'm being difficult. I'm not. I'm just not willing to jump on this bandwagon when it's not for me.

'You'll need to talk to your mother either way. You'll need to get both of your parents on side before this investigation goes any further. And you will have to tell them everything before someone else does. Because you can guarantee, because of who your mother is, they are going to leave no stone unturned . . . And, it's a risk me representing you. I'm only doing so to protect you from a lot of things by not making official notes just yet, but you need to tell your parents And tell them about you and me.'

'That's a big fat no from me,' I reply.

'It's not a request or a suggestion, Verity, it is imperative that you tell them. If the police investigate you as thoroughly as I suspect they're going to, they may well go asking for security camera footage from the hotel. We don't know how long they keep those videos, but we do know they will see us kissing in the corridor if they get the chance to watch it. They will see you entering my room. It doesn't matter that you left less than ten minutes later, they could use that to help build the idea that you become involved with older men. That you're some kind of over-sexed femme fatale.

'You need to get in front of this. You need to tell your parents, your brother, the people who you will need to be very publicly supportive of you now and in the lead-up to the trial. Because when it comes to trial, if they are continually blindsided by information presented to them by other people, they will start to crack in public when they need to be emphatic about your innocence.'

Without warning, my eyes are wet and the sea seems to be swirling loudly in my ears. Trial. Public support. This is suddenly very *real*. Very frightening. Before it was like everyone would definitely see it was all a big mistake. But Darryl is skipping ahead – fast. He hasn't said the words, but he is thinking about mounting a defence, needing public support, the possibility of hearing 'guilty' instead of 'not guilty'.

I blink my eyes to clear them. This is silly. This is all going to work out just fine. Just fine.

'If they do charge me, it will take a while for it to get to court, won't it?'

Another ocean-deep sigh from the man I could have slept with all those months ago. 'I'm going to try to get you out of here, but yes, it would take a few months to come to court if they find enough grounds to charge you. But you should brace yourself because I think they're going to find the grounds.'

He is being dramatic, of course, hitting me with the worst-case scenario, so I'm going to ignore those words. 'It'll be easier if I tell my parents when I'm out of here. Sitting in here or on remand telling them stuff will not be a good idea. And I won't know who's listening. Who'll have been paid to keep an eye on me and listen out for information to use against me.'

'Have it your way, Verity, but know this, as your legal adviser, as someone who has been doing this almost as long as you've been alive, being honest sooner rather than later, before you're compelled to by circumstance, is always better. Always.'

It was all right for him to say that. But he doesn't know that these truths, the ones I've been keeping to myself, aren't the type you can shout from the rooftops, or even stand up and boldly proclaim; they are things you have to speak of in hushed tones, with lowered eyes and clenched hands.

The door opens and Darryl moves from his place on the other side of the desk and comes to sit beside me before the police arrive for the first interview.

Telling the truth is no way as simple and straightforward as Darryl has been trying to make out.

serena

Now

Evan sits in bed with his knees drawn up to his bare chest. Like me, he's starting to look his age. Like me, he wants to go over and over what is happening, but, like me, fears that once he starts talking he'll never be able to stop, and during that talking, uncomfortable truths will escape.

'Why is this happening?' he says.

'I don't know,' I reply.

We'd both been devastated, truly heartbroken, when we were told Verity would be spending the night in police custody. It didn't seem real, somehow. I remember . . . I remember the concrete bed with its thin blue mattress underneath you that never gives even the slightest bit so you are always uncomfortable when you try to sleep or just sit . . . I remember . . . the door, sealed so tight, so flush against the wall, it looks drawn on and not capable of being opened ever again . . . I remember . . . the smell of the toilet, used or unused, and how it smeared itself inside your nostrils causing a sickness to rise that would not leave.

Verity is there. My little girl, who not five minutes ago was asking me for a bunny, who had written me a list of reasons why I should say yes to a bunny and had promised – in writing – that she'd look after it if I said yes, is now locked up for attempted murder.

'It's going to be fine,' Evan says. 'She didn't do it so she'll be fine.'

'How do you know she didn't do it?' I ask quietly.

'What?' he asks, completely affronted by what I've just uttered. He spins slightly on his bottom and leans back to look at me. 'What are you saying?'

'I'm saying, how do you know she didn't do it?'

'Because I know our daughter and I know she wouldn't.'

'You don't know her at all. None of us know each other; what we'd do if we got desperate. When I was with . . . M-a-r—with *him* you don't know the amount of times I wanted to kill him.' I haven't admitted this to anyone, ever. 'I wanted the pain – mainly the mental and emotional anguish – to stop, and I would have done anything to stop it. How do you know it wasn't the same for Vee? How do you know Logan wasn't abusive and she wasn't in so much agony she just snapped?'

'She wouldn't,' Evan snarls at me. He's daring me to keep going, to basically keep calling our daughter a murderer, because he will fight me all the way.

'You don't know that.'

Evan rips back the duvet and gets out of bed in angry, jerky movements. Those movements don't fit with the usually easy fluidity of his frame so his anger is apparent and amplified. 'What are you saying, Serena?' His hands are on his head in sheer frustration, downright disgust. 'What are you saying about our daughter?'

'I'm saying what you won't even consider.'

'I won't consider it because she didn't do it. She wouldn't do it.'

'How do you know?'

'The same way that I know you didn't do it.'

'You know I didn't do it because I told you I didn't do it. Has Verity said anything like that? Anything at all? No. She hasn't.'

'Sere—'

'Evan, you have a huge blind spot when it comes to your children, when it comes to Verity. They can do no wrong in your eyes.'

'That's normal for a parent to feel like that.'

'And is it normal to use someone else's feelings for you to help solve a problem for your daughter?'

That stops him short, halts his dramatic anger. 'What are you talking about?' he says, even though from his ashamed face it's obvious he knows exactly what I'm talking about.

Years ago, Verity had a sleepover at Zephie's house, which had turned into Zephie inviting her much older boyfriend over. It'd ended badly for her, and Verity had called her dad to come and help. He, not able to treat a teenage girl who had been sexually assaulted, had called one of the doctors who worked with him – who'd had a crush on him since they were in medical school together – to go and see her. They had kept it secret because they could have lost their jobs.

'Did you think I had no idea that the doctor who helped Zephie after she was assaulted and kept it quiet was Colleen, who just so happens to be completely in love with you?'

Evan's silence reveals quite clearly he did think I was oblivious.

'It was obvious that's who you would go to. And why. I knew it was her. And I was pissed off about it for a long time but you did it to help a young girl so I let it slide. But Evan, come on, that's pretty shitty behaviour. And you did that for Verity. Yes, it was to help Zephie, but ultimately it was for Vee. And that is fine. But let's not pretend that you're not basically blindly supporting someone who hasn't actually said she's innocent.'

'We haven't had the chance to speak to her yet.'

'Don't change the subject. You used Colleen's feelings for you to help our daughter, didn't you?'

Evan, my stoic, solid, dependable husband, folds his arms across his chest and stares off to the right of the bed as he gives a couple of short, curt nods.

'If someone had asked me up until you did that, I would have said you would never do something like that. And they would have said, "How do you know?" And I would have said because I know you would never do something like that. And I'd have been wrong.'

'Don't start thinking like that about Verity. She is innocent until proven guilty. And I'll only believe she's guilty when she looks me in the eye and tells me she is.'

'You're not helping her.'

'Don't do this, Serena,' Evan warns.

'Ev—'

'I know you've never said this,' he interrupts, 'but I know it still hurts you that your dad died thinking you might have killed that man.'

Those words spear me through the heart, right through the centre of my soul. I carry that sadness, every day. I don't acknowledge it every day, I don't give it space in my mind, my heart or my life, really, but it's there; it's blended into the background of my life, a kind of ache I didn't know it was possible to feel. I didn't realise Evan knew about it, had realised that for five years it's gnawed away at me. I didn't realise Evan would use it against me, either. I guess it's one of those quantum things the children always speak about. Two very different or opposite things being possible and true at the same time: I'm claiming he doesn't know me but he knows me enough to use this against me; I'm claiming I don't know him, but I know him enough to know how irrational he will be about all of this – including using painful things against me – until Verity is home.

'That was an awful thing to say,' I whisper.

We didn't talk about it, that's the problem. After we got back together and I told him the whole truth about what happened to *him* that night, we never spoke of it again. I couldn't, not really. Not to Evan. I told myself it wasn't necessary, not when I had confessed everything to him. And I'm sure he convinced himself that hearing it first-hand was enough, he didn't need to go back and check up on this, examine that, get me to explain this bit or that bit. We haven't talked about it and now we're being forced to talk about it under war-like conditions. Not at our leisure, but under siege.

'I'm sorry, I'm sorry,' he returns to his side of the bed and sits down. 'I'm sorry. I didn't mean for it to come out like that.' He takes my hand in both of his, holding me safe and secure. At least it usually feels like that, but right now it feels like he could turn on me at any moment. 'I could see there was something else there, another pain you couldn't talk about, and I'm sorry to bring it up like this.'

He draws me towards him, kissing the top of my head a couple of times as he holds me, tries to console away the agony he's brought up. 'Serena . . . *Sez* . . . I just don't want this to become something you and Verity can't come back from.'

'It won't be.'

'Are you sure this isn't about you projecting all the anger you feel for yourself onto her?'

'I probably am, who knows? But that doesn't change the fact that I can't just blindly believe she didn't do it.'

'I don't understand, to be honest. I mean, you said your sisters told you that your mum never believed you did it. Why can't you be like her? Why won't you give your own daughter the benefit of the doubt?'

Evan doesn't want to hear the answer to that. It's not as simple as he thinks it is. He doesn't understand what it's like to be in that situation. How it changes even the most passive person into someone desperate, someone who could do anything. But then, we don't know anything about her situation. It might have been a case of him being abusive. It might be that she actually did it because she felt like it.

Because I have seen something change in Verity over the time she's been with him. And there was that look in her eyes, on her face, when the police came to get her. It was resignation. Not fear. It was as though she was expecting them and was surprised they hadn't come for her earlier.

'You're right,' I say to appease Evan because I don't want to fight with him any more. I don't want to upset him any more than I need to at this stage. We've got a lot more of that ahead, there's no need to start it right now. 'I need to keep an open mind – give her the benefit of the doubt until we know more.'

That pleases and appeases my husband. He climbs into bed and I cuddle up to him.

I don't know how I know this, I only know that I do, whether by accident or on purpose, my daughter is not as innocent in all of this as Evan wants her to be.

February, 2015

The lights were low and a hush had settled over everything: in the room, in the outside world.

It felt like we were the only two people in the world. I kept staring at the blinds. I was looking for flaws, for anything that made the lines uneven or irregular. I sat in this chair, waiting. Counting down the hours, which had been days not long ago, weeks not long before that. I couldn't remember when it had been months or years. I just knew it was now hours and these were my hours.

These were the moments assigned to me so I could sit here and listen, wait and talk if I fancied.

My dad was asleep. He was sleeping more nowadays but when he was awake he was alert, he was here, he was present.

I'd been reading him a book on Ghanaian politics when he closed his eyes and didn't open them. Terror bolted through me. But this wasn't it. This wasn't the moment I'd have to say goodbye.

I put the book down on the bedside table, and relaxed back against the chair. Immediately, I sat up again. I knew the second I relaxed, the moment I let myself go, that would be it. The moment we were all dreading would arrive.

I looked at my father, my dad. I'd never get used to seeing him like this. Thin and gaunt, fragile. He'd always been strong and big and *there*. I'd taken him for granted, though. Without realising it, I just always expected him to be around. Even when I found out he was ill, I didn't really think about it. I didn't really contemplate it. It wasn't something that was meant to happen so it wasn't something that was going to happen.

I didn't do it, Daddy, I wanted to whisper into the dark, into his sleep, just so he would know. *I was accused, but I didn't do it. I might have thought about it, he might have battered me down so I was almost broken, but I didn't do it.*

I wanted to tell my dad this so he wouldn't leave this Earth thinking that of me. He wouldn't leave this world believing that I could have done it.

I whispered it in my head, so quiet even my mind had to strain to hear. I didn't want anyone to hear me say that. I didn't want there to be even the sliver of a chance that Dad might pick it up.

I couldn't dredge that up, put that out there, even inside my head, in case he heard. In case he heard and it brought it all up for him. And he would leave with all of that unresolved, all of it preying on his mind again. He believed what he believed and there was no way for me to change it. Not now.

'I want you to know that I love you,' I whispered out loud instead. 'It's been complicated and I never said that to you before, but I love you. And thank you. Thank you for being my dad. Thank you for being the man you are. Thank you for being the best grandfather. The children, as big as they are, have loved every second of being around you. I love you.'

And I didn't do it, Daddy. I didn't do it.

verity

Now

'Who is Howard Scarber, Miss Gillmare?'

They have asked me what happened the night Logan was hurt and I have stayed silent. They said I had one chance to put my side forward, to explain what happened at my flat. And I stayed silent. I thought I was imagining it, that they weren't pursuing that line of questioning as rigorously considering that was what I was here for. And now I know why. Howard. Howie.

Yes, Darryl warned me of this, that the police would be digging into the most hidden recesses of my life, but I didn't think they'd get to Howie so quickly.

I don't say anything because I'm still doing the silence thing.

'My client, as advised by me, has chosen not to reply to that or any other questions,' Darryl intones. He does that every few questions, in case they have somehow forgotten. There's a tremor flitting along the curves of his words that only I can decipher. That tremor is saying that he is PISSED OFF. Because despite demanding I tell him everything yesterday, despite him putting himself out for me, he's been blindsided. Exactly what he warned me about. I didn't realise, though, that such a detailed, fingertip, forensic search of my life was possible in such a short amount of time.

May, 2017

I checked my watch for the millionth time (only a slight exaggeration) and sighed. Howard was really pushing it. He was one of those people I'd spotted on the first day of university and decided I was going to be friends with. Much like I had with Zeph on the first day of reception. Howie and I were in the same halls of residence and when we discovered we were both from Brighton, our friendship had been sealed. Because we went way back there were certain things he could get away with – being late was one of them. But only to a certain point. There were limits to my patience.

I forced my mind to focus on the book in front of me, and shivered. It was May, it was meant to be warmer than this, but this dip in temperature had meant sitting out here at the Meeting Place Café on the seafront, waiting for Howie to show up had resulted in a cold nose and numbing fingers.

'Oh, finally,' I said to him as he slotted himself into the bench across from me at the table. I was about to start telling him off, when I spotted his face. 'What happened to you?' His handsome face had been hit a few times, basically. He had a white plaster across his nose, a split on his lower lip that was healing with a thick black scab, and a purple-blue bruise shading the dark-brown skin under and around his left eye.

He went to pull a face, thought better of it, and instead said, 'Muggery, innit?'

'What? Oh no! When? Did they get much?'

'My phone and my dignity. Thought I could handle it, thought I could handle myself in that sort of situation, but . . .' He pointed to his face. 'Not in real life. I should get a refund on my *Streetfighter* and *Ultimate Ninja* games, seeing as they don't translate into real-life fighting skills.'

I knew Howie well enough to know his pride had been hurt way more than his body. 'When did this happen?'

'Yesterday. On the way to the chippie. Was really looking forward to those chippie-shop chips for tea. I tell you, Beccie was not happy that she didn't get her large battered sausage and curry sauce. I think she would have taken them apart with her bare hands if she could.'

'What did the police say? Has there been a spate of these around the area?'

'Police? What you chatting about police? What exactly are they going to do?'

'You were assaulted and robbed. The police will need to investigate that.'

'Last year when our flat was robbed, they barely had enough resources to send someone over to investigate, how are they going to investigate a simple street mugging?'

'But don't you need a crime number for the insurance?'

'Yes, I would . . . if I had phone insurance.'

'You don't have phone insurance?'

'Vee!' he said, exasperated. 'You're actually making me feel worse than I did just after I was punched in the face.'

'Sorry,' I said.

'Are we doing this, then?'

I nodded half-heartedly. I wasn't so keen on this now. About half an hour ago I was all for it; right now, all the waiting around had actually put paid to my enthusiasm.

'Come on, then,' he said and stood up, wincing as he did so. He immediately straightened his face, tried to pretend he was fine.

'Are you in pain?' I asked.

Howie gave me a once-over, scrutinising me as though considering if he should admit what he felt or not. Eventually he seemed to give up as he said, 'Once I was on the ground I got a bit of a kicking. My ribs are a bit tender.'

'Howie! That's awful. I really wish you'd gone to the police. These people sound dangerous. What if they'd had a weapon?' Not helpful I realised too late and jammed my stupid lips into my stupid mouth in an attempt to eat my stupid words. 'Sorry,' I mumbled.

We stood in an uncomfortable silence for several seconds that stretched and stretched themselves into feeling like minutes. 'Tell me you went to the doctor at least.'

'Yes, I went to the doctor. I wasn't going to, but Beccie made me. Drove me there and everything. Even though you know how much she hates driving. And just so you know, she was all for me going to the police, as well.'

'Are you sure you still want to do this?' I replied with a note of hope in my voice that he might actually say no.

'Verity Gillmare, you asked me to help you train and I am going to help you train. Now get your kit off.'

I grinned at him as we moved onto the shingle. It was bobbly and uncomfortable underfoot even in shoes, so I knew the cold was going to make them feel like shards of glass when I went barefoot. We slowly stripped off our top clothes, revealing the wetsuits we were wearing underneath.

I'd decided to do a sea swim to raise money for charity and super-fit Howie was my coach. When we started college he had been the width of a pencil. He was gangly and goofy with it, and no one took him seriously. I liked him because he just exuded 'nice' and he always seemed to be the butt of his mates' jokes.

We didn't manage to meet up during our first Christmas holidays home in Brighton, but when we returned to Leeds I could see why – Howard had been transformed. I was never sure how he'd done it, whether he'd really just done it through diet and exercise or if he'd had 'supplemental' help, but Howard had filled out in all the right places; he'd become solid, strong. And he dropped Howard for Howie. To maintain his recently acquired looks, Howie would work out every day. Every day he would be out on the college track running and running, only skipping days when ice slicked up the gravel too much to run on. Every day he would be at the local council gym to lift weights or to row and swim.

With his new body came a lot of female attention, a lot of male admiration and streaks of vanity that were quite adorable because he'd always be the sweet lad I knew when he was skinny. His determination was what was going to get me fit enough and confident enough to swim in the sea.

I cringed as my bare feet hit the pebbles, some of them smooth, slick and freezing cold; others were small, spiky and seemed to puncture the soles of my feet like tiny shards of ice.

'Whose idea was this anyway?' I said, my voice as bitter as the wind that was picking up around us.

'Yours,' he replied simply.

'Maybe we should postpone this until you're feeling a bit better,' I offered.

'No can do. The second we start to make excuses is the second we give in to not doing it. Do you remember how I got this body? There were days when I just did not want to get out of bed, when the last place I wanted to be was at that gym lifting those weights, but I did it. I kept on going through all of that so I could get the body I wanted. You cannot give up at the first moment you don't want to do something. You have to do this. You're in it for the long haul, so don't let the short haul stop you from achieving greatness.'

'Oh my God, that was cheesy!' I shrieked. 'Are you going to be releasing motivational tea towels or something? Bloody hell!'

'Mock away, lady, mock away. But when you're out in that water, freezing your danglies off, you'll remember those words.'

'I don't have danglies, pie face.'

'Not yet you don't,' he said with a nod to my chest. 'Not yet.'

I stuffed my joggers and my T-shirt and hoodie into my little pink rucksack that Con had bought me before I went to college. Rubbing my palms over my arms and walking like the icicles were spiking me, I moved over the shingle. I was going to do this. Despite mocking him, he was right; I had to do this. As unappealing as it was, if I gave up now, today, I would never get around to it.

The water seemed to dash forward to greet me, desperate to drag me in. The pebbles were smaller, sharper at this point of the beach and in my head I *yowled*. On the outside I gritted my teeth and took another step forward, plunging my ankles further into the water. Cold. Cold. *COLD!* But I couldn't stop. I had to push forward.

'That's it, you can do it,' encouraged Howard, who did not seem at all bothered by the temperature or the spiky pebbles.

I made it to my wetsuit-covered thighs before I had to curse and screech and run back out as fast as my feet would carry me over the shards.

Howard stood with his feet apart, his large arms folded across his chest, laughing at me running for my towel and my shoes and the warmth of not being out in the early chill.

'Next time, you'll get your whole body in. That's my mission.'

'Mine, too, Howie,' I replied, knowing I wasn't going near the damn beach ever again if it was to do that!

Now

'Since you're not talking due to "advice" from your solicitor, shall I tell you what we found out about Howard Scarber? Well, shall I tell everyone around us what I found out about him since you probably already know?' DI Brosnin says.

She makes a big drama of opening the beige-coloured file in front of her, allowing me to see the mugshot of Howie, the typed pages that make up his file, before she pulls it towards her out of my sight. She just wanted me to know that she knows about Howie, and she is going to go through everything he's ever done in great detail.

She hums slightly to herself as she shuffles through the pages. 'Now, where shall I start? Hmm . . .' She pauses. 'That's right, Howard Scarber. No one has a word to say against him. He literally is everyone's best friend. All-round good guy. And he's been arrested, what is it . . . that's right, six times for beating up his partner.'

Those words sound horrific said like that. And they are horrific. But I can't say anything, I have to keep quiet, silent.

'Those are only the times he was actually arrested for his violence; we had call-outs several times but his partner, Beccie Holman, refused to press charges or tell us what he did to her.'

I stare down at my raggedy nails, picked and shredded while I have had nothing to do but sit and wait for the next thing to be done to me.

'He's been convicted twice because we've had to press ahead with charges even when Ms Holman wouldn't cooperate. And just like lots of women in her situation, she kept taking him back.'

I feel Darryl move to say something and DI Brosnin says, 'Before you ask what relevance this has, Mr Palmer, I'll explain that momentarily. Although, I suspect your client knows what is coming.'

She shifts one piece of paper away from the other, makes another big show of reading what's written in front of her. 'Now, where was I? Oh yes, it's amazing he's avoided a custodial sentence, but that's only because Miss Holman has testified to his good character. And, oh, actually said it was her fault he was like he is. She gets him . . .' She runs her podgy finger along the lines of text as she reads: 'She gets him all riled up by being so annoying. She nags him. She prods and prods at him until he lashes out. It's not his fault, it's hers.'

Moving her attention from the file, she examines me over her glasses. 'We know that's not true, don't we? It's just what abused women tell the world and tell themselves so they convince themselves they can control what happens to them. You know, by being a bit less naggy, by being better at walking over those eggshells the man they love has scattered all over their lives. By not minding if their man is carrying on with another woman right under their noses.

'Oh, and not be too nagging when said woman gets him involved in a plot to kill her boyfriend.'

I freeze. I know Darryl said not to show any emotion no matter what, but I can't help myself. I can't pretend that I'm not scared – terrified, actually – that they know this.

She slaps the file shut in another dramatic move and folds her hands carefully on top of it. 'Let's just cut to the chase, shall we? Where is Mr Scarber? I'm asking because we found his fingerprints in the blood at your flat, but when we tried to talk to him, he disappeared and no one has seen him since the night of the attack on Mr Carlisle. And that seems to be, according to your phone, the last time you contacted him. You sent him a message and he called you back. What did you discuss during that call?'

I'm clearly not going to tell her.

'Miss Holman hasn't seen him and is understandably frantic. We had a very *enlightening* chat with her. She seemed to think Mr Scarber was obsessed with you. That his attacks on her usually followed time spent with you. That he wasn't happy when you started seeing Mr Carlisle. That there was an altercation previously with Mr Carlisle, and she suspects – like we do – that he attacked Mr Carlisle to defend you.'

She removes her glasses and settles her face into something so close to caring sympathy I almost fall for it. Almost. 'Is that what happened? Was he simply protecting you and things got out of hand? We would understand, you know.' She's even softened her tone to try to draw me in. 'People protect the ones they love, that's normal, *human*, and if things got out of hand when he stepped in to protect you, or if he couldn't stand to see you upset any more, understandable. Or was it a love affair where you couldn't choose and he decided to force the issue by eliminating the competition? Again, that's understandable. It would also explain why you're keeping quiet to protect him if his jealousy got the better of him and ignited his rage at Logan Carlisle's expense.'

She strokes her fingers along the top edge of the file as though mired deep in thought, as though trying to understand what could have led to this.

'I wish you would talk to us,' she says gently. 'We aren't as . . . stringent and *cold* as you seem to think. We've all been there, when things go wrong romantically and the situation rapidly escalates out of control. I'm sure you didn't mean for any of this to happen.'

DI Brosnin pauses, gives me the chance to jump in, explain, confess that it's all been a huge mistake. That Howie did do it; that I did it; that I didn't mean for any of this to happen, like she says.

If only she knew the half of it.

When I don't oblige, when I don't immediately open up to her, frankly, half-hearted attempt to get me onside, she returns her glasses to her face, slotting them into position like she is setting up her best weapon. She gives a slight, sideways dip of her head as if to say I've had my chance.

'Well, this has all been enlightening,' she says with a smile. 'We all know the clock is ticking until your release, and I'm inclined to let you go. I'm thinking that you're not the one we should be looking at here.' She nods to herself. 'Clearly we should be examining your mother's life far more forensically. Yes, we've been through her house, but, when two men end up in this situation and the connecting factor is Serena Gorringe, maybe we should refocus our attentions?'

Mum wouldn't be able to handle them going through her life again. Finding out the truth about her had made everything so clear about the things she does. The hiding knives, the avoiding ice cream, her fear of letting us out of her sight. Mum has lived in a state of perpetual worry since she was a teenager, probably, and yes, sometimes I wonder if she got away with murder, but she wasn't involved in this thing with Logan, and she couldn't deal with them going through her life again. Having all of this dragged up and splattered out into the world.

Maybe I should tell. *Explain*. Maybe I should break my silence to save my mum? I never realised that I'd be here. That this is a choice I'd have to make.

I moisten my lips, open my mouth to speak. I know I promised, but I can't put Mum through this. I can't let her suffer just so—Before any words leave my head, Darryl puts his hand on my forearm to stop me. DI Brosnin notices what Darryl does, how he stops me from cooperating and she probably notes it down as a line of questioning to pursue. Going for Howie hasn't made me talk, going for my mother will more likely get her what she wants.

'Do you have any other questions for my client?' Darryl asks. 'Because my client isn't the person to tell you where your attentions should be focused.'

DI Brosnin smiles, she hasn't got any more information, but she does have something that might get her what she wants: a strategy that involves moving up the schedule on investigating my mother. They were always going to do it, I'm not green enough to believe they wouldn't, but they probably thought it would keep. Now they know where to prod to get me to open up like you would a stubborn oyster protecting its pearl.

'No, no more questions right now. We'll talk some more, later.' Like she does most things, DI Brosnin makes a big dramatic show of looking at her watch. 'Time is ticking on, so we will be speaking again soon – very soon.'

'Thank you, Detective,' Darryl says. 'I'd like a few minutes with my client, please?'

'Of course, of course,' she says pleasantly. The male officer who has been sitting beside her, in his creased white shirt and tie with its tiny knot pulled right to the top of his shirt collar, gathers up all the papers and stands. He hasn't said a word. Instead he has been openly watching me, so I guess he had been tasked with seeing my responses to the various things she asked.

Alone in my interview room, Darryl waits several seconds, tapping out each one with his pen on his yellow, lined legal pad. He's made a few notes, but I can't read them because his writing is so bad. Deliberately, I'm sure, so no one on the opposite side of the desk can read what he has deemed necessary to get down on paper.

'What part of "everything" didn't you understand?' he asks eventually through gritted teeth.

'I did tell you everything. I didn't know they were going to bring up Howie.'

He grabs the pen with both hands, and holds it like he could quite happily substitute me for it because he would love to wring me so tight all my secrets would gush out like water from a dishrag. 'You didn't know that your violent, abusive "friend" who has already had one physical fight with your partner and has clearly gone on the run since your partner was attacked would be a topic of conversation during an interrogation about an attempted murder? Is that what you would like me to believe, Verity Gillmare?'

'I wasn't deliberately keeping it from you.' I'm blatantly ignoring his calling me out. 'It's really complicated with Howie. It's not as simple as she was saying. And they didn't have a fight, it was a scuffle. If that. It was just . . . it was complicated. The whole thing is so complicated and I just—' I stop abruptly because to tell him any more would be to tell him too much.

'Were you sleeping with him, Verity?'

'No, not at all. Howie and I are close friends, the best of friends at certain times, but never anything like that.'

'Did Logan think you were sleeping with him?'

I shrug because there's no good way to answer that question without getting into trouble.

My boss tosses the pen onto the table and I stare at it so I don't have to face him.

'I'm worried, Verity. I'm worried that you're not taking this as seriously as you need to. If you were any other client, I'd be seriously thinking of walking away because you're not being honest and you're not thinking of how to save yourself, but you won't tell me why.'

He looks at his watch. 'Despite what she said, I think they're going to go back to court to get the full ninety-six hours. And after that, I'm sure they'll either charge you or find another reason to re-arrest you almost straight away.' He shakes his head despairingly; his frustration rolls off him like the thick, white mist sometimes rolls off the sea. 'Whoever it is you're protecting, Verity, I hope they're worth it. I really hope they're worth it. I'll speak to you soon.'

Of course they're worth it, of course they are, I would love to say to Darryl. They are worth everything.

February, 2020

I liked to put my arms around Howie because he was so comfort-able. It was easy to comfort him, to hold him, to stroke his head and soothe his frown.

'Didn't know life could be like this, Vee,' he said softly. 'Which is ridiculous when you think about it. I suppose I thought it would get easier the further into life I got. Everyone expects so much from me and I don't know if I can deliver.'

I kind of knew what he was talking about because we all have expectations placed on us, and sometimes the burden of them becomes too great.

'I'm not allowed to be like this,' he said. I felt him close his eyes, so heavy the simple action was. And his arms around me squeezed me that bit tighter. 'I'm not supposed to feel this. I know the world looks at me and sees one thing and inside I'm another. I'm just not as strong as they expect me to be. There's so much stuff inside that I would like to get out. Like . . .'

He stopped speaking for such a long time that I had to ask, 'Like?'

'Like I'm scared that Beccie will leave me. That after everything we've been through, how I've shown her how much I love her, she'll just walk away. And I'm scared, all the time . . . I'm scared all the time I'm going to be killed. I can only ever say that to you. But I know my mum is terrified about it every time she's not with me. She's terrified that I'll be racially abused, but also that someone will find an excuse to kill me. And I have to tell her not to worry, I have to go out there every day and pretend that it's all good, it's all fine because I don't want her to worry. If I pretend it's OK, then she'll think it's OK. But, Vee, I am scared. I'm scared I'll be walking down the street and someone will jump me. I'm scared that I'll be driving around minding my own business and the police will pull me over for some spurious reason and the next anyone hears of me is that I resisted arrest and died in custody. I'm scared that someone who talks so long and loud about being "colour-blind" will be so good at it they'll see one Black man and think it's me and will get me accused me of something I didn't do, or even get me killed.

'I'm scared that I can do the most to be a good person, to not trouble the world too much and it will mean nothing because I won't get the chance to be anything other than dead at a young age.

'I don't even worry about getting ill that much, Vee. But I fear that I'll not reach the end of my twenties. That I'll not get the chance to live my life. That's why I cling to Beccie, I think. I feel sometimes I have to do it all now so I've left something behind before I'm murdered. And the person who does it gets away with it.'

I held onto him that bit tighter. I didn't know that this was what was going through Howie's mind on a daily basis. His pain was palpable, something almost physical and touchable. He carried this with him wherever he went; whatever he did, he carried this burden, this uncontrollable fear with him. I couldn't imagine living like that.

But then, couldn't I? Wasn't I always mindful of how I dressed, where I went alone, how I spoke and how I looked? Isn't that the fear that is the backdrop to our lives as women but we rarely voice because we'll be dismissed, put down, not believed or laughed at? And I carried the other burden, the fear of being racially abused, too, and just having to smile and put up with it, then to have my experiences diminished or denied if I try to talk about it.

I didn't think about it, though. It was not a fear that haunted my every waking moment like it did Howie. It didn't make me do those things that he did just so he could leave his mark on the world if his life was cut short.

I understood a bit more now. How his fear shaped his reality, fashioned his world.

Just as I reached up to stroke his head, I heard the key in the lock. I immediately looked at the clock on the wall: 23:05. Logan. He was meant to be away for another night. This was not going to end well.

Even though he'd never met Howie, he brought him up with an alarming regularity. He was obviously insecure about our friendship.

I didn't get away from Howie fast enough, so when Logan came into the living room, the 'Babe' on his lips froze when he saw Howie and me cuddled up on the sofa.

'Hey!' I said and untangled myself from my friend, got up and went towards him. 'I didn't expect you back tonight!'

I put my arms around him and he very unsubtly stepped straight back out of my hold. 'Clearly,' he said, glaring at Howie. 'Don't let me interrupt you. I'll go back to my place. Call me in a few days if you've got a moment or two for me.'

Howie understood. More than most he understood. He got up, grabbed his jacket from the back of the sofa. 'Vee, thanks for the take-away and chat. I'm going to bounce.'

'You don't have to,' I said.

'Yeah, I do,' he replied.

'Yeah, he does,' Logan interjected.

I swung towards him. 'Excuse me?' I said to him.

'It's late, his girlfriend will be worried, won't she? I mean, doesn't she mind him cosying up to another man's woman?'

'I'm nobody's anything, Logan. And Howie's welcome to stay as long as he likes.' I turned to my friend to find him facing down my boyfriend. 'As long as you like.'

'I'm gonna bounce,' Howie stated again, still focused on Logan.

Maybe it would be better if he left. The testosterone levels in the room would drop by about a couple of million and I could give Logan Carlisle a piece of my mind without an audience.

Howie kissed my cheek, gave me a bear hug and then began to leave the room. I couldn't work out what happened, who started it, who got in whose way, but suddenly they were pushing and shoving, squaring up and jostling each other. My mind went blank, my body rigid. I couldn't believe what I was seeing, what they were doing. Any second it was going to break out into a full-on fist fight.

'STOP IT!' I screamed at them. 'JUST STOP IT!' My voice was loud enough to get them to listen, to force them to stop, but it was also at the level that would disturb the neighbours, possibly get them to contact the police.

Howie came to his senses first, probably because he'd been arrested six times now, a seventh arrest would be catastrophic for so many reasons. 'Sorry, Vee,' he said, stepped around Logan and practically ran out of the room and then out of my flat.

I was trembling. Shaken by what had happened, terrified that what Howie was talking about would come to pass, possibly because of a fairly innocent incident like the one I'd just witnessed.

'I'm sorry,' Logan said once we were alone and we heard the downstairs door click shut.

'Yeah, sorry's not good enough. You don't get to come to my flat and start a fight, Logan! What were you thinking?'

'I wasn't thinking. I just saw his hands on you and I saw red. I don't like the thought of other men touching you.'

'Oh, give it a rest. Just go home.'

'I've just got here. I travelled home tonight instead of tomorrow so I could see you.'

'Well . . . you should have thought of that before you got all up into being Mr Jealous, shouldn't you?'

'Ver—'

'Don't let the door hit you on your way out.'

Looking mortified but without another word, Logan turned on his heels and left.

Minutes later, a text message flashed up on my phone:

He's bad news, Vee. Really bad news.

I deleted the message and dropped my phone onto the sofa beside me. All things considered, I thought that was a bit rich coming from Howie, but I wouldn't ever say that.

serena

Now

'What have I done now?' Con asks the moment we ask him to come into the kitchen and sit down with us at the table.

I've been lucky, I know that. Until now, my children have been dreams. I used to often wonder what I did to get this fortunate. They didn't go off the rails too much, and whenever Con wanted to do something he knew we wouldn't tolerate, he'd pitch up at Verity's and make her his accomplice. I minded that he did that stuff, but preferred he was doing it around someone who would stop things getting out of hand. His group of friends are a mix of bad boys and angelic boys that Verity has lovingly named the 'Brain's Trust' because while they are all really intelligent, when they're together they seem to share one brain and do the most ridiculous/stupid things. Again, I've never minded because until recently I knew someone – Verity – was watching over them.

'What do you think you've done?' Evan asks his son. I don't know why he's trying it on, Con could run rings around us both by the time he was twelve. He knew how to use his big eyes, cute looks and sweet charm to get exactly what he wanted whenever he wanted by the time he turned eight. And my husband is trying this on now?

'That's for me to know and you to bring up in its entirety in your case against me,' Con replies.

I shoot Evan a dirty look. This is a serious conversation, I don't want to start it by being silly because I don't want to have to try to convince our son what we're saying is true.

'Can we just talk about what we called you in here to talk about, please?' I say to my son but mean it for my husband.

Evan glances at me and I give him a 'come on!' look. Mollified he returns his attention to Con. Evan has his doctor's face on again because he's back where we were when we made the decision to tell him sooner rather than later. To explain why Verity is now sitting in a prison cell. Why the police will probably be taking us all in for questioning.

'This is about me and Verity,' I say to Conrad. 'And why she's been arrested and held in custody.'

'Is this about you being accused of murder when you were a teenager and almost going to prison? And that other girl, well, I suppose she's a woman now, going to prison for the crime? Ahhh, sick, she was a Carlisle. Is that guy related to her?'

'What?' I say to my son, my eyes wide with shock.

'What?' my husband says to our son, his face set with alarm.

We stare at each other, confused, then turn to Conrad, ultra-confused. 'What?' we both say at the same time.

Conrad looks back at us like we're the ones who are a bit on the odd side.

'You know about that?' I say cautiously.

'Yeah, course.'

'How?'

'I searched you up. I've searched up everyone in this family, especially you two. I've got to know who I'm dealing with.'

'What do you mean, you've got to know who you're dealing with? We're your parents.'

'Yeah, and?' he replies earnestly because he can't see what we're surprised about.

'You searched us up? I mean, you did searches on us?'

'Mum, Dad, it is on you if you're not curious about the people you're around. Me? I've gotta know what you people are all about.'

'And it doesn't bother you?'

Conrad shrugs, pulls a face. 'Why would it?' He puts his hands up, then reaches forward and gently places his hand on mine for a moment in what feels like a comforting and slightly patronising gesture. 'I mean, Mum, that must have been some difficult . . . *stuff* to deal with. But it doesn't bother me at all. What you did is what you did.' He takes his hand away, robbing me of the calmness his touch gave me. 'And they found you innocent, set you free.' He shrugs again. 'All in the past as far as I'm concerned. And doesn't stop you being the excellent mother you are.'

I side-eye my husband for managing to give our son this excess of charm, no matter what the situation.

'When did you find this out? Did Verity tell you?' Evan asks.

He shakes his head. 'I found out back in the day.'

'You're seventeen, there isn't a "day" for you to hark back to, son,' Evan replies.

'I searched you both up about two years ago. Found you linked to that Poppy Carlisle girl. I didn't tell Verity. I didn't tell anyone. It was none of my business. You're always telling me to mind my own damn business and that's what I do – even if I know everyone's business.'

'Did you know about Verity and Logan Carlisle?' Evan asks.

Conrad looks a little troubled and shakes his shaved head. I remember a time when he wanted to grow the biggest Afro. The amount of trouble it caused at school. The number of letters we were sent, meetings we had, threats to exclude him we had to field. The school's attitude got mild-mannered, laid-back Evan's back up. Usually, I deal with school stuff but with this . . . he took it as personally as anyone could or should. No one was going to criminalise his child for how they wore their hair and Evan went to war with them after the first threatening letter.

Several legal letters in response later, and the school backed down. (I'm sure it had nothing to do with it being pointed out in one of the last letters we sent that Conrad was one of the brightest students in the school and his loss would do nothing for their grades come GCSE results time.) The day the school reversed their thoughts on how Conrad wore his hair was hugely celebrated in the Gillmare house. Conrad, in particular, celebrated by shaving his head in the bathroom using Evan's clippers, then calling his dad to ask him to do the back.

When Evan came to bed that night, I'd thought he'd be annoyed that after all that battling, all that money, all that energy, Conrad had decided to de-hair himself. But no. He climbed into bed and said, 'You know why he did it, don't you? He knew we'd go all the way, we wouldn't stop until he got to wear his hair how he wanted. He did it because he wanted everyone else to have the same freedom. The kids whose parents can't afford it, who don't have his marks, who don't have parents with that fight in them can now wear their hair how they want, too. Without the fight.' He'd cuddled up to me and I could see tears of pride shining in his eyes. 'We've got a good kid there. And we did that. We raised a kid like that.'

In the present, my youngest child continues to run his hand over his head. 'I had no clue.' He hesitates, looks unsure whether to say what is sitting there at the back of his throat. 'Vee and me haven't been close for a while. She's not been available for a while now and . . .' He stops speaking and looks at each of us as though trying to work out if we can handle what he's about to say. 'And about six months ago she changed the locks on her flat and didn't tell me.' He shrugs again, but this one isn't as unburdened. 'I probably should have guessed something was up. But I just figured she was done with me using her place as a crash pad so left it.'

'This isn't your fault,' Evan and I say together.

'You think she's going to prison?' Conrad asks.

Evan is about to say no. I can tell he's about to declare that with certainty, but my husband can't promise that. He has no idea what is coming, what it's going to be like. He has no idea what things will be twisted and found and torn apart, dissected and micro-examined to find anything that will make her guilty.

'We don't know anything,' I say quickly. My voice is like a scalpel that has been inserted into a bubble of delusion and lanced it. Now it will cut away any of the hope that is starting to grow. All of that needs to be removed as quickly and cleanly as possible because we need to be on the other end of the scale. We need to be as pessimistic as possible so anything other than a worst-case scenario is a bonus. 'Her solicitor is advising her and since he works with her we can be sure he cares. But no one knows anything, no one can say anything for sure. We all need to hang in there and wait to see how things pan out. See what the next few days and weeks bring.'

It's Evan's turn to cast a sour look in my direction. 'And stay positive. What Verity needs right now is for us to stay positive, focused on her coming home and being hopeful that this is all over soon.'

Do you know why I'm sitting here like this, with two children and a twenty-five-year marriage? I want to scream at Evan. *Do you know why you get to love me and fuck me and live your life with me? It wasn't staying positive, it wasn't people focusing on me coming home, it wasn't hoping that it would all be over soon. It was because my fingerprints weren't on the knife. After all of it, after everything that was said in court to trash me, my reputation, my personality, my humanity, I only 'got away with it' because they couldn't prove I had even touched the thing that killed him.*

I look down to stop myself getting to my feet and shouting this at my husband in front of our son.

Conrad reaches for me again and rests his hand on mine. 'It'll be all right, Mum. No matter what happens, it'll be all right.'

Evan slips his arm around my shoulders and for the first time ever, I want to tell him to get his hands off me. For the first time ever, I don't want Evan anywhere near me.

Part 6

poppy

Now

If I didn't have Betina, I would start smoking again.

I'm drinking too much, but I need the edge that smoking brings to deal with this. It's only been three days, but everything about me seems to have stopped functioning properly.

Work? What's that? When I'm there I'm going through the motions, sending out invoices, interviewing people, doing spot checks, admin, bookkeeping, accounting on autopilot. I barely notice what I'm doing until it's done and then I wonder if I did it to the best of my ability.

Parenting? What's that? When I'm home I'm going through the motions and leaving the rest of it to Alain who, without being asked, has moved in. I crumpled when the police liaison woman told me that Serena's daughter had done this to Logan, burst into noisy tears that Alain had to console me through, and after that he went to his house, got his stuff and didn't leave again.

I'm still processing everything. Still.

There was evidence of a struggle at her flat. Two types of blood found. Splatter consistent with a knife wound in one room, but nothing definitive. She, the family liaison officer, has been strangely forthcoming with information. She has told us stuff that I don't think they'd normally share, but she only does it when I'm there. I'll get a call summoning me over to my parents' house because the family liaison is paying a visit and once I get there, she will speak and retell in great detail something about the case, all the while watching me closely. I've noticed that she studies me while she overshares, visually notes my every reaction.

Alain thinks it's paranoia, but I don't. Why tell us about the other blood? It's not like we're going to know who Verity Gillmare has had over at her place. Why tell us about the splatter consistent with a knife wound? It's not as if we know what type of knife it might be.

My family are blaming me for what happened to Logan and the police are trying to work out if I'm involved.

I am blaming myself, hating myself every second of every day. I constantly wish I could smoke as much as I drink; I continuously wish I could slice at my flesh to release the agony – the monumental pain of guilt that flows through my veins.

If I didn't have Betina, I would start smoking again and I would ribbon my skin as often as I could.

serena

Now

I am hiding from Evan at the supermarket.

We've both been pretending over the last few days that we're on the same page, but we're not. We're so not. And it's difficult. Apart from when he made me leave, we've never been like this, Evan and I. We are usually balanced. We're a team that almost always works things out, but this time, we're both on our own sides of this argument and we are not changing.

He thinks Verity couldn't have done it; I need him to consider the possibility.

I've been in the supermarket a while now, and I've been working on autopilot so there is stuff in my trolley, stuff that I pick up normally, but I'm not there. I'm somewhere else. Probably that place where I can work out how Evan and I are going to sort this out.

I turn my trolley into the frozen food aisle. I don't really know what I'm doing here. Since we found out that Conrad is allergic to peas, I don't buy frozen veg, and I don't buy frozen chips or pizzas. I continue pushing my trolley down there, though, passing sections and sections of food I'm not going to buy. No frozen fish, no frozen veggie meals, no frozen burgers.

And then here I am.

My trolley seems to have stopped itself in this specific spot, stalled here in this particular place, so I can stand and stare at the tubs, the boxes, the packets of the stuff. Ice cream.

It didn't start there. It didn't end there, either. It began when I didn't tell. When I didn't tell that a teacher had touched me, had taken me to his house, had kissed me, had taken me to his bed. It began when I thought I could handle it, when I didn't believe that what was happening was wrong on every single level.

I thought, I really thought, my relationship with Verity was different. That she would talk to me, would confide in me. And if not me, then at least my twin sisters, her aunts, Medina or Faye. When she was growing up I tried to impress upon her that talking was the best way to empower yourself. And it didn't work. I was smug about my relationship with my daughter and it has led to this.

I've let her down. So badly.

By being an Ice Cream Girl, by not telling her the truth about myself, by not pursuing it as she changed and altered over the last year.

I know Evan can't see it, but the fact Mr Palmer has advised Verity to keep quiet is terrible. It means there is something awful there that will see her charged and convicted. I know because when I realised the police were not going to believe me, were probably not going to believe Poppy, I shut up. I stopped talking, I stopped answering questions about anything. And I did that because I did not want to let out the truth about what I'd done.

I tear my eyes away from the freezer cabinet, from the rows and rows of food that remind me of things I should have forgotten by now. I should have moved on from all of that by now. I shouldn't still have a reaction to history lessons, I shouldn't still be stuck in a world where yellow dresses turn my stomach and ice cream brings the torture of 'let's make up' shuddering through my skin.

Move on, I tell myself. Emotionally, physically, I need to do just that. I need to move on, live in the here and now.

I push my trolley in an arc to veer away from this side of the frozen food aisle and all the memories it conjures up, and it clashes with another trolley.

'Sorry,' we both mumble at the same time, without properly acknowledging each other. It's the tingle which zigzags down my spine when I hear that voice that makes me look up. It's her. Of course it's her. Why wouldn't it be?

'Poppy,' I say.

'Serena,' she replies.

'You live round here?' I ask after a moment or two of tense, almost violent silence has passed between us. Neither of us is sure what to do, how to handle this. We're not supposed to meet, we're not meant to be in each other's lives.

She nods.

'Right,' I say. At least now I know so I can go to another area of East Sussex when I want to escape from my husband.

'How's your . . . is there any change?' I don't know if Evan has called up about Logan Carlisle because he was one of the doctors that helped him, but I haven't. I've left well enough alone so I have no idea how he is; all I know is that my daughter is spending another day in a custody cell because of him.

Poppy shakes her head, her brown hair bouncing as she moves. 'No. The swelling on his brain hasn't gone down as much as they expected it to. There's less pressure inside his skull, but they're getting concerned, I think. That's just the way it feels, anyway.' Her brown eyes look me over, probably in the same way that I have been visually frisking her for weapons of any kind. 'How's your . . . Anything happening?'

I shake my head. 'She's still answering their questions. I haven't spoken to her directly yet.'

'Did you know about them?' Poppy asks. 'That they were . . . ?'

'No. Not a clue. Did you?'

She glances behind her, as though checking for an attack from behind. 'No idea. It's been a shock, to say the least.'

I have the urge, a strong, almost overwhelming urge, to tell her that Verity didn't do it. That she wouldn't do it and when he wakes up – if he wakes up – he'll confirm that. To stop myself lying, trying to make those lies a truth, I grip the handle of my trolley that bit harder, bite down on the inside of my lip, and redirect my gaze to Poppy's shopping trolley.

It's so weird seeing her do something as mundane, ordinary, normal as shopping. I remember how much I resented her. How every time I saw her or heard her name I wanted her to disappear.

Her trolley is as full as mine with fresh fruit and vegetables. She has full-fat milk and full-fat cheese; she has breadsticks and hummus. She has eggs and whole-wheat pasta. And she has organic junior cereal bars and mini yoghurts and strips of dried fruit packaged up in brilliant-coloured sleeves. This is what my trolley looked like when the children were younger. When they needed snacks for school and something small for them to devour on the way home.

Poppy has a child or possibly children.

Poppy, a mother. If seeing her do something as mundane as shopping is weird, thinking of her as a mother is *wild*. I look her over again, this time noting what could be signs of motherhood. But she's no more doughy round the middle than anyone else in this supermarket; she has a smudge of grey under her eyes, but no more than the last time I saw her, I think. She has a haircut like anyone else, her skin is pale but not overly blemished. She doesn't wear 'mum jeans' or a 'mum jacket'. She doesn't have a wedding ring. There are no clues about Poppy at all in the way she is, and the only thing that gives her away is her shopping trolley.

'Do you think she did it?' Poppy, my ancient rival, my so-called co-conspirator, asks out of the blue.

Our gazes snap together, and the years from then till now unravel themselves into seconds that elongate the silence between us.

'If she did, I'm sure she had good reason,' I reply eventually.

'What's that supposed to mean?' she asks, our stares still battling it out with each other.

'It means my daughter is a kind, gentle, thoughtful young woman who wouldn't hurt anyone unless she had no other choice.'

'Like you, you mean?' she replies.

'My daughter is nothing like me.'

'And my brother wasn't "asking for it",' she retorts.

'I never said he was.'

'Yes, you did. You literally did. When he wakes up, we're going to find out what really happened.'

If he wakes up, I almost say. 'Yes, we will, I suppose.' I unhook my trolley from its position almost melded to hers. 'I'll see you, Poppy.'

'I'll see you, Serena,' she replies.

I'm about to turn the corner into the next aisle when she calls me again. I turn back to her. She smiles and says, 'Give my love to Dr Evan,' in a voice drizzled with so much honey, so much affection, I abandon my trolley and go straight home to my husband.

verity

'Gillmare, visitor.'

'Visitor' has to mean Darryl since, as my solicitor, he's the only person I'm allowed to have 'visit'. This particular police officer doesn't like me. I don't know why, and she hasn't said anything directly, but she does not like me and often gives me the stare of someone who would just love for me to try to escape. I know she wouldn't hesitate in trying to take me down – a well-placed fist in the gut, a kick to the back of my knee, anything that would stop me in my tracks.

I swing my legs off my cold concrete bunk and stand, unkinking my back and my frozen, locked limbs with careful, big, slow movements so I don't get myself into trouble. *Could I take her?* Absolutely. *Would she have lots of mates to back her up?* Absolutely again. Because I've found out something over these hours that I've been here: people have long memories.

From the looks and whispers and attitude I'm getting, being the daughter of the Ice Cream Girl Who Got Away With It is almost as bad as being her.

Hilariously (!) I'm sure half these people wouldn't have been in big school when my mum was notorious, but that doesn't stop them having

276

an opinion about the 'fact' she 'got away with it'. About the 'fact' that it looks like her daughter is about to do the same. I'm sure a few of them – including this woman – would love to get their licks in. I'm not actually sure how many of them I'd be able to hurt before they really hurt me, though.

As I move to my cell door, she leaves it that beat too long to step aside; she contrives to make us collide, to start that altercation she would so love to have. I'm not silly, though. I leave it that bit too long to step through the doorway, so we don't touch.

She walks behind me, not in reverence or out of respect, but so she can keep an eye on me and I lead the way to the interview room that I've started to think of as *my* interview room. I know the kinks of the wall, the bumps of the table, the flaws of the chairs, the mottles of the two-way mirror. Whenever I'm brought in here, I immerse myself in the feel of the room, its unsubtle stench of sweat and tears and fear and confession. Those things cling to the molecules of air, to the auras of all who enter and exit.

There is a woman sitting in Darryl's place. Even in this dingy, depressive light, I can see from the way she is dressed, the manner in which she holds herself, that she is a barrister. She wears a black skirt suit over a white shirt with the top button open; she sits rod straight even though she has crossed her legs. Her shoes, though, are not those of a woman who stands on her feet all day – they are shiny black and have pencil-thin heels that would make her tower over most people she stands near. I wouldn't have thought I'd need a barrister at this stage. Yes, the police have, unusually, been almost outright telling me they are going to try to hold me for the full ninety-six hours they officially can, even if it means going back to court after seventy-two hours, but that doesn't mean I'll be charged at the end of it. It just means they think they can find something. I don't need a barrister.

'Take a seat,' she says with a voice as smooth and delicious as syrup.

When I do sit opposite her, I suddenly feel as scruffy as I am in this grey tracksuit.

Not only is this woman well put together, she is very beautiful. Under her flawless make-up, her dark-brown skin is so smooth, I have to wonder why she bothers with foundation and the rest of it. Her large, mascaraed eyes are quick, they have the look of someone who nothing escapes no matter how she outwardly responds to the information that she's given. She's Mum's age, or thereabouts, and doesn't look weary or cynical. I'm sure she's probably practised that, found a way to give nothing away so in court the witness has no idea what to expect from her – even if she's on your side.

'My name is Nerissa Bawku,' she says in her syrup voice. 'I know Darryl Palmer from the Society of Black Lawyers and I work with him sometimes. He has asked me to come and talk to you, to see if I would consider representing you.'

'OK, I didn't realise it'd got to that stage. Does he know something I don't?'

She grins at me and I'm sure that smile has thrown many a guilty and innocent person off, I bet she brings it out and dusts it off in those moments when she either needs to put someone at ease or terrify them. I'm not quite sure which situation this is.

'You may very well need to go to court when the police ask for the additional twenty-four hours that will take your questioning up to ninety-six hours,' she says. 'He asked me because I'm not connected to your firm and he . . . he was worried that you weren't taking this seriously. I must say, I have to agree with him.'

'You've talked to me for all of three seconds, how can you know if I'm not taking this seriously?' How dare this woman say that to me. How dare she! 'Believe me, I am taking this seriously. And you can tell Darryl that.'

'Verity, if I may call you that, Darryl is extremely worried about you. He knows how them out there' – she points a manicured nail towards the door – 'are working around the clock to find the evidence to prove you guilty. And you are guilty . . . according to them.' She left that a moment too long, she obviously thinks I'm guilty, too. 'Darryl knows first-hand what a manipulative young woman you are, and he's concerned that the police will not only see it, they'll find evidence to prove that it was your manipulative nature that led us here.'

Hang on a second . . . ! 'Manipulative? Darryl said that about me?'

'He told me, *everything*. He told me about how when he had a rare moment of public vulnerability and opened up to you about his late wife, you used it to make a move on him.'

What?!

'That seconds after he talked to you about his wife, you manoeuvred yourself into a position where he felt compelled to kiss you.'

WHAT?!

'That you invited yourself back to his hotel room and set about trying to get him into bed.'

'No, no, that's not how it was.'

'He told me that when he very quickly came to his senses, you weren't happy. You tried to get him to change his mind, to make him take you to his bed.'

'No, it wasn't like that.'

'He said, when he suggested being honest with human resources so everything was out in the open, you basically threatened to tell them that he had sexually harassed you because you didn't want anyone to know that you'd done this sort of thing before.'

'No! I didn't. I wouldn't. That's not what happened. That's not what happened at all.'

'He added that when he asked you to leave, you told him that you didn't want to. You basically tried to stay by saying you couldn't leave because you were desperate for him to make love to you.'

'No! No! No! None of that is true. None of that happened.'

'So you didn't kiss him outside the lift at the Marriot Hotel in June 2018?'

'Yes, but I—'

'And you didn't go back to his hotel room, room 612?'

'Yes, I did, but—'

'And you didn't ask him not to tell human resources about the two of you in case you got a reputation as a girl who cried sexual harassment?'

'I didn't mean it like—'

'And you didn't say that you were having a hard time going when he asked you to leave his room?'

'It wasn't like that. None of it was like that. It was— We were—'

Nerissa Bawku slams her hand down on the table in front of me so hard it immediately stops me mid-self-defence. My horrified, widened eyes become fixated on her nails, manicured with clear vanish. All neat and perfectly shaped.

'They are going to eat you alive,' Nerissa declares quietly, viciously, with the knowledge of one who has literally seen it all before. 'That was just a fraction of what you're going to face. I didn't even break a sweat. You need to wake the hell up! You are not a posh white boy whose parents dine with the judges and who'll have his coke-fuelled assault dismissed as a youthful indiscretion and will avoid prison because he can't emotionally deal with it.

'You are a Black girl who went to state school. Talk to any of the working-class white girls who went to state school who are sitting in prison right now if anyone cared whether they could emotionally handle prison because they stole a tin of beans so they could feed themselves. Talk to any of the Black boys who were arrested because they wore their hoods up while being in a crime-heavy area whether the judge cared that there was scant evidence against them. You are a Black girl who is here because of attempted murder. You have none of the privilege that will get you a fair hearing from the outset. Add to that the fact your mother is notorious, and you haven't a cat in hell's chance of this not going to trial.

'They will find the evidence they need to get you to trial, you can be certain about that. They will dredge up every little thing about you that will point to you being slyly manipulative, highly sexed and aggressive. They will do everything they can to pin this on you, evidence or not. They are going to make an example of you.'

I knew I was in trouble, I knew things were dire but I don't think I ever allowed myself to think of it in these terms. She's right, they are going to eat me alive. They are going to chew me up, macerate me into the tiniest of pieces, and then they will spit me out.

'If you want an even halfway-decent defence you will have to start helping yourself. Tell Darryl the truth. Tell him everything so he can help you.'

But it's not that simple because I promised. I promised I wouldn't tell.

And I have to keep this promise.

Even if it means I end up going to prison.

Now

'Daaaad,' I began.

'No,' he stated without even looking at me or anything. Dad loved sitting out there having a beer when the football wasn't on and the nights were clear. He didn't even mind it being cold, he just liked being outside.

'But—'

'No.'

'The—'

'No.'

'I just—'

'No.'

With a sour look on my face and a bitter taste in my mouth, I harrumphed, my arms folded. 'I shouldn't have led with the "Daaad",' I murmured so quietly I barely heard myself.

'You're right there,' Dad replied to my statement he wasn't meant to hear.

'I just want to ask your advice on something. I promise you won't have to do anything doctory.'

My dad, the doctor, squeezed his forefinger and thumb over the bridge of his nose and winced a little as he lowered his hand and took a swig from his bottle. 'You do realise that "doctory" can also cover things like something that is happening to a vulnerable person? Or something that is about someone who is in danger of being physically harmed? In those cases, if you tell me something, I will have to report it as a safeguarding issue.'

I hesitated. I did know that, but I was kind of hoping he'd forget about it for the length of time I was going to talk to him.

Slowly, he swivelled in his seat to look at me. 'Do you realise that, Verity?'

I nodded.

'Well, then, now you know why I said no.'

'But, Dad—'

He shook his head. 'No.'

'Dad,' I said quietly and seriously, 'can I just talk to you like you're someone I would talk to?'

'If that's what you want, why aren't you talking to your mother about it?'

I shrugged.

'Shrug is not an answer,' Dad said. Mum used to say that to me all the time when I was a kid. She'd say that then tickle me. I missed that Mum. The one I didn't know anything about. Who was just the most honest, straightforward, neurotic person on Earth. I could love her without question back then. She had so many faults and she got so many things wrong, but it didn't matter. She was just my mum and that was who she was. Now all I could see were the lies, the things she did; they coated her like a layer of thick slime that I was surprised no one else could see.

'What's going on with you and your mother?'

I shrugged again.

My father's face contorted slightly as he seemed to be thinking something through while he put his beer bottle to his lips and chugged down a couple of mouthfuls. He wanted to say something, but instead drank his beer. His silence allowed me to say: 'What would you do, Dad, if you found out someone was in a bad situation?'

'What sort of bad situation?' His voice was tired and taut, a solid ball of resignation that I was dragging him into a conversation that could become a safeguarding issue which could cause problems for him.

'I mean, what if you know your friend is in a bad relationship, where stuff happens and you can see the effect it's having on them and you know they should leave but they don't. Or won't. Or can't. What would you do?'

'Is this person a child, an elderly person or vulnerable in some other way?' he asked.

I shook my head.

He physically relaxed; his body, which he'd been holding ready to leap into rescue mode, was able to stand down for now. 'My friend . . . they feel *trapped*, I guess. They've got old issh, yes, but it's not major. Or maybe it is. Thing is, I can see what it's doing to them. They feel powerless and scared all the time. Not of getting hit, that doesn't always feel as bad, it's more everything else that comes with it. The fear and worry and the trying to work out what to do to make life easier and not have things kick off.

'It's a constant churning feeling along with everything else there is to worry about . . . what if they retaliate and become worse than the other person? What would they do then if they retaliated and someone found out? It would look bad, wouldn't it? I know from the law point of view it'd look bad if it wasn't a clear case of self-defence from an imminent threat, but from your point of view, how do you think it would look? Would they have had to tell someone official at some point for them to be taken seriously?'

My father was watching me very closely. He was taking in everything, absorbing every word and filtering it through his experiences of life as a man, a doctor, a father, a human being. 'You seem very invested, Verity, for someone who is talking about a "friend".'

Huh? 'Wha—oh, you think I'm talking about me? I'm not.' Convinced he did not look. 'Honestly, Dad, it's not me. It's a friend who confided in me and I don't know what I'm supposed to be doing. Do I just listen like I have been doing? Do I say something? Do I get them to leave? Should I offer to put them up? Find a shelter? Do I call the police myself?' I flapped my arms up and down hopelessly. 'I don't know what to do. There is so much I could do and say, but I'm not sure if it's right. Which is why I'm asking you, as someone older who will have seen other people who've been through this.'

'I don't know, is the answer, Verity. If someone comes to me as a doctor and tells me they're being abused then I have to do all I can to help. If I see signs from injuries or other things that suggest abuse, I have to ask them about it. If they deny it, or if they retract what they say, I still have to follow it up with them at some point in the future. If things are escalating and I think they are in danger of being seriously injured or killed, I have to do something. Basically, I'm saying you should talk to your mother about this sort of thing because I can't answer as an average person. There are certain laws and procedures I have to follow.'

What he's telling me without saying the actual words is that what he did back in 2011, when Zeph's boyfriend basically assaulted her, couldn't happen again. He and Dr Joiner would be struck off. We have never discussed that since it happened. The only acknowledgement is that periodically Dad will ask about Zeph, and at the time I wasn't allowed a phone, computer or to leave the house for anything other than school and food shopping for a month. That meant I couldn't do all of my homework, which meant I got into a LOT of trouble at school, which was kind of the point, I guess, because low grades and detention were my kind of hell.

'I suppose I want to know I'm doing the right thing,' I pressed on. 'From someone official.'

'Which is why I said no.'

'How do you do it, Dad? It must be so hard when you see someone and they've got injuries and they won't admit it. You must just want to shake them and tell them to get out while they can. Or to ask them why they won't leave.'

'I do want to tell them that they deserve better. That there will be help available if they're ready to leave. And I want to protect them from the situation they're in. Until someone is ready, though, nothing I say will change anything. Doesn't mean you shouldn't say something . . . Look, Vee, you should speak to your mother about this stuff. She will give you much better advice.'

'Doubt it,' I snarked in disgust. It was meant to come out silently, but it didn't and my father heard.

In response, he settled his bottle on the table and turned his whole body to face me. 'What did you say?'

The thing about my old man was that he was nice. He was cool and calm and *nice*. He was patient and fair and noble. He was also someone who was hyper-protective of each and every one of us, including Mum, and he would respond in this way no matter who said something like that about someone he loved.

'I meant you and her give the same quality of advice. I seriously don't think her advice will be any better than yours.'

My father's gaze continued to eviscerate me, and I grew hot and uncomfortable under his stare.

'Thanks, Dad,' I said. That was one of the good things about being an adult with her own place – I could leave whenever I chose. And leaving then was the best thing to do. 'It's been a really helpful chat. I'll see you soon.'

'Drive safe,' was all he said as I raced out of the house and through the front door.

I left without knowing what to do. I couldn't force anything, couldn't change anything. Just keeping the secret felt wrong, but right then, there was nothing more I could do, was there?

poppy

Now

The police have given me access to Logan's flat so I can tidy it up. I need to be doing something and since the sitting beside his bed all the spare hours bit has been annexed by my parents and a little by Bella, I need to be doing something else. Somewhere else.

I didn't realise things could get so awful between us. Bella's behaviour towards me has become almost solicitous whenever possible. She wants to spend every moment stuck to my side and she asks me copious amounts of questions to get me to engage with her.

Mum and Dad, on the other hand, have obviously sensed a change in me, probably largely to do with the fact I don't bother to speak to them unless I have to. Their response to this is to be falsely bright without actually engaging in conversation (Mum), and to be curt and sullen after acknowledging my presence in a room with a nod of the head (Dad). Dad obviously tunes in when Mum asks after Betina. They both wait for me to answer 'How is Betina?' with 'She's fine, I'll drop her over in the next few days.' And they're both disappointed, openly so, when my words end with 'She's fine'. I am not playing. Times like these are meant to bring us together. But my role in our 'together' has changed and I will no longer allow them to merely tolerate me just so they can enjoy seeing their only grandchild.

I'm allowed access to Logan's flat because there is no sign that anyone other than Logan was ever there. Certainly not Verity Gillmare. No hairs, no bodily fluids, no skin cells, no fingerprints. Whereas, apparently, he was all over her place, was so ingrained into the fabric of her flat that they were convinced he'd all but moved in.

That immediately set off alarm bells about how equal their relationship had been. Because of the nature of our relationship, I was only ever able to go to Marcus's place. That meant he was in control of everything. Why did Verity Gillmare never go to Logan's place? Not once, it seems. It couldn't have been because they feared being caught. We very rarely went to his flat. In fact, since Serena and her daughter seemed so close, it was more likely they'd get caught at her place. So why not base themselves at his?

The answer is obvious, of course: it was easier for Verity to never leave her place, so she didn't. She required Logan to make all the effort in their relationship.

I stand in the living-room doorway, looking around. 'Amateurs', is the first word to come to mind. The people who searched my parents' house in London were professionals. Whenever they had finished their multiple searches, it looked like a hurricane had blown through the house. A vicious, targeted hurricane that was determined to upend, disrupt and uncover everything, right down to the smallest dust mote.

I still think it's a miracle they didn't find my diary and clothes from the night Marcus died. Whereas Logan's place looks as though a friendly breeze has rattled a few things and I wonder what secrets have been missed. I wonder what Logan put away that he did not want any-one to see.

I bit back at Serena in the supermarket, wasn't having a bar of what she was implying about my brother and her daughter. But what do I know? How do I know that Logan didn't provoke the attack on himself?

What if she was right? What if my brother was abusive? How would I cope with that? How will I square that circle in my head? I love my brother. How will I cope if he turns out to be like Marcus?

Yes, my secret that I still love Marcus is loose in my head now, but that doesn't change the fact that I hate him as well. For every molecule of love I have for Marcus, there is one of pure hatred, too. I do not want to have any love for him. I want to just hate him, but I can't. And that hurts me, that churns me up inside. I do not want conflicting emotions when it comes to my brother. I want him to piss me off, like everyone pisses off everyone at least a few times in their life. I do not want to have reason to hate my brother. I do not want my brother to be like Marcus. I do not want another woman to have suffered at the hands of a man, especially not a man that I love.

September, 1987

'Poppy, why have you still got your clothes on?'

I was confused. He'd told me to go upstairs, lie on the bed, take my knickers off and keep everything else on. 'You told me to keep my clothes on.'

'I didn't.'

My heart rate leapt up several notches. He did. I was sure he did. 'You did. You told me to go upstairs and take my knickers off and leave everything else on.'

Emotion rippled across Marcus's jaw and my heart rate went from racing to galloping. I was sure that's what he'd said, but his face, his rising anger, told me that I was wrong. That he'd told me to take everything off.

'I told you, *Poppy*,' he enunciated every word with menace, 'to come upstairs, take off all your clothes except your knickers and then to lie down on the bed waiting for me.'

He didn't. I was sure he didn't. I was sure he told me to leave everything on. I was sure. 'I thought you said it the other way round.'

The ripple moved across his jaw, slid over his face, then settled in his eyes, twin pools of anger at being questioned. 'I didn't say it the other way around, *Poppy*. I know what I said. I know what I wanted and I told you. I asked you to get ready.'

'I . . . I thought . . .' *I hadn't been listening, had I? I hadn't listened properly and now he was angry with me.* Now he was angry and he would . . . 'I'm sorry,' I said desperately. I scrambled off the bed, picked up my underwear and pulled it on. Sobbing out sorry after sorry after sorry, I took my clothes off with shaking fingers. Then lay on the bed. Finally doing as he had asked.

'I'm sorry,' I said again as he came towards me. 'I'm so sorry.' I was hoping he wouldn't hit me. And he didn't. He didn't hit me.

He didn't punch me or shove me or kick me. But he was rough. He was brutal, he left me hurting and trembling and doing all I could not to cry. Because if there was anything he hated more than me getting something wrong, it was me crying because sex had hurt.

'I think you were right, actually, Poppy,' he said, stretching before he went to sleep. 'I did tell you to keep your clothes on and take your knickers off. Must have got you confused with Serena. That's what we did earlier. I'm silly sometimes.'

We both knew he was lying. We both knew he hadn't got confused. And we both knew I wasn't going to say a thing about it.

Now

Logan's flat is tidy now. Righted. Straightened out and perfect. I've cleaned as I've tidied and now you wouldn't be able to tell that the police have been through here.

I still think they missed something. I still think that here, his safe place away from the madness of the outside world, away from his intense, secret relationship, he has shared something. It must have been driving him wild being with her, wanting to talk about her, but not being able to.

Pictures. There must be pictures of them together. Out of all of us, he has the most photos on display in his home, he *must* have photos of him and Verity somewhere. He wouldn't be able to keep them on his phone in case someone saw. But I'm sure there'd be pictures of them together somewhere. Or even just photos of her. She's the kind of pretty that men take photos of, let's face it.

Letters. I know they're old-fashioned, but I can imagine them sharing letters.

I don't know what I'm hoping for. What it will prove if I do find something, but I'm looking for it. I'm running my eyes over surfaces, over areas of walls and carpets, over anywhere that might be hiding the treasury to Logan's love life. I feel like there is a missing piece in all of this. Until he wakes up, there doesn't seem to be much we can do but make up what fits into that missing piece.

I move to the kitchen, to his spare bedroom, which doubles as an office, back to the living room.

If I were a man trying to hide my relationship, my passionate, 'complicated' relationship, where would I store stuff? She's never been to my flat. She'll never know if I bring some of her stuff here. But I don't want anyone asking questions. I don't want anyone to see the photos or one of her scarves or read something I've written to her on one of the nights I'm not with her.

If I were a man trying to hide my relationship, where would I store stuff? Not hide, exactly. Store, keep, treasure. The police – as amateur as this lot seemed – have looked in all the obvious places. Is my brother a plain-sighter? Would he put things in plain sight for all to see and not notice? I unhook the pictures from the walls, gather up the others that are standing on the fireplace and bookcases and then take out the various photos of the three of us together: Christmas at our parents', Betina and him. Nope. Not the place. All that is kept in those photo frames are the photos that should be there.

The police have his phone and his computers. Maybe they're on there. But I don't think so, not when he's gone to so much trouble to hide them. Where would I hide something like a USB drive? Everything I ever hid was under the floorboards. So down low. If not down low then up high? I look up – the picture rails are too thin. The shelves have been searched, including the tops I'd imagine.

Where else, where else, where el—? I can only really see it when I am standing in the exact spot I am now. Above the window is a short wooden pelmet that sits just above his white, slatted blinds. On top of that pelmet, where no one would think to look, is something that shouldn't be there. From where I am standing, if my eyesight was any worse, it would look like a bump, a flaw in the woodwork. But I am looking for something so the white 'bump' is a different shade to the wood on which it sits and it is plastic. And is it . . .? I go closer and yes, yes it is; it's a USB stick.

I knew it!

I have to stand on a chair from the kitchen to reach it. But once it's in my fingers, I know that I've got something significant. Something that will allow me an insight into what he was up to.

I have to get home, get my computer. See what he has here.

I'm about to gather up my belongings when the buzzer sounds. And, 'It's me,' Bella says into the intercom.

I sigh. I don't want to talk to her. We haven't properly talked in days and I still don't want to talk to her. What I want to do is go home, get my computer, put this USB into it and hope it's not password-protected. Hope that it will tell me something about my brother and what he was up to and how he got together with Verity Gillmare in the first place.

I don't say anything, but do buzz Bella in. I have to cope with her for now. I don't like that we're not friends. We've already lost so much time, I don't like that we're losing more like this.

She throws her arms around me the second she enters Logan's flat. 'I'msorryI'msorryI'msorryI'msorryI'msorry.' She doesn't give me a chance to do anything else except stand there and accept and experience this full-body apology.

After a few minutes of 'I'msorry'ing me, she finally lets me go. 'I'm so stressed, so upset, I lashed out at you. You, of all people, don't deserve it.'

'How did you know I was here?' I ask because I'm not sure what to say. It's not OK, and I'm not prepared to say it is OK. At some point, I have to do what Tina was always trying to tell me to do: stand up for myself; rescue myself.

'A-Lane told me. I went by your place and he said you were here, cleaning up. As if I couldn't be any more ashamed.' As she speaks, she walks into the corridor and then straight into the living room. 'Wow, you've done an amazing job. I don't think my clean-freak brother has ever had it *this* clean!'

Our clean-freak brother, I want to say, but it's a small thing. An unintentional slip of the tongue.

'The question on everyone's lips, though' – she spins on her heels to look at me – 'is does the boy have any booze in the house?'

'Oh yes, if there's one thing our brother has, it's booze.' I indicate for her to sit down. 'Sit and I'll get a selection of stuff.'

When I return with a tray full of bottles and glasses and carefully settle it on the floor beside her, before sitting down on the other side, Bella looks distressed. I pour her a glass of white wine in a short water tumbler and hand it to her.

She takes the glass, still looking distressed. Eventually she spills: 'Do you think this is a bit morbid? I mean, he's on the other side of town in a coma with our parents keeping vigil and we're here in his house drinking his alcohol.'

I drink the wine and it is good. Light, fruity, the right type of tart. Is it morbid? Is it? 'Probably,' I say with a shrug. 'But he's not drinking it, is he?'

She spits out the wine and stares wide-eyed at me.

'What?' I ask her. 'Oh, come on, it's true.'

'I've messed up,' Bella suddenly says. 'I've really, really messed up. This is all my fault. That's why I was trying to blame you. It's my fault Logan's lying in a hospital bed. That he may never wake up.'

'How is it your fault?'

'I should have . . . I should have stopped him. He told me what he was going to do. How he was going to track down Serena Gorringe and get her to confess. I mean, we both knew it was a batshit plan. The woman has lied for over thirty years, how is Logan talking to her going to change it? I should have stopped him. I tried. I thought, I convinced myself I'd talked him out of it, but you know Logan, it'll take more than a couple of chats to stop him.'

Do I know Logan? Do any of us?

'It's not your fault,' I tell my sister. I'm staring at the array of drinks that sits on the wooden tray between us. I'm wondering what to go for next. I'm not enjoying the wine any more. It's taking too long. I want the hit and buzz thirty minutes ago, I do not want intoxication to stroll up to me and offer me a nice meander into its embrace. I want a smackbang 'AND NOW YOU'RE DRUNK!' feeling. That is the best kind of drunk nowadays. It means the crying only comes once I'm too out of it to care. With the slow type of drunk, there are far too many tearful avenues to take myself down, numerous cul-de-sacs of sobbing to visit before face-down, care-about-nothing drunk arrives.

'You have to say that, you're my big sister,' Bella says.

'I really don't have to say that. I'm not sure what I'm supposed to say most of the time, Bella. I spend so much time not knowing what to say, I stop talking. I just sit there chewing the inside of my mouth, biting my tongue and fuming. I do a lot of fuming.'

'What was prison like?'

I stop scoping out the booze on the tray and look at her. She's never asked. Neither of them has ever asked. Not directly. Logan has asked more questions that lead into conversations about prison than Bella, but neither of them has ever asked what it was like.

'Horrible,' I state. 'It was horrible. And even though I met Tina, who I loved more than life itself, even though I got time to read, even though I learnt stuff and I met great people, prison was horrible. I wouldn't wish it on anyone.' Except Serena. I think I'm at that stage where I would wish it on her. And her daughter, if she did this. They need to go to prison if she did this.

'Not even the person who did this to Logan?'

'I would totally wish it on them.'

'Do you think Verity Gillmare did it?'

'Can we not talk about it? I'm not in the place to talk about that. I just want to forget about it for a while. OK?'

'OK.'

I pour myself a huge tumbler of Bailey's, then top up Bella's glass with wine. She's not on my drunk-fast road yet and I'm trying to respect that while making sure I don't slow down at all. 'How come you were here this weekend?' That's been bothering me for days. Saturday night, she got the call first and she met me at the hospital. 'I thought you were in London with the fella this weekend.'

'Yeah, well,' she replies. 'You thought wrong.'

'OK, then. I'll just remind myself *never* to ask you anything again and shut myself up, shall I?'

'No, no, sorry. I just hate that I've joined you and Logan in the messed-up stakes.'

'How do you mean?'

'Myron and I had a huge falling-out and decided not to see each other this weekend. I mean, come Saturday, I was all kinds of pissed off and did not need the Logan situation heaped on top.'

'What was the falling-out about?'

'He wants to move here sooner. He thinks it's ridiculous to wait another eight months. Eight months is practically no months as far as he's concerned so he's all for putting his place on the market and then moving as soon as possible.'

'What's wrong with that? It sounds like he can't wait to be with you. That's nice. That's the very definition of not messed-up as far as I can see.'

'But that's not the plan!' she wails. 'The plan is for us to pay off the mortgage and *then* for him to move down. Not the other way around. That's not the plan.'

'Oh, I see!' I say, and I really do. 'The plan is for you to enjoy living on your own and occasionally visiting your boyfriend and having him visit you, but you essentially live the single life for as long as is humanly possible, yes?'

'Get lost,' she says, refusing to meet my eye.

'I love it when a sibling joins me in the messed-up stakes,' I laugh. 'Just love it.'

'Get lost,' she replies.

I am, I think. I am completely and utterly lost. And I have a feeling that once I see what's on the USB, I'm going to be even more lost. Even more in need of something to anchor me. I watch my sister sip her wine, her short brown hair is in a newly acquired sexy little pixie cut, and her face is looking happier than it has since Logan was hospitalised.

I should probably tell her what I've found. Look at it with her. But I'm scared that it may be something hideous. It might be something so damaging she'll never recover from seeing it, so I quiet the small part of me that wants to share it with her by downing more Bailey's. The rest of me knows that, for now, I need to keep this discovery to myself.

Part 7

serena

Now

I've pretty much erased from my mind what it's like to be in a magistrate's court. Or maybe it's one of the things that was removed with my memory loss.

I wasn't in one for an extensive amount of time, just long enough to hear the charges read, to be asked if I understood what I was being charged with, and to be told I would have to stay at home under curfew for the months and months before the trial.

Verity might not be in court for long this morning. The police have come up to seventy-two hours and haven't found anything to prove she did something to Logan Carlisle, so they've had to return to court to get her time in custody extended to ninety-six hours.

It's rare for the full ninety-six to be awarded, explained Mr Palmer, but it might be. Because of that possibility, we've all put on suits to make us look respectable. It's not as cynical and calculated as it sounds, just sensible. Easier. Verity doesn't have any smart clothes and I know she will look tired and bedraggled; like someone who could have done what she was accused of. So the rest of us have to show that this is not how she normally looks, that's not where she comes from.

There is a lot of wood around the court; that hasn't changed in all these years. Lots of wood, imposing and grand; overtly menacing. You can't help but feel intimidated sitting here surrounded by all this wood and worry.

We told Conrad he didn't have to come to court, but he insisted because he wanted to see his sister. We don't speak as we sit in a line on uncomfortable chairs, waiting to be called. It feels small in here, maybe because of the wood, maybe because of how oppressive being surrounded by so much emotion is, but I feel ridiculously oversized, like a giant in a miniature world.

When I look up at the doorway to the waiting area, I see Medina and Faye. They are also wearing suits – identical suits. I bet that's an accident. They used to hate dressing alike when they were younger, so I suspect this morning, when they grabbed clothes to come down here, they didn't intentionally coordinate and pull on dark-grey trouser suits complete with waistcoats and pink shirts. If we weren't in this situation, I would laugh. Their faces when they saw each other first thing must have been a picture.

Medina indicates her head for me to come out rather than wait for them to go in. I stand and pull my bag onto my shoulder, mumbling, 'I'll be back in a minute' to the other two, and head outside.

Once in the corridor, Medina pulls me into a hug, clinging onto me tightly. 'How are you, babe?' she says. I'm not sure who the hug is for – her or me. Faye, always more reserved, rubs my back while Medina squishes me. 'Are you OK? Have you seen her? Is she OK? What can we do? Will she be let out today?' Medina's questions are rapid, frantic, a sure sign of what she is feeling inside.

'Give the girl a bloody chance,' Faye says, rubbing my back a little firmer. 'How is she supposed to answer those questions when you're firing them at her like your mouth's a machine gun?'

'Don't start with me, Fez,' Medina threatens.

'Or you'll do what? Go and get your own style so we don't dress like fifty-something twinnies?'

'I said don't start with me.' Mez is crushing me to her chest so she can remonstrate with our sister over my shoulder.

'I'll start all I want,' Fez replies. She's now rubbing my back so hard she's about to break a rib.

'Really? My two big sisters come to support me in my hour of need and this is what they do?' I struggle to loosen Mez's hold for long enough to break free. 'Really? Well, thanks for coming girls, couldn't get through this without you.'

'Sorry, sweetheart, sorry,' Medina says, scowling at Fez.

'Yes, sorry. I know you didn't need that,' Faye adds, side-eyeing Mez back to the dawn of time.

'I can't believe this is happening again,' Medina declares, even though the words from the apology for their spat aren't even dry.

'Don't say that,' Faye says, trying to tell Medina to stop because she can see I can't take it.

'It's fine,' I say. 'In a way it does feel like this is history repeating itself. But Verity is not me. She's an adult and she's way smarter than I ever was.' My confidence in what I am saying is thin, papery, blatantly apparent to the other two.

'We know,' Faye says. She slings her arms around me and pulls me into one of her rare hugs.

'We absolutely know,' Medina adds and throws her arms around the two of us.

This feels more genuine, more comforting, like they're here to prop me up in a way that I definitely need right now. My body relaxes, only for a moment, a time when I don't have to keep myself upright because my two big sisters are doing it for me. My eyes are about to slip shut, to allow Faye and Medina to keep me up for a few moments longer before I have to go in and be a respectable parent in front of the magistrate while they pass it over to the crown court and let us know the conditions of her bail, when something familiar catches my eye.

Someone familiar.

They are outside, beyond the revolving doors, talking to someone else. I don't have my glasses on, I can't see properly, completely, but this person is . . . My eyes widen rather than shut as I stare through the smoky, slightly darkened court glazing at the person who stands at the top of the steps, hands in pockets, having an intense discussion with another person in a suit.

My whole body grows icy and I'm glad my sisters have their arms around me because if they didn't I would probably pass right out cold on the floor.

Standing outside is a person I never thought I would see again. Literally thought I would never see again because it would be impossible.

Standing outside, just beyond the doors is . . .

Sir.

Him.

Marcus.

poppy

Now

My hangover is brutal. Earned and deserved. I must have put away at least twice as much as Bella, if not three times. Every time I thought about what had happened, what I'd found, what it could mean, I had to take another large drink.

The net result was that Bella and I both fell asleep sitting on the floor of Logan's flat, one of us having put on a CD of Christmas songs at some point. Winning. Totally and utterly winning at everything, as Alain would say.

At another undefined point of the night, I came round and managed to coax Bella into Logan's bed. We'd both slept there until six a.m. when I called us a taxi to take us to our respective homes.

I'd been aware enough to be quiet as I crawled into bed beside Alain. He was awake and hadn't said anything – he just stared at me with his lips a grim, flat line and his eyes dark mirrors of reproach, then got up to take care of our child. He even let her come in and say goodbye and managed to make it seem normal that I had slept out and hadn't called.

'Eat something,' was all he said while Betina was putting on her shoes in the corridor.

Now I am sitting at the table with my laptop, my hangover and my new-found sense of terror. What if I can't get into this USB drive? What if I can get in and I find something awful?

The first few password attempts don't work. And I don't know how many more times I'll be allowed before it locks me out permanently.

Think, Poppy, think.

I massage my temples, tap my fingernails on my teeth, jiggle my legs until my bottom feels less numb.

Think, Poppy, think.

I can't think. I can't think at all. My brain has been dulled by alcohol, by shock, by battling thoughts of still loving Marcus and so still being in the thrall of that monster.

Well I know what I'd be trying, Tina tells me.

'What's that then?' I ask. I'll take help from anyone right now.

What's he been doing all this for? Sorry, WHO has he been doing all this for?

'Me?'

Exactly!

'You think it could be my date of birth or something?'

Maybe. Or how about the day that your life, his life, your family's life changed for ever?

'The day I was found guilty? He can't have remembered that date. Not to use it as a password? Could he?'

Tina shrugs her ethereal shoulders. *What have you got to lose?*

I stare at the keyboard. Stare at the screen. Is it really that simple? Would he really use that as a passcode?

My fingers still hesitate. I always hesitate when I'm about to do something associated with that time, when it's a moment that will drag me back to that hell called my past. Then I push through. Remember

Logan lying in that bed, powerless and close to death. Recall my parents, every day sitting by his bedside as more and more of their strength drains away. Recollect Bella, devastated by the state of her best friend. I conjure up all of these things to force myself to find out what was really going on.

Tina is right. It is the date I was sent to prison.

And I am right, this white plastic rectangle does hold some of my brother's secrets.

It's hiding pictures of Logan next to Serena as she was thirty years ago. This younger, prettier version of my 'rival' smiles in every picture she is with Logan.

Snap: their heads are close together, and he is holding the phone up for a selfie.

Snap: she is laughing so much she can't look at the camera while he takes the picture.

Snap: they're sharing a peck while he takes the photo.

Snap: someone has taken a shot of their hands intertwined.

Snap: she's smiling at him over the top of a coffee mug.

Snap: she's on the seafront, in front of the bandstand, and he's made some kind of error so you only see half of her face. And even then, even with one eye, half her nose, half her lips, she looks stunning.

Snap. Snap. Snap.

There are hundreds of pictures. Hundreds! He is obsessed with her. And the way she looks at him in some of the photos, it's clear she loves him, too.

I think this is what I needed to see. It's not easy, especially not when Verity Gillmare is almost identical to Serena Gorringe, but they were in love. It wasn't . . . I don't know . . . at its core it wasn't wrong,

I suppose. She wasn't using him, he wasn't in her thrall. He wasn't using her, he wasn't abusing her.

The only other folder on the drive is also password-protected. I try many more combinations of the date I went to prison, but none of them work. Then I have an idea. The day his life and my life changed again – the date I came out of prison.

Bingo!

There's a Word document called '**Untitled.47**'. I open it and immediately see that it is a diary. It runs to a couple of hundred pages.

It doesn't take me long to see that the horror I thought I had been searching for, thought I had prepared for, was so much worse than I could ever have imagined.

serena

October, 1987

'Do you know when I first noticed you, Serena?' *he* asked me.

'No,' I replied. Straight away. He didn't like to be kept waiting, didn't understand that sometimes I needed to think about the answer to a question.

'You were walking down the corridor and you looked so lost. But determined as well. You were all these contradictions at once. It was the lost thing that caught my attention, though. It made me want to take care of you. I really wanted to take care of you for ever.'

He looked down at me, a croissant shape on the floor, my arms wrapped around my stomach, trying to hold myself together until the pain ebbed away. 'Let's make up,' he said, bending down to hoist me up into his arms as though he wasn't the one who put me on the floor. 'Come on, baby, let's make up.'

Now

It was him.

I was sure it was him. And he looked exactly the same. *Exactly* the same. As though he hadn't aged a day, as though he had crawled his way out of the past, out of wherever you go when you die to come back and oversee the long, slow destruction of my family. When *he* died, he would have been mid-thirties; if he had lived, he would be mid-sixties now. The man outside the court was not mid-sixties. He looked how he used to.

How he was when I developed a crush on him. Dark hair slightly wild to show how young he really was, strong cheekbones smoothed over by his pale-but-healthy-looking skin; eyes that were striking and stood out. I couldn't tear my eyes away earlier. I kept staring and gawking until Faye and Medina's arms slipped away and they had to shake me slightly and Fez told me that we'd been called.

Even then I didn't want to tear my eyes away; I wanted to go closer, see if my eyes were playing tricks on me without my glasses and with the distance. I shook myself out of it, slotted my game face into place and followed my sisters back into the waiting room to collect the others before we filed into the court to see if Verity would be able to come home finally.

'For pity's sake, Serena!' Faye says in my kitchen. She's obviously been calling me for a while, and I have been standing in front of the stove replaying what I saw earlier. *Was it an apparition? Was it my eyes playing tricks on me? Was it . . . ?*

'Sorry, Faye, what's going on?'

'Where were you just now?' she asks. 'Because you weren't here. I've had to call you so many times.'

I have the urge to tell her. To explain, to ask if she saw him and if not, what she thinks might be going on. Is this the start of it? Me driving myself into a mentally unstable condition because of all this blowing up again? I don't want to worry her, though. 'I'm just . . .'

I dismiss the whole thing with a wave of my hand. 'I'm just a bit, you know. It's fine. It'll pass.'

My sister, who is dressed like and has the same features as my other sister, comes closer until she is right in front of me – so close the words we speak can be quiet and hushed. 'What's going on?' she asks. 'I'm not going to let this happen again, OK? Thirty years ago I knew something was up, you changed and I just let it go. Almost every day I wish I had made you talk to me, tell me so things might have had the chance to turn out differently. I'm not going to let that happen again, all right? Tell me what's going on.'

She's right, of course. If I had told all those years ago, things may have turned out differently. If I hadn't lied about my injuries, about the brutal way he started to have sex with me, the emotional torture of trying to be perfect all the time so he wouldn't get upset, the mental pressure of knowing one day he would use the knife he regularly held to my throat to actually kill me if I did try to leave, Verity might not be where she is today.

'Evan and me, we're not getting on,' I confess. 'Or rather, I'm not getting on with him because . . . I . . .' I step closer to my sister, lower my voice to barely above a whisper. 'Because I think she could have, might have, done it. He hates me for thinking like that. And I hate me for thinking like that.'

'Isn't the last part the bit that's responsible for everything else?' Faye asks, not at all fazed by what I've just said. I just told her that I think my daughter is guilty and she hasn't flinched.

'I don't follow.'

'You hate yourself for this. You think it's all your fault and you're angry at yourself. And you're angry at Verity because she's essentially

311

you in this situation, and she represents everything you did wrong. You still hate yourself for what happened, don't you?'

'You make it sound like I wasn't there. Yes, I still hate myself for what I did. Not "what happened", that takes away the responsibility.'

'Serena . . .' My sister's face becomes a rainbow of emotions, she's struggling to control herself. 'Serena, we all know so much more than we did back then. You were groomed by a person in a position of trust and authority. I mean, back then we didn't know half of what we know about grooming now. None of us understood how powerful and dangerous it can be when someone focuses on you in that way. You were fifteen and you were essentially brainwashed to accept anything, including being coerced into sex with him. After that, he regularly beat you, he repeatedly raped you, he threatened to kill you if you left him. Those *were* all things that happened *to* you. Those were all things that someone else forced upon you. You didn't do that. You're not responsible, someone did that to you.'

It doesn't sound possible and it doesn't sound right. Because that wasn't the complete picture. He was nice to me. So often he was nice to me. So often he would be caring. And sometimes the sex was gentle and close and loving. And sometimes he would stop himself lashing out at me, he would think twice and say he was disappointed instead. It wasn't always as bad as she's telling me.

'I know Vee being involved with Carlisle complicates things and makes it feel like it's the same as what you went through, but it's not. She's not you. And even if she was you, you still deserve all the compassion you'd show anyone else in that situation.' My sister rests her hand on my shoulder, calms me with her touch and the timbre of her voice. 'Give her a chance. Give her the space to have messed up, completely fucked up, and it not being about you.'

'You're right,' I say to her. And she is. This is about Vee, not me. And if she did do it, if she did try to kill Logan Carlisle, then I'll have to deal with that when the knowledge comes.

'How did you get to be so wise?' I ask Fez. She's undone a couple of buttons on her waistcoat and several on her shirt. My older sister is pretty darn sexy. She's taken to shaving her hair because she can't be bothered with the upkeep and it makes her even more striking. Ten years ago she would never have even contemplated it.

'A fuck-ton of therapy,' she replies happily.

'Are you really in therapy?' I ask, surprised. Out of Faye and Medina, I would never have thought she would be the one telling me she does this.

'Yes, no shame here about it. I had to find a way to deal with the fact that I wasn't ever going to have children while you and Mez were mothers.

'It started as couple's therapy with Harry. I thought, ahhh, why deny it? I thought I'd be able to change his mind about the baby thing. I mean, I just needed someone who he respected to back me up and it'd work, right? Wrong. It just showed me that, actually, it was a good thing we didn't have kids.

'I had so much resentment for that man. He had basically wasted my time all those years. I didn't even realise how much I'd built my life around him and his career and what he needed and wanted. All because I loved him. When really, it was because I was scared to be alone. And he had – probably unknowingly – used that to make the relationship exactly how he wanted. So, after six sessions, I kept the therapist and kicked Harry out.'

'What?' I say. 'When was this?'

'About a year after your non-wedding renewal.'

'I had no idea! And you and Harry are still together.'

'Yes, we are. But that's because we got back together. There were so many conditions on us trying again and, funnily enough, none of them involved trying for a baby because that ship had sailed.

'I just wanted something like you and Evan have. Something that's equal and honest. And I know I was a bitch to you about you not telling him everything about yourself and I was devastated when you split for that time, but you two are like the gold standard of relationships. Turns out I could have that with Harry if I stopped letting him walk all over me and my boundaries. So now, I have boundaries and I have a relationship that is equal and I have a whole new way to big-sister you and Medina.'

'Did Medina know about this?'

'Yup. Mainly because it was around the same time that she gave Adrian an ultimatum about his involvement in their family life. Either get all in or get out. He cleaned up his act for a bit, then just got progressively worse. Until he came at her with the "I'm not sure I love you any more" line. I think he thought she'd buckle and would do anything to keep him. Instead she told him to jog on. Literally. She said, "Jog on, buddy." He realised too late that he'd overplayed his hand and basically had to work incredibly hard to get her back.'

'How come I haven't noticed all this? It's like I've been asleep.'

'Life is busy, and it wasn't exactly what we wanted to talk about. You and Evan had just got back together, the last thing you needed was to hear our stuff and find another excuse to blame yourself for shit that's not your fault. And it's been more than fine for years so no need to bring it up.'

'Wish you'd told me.'

'I did, just now. This was the right time to tell you. Everything happens when it's meant to.'

'You've really taken to therapy, haven't you? But why are you still seeing her – I assume it's a her – if it's fine with Harry now?'

'Are you joking? I have so much to unpack. I don't see her all the time, but she was my lifeline when Daddy died. I couldn't have coped without her.'

Medina enters the kitchen almost at a run. 'What are you two doing out here? Everyone's gasping and you're out here gassing.'

I move away from Fez and go to her, wrap my arms around my younger big sister. 'Oh God, what's happened?' Medina asks. 'Why are you hugging me like this? Am I ill? What's going to happen to me?'

'I just told her about you and Adrian splitting up. And me and Harry splitting up and me being in long-term therapy,' Faye says. She really is a different woman. I haven't really noticed that. Faye was always pretty taciturn and slightly removed, but thinking back, she has been more open, less critical in the past few years.

'Oh, that,' Medina says.

'Yes, that, sister who doesn't tell me anything.'

'There was nothing to tell. It's all sorted. Just like all of this is going to be sorted out in no time.'

I'd forgotten. For a few short minutes I'd forgotten why they were here. I step back and as I leave the huggableness of my sister, worry clambers back into place.

'Trust you, Mez,' Faye spits. 'I swear . . . I had taken her mind off it and you've brought her right back down again.'

'Well, if you'd bothered to engage that twin telepathy you tortured me for hours trying to perfect when we were kids, I might have known your grand plan.'

'I don't have grand plans, remember? That's on you.'

'You don't have grand plans? All you live for is to plan stuff.'

'Well, at least I know which college I went to.'

'I know which college I went to,' Medina says.

'Are you sure? Because weren't you the one who "forgot" which college you were enrolled in and only "remembered" when you'd got Daddy to drive you halfway to another place?'

'It was an honest mistake. Anyone could have made it.'

'Funny how it was only you, Messy Mez, who made it.'

My squabbling sisters don't even notice when I leave the kitchen. Once they've got themselves into this mode, there is very little that will stop them. Verity is just leaving the living room at the same time and stops, a terrified rabbit caught and literally petrified in the head-lights of my presence.

'Is it OK if I go to the loo?' she asks.

'Of course. This is your home. You can go to the toilet whenever you choose.'

'Thanks,' she mumbles.

I stand and watch her go. I'm going to have to talk to her.

But will she want to talk to me?

serena

Now

'We're the gold standard, apparently,' I say to Evan.

He's reading in bed, bare-chested with his glasses perched at the end of his nose. 'That's nice,' he says dismissively.

This is the closest we've got to normal conversation since this all began and I'm sure he's still a bit annoyed with me. Just as I was – am? – with him. I pull back the covers on my side of the bed and slide in.

'Don't you even want to know what for?'

I see him grit his teeth, almost roll his eyes, but not turn to me as he asks, 'What are we the gold standard for?'

'I'll tell you when you're a little less *distracted*,' I snipe because I'm trying here and he's giving me nothing. Since our row, since we silently agreed to disagree, which actually meant we hid our testiness with each other in front of Conrad and barely spoke at other times, neither of us has made the effort I am making now. Yes, I want us to start speaking again, but I'm not trying alone.

Irritation oscillates across Evan's face, his eyes stare into the mid-distance beyond his book before he fixes his expression and turns to me. 'What are we the gold standard for?'

I carefully take his book from him and place it on my bedside table.

'What are we the gold standard for?' he asks again. He's looking tired, frazzled and frayed around the edges. This is what I noticed about myself when I looked in the mirror earlier. Life seems to be catching up with us; things seem to be nibbling away at the sorted life we thought we had and one of the side effects of those nibbles is this: looking older than our years.

I move up the covers so I can climb up and sit astride him. He is suddenly willing to take me seriously now that I'm in front of him, not giving him much choice. 'Faye and Medina—'

'Oh, it's a Witches of Ipswich thing, is it?' Evan asks.

I slip my hands into the waistband of the Brighton and Hove Albion footie-kit shorts he wears to bed and tug them down past his hips to his thighs.

'Yes, it's a Witches thing.'

I grip him firmly then run my hand up and down the full length of his erection. I grin as this contorts his face in pleasure, causes a groan to escape his lips.

Slowly I take off my nightshirt and toss it to one side. Then my hand is back on him, moving up and down, tantalisingly slowly, drawing out the seconds of delight.

'Tell me,' he says, trying to sound normal while I'm teasing him.

'They think we have the type of relationship they've both been striving for all these years.'

Still holding him, I shift forward, push the tip of him against me and rock back and forward.

'Do they?' he pants.

I place one hand on his shoulder, lift myself up and then guide him into me as I sink down onto the full length of him.

We both softly groan this time as we become one. 'They do,' I reply when I can speak.

I rock against him, making sure we keep eye contact. 'That's nice,' he says between his teeth.

'Isn't . . . it . . . just,' I eventually manage. 'Isn't . . . it . . . just.'

Suddenly Evan takes control by grabbing my hips. He holds me in place as he starts to forcefully thrust into me.

I bite down again, try to move but he refuses to let me, keeps me in place while he drives himself into me. Our eyes are linked as he finally loosens his grip, but only so he can move me up and down on him, shifting gear again.

Everything is fierce and fast, full and pulsing with pleasure and need and a desperation to connect like this. My hand claws into his shoulder, and 'UHHHHH,' Evan cries loudly, forgetting himself.

'Shhhhhh,' I hush before I clamp my hand over his mouth. 'Shh-hhh!' Our children are down the hall, they do not need to hear this.

Grimacing then smirking, he doesn't break stroke, instead he speeds up, intensifies how forcefully he moves me on top of him. My fingers curl into his shoulders as I let myself go, allow him to take me, move me, fill me, pound at me until I can feel the pleasure rushing through my bloodstream, careening and galloping, going on and on until I throw my head back, bite down hard on my bottom teeth and let the orgasm flood through me, through every part of me and into Evan, as he stops mid-thrust and silently, almost violently, comes with me.

Minutes later, Evan says, 'Gold standard, huh?' He's composed himself, redressed himself and gathered me in his arms.

I've missed this these past few days, I've missed the closeness that's always been effortless between us. Even after we split up and got back together, cuddling and holding each other wasn't an issue.

'That's what the other Witches say.'

'I'm glad the outside world can see how perfect we are for each other.'

'Let's not do this again, Evan, OK?' I say.

'What, you don't want to have sex any more?'

'No, silly. The other thing. Where we fall out and just sort of drift apart. Let's not do that again. Because it doesn't have to be rowing that splits people apart: it's not talking, it's letting the resentments grow until they're insurmountable.'

'Yes, I know.'

'We are the gold standard, after all.'

'Yes, we are. But, Serena . . . I have to tell you, it's always going to be the kids before you. You know that, right?'

'Yes, it's always been the kids before you for me, as well. But . . .'

'But?'

'But this thing with Verity is complicated by so many factors. And until we know what's going on, I'm just . . . Faye told me that I'm seeing me in her so I'm being harder on her than I normally would be.'

'She's right. And that's sort of what I mean. I'm not completely closed off to the idea that she might have done it.' He lowers his voice to say that in case she can hear down the corridor. 'But until I know otherwise, my daughter is innocent until proven guilty. And it doesn't matter who says otherwise. Not even you.'

He's right, of course. Just like Faye was right. 'Yes, I agree. I've got to stop thinking she's me.'

'Yes, you do. She's going to need you. Not only because you're her mum but also you've been there. You need to remember what it was like and how scary it was. And what you wanted from your parents when it was happening to you.'

'You're right,' I say to him. 'You're absolutely right.'

'Wow, I should buy a lottery ticket or something – you've just said I'm right about something.'

'Watch it you, Gold Standard Man.'

Evan smiles before he reaches for the bedside table lamp and flicks it off. 'Come here,' he says and pulls me back into his arms. He gently strokes his hand down my face. 'I love you. And I love this face. And I never want to be without you.'

'Me, too.'

'Go to sleep now, Sez. I know you haven't been sleeping these past few days, go to sleep now. It'll make everything seem so much better in the morning.'

Better is going to be impossible, but I don't tell Evan that. Better is what we can hope for. Not as bad is probably what we'll get.

I close my eyes and it comes to me suddenly.

Sir. Him. Marcus.

He was there today.

verity

Now

Beccie: Where's Howie?

Beccie: He was coming to you. I know he was.

Beccie: I heard him on the phone. He was whispering, but I heard him saying he was coming. I heard him say he loved you.

Beccie: Don't ignore me, Verity.

Beccie: Where is he?

Beccie: Verity, where is Howie?

Beccie: The police think he's gone on the run because he was protecting you from your boyfriend. Where is he?

Beccie: Look, just tell me what happened. I won't tell anyone, not even the police. What happened?

Beccie: Did you know we were thinking of getting married? Next year. He was saving up for the perfect ring. It's not like him not to be in touch.

Beccie: Verity, please. I love him. He's my everything. I love him. I love him. I love him.

Beccie: Why don't you at least reply. You're so rude!!!!

My phone has been blowing up with messages all day. Actually, since the moment I left the police station and came home the messages started. Then, though, it was only one or two. Today, she must have had a cup or two of the neurotic lemonade because she has been messaging me non-stop.

'Who's desperate to get a piece of you?' Dad asks as he enters the kitchen and sees my phone lighting up, the other messages lit up with it.

'Howie's girlfriend/fiancée/wife/babymother-to-be depending on which message you read.'

'Beccie, her name is, yes?'

'Yes.'

'So why does she want you so badly?'

'She thinks I know where he is. I don't know where he is. Even if I did know, I wouldn't tell her.'

Dad sets about making a cup of tea and I watch Beccie continue to meltdown on my phone. Darryl told me quite clearly that they never give people back their phones in my situation. *Never.* He'd been at pains to tell me this, because he wanted me to know that they were monitoring it – the police would be using my phone as a way to find out if I would try to contact Howie, if Howie would contact me, or if I would try to go and meet him. Darryl didn't explicitly tell me not to send or reply to any texts or messages nor not to do any internet searches, nor to go anywhere that wasn't the local shops, he just said, after the fifth time of telling me they never give people back their phones, 'You like television and reading, don't you? You like staying at home, don't you?' as a way of saying my phone would be used to track my every move.

'You don't like her, then?' Dad asks.

'That would be correct.'

'Is that anything to do with her being the person your "friend" is in a bad relationship with?'

I am clearly as subtle as a brick. 'What do you mean?'

'How bad is it?' Dad replies. He stands in front of the kettle as it starts to boil, arms folded across his chest, staring at me.

'If I tell you, you'll have to report it and I can't risk that.'

'I didn't say I'd have to report it. I said if they were vulnerable or in danger of being immediately hurt or killed, I'd have to do something about it. How bad?'

'It's bad, Dad. He didn't want me to tell anyone. He was so ashamed. The worst thing in the world for him was anyone finding out, anyone guessing what was happening.'

'How long has it been going on for?'

'I don't know. He's been having accidents for years. Told me he was mugged, bashed himself on gym equipment, fell down some stairs. So many things, all plausible. Until he was arrested for the second time for hurting her. He called me to come and get him because he couldn't go home. That's when he told me. I couldn't believe what I was hearing.'

Another message comes up on my phone. Then another. And another.

'He's been arrested a few times because other people have heard and have called the police. She always manages to convince them that he's the violent one. And because he doesn't want anyone to know, he never tells them what happened. You know she actually says, "It's my fault, I did this," and no one realises that she's actually confessing. No one ever believes the man in these situations.'

My father ignores the boiling kettle and comes to the table, sits down opposite me.

'It's not that simple, Verity,' he says. 'Women are far more abused than men.'

'Yes, but men are abused, too.'

'I know they are. I'm not saying they're not. But, Vee, it's a reality that a lot of abusive men spend a lot of time convincing the world that they are the victim. They create a reality and a story that is completely separate to what the real victim is living with and they gaslight her, and friends and family, colleagues, and sometimes even the police, into giving them sympathy and support that they don't deserve. At its core, abuse has manipulation, and abusive people are excellent at manipulating others.'

I go to speak but Dad continues, 'And yes, abusive women do that, too. But I'm telling you, the "no one believes men" line is not helpful. Not for anyone. It pushes well-meaning people to start giving the benefit of the doubt even when all other evidence suggests the abuser isn't the victim but the perpetrator.'

'I see what you're saying.'

'Do you know where Howie is?' he asks.

I shake my head. I really don't and I feel awful for dragging him into it. *Dreadful.* I am literally full of dread about what happened and where he is.

'Seeing what Howie went through, reading other stuff, that's why I know Darryl – Mr Palmer – was wrong about Logan being abusive.'

'Your solicitor thinks he was abusive?'

'He wasn't, Dad. Isn't. Logan isn't abusive. He didn't do anything like what Beccie did to Howie.' I shake my head. 'She didn't just hit him, she made his life a misery.' I pick up my phone, show him the number of new messages that have come up. 'This is nothing compared to what she'd send him if he dared to go out without her. I mean, I didn't care. She could ring a million times when we were out together, it didn't bother me if he was late or if he had to leave early. If she turned up unannounced, I welcomed her joining us. He was always trying to please her, keep her happy so she wouldn't freak out at him. And also so she was happy. He wanted nothing more than for her to be happy. That was nothing like what I had with Logan.'

Dad nods while staring at my phone, which continues to flash up with message after message after message.

'When was the last time you saw Zephie? Before the party, I mean.'

'We're both really busy.'

'She's your oldest, closest friend.'

'We're both just really busy.'

'When was the last time you saw Howie, before all this kicked off?'

'It wasn't easy when Beccie was so controlling.'

'But up until what, six months ago, Beccie's controlling nature wasn't a problem with seeing him, was it? I mean, he came for Sunday lunch that time and he was on the list for my party.'

'I don't know. I've been really busy.'

'And what about your brother? When was the last time you saw Conrad, Verity? You and him used to go to the same clubs, and you let him crash at your place whenever he wanted. When did you last spend time with your brother because you woke up and found him asleep on your couch?'

Dad stares at me so intently I have to redirect my eyes to the phone he was just staring at.

Logan wasn't abusive; I wasn't abused by him. I know what abuse looks like and it was what Howie went through, what Mum went through, it wasn't the normal ups and downs of a relationship.

'I know you've had your problems recently, but I think you should talk to your mother,' Dad says gently. 'Abuse isn't always what you think. It doesn't look the same for every relationship.'

'I suppose it wouldn't,' I say.

He stands. 'And think about turning your phone off. It's not going to do you any good seeing those messages one after the other.'

I nod.

But I can't, of course, because Howie might call me. Text me. Find a way to contact me. And I need to know what's happening to him. I need to know that he's OK. And I need to know it wasn't him who tried to kill my boyfriend.

August, 2018

'She's going to kill you, you know that, don't you?'

I was angry with Howie. More frustrated, actually. And scared. So panicky my heart was fluttering in my chest. We sat in my kitchen with my first-aid box open on the table. His lip was split, his eye was going to be swelling very soon and his top was off because I'd had to tape up his ribs. He hadn't done anything to defend himself except curl up into a ball and wait for her rage to burn itself out. 'She's going to kill you because – what was it this time? You didn't put the guest towels away in the guest towel drawer?'

'It wasn't that simple, Vee. She's told me so many times about doing that. It makes her life more difficult because she's the one who has to get the flat ready when people come to stay.'

'Well, that's all right, then. I think it's so much more important that it's easy for her to get her hands on coordinating towels than it is for you to walk around with unbruised ribs.'

Howie grabbed my hand, stopped it dabbing at his lip and slipped his fingers through mine. 'Don't be angry with me,' he said.

'I'm not angry,' I said. 'I'm frightened. She's getting worse; the cycle of good to bad times is getting shorter, and the violence is getting worse. She's not even bothering to find proper reasons any more. I'm scared she's going to kill you. Over fucking guest towels. Not even proper towels, guest ones.'

That made Howie smile, as it was meant to.

He dropped my hand and instead put his arm around my waist, pulled me towards him.

'Why did we never get together?' he asked. 'I mean, we're perfect for each other. How come it never happened?' He was trying to distract me from bringing up the horror show that was his relationship, how he was defending his girlfriend's right to beat him up because of towels. (This time it was towels, last time it was not wiping his shoes on the mat.)

He was trying that distraction technique with the wrong person – yes we could talk about this, but it wouldn't stop me going back to the original conversation. 'Oh, I don't know, Howie, I guess it was never really meant to be. I mean, I wasn't interested in a relationship, you don't fancy dark-skin girls . . . So . . .' I shrugged.

In the bright lights of my kitchen, Howie had the good grace to look thoroughly ashamed. 'I do fancy dark-skin girls,' he replied quietly, redirecting his gaze away from anywhere we might make eye contact.

'All right, you don't go out with dark-skin girls.'

'I admit I didn't go out with dark-skin girls when we met.' He was trying to deny it without denying it. 'I may have changed my ways since then.'

'Really? Been out with any dark-skin girls since college?'

'I go out with you all the time,' he replied.

'Yeah, thought so,' I told him, cutting my eyes at him. This was not the time for this conversation, although when would be was never quite clear. 'You asked why we never got together and that is the reason.'

'Hey, back up there, sister, you said you weren't interested in a relationship, don't be putting all of that on me.'

'Howie, if your fine self had asked me out, I would have said yes in a heartbeat. Why do you think I came and sat down next to you at college on the first day? There were other Black guys in the canteen that day, but even when you were goofy Howard I was . . . I didn't fancy you so much as completely fall in love with you at first sight. You were like my soulmate from the moment I talked to you. I mean, I wasn't interested in going out with anyone or having a relationship, but if you, the person I could talk to, just chill with, laugh with, cry with, had shown any indication that he could fancy me, that he thought of me in the way he saw white and mixed-race girls, I would have been there for it. No messing.'

My best male friend, my soul mate, stared at me, his unbattered eye wide with shock. He had no idea what to say because he had had no idea that I was completely in love with him. He was probably also shocked that he'd been called out on his particular type of misogynoir by me of all people.

'Don't get me wrong, Howie, I wasn't pining for you or anything like that, and I haven't put my love life on hold for you, but up until quite recently, if you had asked me out, I would have said yes before the words had finished leaving your mouth. But that wasn't in our story, was it?'

He shook his head, still a little discombobulated.

'And don't worry, my mother and father brought me up to see how beautiful I am. So I have more than enough self-esteem to see my beauty and not worry about why you don't fancy someone as dark as me. And I can still be your friend as well.' I rested my hand lightly on his shoulder. 'Your best friend at that.' I lowered my face to his level. 'And as your best friend, I am going to say again – she's going to kill you.'

'Vee, don't—'

'I have to, Howie. That's what best friends are for. I need to tell you this. I don't know what to do but I have to tell you that she's going to kill you if you don't get out.'

'Thing is, Vee, I love her. And I know she loves me. It's just things are difficult for her right now. It'll be fine. She doesn't mean for things to get out of hand. It'll be all right. I just need to try a bit harder. Romance her a bit more. It'll be fine. It'll be fine.'

I nodded because I couldn't co-sign that nonsense he was talking. I couldn't pretend that she wasn't going to do anything except get worse until she did kill him.

Now

I keep watching my phone receive message after message from Beccie. Logan was nothing like her. He was nothing like Marcus Halnsley. He wasn't abusive. If there was one thing I was sure of, it was that Logan wasn't abusive.

poppy

Now

I hate her.

I actually hate her. I can't believe she's done this. She's been doing this.

You see her, with those cheekbones, those eyes and that smile. When they're together in the photos, they look so happy. Joyful. I think that's what Alain and I would want to look like if we did loved-up selfies.

But it wasn't how they made it look. Maybe those were the easy times, the happy times, the times when being together didn't hurt.

I have read his diary and I hate her. I just hate her.

verity

Now

I keep thinking about what Darryl said to me *about* me.

'Women in your situation.' Was I really in a 'situation'?

I didn't feel like I was. I had seen abuse. I had seen when someone had their lives limited, when they'd been hit and couldn't leave. I could have left any time. Did I need to leave? Or was what I had with Logan part of a normal relationship, part of the peaks and troughs a woman had with her significant other? That's what it felt like. Normal.

Logan didn't control me. He didn't isolate me. He didn't stop me doing what I wanted.

November, 2019

'From the state of the place, I think your brother was here earlier,' Logan said to me over dinner.

I'd come back late from work and found Logan in the flat. He'd borrowed my spare key to let himself back in that first Sunday morning when he got breakfast and had sort of kept it. I didn't mind too much and it seemed petty to keep asking for it back when he made the same trip every week. He had originally only used it on Sundays, but lately I'd come home to find the alarm off and Logan in my flat.

I still hadn't worked out how I felt about that. It felt, in an odd way, like an invasion; him pushing us into something I wasn't sure I was ready for. But it wasn't unpleasant. Especially if, like this evening, I came home and the flat had been tidied, the washing-up done, dinner cooked and lowlights were on with soft music.

'Yes, he was definitely here earlier. He went out with his mates in town and wasn't going home to deal with Mum and Dad in that state so he crashed here.'

'Has he always had a key?'

'Yup. He's my annoying little brother but, you know, mi casa su casa and all that.'

Logan nodded. 'OK.' He carried on nodding, avoiding my eye and concentrating very hard on the ribbons of pasta he'd made from scratch using the pasta maker he'd brought from his place, and the red sauce he'd also made from scratch. I'd got to know him these last few months and it was obvious that he had something to say but knew I wouldn't like it so was staring at his delicious meal instead.

'What's the problem?' I asked. I was concentrating on my food now, too.

'No problem . . .'

But . . . I thought rather uncharitably.

'But,' he obliged, 'he left the place in a mess.'

'I know, he does that. I saw it this morning and knew I'd be tidying it later.' I shrugged happily. 'But turns out I didn't have to cos you did it for me.'

Logan was not happy. Or amused. Not even in the slightest. 'He should really be tidying up after himself. Especially if he's staying in someone else's house.'

'He does, usually. He just had to dash off to school this morning.'

'OK.'

It was not OK, clearly. 'If you've got something to say, I really wish you'd say it.'

'Look, it's not my flat, not my life and not my brother . . .'

But . . .

'But I could smell drugs when I came over. Someone had clearly been smoking weed in here.'

Is that it? Is that what he was so bent out of shape about? 'He smokes a little weed every now and again with his friends. It's really no big deal.'

'Thing is, it could be a big deal. If one of your neighbours smells it and reports it, you could seriously damage your chances of being offered a job when you finish training. Or at the very least be in a lot of trouble.'

He was being melodramatic. A bit. No one was going to report me. Why would they? I got on well with my neighbours, my neighbours got on with me. Why would anyone report me? 'Why would anyone report me?' I asked him.

'People do all sorts of strange things for strange reasons.' He stabbed at his pasta, looking dejected. 'I'm only trying to help. I shouldn't have said anything.'

'No, no, I appreciate it, I really do.' I played sadly with my pasta. He was probably right. I shouldn't have let it go as far along as it had. Con was soon to do his A-levels, smoking drugs was probably the last thing he should be doing right now if he wanted to get into his first choice of college. And it would be disastrous if I was caught with drugs. Even if they were someone else's, it would still be bad enough to be associated with drugs. Because I wasn't one of the bigwigs at work for whom people would turn a blind eye if they did a few lines in the toilets or at home on the weekend, or a bit of puffing to relax. Those rules would not apply to me. Nor to Con.

Mum and Dad ignored what he did because he was generally with me and they knew he was safe, but he would be in a world of trouble if he got caught. His college prospects would disappear.

I didn't want to hear it, but Logan had a point.

'You don't have to talk to him about it or anything,' he said. 'I was just raising it because I care about you. And I'm not sure how wise it is for him – and particularly his friends – to have access to your home when you're not here. Like I say, I'm only bringing it up because I care.'

'I know you do.' I squeezed his hand across the table. 'And thank you. It's nice that you care.'

Now

Was that an abusive act? It didn't feel like it. He was looking out for me and he did have a point. But that was about the same time I lost my keys. They just disappeared and I couldn't be sure where I lost them so I had to change all the locks. And I didn't get around to giving Con new keys or even telling him the locks had changed. He didn't mention it, so I'd just assumed that he hadn't been over in a while. We didn't talk as much after that. We didn't spend as much time together. I didn't see the Brain's Trust at all. And, looking back now, into the vacuum that the absence of Conrad and the Brain's Trust created in my life stepped Logan. Not even my other friends. Logan. Only Logan. Was that what Darryl meant?

January, 2020

I wasn't sure whether to roll my eyes, laugh or scream.

Things were going wrong for Zeph again. I loved Zeph, right from when she was Zephie and I was VeeGee and we wore Afro puffs and over-the-knee socks and didn't get what most people were into at school. We were tight, we were closer than sisters and nothing could come between us.

Zeph was a love warrior; the bravest of love soldiers who was always trying to find the person who would match her heart, whose soul would align with hers . . . But she was constantly being thwarted. Her latest thwart involved a man who had seemed perfect, so perfect we'd been making arrangements for me to meet him. I liked the sound of him. I liked the sound of the happy sparkles in her voice when she talked about him.

Only a couple of times had I wondered if he sounded too good to be true. And, ultimately, he was. No affair, no drugs, no gambling, no dodgy sexual practices. He just decided that he didn't want to be with Zeph any more. As simple as that. He wanted to concentrate on his art and that was it.

'I know he means it,' Zeph wept on the phone to me. 'It'd be easier if he was leaving me for another person, or because he was an addict cos then I'd have an excuse. But to just leave me for nothing. Nothing! I mean, he even told me he loved me and he cared about me but he just wanted to concentrate on his art.'

'That sounds like the old "it's not you it's me" bollocks,' I'd replied.

'That's totally what it is. And everyone knows that's a load of lies, except he meant it. He actually meant it.'

I was so frustrated for her! Her heart deserved to find its twin, its beloved. She did not deserve this.

I climbed into bed beside a should-be-sleeping Logan. He'd been about to turn off the television when my phone had flashed up with the call.

'Who was the S.O.S from?' he asked. He flicked off the bedside lamp and snuggled up to me. Logan's snuggles were the best. Apart from his smile and his laugh and cooking and his jokes and his ability to make sex feel out of this world, he was also excellent with the snuggles. With wrapping himself around me and transferring not only his body heat but the feeling of being completely, totally adored.

Being with Logan had given me a bit of insight into what Zeph was craving, what a lot of people were probably desperate for. To be honest, until Logan, I'd never really known what the fuss was all about. What the feelings were all about. Now I had it, I didn't blame Zeph – and others – for doing almost anything to feel it again.

'Zeph.' I'd told him about Zeph, mainly because I couldn't tell Zeph about him. I'd wanted to, but the complications . . . whew! Explaining about Mum . . . double whew!

'What's happened now?'

'I can't even tell you. It's complicated but not – the short of the long of it is that it's over with the latest guy. Artist Dude is no longer.'

'Of course not.'

I lifted my head from Logan's chest and frowned at him. He could see my frown in the dark. 'What's that supposed to mean?' I sounded a little more stern than necessary. I was fiercely protective of my girl.

'It means the world was waiting with bated breath to find out how Zeph was going to end up on her own again.'

'Don't talk about my girl like that.'

'I'm not talking about her like anything.'

'Yes, you are. And I don't like it. I've known Zeph since we were five. Don't trash-talk her to me. Or anyone. Don't trash-talk my friend, Logan. It's not cool.'

'I wasn't trash-talking her. Why would I? I like the sound of Zeph very much. From what you've said, she's a great person and has been an excellent friend to you over the years. I am not trash-talking her. I am merely saying she is drama.'

Zeph *was* drama. Always had been. But that wasn't the point, was it? She wasn't harming him, or anyone except possibly herself. It wasn't for Logan to say such things, even if it was true. And he didn't get to have an opinion when he hadn't even been told by her that his knees were ashy and he needed to moisturise. Until you were *that* close to a person you didn't get to make such loud, bold pronouncements.

'You only know what I've told you. So if you extrapolate what I've said into anything other than "she's a good person who has had a run of bad luck in love" then I'm not a very good friend and you're out of order for joining up the things I've said in that way.'

'I didn't mean anything by it.'

'Yes, you did.'

'I didn't. It's just—'

'It's just what, Logan?'

'*Nothing!*' he hissed. '*Absolutely nothing. I shouldn't have opened my mouth.*'

'Come on, tell me.'

'Only if you don't come for me again.'

'I can't promise that if you trash-talk my friend again.'

'I wasn't trash-talking her!'

'What were you doing? Cos that's what it sounded like.'

Logan's sigh rose up in the dark, seeming to grow rather than dissipate. 'All right, Zeph sounds like a great person. But what is it about her that attracts these kinds of relationships? These kinds of men? I mean, you and her grew up together and went to college at the same time and I'm betting it's always been like this with her. That men treat her badly, dump her, put her down, make her feel awful. That's all I meant – of course it was over with this latest guy, who you made sound perfect, because that's what happens to Zeph.'

I didn't say anything because it was nothing I hadn't thought myself. I didn't understand how these things always seemed to happen to her. I could fill a book with the disasters that had befallen Zeph in her search for love.

'She's a really good person and people take advantage of her,' I replied.

'I know, I know. And I feel for her. But aren't you sick of the drama?'

Of course I was. So was she. I wished so much she would finally get what she wanted. That someone would love her and see her for who she was – a beautiful soul inside and out.

'Logan, it's not for you to say that. She's my friend and I'll always support her, no matter what. And no, I'm not sick of her drama. There is no "drama".'

'I know, I know, and your loyalty is one of the things I love about you most.'

He cuddled back into me, trying to charm his way back into my good books. 'Boy, you're fierce when you think someone you love is under attack.'

'Of course, isn't everyone?'

'Well, I hope you get like that about me one day. Because that would mean I'm someone you love.'

'Maybe I will, who knows?'

'I can't believe I've just told you that I love you and you've ignored it,' Logan stated.

'I didn't ignore it as such, I just wasn't going to let you say it by stealth. Either say it properly or leave it out.'

'All right,' he began as he stared at me. 'Verity Gillmare, I'm pleased to report that the process is complete – I love you. I completely and utterly love you.'

'And I . . .' I felt a sudden flutter of nerves, the butterflies of anxiety flitting up and filling my chest with frantic worrying. I'd never said this before. And I was going to say it to a man I couldn't talk to my parents about. Really? *Really?*

'Don't worry about saying it back.' Logan must have read my mind or something. 'You don't go from fiercely protective of a friend to dropping the L word. You just say it when you're ready. It's enough to know that I love you.' He dropped a kiss on my lips. 'Because I absolutely do.'

I received his kisses as, inside, a tidal wave of emotion welled up. Poor Zeph. I could never tell her about this. About how easy this was. Despite the obvious, being with Logan was easy. I could never tell Zeph about any of it because it would wound her. And I didn't want to hurt her by flaunting the fact I had what she craved.

I hated keeping this from her, but I had to protect her. And she would know if she saw me that I was with someone. And I couldn't tell her about it. Not even a fraction of it. Logan was right about one thing: this happened to Zeph far too often, and my being happy on my first go? Oh, Zeph – I couldn't rub her face in it like that. I'd take a step back from seeing her as much, at least until things calmed down with Logan and I wasn't so loved up.

'I love you, Logan,' I whispered in the middle of the night when he was fast asleep. And I swear, I'm sure I saw him smile.

Now

And there. Because of what he had said, how brilliant he made me feel, I had backed away from Zeph. No one made me, he didn't have a bad thing to say about her, but still, the net result was me retreating from her. She told me as much at Dad's party. I'd been trying to be kind to her. But wasn't that patronising? She was an adult, she could handle my being loved up because she was my friend. And Zeph would be there for the good as well as the bad. He hadn't said anything directly, no, but like the thing with my brother, I had decided to back off after speaking to Logan.

They were the two main branches of my support network. And they were removed. And then there was the stuff with Howie.

'I'm sure your family and friends will have noticed,' Darryl had said to me.

And there were other things. Little things. But did that mean—?

I almost jump out of my skin when there's a small, polite knock at the door. 'Knock knock, who's there? Me, so let me in, and let me in now,' Conrad calls from my doorway.

'Come in,' I reply because he does actually wait for me to do that. When he was small, he used to say that all the time at my bedroom door. Small. That seems like a lifetime ago now. My brother is so huge, so masculine, it's hard to believe he was ever anything other than the man he is now.

Mum used to baby him all the time when he was little and he just never seemed to find anything difficult. And even though it irritated me – a lot – I also used to love him so much it hurt. I would totally, without a second thought, hurt anyone who tried to mess with him. I had a visceral need to protect him. I suppose because I was six when he was born and I felt responsible for him.

I think things changed between us when Mum left ten years ago for a short period of time. They thought we didn't know, but it was obvious that she wasn't staying at home all the time. And it scared us both. Suddenly all certainty that both Mum and Dad would be there no matter what, all the time, for ever and ever, Amen, was shattered like a dropped glass – you could see bits of it, but it wasn't cohesive and it looked like it would never be whole and tangible ever again. That was when we decided that the moments of not getting on and fighting and sometimes full-on hating on each other had to get smaller and shorter, and the rest of it, when we cared and looked out for each other, had to get longer and become the norm.

I remember going into his room one night and finding him crying because he was convinced Mum wasn't coming back. 'Doesn't matter,' I ended up whispering as I knelt by his bed, trying to get him to stop sobbing. 'Doesn't matter if she doesn't come back or Dad leaves, because I'm always going to be around.'

I wasn't sure if what I said was a comfort to him or if the thought of being stuck with just me terrified the tears out of him, but he stopped crying and he let me hug him.

'You got a minute?' he asks as all six-foot-something of him wanders into my room. 'What am I saying, you've got all the time in the world, jailbird.'

'Funny,' I reply and cut my eyes at him. 'And I'm not a jailbird.'

'Not yet.'

'How is that helping?'

'Who said I had to help you?'

'The bro-sis code said so.'

He smirks at me. 'You still trying to make that one stick, Pick'n'Mix?'

342

'You still working that ridiculous link from Verity to Variety to Pick'n'Mix, Connie Boy?'

'So, this is a thing, huh?' Con's voice is fully adult now. I was at uni when his voice first started breaking and conversations were peppered with long squeaky sentences that smoothed out into a deep baritone that didn't seem to suit his slender frame and huge, bubble Afro. I'm convinced that was why he spent a big proportion of his late teens not speaking – he could never be sure what version of his developing vocal chords would take charge at any time.

'You could call it that.'

Con has his arms behind his back. I'm not sure he realises that he is standing like a police officer, and it's making me mildly anxious.

'Why didn't you tell anyone, Vee?' he asks.

Because I didn't want anyone to know. Because he was all mine and no one else's. Because I didn't want to. 'Because I'm stupid,' I say instead of uttering all those other words. 'Because I'm stupid and I didn't think it would end up here.'

My brother seems shocked by my words, the venom with which I speak about myself. He'd be horrified, I think, if he could see inside my head and hear what I say to myself, especially since all of this. I've swapped the prison cell for this bedroom but the thoughts haven't changed. They marshal themselves in my mind like an army awaiting orders – each is ready, always ready – to move into action, to unleash the full stupidity of what I've got myself into.

'Aww, well, you can't help being stupid. I knew all that stuff you used to talk about with quantum physics and the workings of the universe was stuff you'd overheard. I knew my big sister wasn't smarter than me. I knew under it all, she was just a bit thick.'

'Oi, you! You're supposed to be nice to me. I'm going through

343

stuff. Some tough stuff. I could use you being a bit kinder to me, you know.'

'Sis, it wasn't me who got you into that, was it? And besides, you've got parents for that sympathy stuff.'

I can't help laughing to myself.

Con moves further into the room and removes what he has been holding behind his back before he sits down on the floor – Aunty Mez's beauty box that she left here ages ago and keeps saying she will pick up soon. That 'soon' hasn't come yet, not even when she's been here probably a hundred times (minimum) since she left it.

'Give me your hand,' Con says.

'Why?'

'Because.' He dumps the black box on my rug and cracks it open with all the reverence of someone opening a treasure chest.

'Because why?'

'Just give me your damn hand. What's wrong with you?'

I slip off the bed, sit on the floor beside him and hold out my hand.

He starts with the pot of red nail polish, painting broad strokes across the bed of my nail. Then he uncaps the bright orange and uses that to paint the next nail. Vivid yellow is next. Then green. Then blue. On the next hand, he starts with red again.

Once both hands are painted, he returns to the first red nail, uncaps the yellow and dots tiny spots all over it. Then he uses the green at the nail bed to create the green leaves that will turn my nail into a strawberry. He moves onto the next nail, using white and green to turn that into an orange. The yellow nail becomes a bee.

It's hypnotic watching him work; observing him paint my nails. His large fingers don't get in the way of his fiddly task, instead they're deft and precise, wielding the brush and the orange sticks with expert precision.

'Scarily, it looks like you've done this before,' I comment as he starts on the green nail.

'Nah, you're the only crim I'd paint nails for.'

'Seriously, Con, you do realise you could really hurt me with these comments,' I state.

'Yeah, but there is waaay too much seriousness going on around here. M and D look like they're going to combust, you look like you're going to start tearing your hair out and screaming. Everyone needs to lighten the hell up.'

'This isn't the sort of thing you lighten up about.'

'Maybe, maybe not.'

'What's *that* supposed to mean?'

'It means I'm not sure when you became all drama, but, boy, you know how to make it a full-on Netflix, binge-watch ten-episoder when you do dip your toe in.'

'Why are you saying all this to me?'

'Mainly because I can. And because, what you gonna do?'

'Nothing, I suppose.'

'Vee, you know how I care about you, but when it comes to something like this, I ain't going to change who I am. There's been enough of that around here already.'

He's talking about me, I just know he is.

'I feel bad, though. Never said anything about how you changed. I mean, yeah, I thought you'd got sick of me and the boys, but I should have known. Changing the locks, that was low-key. And you ain't a low-key kind of person. Not with me. Not with what you promised me when I was eight about always being there for me. I believed every word you said and until recently you proved that you meant every word you said.'

We stare at each other for a moment before he returns to focusing on the task in hand. Eventually, when the smell of nail varnish is enough to knock me out several times over, my brother sits back.

'There you go. Now you can leave the house without bringing shame to the Gillmare name. You may be a crim, but you are stylishly criminal. And if they come back with the handcuffs, well those hands look good enough for that, too.'

The array of designs he's created on my hands is special. Pretty. Clever. Thoughtful.

'Thank you,' I say carefully and meaningfully to my brother. I'm saying thank you for not piling on the guilt too much after what I did with the locks. I had the right to change my locks, of course I did, but not like that. Not without telling him. That was low-key, as my brother said.

He packs up his tools and glue and sequins. At the door he stops. 'Vee, if he was hurting you, physically or mentally, then I hope you did try to hurt him. I really, really do.'

Part 8

Part 5

serena

Now

When I first came out after being locked up for those few days, I just wanted to keep every single door open, I wanted to be able to see that I could walk out whenever I wanted. At the same time, I wanted to shut every door of every room I was in because I didn't want anyone to see my shame; my thick, slimy shame that was slowly suffocating my skin, my mind, my soul.

I've tried a few times to talk to Verity since she came out, and she's shut me down, shut me out. That changes today. I'm done being the respectful friend; I am not her friend. I am her parent. And I need to take charge. Otherwise, I will have squandered this precious time to help her.

I open her bedroom door without knocking and she looks up from the book she's reading. I toss her jacket at her, and it lands on her head with the arms trailing down over the book.

I used to come into this bedroom every night to kiss her and say goodnight. It was a familiar routine that I would have been lost and unanchored without. The day only ended properly for me when I could say goodnight to my children. Even when she was an older teen she was very rarely not there for me to lean my head around the door and wish her the best night's sleep. Verity almost always slept at home. I suppose I did, too, even when I was being screwed by my teacher.

'Let's go,' I say.

'Go where?' she asks. It's clear from the look on her face, even with her fancy nails, she does not want to go anywhere.

'I need to show you something.'

She's about to sigh, tut, roll her eyes, bring out all the snark, when she stops herself. She looks at me as though calculating something, trying to work out if she really hates me as much as she thinks she does.

Slowly she puts down her book, picks up the jacket and slips it on. Any irritation she feels is tucked away, any resentment brushed aside.

I can tell by her face she thought I was going to take her somewhere dramatic and majestic. A place where we could stand and commune with nature, immerse ourselves in the beauty of the world around us.

Instead we're sitting in the car outside a small B&B about ten minutes from our house. It looks cosy enough, but everything about it needs updating. It is tired on the outside, the paintwork faded and chipped, the awnings seagull-christened and grubby, its sign bravely shining on despite how fatigued it seems. It's just as exhausted on the inside, desperately in need of someone to love it again.

'This is where I ended up because thirty-odd years ago my teacher kissed me and I didn't tell anyone,' I explain to my daughter. 'This is where I came ten years ago when your father threw me out and Poppy Carlisle was stalking me.'

'Poppy Carlisle was *stalking* you?'

'Didn't he tell you that?'

She shakes her head, looking upset and disturbed.

'She only did it for a short time; she was trying to . . . well, that doesn't really matter. What does matter is that it was enough to scare me. It was a trigger point in my life. I don't want this to happen to you, Verity. I need you to talk to me. If I had talked to your aunts, even Grandma, all that time ago, things might have turned out completely differently – not just for me, but probably for Poppy, too. Talk to me, Verity. Talk to me.'

There is so much to say, to reveal, to ask about. I can see it on her face. Eventually she says, 'If I tell you something, will you promise not to freak out? I just need you to tell me what you honestly think once you've heard this story. I'm confused by it. And I don't understand why I'm confused.'

'Yes,' I say simply.

'All right, so, one evening I got back from work late. Not too late, but I had a ton of work to do because we were going to be in a client meeting first thing in the morning. Logan was already there, he'd cooked, cleaned up and everything. He was bored, I suppose, because he had to watch telly on his own and he'd done all this stuff for me. So after a bit, he came and started kissing my neck.'

verity

Logan's lips slowly kissed a trail of seduction from my jaw down my neck to my shoulder.

I paused in typing the report I had been working on all evening and my eyes slipped shut and I sighed. He was showing his boredom not by moaning or sighing or sulking, but by kissing my neck. Once his lips grazed the neckline of my top, he moved to the other side, traced a track of kisses up to my jaw. As he kissed, his hand slid over my shoulder inside my top and into my bra.

I leant back against him, as his hand tightened around my breast and his thumb stroked firmly across my nipple, making me gasp out loud.

'Babe, I've got to work,' I murmured as his thumb continued to work on me.

'Shhhhh,' he hushed and pulled me to my feet. 'Shhhhh.'

'I'm serious, Loges,' I replied. 'I need to get this done tonight. We have to be at a huge client meeting in the morning. I should have stayed at work but I thought I'd get more done and would be able to work a lot later—'

Spinning me around, he covered my mouth with his to stop me speaking. The kiss deepened and lengthened and I wanted to go with it, but I had work. I had so much work. I was still a trainee, this was my last seat, my last bit of training where I was shadowing and being general dogsbody for one of the partners. I had been going all out the last two years. It was cut-throat, all of us trainees desperate to prove how indispensible we were so we would be in with a chance of a job at the end of our two years training. I wanted to stay at Frost, Palmer, Cummings, Quarry and Carter, desperately.

I was in early, left late, made sure all my work was 110 per cent perfect. I had work to do and I didn't want Logan to distract me.

'Loges—' I began when he pulled away, so he kissed me again. Harder this time, for longer, undoing the small pearly buttons on my white shirt as he kissed me. When he pulled away I almost fell over from wanting the kiss to continue.

'I have to work,' I said feebly, even as he was leading me towards the bedroom. 'Loges . . .'

He moved faster, tugging me along with him until we were in the bedroom.

'I have to—' Another silencing kiss, one that was huge and grand, like they were in the movies. As we kissed, he eased me back until my legs butted up against the bed and then he was easing me back onto the bed and climbing on top of me. There was no point arguing at this point, no point protesting, whether or not I had work to do, I was here now and the quickest way to get back to work was by going along with it. It wasn't as if it was awful, this, it wasn't terrible being undressed by him.

It wasn't a chore undressing him while we kissed and his fingers moved over my skin. It wasn't difficult to tear open the condom wrapper and roll its contents onto my waiting boyfriend. It was nothing but divine to curve my back and let out a deep sigh as he pushed his fingers into me, then immediately withdrew them, and then drove himself where his fingers had been. I really didn't know that sex could be like this. My hook-ups and short flings had been good, enjoyable, but none were as satisfying as being with Logan.

As he moved inside me, and I rocked myself against him, he placed his hands around my wrists, eased them up and pushed them gently on each side of my head; with each thrust he increased the firmness of the grip until my wrists were pinned, hard.

Just as I expected him to start to speed up, to lead us to the finish, he suddenly pulled out and moved back a little. His right hand let go of my left wrist, and moved down between my legs, to his erection, and I felt him tugging at the condom, trying to remove it.

No, this wasn't what I wanted, we weren't at that stage yet. 'What are—' I began, but he covered my mouth with his, kissed away my words again. He kept his lips on mine, stopped me from protesting as he entered me again, but without the condom. Without protection.

I moved my free hand to push at his chest, but he gripped that wrist again, forced it back onto the bed and held it firmly in place as he continued to plunge deep inside me. I felt him groan against my lips right before he began his familiar fast, hard thrusts; harder and faster he moved, speeding to get to the end, to finish. He was going to . . .

I didn't want that. I'd never done that before and I didn't want it.

No. The word bubbled up in my mind.

No. I tried to form with my covered-up lips.

No. I tried to express with my now still, unresponsive body.

No. No. No.

'Why did you do that?' I asked him the moment he had finished and rolled off me.

He was breathing as though he had run a race and took a few

seconds to steady himself. Eventually he propped himself up on one elbow and began tracing his fingers down the centre of my chest. I slapped his hand away. I could barely stand to look at him, let alone have him touch me right now.

I felt his frown but didn't properly see it in the dark of the bedroom. 'Do what?' he asked.

'Why did you take the condom off?'

'Didn't you want me to?'

'No, I did not want you to.'

'But we talked about it. We agreed that we'd stop using them.'

'No, *you* brought it up, I said I'd *think* about us stopping condoms *at some point in the future*.'

'But it's much better without it. I feel so much closer to you. And anyway, what's the problem? We're together, neither of us is seeing anyone else. It's not like I'm looking elsewhere. Are you?'

'No! Of course not.'

'So what's the problem?'

'The problem is, I didn't want to do that. I wasn't ready. And I'm not on any other contraception.'

'You'll be fine.'

'How do you know I'll be "fine"? I don't mess about with contraception, Logan. I don't ever want to be in a situation where I have to decide what to do about a pregnancy.'

'Would it be a big deal if you did get pregnant? Really?'

'Yes, it would be a *huge* deal.'

His almost jovial, carefree attitude dissipated then, and he looked very troubled; upset and hurt. I hid from his pain by scooching myself up, pulling away the duvet and sliding into the cold, cotton embrace of the bed, pulling the duvet right up to cover most of my face.

'Why would it be a huge deal?' he asked in a tight voice. 'Don't you love me?'

My stomach flipped. 'Of course I do,' I replied straight away because if I didn't, he'd think I didn't love him.

'So why would it be such a problem? We love each other.'

'I am literally on the verge of getting my dream job. I'm twenty-four, I haven't even done a fraction of what I want to do with my life. A baby is not part of my near-future plan.'

'Not even *my* baby?'

There was no way to answer that question without getting myself into trouble, I realised, so I said nothing.

'Well, your silence speaks volumes,' he stated, looking and sounding wounded. 'I thought we had something special, unique, but clearly I was wrong.'

I carried on with my silence, because very quickly this conversation had moved into tricky waters.

'Look, Vee, is our relationship just some stop on the way to you finding the man you want to settle down with? Tell me now if I'm nothing more than a consort and I'll try to prepare myself for when the end comes.'

What was I supposed to say? I loved him, had never felt like this about anyone, but I wasn't ready for a baby. And no one could convince me otherwise.

'Wow, did I read this whole thing wrong?' he breathed to my continued silence.

A familiar feeling crept across my chest. Sometimes it was all I felt, this sensation that I was doing something wrong. I loved being with Logan, but the guilt – from how we met, from not telling my parents, from sometimes feeling like he was more into me than I was him, that

I wasn't giving him enough of myself and my attention and my heart – was a constant, unwelcome companion.

I closed my eyes and counted to ten. Tried to centre myself, tried to find a space where everything was cool and I wasn't feeling so many conflicting emotions about the man next to me. I held my eyes closed, sure that it was there in the dark somewhere – a place that was safe and secure.

'Shall I just go?' he asked as though defeated.

No! I screamed inside. *No! Don't go. When you go and it's like this, I feel sick with worry and guilt. And I want you back here with me.*

Yes! I yelled internally. *Yes, go! And take all the guilt and stress and uneasiness you push onto me with you.*

I don't know, I whispered into my safe, dark space. *I don't know if you should stay or if you should go. I don't know anything because I sometimes wonder if things shouldn't be simpler than this. If these times shouldn't happen with such regularity.*

'If you want,' I replied to my boyfriend.

'No, what do you want?'

To be sitting at the table working, like I should be. I shrugged slightly but kept my eyes closed. I couldn't deal with this conversation so I decided not to engage.

'Look,' Logan said after a few moments; his tone had changed. 'I don't know where all the baby talk came from, but can we shelve it for now? I mean, it's quite an emotive subject because it has so many implications for our future. And I'm not sure if either of us is ready to be talking in such terms right now.'

'Yes, you're right,' I murmured, relieved that this conversation was over, but slightly annoyed that he was making out I had brought it up. This was all in response to what he had done. But I relaxed a little, knowing we weren't going to keep on talking about it. 'Let's change the subject.'

It felt safe to open my eyes because we'd agreed to park that topic.

Logan was still leaning up on one elbow and he looked so cute. *Fine*. The gorgeous man that I did truly love. I wished things with him weren't so complicated. That I could talk to my mum or my dad about what was going on. Even in general terms.

'Hey, good-looking,' he said with that smile that melted every part of me.

'Hey, yourself,' I replied as he leant down and kissed me. This time when I closed my eyes it wasn't to hide or find comfort in the dark, it was to fully enjoy the sensation of being with the man I loved.

Now

The muscles in Mum's jaw are undulating like waves in the sea by the time I finish my story.

She drove us to Devil's Dyke before I started to talk because neither of us could stand to keep looking at the sad B&B that had been her home for a little while. And I wanted to be outside, to share this story in a wide-open space.

We lean against the bonnet of the car while I talk. I've told her the story as briefly as I could, not adding in too many details but keeping in enough for her to understand what I am trying to say.

And now the story is done, she stares furiously down at the ground in front of us, her jaw working overtime as she struggles with something. I can't tell exactly what she's thinking, but she's not happy. Is it because of breaching that barrier most of us should have with our parents and letting her know about my sex life? I had warned her about freaking out.

I had to tell her, though, because it's one of those things that's confused me ever since it happened. It's niggled and fretted away at the back of my mind, like a movement just on the periphery of your vision – it is constantly there, it takes up the tiniest fraction of your attention, but not enough to make you turn your head. There are a few things like that that I need to talk to someone about. And since Mum has told me talk to her, I have braved it.

'Is it too weird hearing about me, you know, doing adult things?' I ask her when she doesn't lift her eyes from the ground and the rippling in her jaw doesn't stop or ease off at all. I don't say 'sex' because that would probably traumatise her more than she already looks.

She shakes her head, attempts to smile but it dies before it has a chance to get a foothold on her lips. 'No,' she says quietly, still staring at the scrabbly ground beneath our feet. 'Not at all. I'm glad you told me.' She lifts her head and, despite her upset, she gazes adoringly at me. She used to do that all the time. She would look at me with such adulation I was sometimes embarrassed. She was quite clear and open and blatant about how much she loved me and Con, which was all the more surprising given what she'd hidden about herself all these years. 'I'm sorry it happened.'

'I'm glad I told you, actually, because now that I've said it out loud, it doesn't seem to be as big a deal as I thought it was,' I say.

Mum's brow crinkles quite dramatically. 'In what way?' she asks as though she suddenly doesn't understand the language I'm speaking.

'I mean, it's felt like something huge sometimes, but talking about it, I can see now that it's just a case of getting our wires crossed.'

She nods thoughtfully at that, as though the language she didn't understand is slowly filtering through to the area of her brain where she can translate it. 'Did he apologise?'

'What do you mean?'

'It was a total misunderstanding, so did he apologise for doing that to you?'

'Doing what to me?'

Mum inhales deeply, the agony ripples across her jaw and face again and she breathes out deeply through her barely parted lips. 'For . . .' She stops speaking for a moment. 'For having sex with you without your consent?'

What? Is that what she heard? 'He didn't do that,' I explain. 'I was totally up for it. Sorry if that's TMI.'

'OK, but did you agree to him taking off the condom?' she asks.

'No,' I say.

'Had you discussed in the past that he could decide to do that at any point in the future when you had sex?'

'We'd discussed stopping condoms,' I reply.

'But had you agreed to it and said that he could do that whenever he chose?'

Without warning, it feels like my head is burning, like it's just spontaneously combusted and blue-orange flames are leaping high into the air. *What is she saying? What is she saying?* I shake my blazing head.

'Did he give you the chance to say no when he did take it off? Did he ask if it was OK? Did he give you the chance to say no? Or did he keep going without checking with you if you were all right with him unilaterally taking such a huge step?' she asks gently, quietly, devastatingly. Because her words are devastating me. They are taking a sledgehammer to my very being and slamming away chunks of my certainty about the world, about my boyfriend, about my recollection of my life to date. 'Or did he force you to have unprotected sex and then pretend it was what you wanted afterwards?' My mother looks like she's going to cry again. 'Did he become the victim in that scenario when you mentioned it wasn't what you wanted or would have agreed to?'

He'd kept hold of my wrists, he'd kept kissing my mouth, he'd kept me pinned and silenced while he did what he did. I feel sick. My head is on fire and there is an ocean of nausea filling up my stomach.

I manage to nod my head as it continues to cremate itself. Yes, he became the victim, the wounded one. I was scared of getting pregnant because he'd forced me to have a type of sex I didn't want and the whole conversation became about whether I loved him enough.

'And if it was truly a misunderstanding, a case of getting your wires crossed and him getting caught up in the moment, was he horrified with himself when you told him how you felt? Did he apologise afterwards and promise never to do it again without your explicit say-so?'

I can't tell her. I can't tell her that after we agreed to not talk about the baby stuff and my commitment to him, after all of that, he kissed me. Then he climbed on top of me and he entered me and had sex with me again without a condom. I can't confess that I didn't want to have sex without contraception again, not that night, not ever, but after the trouble it'd just caused, the argument it'd led to, I couldn't say no. I just lay there and let him do it.

And I can't tell her that after that night, he wouldn't wear condoms even though I never agreed to sex without them. He just didn't put them on. He would pretend I hadn't spoken if I asked him to wear one. Even when I made a point of putting one on him as part of foreplay, he would always take it off before penetration. If I tried to move away when he did that, he would kiss me to stop me talking, stroke and caress me while I was under him – all gentle and loving, but all essentially pinning me in place, refusing to let me go until I let him do it to me. The worry about getting pregnant was too much after a while and I had to try to make an appointment to go and get the Pill.

But wasn't it my fault? I had a voice, I could stand up to unreasonable people at work, stand up to police officers, could argue with people who were rude to me in shops, so why could I never use it with Logan? Even though I had the biggest voice in the world, I couldn't say anything to the man I loved about him doing something in my body I didn't want him to.

I slowly rub away the tear that has crawled out of my eye.

'After the first time we had sex, *Marcus* . . .' Mum says his name like she is on unsteady territory, that the mere mention of those six letters in that order would open up the ground and make her tumble down into the bowels of hell. '*Marcus* . . . he drove me home. He was meant to be tutoring me in history after school *at school*, but he managed to get me to convince him to take me to his house. It was about ten times after that we had sex. And it wasn't awful, it hurt a little, but I was so confused. I didn't understand why I was so confused until your aunt Faye told me he wasn't allowed to do that with me. That it was against the law and it was statutory rape. That all came so much later though. After that first time, he drove me home and dropped me off at the end of the road. I was still really confused because while it hadn't been terrible, it hadn't felt good. I'd gone along with it because it was what he wanted.

'Just as I was walking away, he called me back. And I knew it would all have been worth it then because he was going to tell me he loved me. And more than anything, more than breathing sometimes, I wanted him to love me. And instead of saying he loved me, he told me to go to the doctor for the Pill so I wouldn't get knocked up.' Mum reaches up and wipes away a tear that's sitting in the well of her eye. 'It's only now I can see it all clearly. He was in control of everything. It didn't start when he started to hit me. It started with seemingly little, insignificant things like that – he had decided when we were going to have sex, then he decided that the burden of contraception would be mine because he wouldn't wear condoms any longer.

'And I did it. Without question. I started to hide things from my parents, I started to sneak around to meet him, I went to the doctor and got the Pill. And in those days, that wasn't easy. There was a woman who'd made a big deal about under-sixteens getting the Pill without their parents' consent and took it to court. Even though she lost her case, the doctors had to ask you a lot of questions to find out if you were competent enough to be having sex and therefore to take the Pill. I was mortified sitting there, lying to the doctor about my boyfriend, saying he was the same age as me. He got me lying for him right from the start.'

'But you were a teenager, Mum. I'm an adult.'

'Nah, you're a superannuated teen,' Mum replies jokingly and nudges me with her shoulder. 'You'll always be the little girl with the two neat puffs and the supersonic Vee voice to me.'

I manage a smile when I think of all the times Con and Mum and Dad had to clamp their hands over their ears because my voice went so high in outrage it was virtually supersonic.

'Do you think Logan was abusive, Mum?'

'I think . . . I think . . . That night you were telling me about, did you finish your work in time?'

No, I didn't. After he'd initiated sex again and kept me up talking for a couple more hours, I fell asleep. And when I woke up, it was too late to finish it off. I'd had to go to work unprepared and we'd had to rush to get it done before the client meeting. That had been the first time in my whole life that I hadn't done my work to the best of my abilities. It had been frowned upon. It hadn't gone unnoticed. Is that what Darryl had meant when he said he'd seen a change in me? Is that what Dad had been trying to say when he was pushing me to examine who had been manoeuvred out of my life? After that night, after the surprise and disappointment on my colleagues' faces the next morning, I'd started staying at work to finish anything that needed doing. Again it wasn't a wholly conscious thing, but it was easier to get texts and calls asking where I was and when I'd be back than to have to resist Logan dragging me to bed when I had to get stuff done.

'No,' I reply. 'No I didn't finish my work that night.'

'And was it important to you?'

'Yes, I was so close to finishing my training and there are so many of us who would do anything to get the job at the end of it. And it just looked bad.'

'If someone consistently interferes with something like your job or your studies or your family life or your health, then they don't have your best interests at heart.'

'But does that make them abusive? Does that make Logan abusive?'

She says nothing for a long time. And I can see she is thinking it over – either considering the evidence or trying to think of the best way to say it.

'Sometimes it seems like I see abuse everywhere,' Mum eventually says, rather neatly dodging the question.

That's because she doesn't want to say it. Like Darryl, like Dad, like Conrad even, she's hinted at it, walked right up and brushed against it, and if anyone was going to be brave enough to say it to me,

I'd have thought it would be my mother. But no, even she is ducking out at this point in the conversation.

She obviously doesn't want to say that my burning head and churning stomach and the incidents that keep popping up in my mind like jack-in-the-boxes at a toy factory, all tell me this one simple truth: I was in an abusive relationship. And because he never hit me, because I was feisty and forthright in other areas of my life, because he was good-looking and intelligent and sweet and kind, I hadn't even noticed it happening.

serena

Now

Hell is listening to your daughter describe how she was violated, raped, manipulated and abused.

Hell is listening to your daughter describe how she was violated, raped, manipulated and abused in many different ways, and knowing it is your fault.

I am trying not to cry. I am trying not to let it show how truly horrible her relationship was. She doesn't realise. She doesn't see that, no, he didn't hit her, he didn't shove her or kick her, but he was violent in so many different ways.

He tried to break her mentally and emotionally, he almost severed her bond with her family, and he has shattered her faith in the world. And she doesn't fully realise it yet. She wants me to name it for her, contextualise it for her, and I can't do that. If I do, there will always be seeds of doubt in her mind about whether my experience is clouding how I see her experience.

All I can do is listen and question and suggest. The rest she will have to come to herself.

But, oh, hell is listening to your daughter describe how she was violated, raped, manipulated and abused and knowing you can't do a thing about it.

Nothing, except put your arms around her and try to hug away the pain.

Part 9

logan

20 July, 2019

Am hypersensitive to this. But she pushed my head. Sounds pathetic written down but we were talking about who could have killed Marcus Halnsley and when I said it could have been her mother, she kind of pushed my head. Sounds pathetic, but felt unnecessarily physical. I didn't say anything, but it kind of sat in my head for a long time afterwards – how easily she could do that to me.

5 August, 2019

Don't know how I feel about this. Something happened that I think most men would be all right with. But I'm not sure how to feel. Woke up and I was in her mouth. Tried to get her to stop, gently tugged at her head to move her away but she wouldn't stop. And ended up with my hands in her hair and letting her, I suppose. It was all right in the end, you know, I mean I came and all that, but it felt strange. Odd. Because I had no say in it. I mean, woke up and *boom* she's doing it to me and I'm having to go along with it. Feels strange, that's all.

14 August, 2019

Good day today. She was in a good mood. Came home from work and she was all happy. I'd spent a couple of hours cooking and she loved it. None of the usual grumpiness about it being unseasoned or over-seasoned or too fatty. She just ate it and said thank you and kissed me several times. Ended up cuddling on the sofa. Remember why I love her. This is the real her. Not the other one. Not the one I have to deal with sometimes. Actually, not going to spoil today by thinking about that.

1 September, 2019

Devastated. Absolutely devastated. She hit me. First time. Keep trying to find a way to get around it, to pretend it didn't happen the way it did. Was behind the door in the living room, putting up one of those sticky things because she wants a hook behind the door. Next thing I know, BAM!!!! Door was slammed into my face. Surprised my nose didn't break. And then she started laughing. Claimed she'd forgotten I was behind the door and had reacted instinctively when the door moved. She wouldn't stop laughing so have come home. She's left a message on the answer machine which is nonsense. No real apology. Just shite, really. Feel awful. Understand what those women mean when they say they don't know what to do when a man hits them. I know I should just walk away, but we've been through so much together. All the Ice Cream Girls stuff. We've become so close, and no one else really understands all that like she does. Don't know what to do. Just don't know what to do. Love her so much. But can't stay with her if she's going to do this.

5 September, 2019

She did it again. Woke up and she's on top of me. She's working on me until I'm hard and then I can't stop her. Not really. Not without hurting her. I kind of lay there and let her. She even took my hands and put them on her breasts and made out that I was enjoying it. My stupid body was responding right until I came but it wasn't what I wanted. Is this what it's going to be like from now on? Asked her not to do it again. And she agreed. Hopefully she'll stick to it.

16 September, 2019

I miss her. The her I met all those months ago. When we were working together and nothing had happened. I remember how happy she was when I told her I had tickets to see that science guy she's so keen on. She threw her arms around me and squealed. That was the happiest I'd seen her. That night, the science guy night, was the first time I kissed her. The first time I took her to bed. Didn't think I could be happier. I remember the feel of her underneath me, the look in her eyes. I had completely fallen for her by then. I like to think she'd fallen for me, but with some of the things she does, I have to wonder if she does love me. If she even likes me.

21 September, 2019

Life and love are good. Totally loved up. Totally blissed out.

9 October, 2019

She did it again. It's like the conversation we had about her not having sex with me when I was asleep didn't happen. Woke up to find her mouth on me again. Wasn't going to tolerate it this time.

I tried to push her off and she just wouldn't stop. She was determined not to stop, she kept at me, almost holding me down until it was over. I kind of went weak. Couldn't fight her off. And when I tried to say something afterwards she said she had evidence that I'd enjoyed it. And who would believe me? Don't know what to do about this. Just don't know. But I can't leave her. If I can't leave her, does that mean I have to put up with my body not being my own for ever?

17 November, 2019

Another day, another argument. Why can't she see that her brother is going to get her in trouble? Came over and he'd obviously been there Monday night. Smoking weed with his loser mates. I told her that it wasn't great, especially when she's so desperate to be a solicitor and get a job at her firm. But she got all defensive and threatened to kick me out. She kind of conceded my point in the end. Or so I thought. Guess what happened last night? Full sex, no choice, just woke up to her doing it to me. Felt so much like a punishment. I speak up, she does that to me. Wish my body would stop responding to her at those times.

24 January, 2020

She screamed at me today. Was trying to talk to her about her friend, the one who is all drama and never seems to be there for her. I mean, I've never known her call her friend just to vent. And she got so mad she shoved my head away from her. It was hard, but more than that, it was the viciousness of the action that felt more violent. She does get so annoyed sometimes that I am scared of her. Wish she'd understand that I only want what's best for her.

16 February, 2020

Think she's shagging someone else. Well, not someone else. Her 'friend' Howie. Always knew there was something dodgy about him, about their relationship. Came over and they'd been together. They were dressed, but there was an atmosphere in the air. Intimacy. Maybe they hadn't had sex, but something had happened, a line had been crossed. He got all uppity and cross when I arrived. Maybe he'd been working his way up to fucking her. I don't know, I feel so jealous but at the same time a little bit relieved that I haven't been going crazy all this time. She and Howie aren't as innocent and 'friendly' as she likes to pretend. Bit of a scuffle on the way out, thought he was going to pulverise me. She got rid of him, then she turned on me. Think she was upset cos I came back unannounced. She shoved me and threw me out. Told me to do one. I hung around for ages outside to see if 'Howie' came back but he didn't. That's something, I suppose. Don't know what to do, though. She's my world.

19 February, 2020

Hot on the heels of the Howie thing is her not wanting to tell anyone. I want it to be out there. Want everyone to know so I can, I don't know, claim her as my own. So she'll claim me. I know there'll be fallout, but everyone will understand in the end. They'll see how much we love each other and they won't care. They'll be happy for us.

28 February, 2020

Found texts from Howie. He's clearly in love with her. His girlfriend is suspicious and wants to kick him out if he won't stop seeing her. Wish I could get the image of them out of my head.

5 March, 2020

Can't find the words to describe this. She's implying that I did to her what she's been doing to me. We've talked about stopping condoms, we've talked and talked and we agreed we would. And then the first time we did it without a condom she says it's not what she wanted. That I've forced myself on her. I'm so confused. We agreed not to use them. We agreed to at this stage of our relationship. And now she's saying these terrible things. What if she tells someone? They'll think I'm a beast. And they won't believe me when I say she's had sex with me against my will. They'll think I'm being pathetic. I'm stuck. I'm so stuck.

7 March, 2020

It's all right now. It was a misunderstanding. She doesn't think I forced myself on her. She's fine with it now. Feel so much better. And she's going to stop with the other stuff. She's going to check with me, make sure I'm awake before she does anything.

21 March, 2020

I hurt all over. Every part of me. Can't believe she's done this. Can't believe it's gone this far. And then she did that afterwards. She used my body against me. In so much pain. So much pain. Wish I didn't love her.

25 March, 2020

Something's going to happen soon. I can feel it. Everything's going to come to a head. I hope there isn't too much fallout.

26 March, 2020

She's my life. I keep reminding myself that she is everything to me. I don't know how I managed to get here, get myself into this situation where she is all I can think about, but she is. Is it going to work out? I hope so. I want to be with her for ever. I want to be her BAE. Not sure if she feels the same.

28 March, 2020

What do I do when she won't stop doing it? And now it feels like the hitting – all accidental, of course – is happening more often, too. I'm so confused. So confused.

19 April, 2020

Think if we have a proper conversation about settling down, it might help things. I'm going to sit her down and tell her I love her. Tell her she's all that I want and we can work things out. I don't like ultimatums, but think I may need to give her one.

20 April, 2020

Didn't quite go as expected. She doesn't want to split up but she doesn't want to settle down or tell anyone about us. I'm stuck here. She says we should separate for a while and come back together to talk things through. But . . . we should split up. Maybe some distance would be good for me. Clear my head. Reading back over these pages I see how broken I am. The sex thing. How am I going to trust another woman after this one has crossed so many boundaries? I get nervous going to sleep around her. But I can't really sleep without her. This is so complex. So complicated. What do I do? What do I do?

poppy

Now

'I'm sorry, Logan.'

I am sitting at my brother's bedside and I am apologising for what he went through. It's because of me. He got involved with her because of me and he paid the price. He's the victim of a crime, he could be a target for another attack, so he has been assigned a room on his own. Which is good. Because what I need to say to him needs to be said when we're alone.

'I'm so sorry, Logan.'

I still feel sick every time I think about the things he wrote. How it went on and on, how it didn't get better, didn't change, was just a cycle that ran shorter and shorter. And how much he loved her. No matter what she did, he still loved her. Wanted to be with her, wanted to please her, wanted to find the woman he'd fallen in love with and have her come back to him.

Every single painful word he wrote haunts me. As I was reading, I wanted to shout at him to walk away. To let that be the last time. To stick to his promise of not being treated like that. To just choose himself and run.

But he didn't. He stayed. He kept trying.

It was like reading my own words. My feelings, my emotions, my actions that wouldn't let me leave. It was like looking into a mirror from the past and knowing that nothing can be changed, altered, bettered. Everything would have to play out exactly as it did before. Except this time, it is the other way round. It is the victim who has ended up (nearly) dead, not the abuser.

'I'm so sorry you went through all of that because of me. I read why you did it, how you met her, how you spent all that money trying to find something in the transcripts that could help me. Thank you. And I'm sorry. I wish you could have met someone nicer. Someone who cared for you and saw all the amazing things about you.' I take my brother's hand in mine. 'Don't worry, though. They're going to get her. I'm going to give the drive to the police and they're going to get her. She is not going to get away with it. Any of it.

'I'm going to make sure she gets what's coming to her. For you. And for me. And for all the other people out there like us.'

I have to leave before my parents arrive. I came here because I wanted to tell him that I knew. That I was going to do something about it. I'm his sister, this is my fault and I am going to sort it for him.

I know he can hear me. And I know I have to do everything I can to get him justice.

'Poppy,' Mum says to me when we meet in the stark white corridor outside Logan's room.

'Mum,' I reply. 'Dad.' I'm tired, I realise, when I see how deep the lines of worry have scored themselves into Mum's face; when I note how the anxiety has slowed Dad's movements. I'm tired – I feel how they look.

'Why don't you come over for dinner one night this week?' she says. My gaze moves back to my father, who, I'm surprised to find, is looking at me. Directly.

But I shake my head. I'm not taking my daughter to see them so they'll be nice to me – actually, so they'll tolerate me. 'I don't think so,' I reply.

'Not Betina or Alain,' Dad says. 'Just you, Pepper. Just you.'

That makes me swallow. Why the sudden interest in me? Why the nickname coming out again? Do they need to get me alone so they can finally say all the awful things they've wanted to say since Logan has been here? Since I rocked up to their door ten years ago, requesting a place to stay and them to talk to me?

'We miss you,' Mum says.

'We miss you a lot,' Dad says.

'Me? This is Poppy you're talking to, not Bella. You do realise that? Bella's at work. This is Poppy.'

'We deserve that,' Mum says. 'We just . . . these past few days without you around, it's shown us how much we've missed out on. We've taken having you back for granted. These last few days with Logan . . . with not knowing . . .' Mum starts to sob. It's quiet, discreet, mainly hidden by the lowering of her head, but it's significant.

'With not knowing what will happen to Logan, we've realised that we love you, Pepper. We need to reconnect with you. It won't happen straight away, we know that, we've treated you badly. But we want to try.'

I stare at my dad. I've waited so long to hear those words, so long for them to behave like this. And now they are. It's not real, is it? It's not real. It's the hangover. It's the drinking too much and eating too little and not sleeping and not grounding myself in work and my daughter. It's the hallucinating, the desperation to get back all that I've lost because I was stupid enough to fall for Marcus. This conversation with my parents is pure fantasy.

This is my reality: 'Poppy,' Mum says to me when we meet in the stark white corridor outside Logan's room.

'Mum,' I reply. 'Dad.'

'Any change?' she asks.

I shake my head.

They both deflate a little, they both continue to avoid my eyes. This is what it's really like. This is reality.

'I'll see you soon,' I say and walk away. I can't let them derail me. All I can do is focus, focus, focus on getting my brother the justice he truly deserves.

poppy

Now

Breathe, Poppy, breathe.

I've been up and down this road what feels like a million trillion times. I keep telling myself to breathe. To pause here, to bend over and rest the palms of my hands on my thighs and breathe.

I can do this. I can do this.

I can walk into this police station. I can walk through the doors, I can walk up to the counter and I can hand over the evidence I have found. It will be fine. They will not put me in an interview room. They will not read me a statement that tells me they're arresting me. They will not detain me overnight.

Breathe, Poppy, breathe.

I can do this because I'm not a convict any more. I have served my time and I am a free woman.

Breathe, Poppy, breathe.

You're doing this for Logan. For your family. For fifteen-year-old Poppy who was in this situation, too, and no one did anything to help her.

Breathe, Poppy, breathe.

Walk in there and do this. Walk in there and save your brother.

Breathe, Poppy, breathe.

I stand upright, straighten my spine, remember who I am. What I have been through. What I have survived.

I remind myself that I can do this.

I can absolutely do this.

I have to. No one else is going to do it for me. Or for Logan.

Part 10

poppy

Now

I thought it would be much more dramatic, bleeping machines and running nurses and doctors. I thought we, his family, would be standing in the background, clutching on to each other, desperate for things to turn out OK while everyone rushed about making sure he stayed with us.

As it is, the machines kept beeping steadily along, he squeezed my hand and then his eyes edged open. It was all so undramatic I felt almost *robbed*. And now he has been checked over, he has been prodded and scanned and punctured for blood, and the verdict is that he is fine. Pale, bruised-looking, drained, exhausted, but generally fine.

The nurses couldn't stop us all cramming ourselves into his room this time. None of us were willing to wait for the others to finish and they were kind enough to turn a blind eye, just this once. Mum is on one side of the bed, Dad is on the other, they both have one of his hands in theirs and they're not letting go any time soon.

One of us is going to call the police, but probably only when we can tear ourselves away from him.

'Is he going to be all right?' Bella keeps asking the doctor. 'Will he be OK?'

The doctor, to her credit, answered the first six to ten times, and has now taken to pretending Bella isn't talking. I can't speak. Mum is shedding tears of gratitude, Dad keeps patting Logan's shoulder and nodding like they're communicating without words. My brother lies bare-chested in the bed, a bit removed from it all. He keeps staring at me, though. As though he could hear me when he was in his coma and he knows that I know everything about his relationship, about the abuse, and he's scared I'm going to voice it in front of everyone.

He's probably scared it will make him seem less of a man in front of the four people he wants to maintain his masculine image with.

'You can only have a few more minutes,' the doctor says to no one in particular. 'Logan needs to rest.'

'That's all I've been doing,' Logan says. His voice is croaky; musted and fusted by his time unconscious.

'Maybe so, but you still need to rest. If you want to recover quickly and get out of here as soon as possible, I suggest you listen to what I'm telling you – all of you – and get some real rest. Coma sleep is not rest.'

Once the doctor has gone, presumably to find a nurse who is scarier and who we're more likely to listen to, we all focus on him again.

'Who did this?' Dad asks him now we're alone and it's safe to ask because the people in the room love him. 'The police have been working on it, but they've been waiting to find out from you who did this to you.'

Logan looks at Bella, then at me. Ashamed, cornered. A little scared.

'It's all right,' I say gently. 'We all know about you and Verity Gill-mare. We all know that you were involved and that you didn't always have the smoothest of relationships.' I am trying to talk around the subject because the other three don't know what I took to the police. They don't know the contents of the USB drive. They don't know I

388

was involved at all in finding the 'additional evidence' that is helping the police to take their enquiries in a different direction.

'Who did this to you, boy?' Dad asks again. And the affection, the concern he has in his voice for his third-born unplugs a well of sadness in my chest. I wish my dad was capable of feeling that for me. I push those thoughts to one side. It's not about me, it's about Logan and finding out who did this to him. Well, confirming who did this to him. We all know.

'I don't want to say,' Logan eventually says.

'Stop protecting her,' I say sternly. It'll do no one any good to protect her – she'll only do it to the next person who crosses her path. 'Just stop protecting her. She could have killed you.'

'It's not like that,' Logan says, and shifts his position. Pain shoots across his face.

'Logan, look at—'

'Love, you have to tell us who did this. We need to keep you safe.' This is Mum, rubbing his hand and trying to get him to open up. *Would I have talked if she had done that to me? Would I have confessed all?*

'It's not that simple, Mum,' Logan croaks. He's exhausted, there's no hiding it. Soon a nurse will come and chase us out so he can get some proper rest. And then this opportunity will be lost. He'll sit and he'll think and his first instinct to protect her will kick in. Our window of opportunity is dwindling. Left alone, he will stop himself from telling.

'Don't do this, Logan. Just tell the truth. No lies, no hiding, no twisting. Just tell the truth. Tell who did this to you.' Bella is direct, sharp. Her voice is like a precision laser, carving out the truth hidden in all our words in a clear, concise manner. She knows him better than any of us; she knows what to say to get him to open up. 'Just do it. Please.'

'Please,' Mum adds.

'Please, son,' says Dad.

Logan looks to me for the final word and he gets none. I just stare at him. The decision is his, but telling is better than not.

My brother closes his eyes and is very still for more than a few moments. I can hear the nurse's footsteps as she approaches, tasked with getting rid of us. It's now or it's at some unspecified point in the future. The footsteps are coming nearer, she is on her way to our room for sure. I want to hurry him up, but say nothing, do nothing. Neither do the others. It has to come from him now.

The footsteps are almost here. I can practically feel her weight leaning against the door to push it open.

'From what I can remember,' he says quietly as the door swings open, 'it was Verity Gillmare.'

Thank you, Logan, I think. *That bitch is all mine.*

verity

Now

A knock, a sharp single knock is how it starts.

Then knuckles rapping on the wooden panel that separates the two pieces of stained glass in the front door. By the time I have put down my book and swung my legs off the bed, it is a braying; the loud, angry hammering of someone who hasn't been answered quick enough and is now both trying to draw as much attention to themselves as possible or enter the house the hard way.

I reach the door a fraction before Mum, two fractions before Conrad, and as the door pops open it reveals a woman with a familiar face, and who is terrifying *because* of her familiarity not despite it.

'You!' she snarls, her finger raised, the other hand a lump of fist at her side. She comes through the door at such a speed I have to step back, straight into the solid form of my mother. 'You did this!' Her voice is louder than her knocking. Mum steps back, which is essential because Poppy Carlisle is coming at me, finger raised, fist ready to lay me out.

I'm not scared of her physically, I'm terrified of who she is and what she represents. Logan has two sisters, two parents, friends for whom he is the world. Poppy Carlisle could just be the advance party for all I know. Whether there are others coming or not, she is terrifying.

I don't even notice Mum moving, I'm fixated on the woman who seems to be growing exponentially by the second as her anger unleashes itself at me. Then I realise Mum has been moving because I am being shifted behind her, so she can take my place in front of the raging woman. Mum pushes me backwards slightly, into Con's arms and then steps forward to take on the woman who is screaming, filling up our corridor with her fury.

'You couldn't stand it that he didn't want to be with you any more. That he had finally got the courage together to leave and you did what all people like you do: tried to make him sorry! How could you do that to him? How could you?'

She comes forward and I shrink back against my brother but Mum doesn't move, doesn't flinch, doesn't step back from the onslaught.

'You're not going to get away with this! Any of it. Your mother might have got away with murder, escaped prison on pure luck, but you're not going to! I'm going to make sure you pay for this. I'm going to make sure you pay for everything!'

'Don't talk to my daughter like that, Poppy,' Mum states calmly.

Poppy Carlisle is scary, a ball of flaming anger, but Mum . . . the quiet menace in my mother is all the more frightening. 'If you have something you'd like to discuss with her, then by all means talk, shout if you must, but don't threaten her.'

'Why, Serena, what are you going to do?'

'You don't want to know what I'll do, Poppy.'

'You think I'm scared of you?' she scoffs in response.

'I think you need to think about what you're doing by coming here and throwing threats around and shouting at my family.'

'Family. Your family. I regret the day I set eyes on you. I should have got rid of you back then but I didn't. Well, I'm not going to make that mistake again. I'm not going to let you get away with destroying my life and *my* family again.'

'Me, destroy your life? I always suspected you were deluded, but now I know you are not only deluded but also stupid. How did I destroy your life? You were the one who wouldn't stay away from him. You were the one who was always hanging around waiting for my sloppy seconds. If your life was destroyed, you did it to yourself.'

'If you were enough for him, why would he have had to look elsewhere? Be with someone else? He always used to say that you were tainted. I was pure.'

'Pure! Ha! Don't make me laugh! He gave up teaching at a job he loved for me. What did he give up for you, Poppy? What did he ever give you, Poppy, apart from the same clothes as me? And the same bruises and broken bones as me? Come on, Poppy, tell me, what did he ever give you that wasn't just an extension of what he gave me?

'Nothing to say? No, thought not. At least I could pretend to myself that he loved me. At least at fourteen, fifteen and sixteen I was still naïve enough to be able to pretend that he loved me. At least I had presents and help with homework and celebrating my exam results to keep me brainwashed into believing he actually cared. What did you have, Poppy?'

'You really think he loved you?'

'No, I don't. I don't think that at all. I *know* he didn't love me. I know he liked me because I was young and easy to manipulate. I *know* that he wasn't capable of love, only of controlling and the very worst emotional and physical violence. But at the time, I *thought* he loved me. The way he treated me made me believe he loved me and I had all these things I could point to that would balance out the horror so I could believe he did.

'And I wish – wish, with all my heart – that I had told my daughter about him, about what he did and how to spot the signs so she would have known to walk away from your *brother* the second he started manipulating her so he could abuse her.'

Poppy Carlisle rears up again, comes right up to Mum's face. 'MY BROTHER DIDN'T DO ANYTHING!' she screams before she points around my mother at me. 'She is the one who did this. She is the abuser in this. And she is the one who is finally going to get what's coming to her.'

Conrad circles his arm protectively around me.

'I told you, don't threaten my daughter.'

'I don't need to threaten her, Serena. Logan's awake.'

Oh God.

'And he's told us everything.'

Oh God. I'd hoped, actually hoped, he wouldn't wake up. If he stayed 'asleep' that would mean no one would ever know.

'Including who hurt him.'

Everyone is going to know. Everyone.

'He was talking to the police when I left. He has evidence. They are going to be here really soon to put you away.'

Evidence? He has evidence?

'Can't wait for you to find out what it's like to go to prison for hurting someone.'

'I didn't—' I begin.

'He told me!' Poppy Carlisle roars, almost knocking my mother over to get nearer. 'He told me all about what you did to him. He told all of us about—'

Her words are cut short by the arrival of a tall, white man with dark hair. He comes sprinting up the path and through our front door. 'Poppy,' he says, breathlessly, interrupting her invective.

She stops and turns to him. 'What are you doing here?' she snarls at him, turning the full weight of her anger on him.

'Bella called me. She was worried about where you were going. She said Logan was awake and that when he told you what had happened you just tore out of there and she was scared of what you were going to do.'

'Just go away, Alain. I don't need you here. I can handle this on my own.'

'You shouldn't be here, Poppy. Especially not when you're this angry. You could be violating the terms of your licence, you could get yourself arrested. You should be at home with Betina. None of this is helping you or her.'

'Don't try and use my daughter against me.'

'*Our* daughter. If the police find you here it's not going to help anyone. Especially not Logan.'

As if he has invoked them, conjured them up with the power of his words, DI Brosnin arrives in the rectangle of the doorway, followed by two uniformed police officers. Different to the ones who came for me last time, but still with the same grim expressions; still with the look that suggests this is just another day for them, just another arrest, just another thing they have to do.

I didn't expect it to be special or anything, I just didn't think arresting people would be so mundane to them that they don't even look bothered by it.

DI Brosnin smiles at me; it's such a genuine smile and she clearly doesn't mind the crush in the hallway. In fact, it looks like it gives her an extra thrill that she has an audience. Clearly nothing mundane or everyday about this for her.

'I see Miss Carlisle has beaten me to the punch,' she says. 'No matter. Now that Mr Logan Carlisle has awoken from his coma, he has been able to tell us what happened in the lead-up to his attack. And he told us it was you. That he had been planning on telling your family about your relationship and you grew incredibly angry. More angry than you'd ever been with him previously and you attacked him when it became clear he wasn't going to keep things secret any longer.' She puts her head to one side, looking at me as though I am a curiosity, as though she can't quite believe I truly thought I would get away with it. 'So, Miss Verity Gillmare, I am arresting you on suspicion of Grievous Bodily Harm with Intent and, now, coercive control.' She smiles at me again. 'I do hope you're not going to resist arrest or anything like that, Miss Gillmare,' she states. 'Now that we know what you're really like.'

Conrad doesn't let go of me, and Mum doesn't step out of the way to let them past. I can see what is going to happen. My family are going to be even more hurt because of me. This time, physically. They'll happily arrest them just to prove a point, I can tell that from the weight of DI Brosnin's gaze, the way she has kept her head to one side, the smile that she doesn't even bother to hide. At the end of the path, there are two more police officers. How she managed to get so many when everyone is aware of the police's stretched resources is a mystery; why she decided to bring them is not – she has a narrative in her head about how violent I am. Now that Logan has told them, confirmed it for her, she can proceed without any caution or second thought.

I carefully lower my brother's arm and I step towards my mother. I pause, rest my hand on her shoulder to let her know that I'm fine, that I'm going to go and I'm not going to cause a fuss. Immediately Mum gathers me in her arms. She's soft and comforting, a safe place to pause while I screw up my courage enough to go with the police.

'It's going to be all right,' she whispers into the curve of my jaw. 'It's going to be all right.'

She wants to hang on to me, to hold me tight, keep me safe, but I step away from her. I know my mum has always had trouble letting us go. She would keep us with her twenty-four seven if she could. She would keep us under her watchful gaze so no one could ever do anything to us.

Poppy Carlisle glares and glares as I walk past her. I don't blame her, not really. I would be exactly the same if I thought someone had hurt Conrad.

Her partner, Alain, who Logan had told me about, reaches for her. She doesn't resist when he pulls her into his arms, but she doesn't melt against him or give any indication that she feels anything for him.

Is that what I'm going to be like when I eventually get out of prison? Will I be scary and rock-like, not responding to any type of touch no matter who it's from? This is why Logan started this in the first place – he wanted to help her. He wanted to find a way to get her to feel again. He'd spent the better part of a decade watching her try to connect, try to put her life back together, and he wanted a way to end her pain, find her heart.

I'm sorry it's come to this. I'm sorry that all we have left is more pain, more reasons for Poppy Carlisle to rage against the world; to hate on the Gorringe bloodline.

DI Brosnin's smile widens as I meekly stop in front of her, waiting for them to put on handcuffs. They don't need to, of course; I've got no history of resisting before, but she needs it for present and future optics, I'm sure. She needs the neighbours to see me being led away in cuffs again; and she needs to be able to note down in the file for the CPS that I am a violent criminal – so much so, they've had to take extra precautions by deploying the handcuffs every time they've come for me.

I can feel many, many sets of eyes on me as I walk down the path to the other two waiting police officers. Those eyes stare, watch, observe and look from behind slightly parted blinds, nudged-aside net curtains and bare, unadorned windows. Anyone who didn't see the police car before, will now; or they'll hear about it. 'The doctor's daughter was arrested again. They sent two police cars and six officers [I'm sure there were officers covering the back in case I decided to abscond that way] and they led her away in handcuffs!'

Most of the people now watching will have needed Dad at some point. They often came to us if there was an accident, if their child had an extremely high temperature, if they couldn't get an appointment at their regular GP and wanted to find out if they would be all right to wait or not. And now I have done this to my father's reputation.

I duck my head but the male officer places the flat of his hand on my crown and pushes my head down anyway to 'assist' me getting into the car. Before I get in, I look up at the house and meet my mother's eyes. She is at the end of the path, her hands curled around the gate. She's looking at me like she knows.

She's looking at me like she knows I deserve all of this because I did it.

Part 11

logan

Extract from statement by Logan Carlisle

I wanted to go to her party.

I thought it'd be a good time to finally meet
them. I know it wasn't ideal, but with lots of other
people around, I thought they wouldn't overreact or
be too upset about it all. I know I shouldn't have
kept texting her, especially when I knew she was so
volatile. But I just wanted her to give me a chance.
Let me be a part of her life, properly.

She eventually suggested we meet at her flat to
talk about it. I knew she was probably going to try
to get me into bed and then give me the brush-off,
but I had to try. I loved her so much. I just wanted
to be a part of her life and not a secret any more.

When we arrived at the flat she was really angry.
More angry than I'd ever seen her before. We started
talking and then it turned into a fight. I know, I
know I shouldn't have said some of the things I
said, how she made me feel cheap and how she'd been

using me for sex all this time, but I was angry,
too. I was fed up and hurt and I wanted to hurt her.

When I said that thing about sex she blew up.
She flew at me, lashing out and calling me names.
I reacted. I know I shouldn't have, but I threw my
hands up to protect myself and caught her slightly
in the face. I feel awful about it, even now. She
paused in her tracks, clutching her face and
started crying. Then she stopped cold and said she
had to make the tears look good for when she
reported me. She said she was going to tell
everyone that I hit her and not for the first
time. If I came anywhere near her dad's party,
that's what she would do.

I felt stuck. What could I do? If I dared defy
her, she'd ruin me. I can't have any kind of
allegation made against me at work. I begged her
to reconsider and she just laughed. Eventually,
when she could see how distraught I was, she
suggested we make up, that we go to bed. I said
no, and she sort of smirked at me, called me
pathetic and said she'd only offered that as a
consolation prize. She said: 'Did you really think
fucking you was any real fun? The fun went right
out the window when you stopped presenting a
challenge.'

I was just devastated. I love her. When she went
to leave, I touched her shoulder, asking her to
reconsider. And she completely lost it.

She grabbed the award she keeps on the mantelpiece and swung out at me. I was totally not expecting it, and it connected with my temple. Here. I kind of reeled back and she came after me. She hit me with it again and again. I don't remember much after that.

I think I hit my head on the fireplace as I went down. I think . . . most of it is gone, I'm sorry. I know she hit me again when I was on the ground. I think, think I woke up and there was a male voice. I think she was there, too. I don't remember anything else - I don't remember getting into a fight, as you said. But maybe that's where the male voice came from? It did sound familiar, I think. It might have been the guy I thought she was sleeping with - Howie. Although I don't know what he would have been doing there so maybe I've made that up in my head.

I do remember waking up at one point and having this need to be with her. This urge to desperately find her. I think I probably thought she was in danger. And I remember the sound of the sea, the seagulls. Pumping, pounding music. And the desperate need to find Verity.

But that's it. That's all I can remember clearly. There are other flashes, but I'm not sure when they're from or if they're partial dreams.

Signed: L Carlisle

Extract from interview with Verity Gillmare, as transcribed by Darryl Palmer

Logan was obsessed with coming to my dad's party.

He kept saying that it'd be the right time to tell everyone about us, but really, nothing could be further from the truth. How was Mum going to feel seeing a Carlisle at something she'd spent so much time trying to organise? And I'd already given Mum enough grief about the party. So when he started texting me non-stop asking to come to the party, I ended up saying we should meet at my flat.

By the time I got there, he was really wound up. He was walking around and ranting about me not allowing him into my life. He just wanted me to acknowledge him. But it wasn't that simple and the more he was pushing for it, the more I realised that it was about a lot more than just telling people about us. He wanted to hurt my mum and I couldn't let that happen.

When I said no for a final time, he lost it. He started screaming at me that I had wasted his time, that I'd used him. That he'd been a convenient dick for me who serviced me as well as tidying up my flat and basically anything else I ordered him to do.

I was really shocked. I'd never heard or seen him like that before, I was genuinely scared of him. I asked him to calm down, which made him even worse. He wouldn't stop shouting so I said I was leaving. He said I wasn't going anywhere until he'd . . . until he'd serviced me like I'd forced him to do for the past year.

I was terrified at this point, and tried to run for it and he lashed out. I don't think he was trying to hit me, I think he was just trying to stop me leaving but his hand caught my cheek. I was horrified. I grabbed my cheek and just stood there looking at him, shocked. My eyes started watering from being hit like that and he started saying I was going to dox him, I was going to lie about him and tell everyone he hit me. I wouldn't do that, I didn't do that. I said no and that I was leaving and he came up to me, asking for a hug.

I didn't want to hug him but with Logan, giving in is often the best way to get something out of the way. I gave him the hug he wanted and before I knew it he was trying it on. He was trying to undress me and get his hands inside my clothes. I tried to get out of his hold and that was when it all went horribly wrong, he just turned and grabbed my throat.

I thought I'd been scared before, but now I really was because he had me completely by the throat and he felt really strong. It felt like all it would take was one jerk and he'd kill me. I started trying to get his hand off me and I was clawing and scratching anything I could to get him off.

He was trying to get inside my clothes again as well and I thought . . . I thought he was going to r- well, you know, I thought he was going to do that and kill me by accident. Except it wouldn't be a complete accident, it'd just be a side effect - I suppose that's the word - of trying to sexually assault me.

I was flailing around, trying to grab something to get him off me and then I felt my award. It sits on my mantelpiece and I've mostly forgotten it was there. I just grabbed it and swung. I think I only glanced a little bit of his head the first time, but his grip loosened a tiny bit. So I swung again and this time it caught him full on the side of the head. He let me go and staggered back and then he tripped over his own feet and stumbled and sort of head-butted the fireplace and smacked his head on the hearth as he went down. He was just out cold in front of me.

I was still shaking and crying from what he'd tried to do and him almost strangling me. When I'd calmed down, I tried calling him a few times but he didn't move. And then I cautiously shook him and he still didn't move. I was trembling too much to check his pulse but he didn't seem to be breathing. I thought I'd killed him and I just panicked.

I ran away. I know I should have called an ambulance or something but I was just so scared. I really thought he was dead. When I got home, I texted Howie. I knew he'd help me. He has keys to my flat because . . . because he needs somewhere he can go if things get too much. So I asked him to help me. He said he'd go over to check if Logan was alive. If he wasn't, he'd go out and call the police anonymously. If he was, then he'd patch him up and send him home.

I didn't hear from Howie again and then Logan just turned up at the party. When he was ranting at me earlier on, he'd told me he'd found out the venue of the party by going to Mum's work and asking various people about it. I mean, that's some crazy stuff to do. And that was why I knew I couldn't trust him to come to the party and have everything be all right.

That's what happened. I know I shouldn't have just left him there after he was hurt, but I was really scared. Just really scared.

Part 12

verity

Now

'Miss Gillmare, in the light of new evidence that we have received and with Mr Carlisle waking up, we are today questioning you about your involvement in his attack.' DI Brosnin states.

'I didn't attack him,' I say quietly. 'As I already explained to you earlier, it wasn't an attack.'

I have to talk now. Darryl and I have agreed that now Logan is awake and there is still no sign of Howie, and Logan is telling them these stories about me, I have to talk. I have no alternative. It's going to look bad enough when it comes to court, but if I don't speak now it's going to be fatal.

'What would you say you did then?' she asks. 'Because from what Mr Carlisle has told us and from the evidence he has produced, this sounds like the end result of a pattern of abusive behaviour that you have been perpetrating over the last year of your relationship.'

'I don't know what evidence you have because I didn't abuse him. I'm not abusive. There was no abuse in our relationship. Not from me, anyway.'

DI Brosnin nods her head thoughtfully. None of us around this table believe for one second that she's listening to me in the sense of she's taking in and understanding the words I'm saying. We all know that she is merely listening to the words so she can dismantle them and refashion them into more weapons to use against me.

'Are you implying that Mr Carlisle was abusive towards you?'

'No. But when I tell people what it was like they all seem to suggest that he was abusive.'

'But you don't think he was?'

'I don't know. I'm very confused about it.' Darryl is not happy. I can feel his body beside me tensing up with every word I utter. I am saying things that can and will be used against me. If I'm not careful, I'm going to talk my way into a longer prison sentence. 'But I'm not confused about whether I was abusive towards him or not. I wasn't. I wouldn't be. I don't know why he's saying I was.'

'How many times did you hit Mr Carlisle over the course of your relationship, Miss Gillmare?'

'None. I didn't hit him.'

'Keeping in mind the fact that we have evidence as well as Mr Carlisle's statement, can I ask you again – how many times have you hit Mr Carlisle?'

'None,' I repeat. I'm not sure what evidence they have but I didn't do that. 'I wouldn't do that.'

DI Brosnin stares at me while she nods at her colleague. He, in response, opens the beige cover of the folder in front of him to reveal a small black tape recorder.

'Let me ask you again, Miss Gillmare, how many times did you hit Mr Carlisle during the course of your relationship?'

'I believe my client has answered that question,' Darryl says. There's a distinct note of wariness in his voice, probably only audible to those who know him. 'Can we move on?'

DI Brosnin pulls a 'you asked for it' face and says, 'We managed to recover this message you left on Mr Carlisle's phone.' She nods again to the detective sergeant next to her and he presses play on the recorder.

'Logan, hello. It's me. Are you OK? You left in such a grump, I didn't get a chance to say sorry. You were kind of asking for it, but I didn't mean to hit you like that, it was—' The tape becomes fuzzy, my voice inaudible as the recording whirrs on. It continues to spew whiteish noise until, 'Look, call,' can be barely heard. And then, slightly clearer, 'I'll say sorry properly again. Bye-bye, love you.'

There's silence in the room after the recording ends. It sounds bad. It is bad. 'How can we be sure that is my client?' Darryl says, rallying first. 'Has the tape been verified for authenticity? If so, can I see the results? If not, can I ask why you are playing this for us when it hasn't been substantiated?'

Darryl is strongly defending me while I'm still stuck on how awful that sounds.

'Is it you?' DI Brosnin asks. 'Miss Gillmare, did you leave a message like that on Mr Carlisle's phone?'

I move my gaze from the recorder, which had just been filling the room with my voice, to the detective across the table. She really does not like me. She doesn't have to, I suppose. For her, I guess it is better if she doesn't like most people – less chance of being torn if you have to arrest or investigate someone you quite like.

'That's not how it sounded.'

'So you did leave such a message on Mr Carlisle's phone?'

'But it wasn't how it sounded.' I take a deep breath, try to sound rational and sane, not the person that recording makes me seem. 'We used to do this silly thing – well, actually, Logan used to do this silly thing of trying to scare me. I used to hate it but he loved it. He was always jumping out at me. And when he started coming over to the flat when I wasn't there, I'd come home and he'd jump out at me. It used to terrify me because I was never sure if it was him or someone else. I used to tell him that one day he'd do it and I wouldn't know it was him and I'd end up—' That sounds terrible so I stop. 'That time on the message, I couldn't find him and I was really scared because I did think this time it was a serial killer who'd broken in. When he jumped out at me from behind the living room door I screamed and totally panicked and pushed the door back, and it hit him in the face.'

'So you hit him with a door?'

'Not like that. I was terrified. I thought I was about to be raped or murdered or both and I just slammed the door back on instinct. He was really pissed off and went home. I left the message because I'd been asking him to stop doing it and he wouldn't and he got hurt as a result of doing something stupid.'

'So when he doesn't do something you want, you hit him to get him to comply?'

'No! Not at all. I'm just explaining how this one incident came about. I didn't hit him in the sense that you mean. I was, I thought, defending myself from an attacker.'

That story, even though it is true, even though he came back and said he was in the wrong, sounds so made up. Something an abusive person would say to counter an indisputable record of their abuse. That's the problem with the truth – it is often so simple, so mundane, it sounds like a lie you haven't made the effort to dress up.

'Miss Gillmare, how many times did you force yourself on Mr Carlisle?'

'What? Never!' I reply. I've replied too soon, though. Not until it's too late do I remember that the police never ask you a question without having some kind of knowledge of the answer – or at least a potential answer. Evidence. Poppy Carlisle mentioned evidence. They have mentioned evidence.

Another cover of a beige-brown cardboard file is opened, and the DI lowers her head as she examines what is on the page in front of her.

'Mr Carlisle's sister found a diary of sorts that he had been keeping.'

'Do I even need to mention the fact we can't verify this diary's authenticity?' Darryl says tiredly.

'Oh, we've done all our checks. They originated from his computer or phone and were added onto the cloud as well as a USB drive, all time-stamped.' DI Brosnin smiles at me. She has something. Something in those 'diaries'. What, I don't know, since there is nothing to tell. 'Mr Carlisle has written here that on more than one occasion he woke up to find you having sex with him.'

'No no no no no no no. No! That's not what happened.' I raise my hands to make a 'no' gesture. 'He went on and on at me about it. He kept saying it was one of his fantasies – to be woken up with oral or full sex. He went on and on about it. I wasn't keen because I've always been really clear about consent – a sleeping person can't consent. But Logan kept going on about it. For months. And then, it was his birthday and he said that was the only present he wanted. And I agreed. He was so happy afterwards, and because it made him so happy, whenever he mentioned it the night before, I would . . . I would . . . It was what he wanted.'

'So you did have sex with him while he was asleep?'

'Not in the bad way that you're saying. It was what he wanted.'

'What about it saying here that you pushed him? You were talking about your mother and her past and you got so enraged about what he said that you shoved him?'

'No, we were on the verge of an argument and he had his head on mine and I moved his head away so we could talk to each other. I didn't shove him.'

'You shouted at him for saying your friend had bad luck with men.'

'No! I barely raised my voice, let alone shouted. He was trash-talking my friend and I wanted him to stop it.'

'You gave him the silent treatment because he said your brother shouldn't be taking drugs in your house.'

'No! I just said my brother was free to do what he wanted in my place.'

'Even if it meant breaking the law, when you're a trainee solicitor, with so much to lose?'

'This isn't about that,' Darryl cuts in.

'No, no it's not, but it doesn't make the general picture we're building up of your client look good, does it?'

'Can we just move on?' he says.

'Miss Gillmare, I could go through all these incidents, and I'm sure you'd have an "excuse" for every one of them.'

'They're not excuses, they're explanations for what happened. They're the truth.'

'Are they? You see, Mr Carlisle seemed to be so concerned about these incidents he made notes of them. They run to pages.' She lifts up a few pages to emphasise what she is saying. 'I have to say, they make for very distressing reading. And they make up a pattern of behaviour that would show *you* to be the abusive one in your relationship.'

'That's not true.'

'Miss Gillmare, Verity, what happened? Were you trying to leave him for Howard Scarber? Was Logan Carlisle just too clingy? I mean, we've all had men like that, the ones who won't get the hint. And you have to be cruel to be kind. Is that what happened here? Did you just have to show him your tough side to get him to back off?'

I shook my head. 'No.'

'Then what was it, Miss Gillmare? Why would you treat this man in the way that is described in these pages? It's not all bad, he does say that you used to say you loved him. But why would you do this to him? And what would lead you to trying to kill him?'

'I didn't do any of those things,' I state.

'You would say that, wouldn't you?' She smiles. 'Now that Mr Carlisle has confirmed you were not only there at the time of his attack, but the perpetrator, could you tell me again, in your own words, what happened?'

I sit back in my seat, my spine almost collapsing under the weight of what is dawning on me.

Logan lied. He lied by twisting things. All of those things happened, but the way he told them, wrote them down – obviously to be read by someone else at a later date – was designed to make me look bad. Make me look *terrible*.

Logan lied. Did he get the idea from the court records, when he saw how easy it was to make one thing seem another? He has painted me as aggressive, moody, sexually abusive, emotionally terrifying. Slowly, carefully, Logan Carlisle has reshaped me in the twisted image of his mind's eye.

Logan lied. It's becoming clearer and clearer that he lied because he wanted to get me. No, actually, he wanted to 'get' Serena Gorringe, and to do that, he had to go through Verity Gillmare.

Logan lied. And it's worked. I am here. Arrested for GBH with intent. Facing charges for being a controlling abuser, backed up by a mountain of evidence that proves I could have done it. Looking closer and closer to being sent down for a crime I didn't commit.

Logan lied. He seduced me, he fooled me, he sucked me into his world.

Logan lied. And unfortunately for me, all his lies are true.

serena

Now

He's there again.

As we approach the court, I see him standing a little way away from the entrance, wearing a grey suit, speaking into a mobile phone.

Sir.

Him.

Marcus.

My sharp intake of breath, an audible gasp when I see him again, causes Evan to look at me. 'Are you all right?' he asks.

'Yes,' I manage through stiff lips. 'Fine. Fine,' I reply, despite my trembling hands. 'I'm perfectly fine,' I add, despite the fact my heart has stopped beating and I can feel the blood solidifying in my veins.

I turn to my husband, yank a smile across my numb face.

'It'll be all right,' Evan says. He says this even though Darryl Palmer told us that it's unlikely she'll be let out because now she is being charged with coercive control and GBH with intent. This hadn't sounded as bad as attempted murder until Darryl Palmer explained it carried the same sentence of life imprisonment as attempted murder. And they were probably charging her with that because it was so

419

difficult to prove attempted murder. As well as the attack, they are saying she abused him and they have evidence. Diary entries mostly, but
other corroboration from the conversations he had with various people.
I know she wasn't abusive, but they're going to make an example of
her. I know they are. Just like they made an example of Poppy and
wanted to make an example of me.

We climb the cream-grey stone steps of the court together, knowing
that it'll just be the two of us today. At our insistence, Conrad is staying at home to revise. I don't want any of this to impact his A-Levels
and his chances of college. We asked Faye and Medina not to come. I
haven't told my mother yet, but I will today, no matter the outcome. I
wanted to spare her this awful trip down Memory Lane for as long as
possible. We enter through the revolving doors into the gloom of the
building and I want to run back outside. I want to find out if that really
was *him*. Obviously it can't be him. But why is his doppelgänger here?
Twice now.

'Do you want to go and find out when we're up? I just need to get
some fresh air,' I say to Evan.

'You do look a bit queasy, are you OK?'

'Yes, I'll be fine. Being outside should sort me out.' I walk quickly
to the exit, not wanting *him* to get away.

The magistrates' court is a huge, grey-yellow concrete box that sits
on a hill in a part of Brighton that always seems barren. The road it's
on has a couple of newsagents, dry-cleaners, and a takeaway but they
all seem to be greyed-out, dull and under-used, as if they need to look
that way to fit in with the area. At the bottom of Edward Street is a
maze of roads that snakes you around to all areas of Brighton, there is
a patch of green, there is a stand for the cream-and-red buses, there are

dozens of people moving here and there, but this place, this area, seems to have had the life sucked out of it.

I exit the court and look both ways, seeking him out. He is leaning against the far side of the building, no longer on his phone, but holding a cigarette and staring hard at the pavement.

My whole body reacts to seeing him properly: my knees buckle, as my chest and stomach violently contract.

It is him.

But him from all those years ago. He hasn't aged, he doesn't look the sixty-odd he would be now. He looks like he is in his thirties, like he was back then. I move down the steps, determined not to let my body, my shock, stop me from speaking to him. As I approach, he stops leaning against the wall and stands upright, then takes another quick drag from his cigarette before he discards it with a flick of his forefinger and thumb.

Once I'm in front of him, and he is standing at his full height, he towers over me.

I haven't planned what I'm going to say, so when I stop in front of him, nothing leaves my mouth, not even the smallest of squeaks.

'I'm not him,' he says in lieu of my words. 'You look like you've seen a ghost, but I'm not Marcus Halnsley. Everyone says I'm the spitting image of him, but I'm not him.'

'Oh, *ohhhhh*.' My entire soul relaxes. It's not him, he isn't haunting me, his doppelgänger isn't stalking me. It's just a huge coincidence. Not that I believe in coincidences.

'You're Serena, aren't you,' he states. He sticks his hands in his pockets and looks incredibly uncomfortable, as though he is being forced to do this.

Immediately, I take a step back, put distance between us before I ask in a shaky voice: 'How do you know that?' I take another step back. Away. Ready to run for it.

This is not a good situation to be in. I know all of a sudden that I should not be talking to this man. And he shouldn't know my name.

'I'm not Marcus. But I am a Halnsley. My name's Jack. I'm Marcus's son.'

serena

Now

I don't really know what's just happened.

My mind is reeling and I'm not taking much in. But like Darryl Palmer had warned us, she wasn't let out. Verity will stay in prison until the trial.

I can't take any of this in properly, though, because of the man outside. *His son.* I knew about him, of course; he'd used his son to make me feel sorry for him, but I had put him well out of my mind. So much so it didn't occur to me when I saw him the other day that it could be him. Jack Halnsley.

'I'm an amateur genealogist,' Jack Halnsley explained, looking like he wanted nothing more than to be dragging deeply on a cigarette. 'I've been researching my family, starting off with my dad, for about fifteen years or so. The Ice Cream Girls thing came up straight away, of course.'

I took another step back at that point because I wasn't sure if the affable persona and demeanour he was currently presenting could switch at any moment. 'It was all over by the time I was old enough to be searching and my mum's not exactly forthcoming about anything to do with my dad. So I set up alerts on my computers to let me know if ever your names came up again.

'It did ten years ago when Poppy Carlisle was released from prison. I live in Birmingham. I actually went down to London to where it said she used to live and found that she'd moved. I chickened out at that point. I'd found out what your married name was by trawling through various records, and had an alert set up for your name. And your surname. Your daughter's name came up to do with this case.'

'What?' I said. I was absolutely horrified. He had been out there all this time waiting for information on me so he could . . . 'This is not OK. This is horrible. Absolutely horrible.'

'I'm sorry, I didn't mean any harm,' he pleaded. 'I just wanted to find out about my father.'

'But you've been stalking me and my family for more than a decade.'

'I haven't. I've just kept an eye out to see if anything happened that might give me a chance to talk to you.'

He took his hands out of his pockets and I darted back a little further, my heart like a frightened bird in my chest, fluttering and fussing, trying to escape: I was arguing with someone who wore the face of the man who would have hit me by this point of the conversation.

My reactions to Jack Halnsley were based on what he looked like, what that face and that physique – lithe but solid – wouldn't usually hesitate to do to me. I couldn't shake that memory. It might as well be *him* in front of me. It might as well be *him* speaking to me because my body and mind were terrified. Scared witless of what he was going to do.

'I'm not going to hurt you,' he said, alarmed at my moving even further back from him. 'It's just . . . I never knew my dad. My mum left him when I was six, and she never went back. She made it as difficult as possible for me to see him. Which, when you find out what I found out, I understand. And then he was gone. Dead. No chance of a reunion. But I basically wear his face without any real concept of who he truly was. You and Poppy Carlisle are a connection to him. It might not be the most positive connection, but it's something. Anything. I just need anything that will help me feel connected to him.'

'I have to go,' I said.

I understood his words – the passion, the need and the craving for history behind them, but I couldn't say anything to him that would be a comfort. I couldn't tell him what his dad did, I couldn't tell him that it took me years to come to terms with the fact I had loved someone who was, essentially, a monster. Jack Halnsley needed to speak to *his* friends. Not me. Not Poppy. How would the victim remember their abuser to his son and not feel pressured to rewrite history? I still found it hard to say anything negative about *him* thirty years later.

'My daughter is about to be— I have to go.'

'I'm staying at the Queens Hotel, down near the Pier, for a few days. Call me if you want to talk.'

I shake my head. 'No. Absolutely no.'

'I understand. Just . . . good luck with your daughter.'

I raced back into the court building, grateful that Evan hadn't come looking for me, horrified that this man was walking around, another person trying to destroy my life.

And now, because of him, because of the fear he's ignited in me, I've missed it. I've missed the important part of what will happen next because Verity isn't coming home.

Verity isn't coming home and the younger version of the man who started all of this is outside this very building trying to stir up even more trouble for me.

Verity turns and looks at us over her shoulder. She attempts a small smile of reassurance. *I'll be OK*, she's telling us. *Don't worry.*

She's five again. Five and about to walk in through the school gates for the first time. She's excited but also frightened. Absolutely terrified. Just as she crossed the threshold, she turned, and gave me the same look. A look that I was meant to understand as this: *I have to do this. I'm scared, but I have to do this. So don't be scared, I'll do it. I'll totally do it.*

I nodded at her back then. Smiled and reassured her with a look that I wasn't scared. I had every bit of faith in her ability to do this.

I nod right now. I don't smile, but I do tell her with my face that I understand; that I know she can do this. And I'll be waiting for her.

'It'll be all right,' Evan says to me without a note of hope anywhere in his words.

'I know,' I tell Evan, for the first time in as long as I can remember, lying to my husband.

poppy

Now

The family liaison and the officer in charge of the case, DI Brosnin, both agree that this is a classic case of an abusive person turning violent when they see themselves losing control.

'She says that she only hit you twice, and only really got you once, and that you tripped and hit the fireplace first, then you hit your head again when you fell down,' DI Brosnin says.

Logan shakes his head. 'No, no. She came after me with the award. It's heavy, she really had to heft it up to use it. I went down after the first hit and then she hit me a few more times. I did hit my head on the fireplace when I first went down, though.'

When they leave, Logan looks exhausted, like the life has been sucked out of him. Remembering it tires him out, talking about it looks like it snatches away huge swathes of energy.

'I don't want her to get into trouble,' he says to me. 'It's crazy, isn't it? I hate the thought of her sitting in a prison cell. I know what it did to you; I hate the idea of the same thing happening to her.'

In response, I fold my arms across my chest. I'm not sure what I'm supposed to say to that. How I'm meant to respond to my brother linking her and me in that way, like we're the same.

'Did you . . . did you go to the hearing? How did she seem?'

'I didn't go. I couldn't face going anywhere near any court. It took pretty much everything I had to take your USB stick into a police station, court wasn't happening.'

'Yes, of course, sorry.'

'But it's good news that they say you're recovering quickly. You'll soon be able to go home. Mum and Dad are gagging to have you back under their roof so they can take care of you.'

'You see this face? Can you see the unbridled joy at the prospect of it?' he says with a small smile.

'Oh please, their golden child at home again? They'll be over the moon. And you'll love being waited on every second of the day.'

'Yeah, and I'll be treated to Mum's finest cooking efforts.'

I smirk. 'It's not that bad.'

'It wasn't until you went away that we realised just how bad her cooking was. I mean, once you weren't around to rescue it or to make the food it was clear how awful . . . urgh. Dad tried, but he was too devastated to cook.' Logan shakes his head. 'You'd think for someone as obsessed with cookbooks as she is and who used to watch all the Delia programmes, that some of it would rub off.' He shrugs. 'But nah, still can't do it. I could weep for the effort she puts in, though.'

'Was it really awful when I went away?'

Just like they never really ask about prison, I never ask about this. We all act as though it was a mutual decision, we all behave as though the years didn't happen; like a pause button was pressed and nothing really went on between that and the play button being hit again.

'Yes,' he says simply. 'It was hell. In ways we couldn't articulate. Dad was like a zombie. We couldn't talk to him about anything for the first few years. He would just fly off the handle. Shout at us. He took us to and from school every day. Even when we were old enough to get there ourselves he'd still take us. He just didn't want to let us out of his sight. You'd think it would be worse for Bella, but no, he was obsessed with keeping the pair of us exactly where he could see us.

'Mum was a mess, but in many ways she coped better than he did, I suppose. I mean, we were all used to her being a bit flaky and you sort of picking up the slack. When you weren't there she kind of stepped up, I guess. Apart from those days when she would cry. Those were times when she'd been to see you, I think. Then Dad banned her from going. They rowed for days about it. And you know them, never a cross word, so Bella and I . . . we thought they were going to split up. And it made us cling to each other more and more.

'In a way, Dad was right. When Mum knew she couldn't go and see you, she sort of, I can't think of the right word. She kind of relaxed? She became what people think of as a mother and completely stepped into the hole you'd left. Apart from the cooking. That never got better.' My brother looks momentarily bereft. 'We never forgot, though. We didn't talk about you, but that doesn't mean we didn't think about you. Every day. Almost every day. Some days I'd forget and then I'd remember and hate myself. I wrote you all these letters in my head. Telling you what was going on, how I felt. I'm sure Bella did, too.

'Dad cried every day. He doesn't know that we know, but he did. You were his favourite, his little girl, and then you were gone. Snatched away from him.

'So, yes, it was awful when you weren't around. It was something beyond awful. When you came back, that was when it felt like that awful time was over. That's why I lost it with Mum and Dad for not telling us sooner that you'd left prison and you were back living with them. I couldn't understand why they would do that to us. And

I couldn't forgive them. I still can't, Poppy. They blocked us being in touch with you when you were in prison and then controlled it again when you left.'

'It wasn't their fault. They—'

'Stop defending them,' he cuts in with such venom, such anger, the words dry up in my throat. 'You don't get to defend them on this. They did wrong and nothing anyone says – not even you – will excuse that. I'll never forgive them for that, Poppy.'

'I could have tried harder to find you. I mean, I found Serena an—'

'And imagine the fallout if you had? How they would have reacted. No, Poppy. There are certain things I can't forgive and—' Logan stops talking suddenly, he grimaces and groans, clutching at his head. He squeezes his eyes shut and leans forward, agony consuming his face.

'Logan?' I ask.

'Arrgh,' he replies.

'Logan? Are you all right?'

He throws himself backwards. His whole body stiff, his face a rigid mountain of pain. I'm about to run for a nurse, when the one machine he is still hooked up to starts to beep loudly. This is the drama we were denied when he woke up. This is the expected room full of nurses and doctors, monitors making noise, me being shunted aside so many times I'm out of the room.

This is the anticipated me standing wide-eyed in the corridor, terrified that my brother is about to die.

serena

Now

I'm only here because I can't see Verity.

Darryl Palmer has said she doesn't want any of us to see her in prison, even though she is potentially going to be there for months until her case comes to trial. The only other place I want to be is at the hospital, shaking the truth out of Logan Carlisle. I know I spent a good amount of time convinced that she might be guilty, but when Mr Palmer told us what had been said, what she was actually accused of under the 'coercive control' banner, I knew she hadn't done it. None of it. Everything she has been accused of sounded calculated, not at all like she had been pushed to do it, as I had originally suspected. I realised the more Mr Palmer talked to us, the more evidence he told us had been presented to back up the story, that Logan Carlisle had spent a lot of time stitching up my daughter.

Evan had been quiet the whole way through. I could tell he was shaken, that he hadn't expected any of this. He – *we* – thought it was just a simple case of 'did she try to kill him?' that could be spun into self-defence. But the additional charges and the 'evidence' have thrown us both . . .

'But it's all lies,' I said more than once.

And every time I mentioned that it was lies, Mr Palmer responded with, 'That's what we're going to have to prove.' When he finished he told us that she didn't want us to see her in prison. 'She'll probably change her mind a bit further down the track but, for now, I think it best you respect her wishes. She needs to focus on herself and not worry about how you're doing.'

'What can we do?' Evan asked a moment before I did.

'At the moment, nothing. Except stay away from the Carlisles, Logan Carlisle especially.'

'But if I talk to him—'

'You'll be charged with witness intimidation. I am serious, Mrs Gillmare, they will throw the book at you.' He was looking at me when he said that. We all knew why. 'Stay away from them all. If you see any of them, cross the street and pretend they don't exist.'

My frustration, my powerlessness and inability to do anything has led me here: The Queens Hotel on Brighton seafront. I'd rung earlier to check he was still there and walked here from our house in Preston Park to give myself the opportunity to change my mind at any point on the journey.

I suppose I felt like punishing myself. His father is the reason why this is all happening. And this man is the closest I'm ever going to get to confronting *him*, so here I am, sitting in the restaurant area of the hotel, waiting for him to come down to speak to me.

I haven't told Evan – or anyone – what I'm doing. Evan is at work, trying to act normal. I can't. I've taken most of my accrued holiday days, and when those run out I will be taking a leave of absence. If I lose my job, so be it. I can't sit there and pretend nothing is happening. That I'm not absolutely frantic every moment of every day about what is happening to Verity.

It's a jolt, again, when Jack Halnsley appears and stands by the lift, trying to see if he can spot me. He really is *his* double. I raise my hand and Jack tips his chin up in acknowledgement before heading towards me. He even walks like *he* did – a strong stride that favours his left leg even though he was right-handed.

'Thanks for coming to see me,' Jack says, taking a seat beside me. I wish he'd taken the seat opposite, it's too freaky having him so close, we're practically touching. 'I didn't think I'd hear from you after the other day.'

'Believe me, it's a big surprise to me, too.'

'What happened with your daughter? I didn't come into the court. I thought it might upset you too much.'

'She was put in prison until the trial.'

'That must be tough.'

'I didn't come here to talk about my daughter, to be honest. You said you wanted to know about your father. Ask me some questions and I'll see if I can answer them. But . . . I'm not sure asking me is going to be best for you. It wasn't exactly the most positive experience for me.'

'Was he like you said in the papers? You said he was abusive. Was he?'

'What answer do you honestly want to that question?'

'The truth.'

'What good is it going to do you to hear "the truth"?'

'I just want to hear stuff about him.'

'But what if it's hideous stuff that you can't ever unhear? You say you kind of understand why your mother left him, but I'm not sure you're ready to hear all of it. The fact you're here suggests you're not ready to hear it. Because, as I've found out recently, you might think you want to

433

know something but when you find it out, it changes you. It haunts you. You're stuck in the present as the world travels to the future and all you'll want to do is get your hands on the past and reshape it.' I shift in my seat, the memory of what Vee told me: the quiet, insidious way Logan Carlisle brutalised her on so many levels floods my mind. I want so much to get my hands on *that* past and erase it. Reshape it. Change it. Anything that would mean she didn't go through all that. And isn't still going through it because of his lies. 'I promise you, sometimes you hear things and you'll wish the other person had lied to you. And if they do lie to you, more than anything, you'll want those lies to be true – even when you know they aren't.'

'Have you come here to lecture me?' he replies after a few moments of silence. 'Because I've got a mum and aunts and uncles and grand-parents for that.'

'Why don't you ask them about him, then?'

'My mum . . . she hated him and she made no bones about it. Every bad thing about him she would recount at length. But I was only small so I only vaguely remember the venom she had towards him. Then he died and no one would say a bad word against him, including Mum. She would either not talk about him or talk about how much he loved me. Same with my aunts and uncles. They only had good stuff to say after he died. And I know that wasn't the case. I mean, if it was, then why would she leave him? Why did I barely see him after we left?

'In recent years, Mum's not been doing too good, health-wise. Emotionally she's quite fragile, too. She's been through some serious bouts of depression. She'll suddenly start talking about my dad, as though he's on her mind. Then she'll stop. It's like she wants me to know about him, she can't keep the stuff in any longer, and then changes her mind and remembers what he was like and how she doesn't want me to know anything but the good stuff about him. So she'll either change the subject completely or she'll start talking about how much he loved me. It's really difficult sometimes.

'And I don't really remember what it was like to have him as a dad. Like I say, Mum made it difficult for me to see him, not that she'll admit that. I just want him to be a real person. Not this saint who used to be the Devil if you heard tell.'

I've tried. I've tried to protect him from himself and he doesn't want my help, not like that. He's determined to find out all the ugly, terrible things about his father. I probably shouldn't have come, but like when I used to meet Poppy, I do want to help. I came because I thought I could be 'doing something' and that 'something' was convincing him he didn't want to hear about his father.

'What do you want to know?'

'What was he like?'

'I only really know what he was like to me.'

'Which was?'

I only know what he was like to me. I don't even know what he was like to Poppy, not really, even though we spent a lot of time together. He was horrible. And he was amazing. He was a terrible, terrible human being who did many horrible, terrible things. I still have the scars from what he did. And not all of them are physical.

I often thought he would kill me. He told me often enough. He showed me often enough. He was unyielding in his structures and rules. If he said something, you followed it to the letter or there would be consequences. I felt sick all the time. I was scared all the time. And I was very aware that he could finish me off at any point and no one would be able to do a thing about it. Once I was gone I would be gone and no amount of handwringing and punishing him and dissecting what went wrong was going to bring me back. When I was with him, death constantly stalked my mind.

And I loved him. I felt sick when I wasn't with him; I felt like I couldn't function and I wasn't real and I didn't exist if I wasn't by his side. And I felt sick when I was with him. He defined who I was for so long. And I thought I couldn't live without him. Even the night I went there to finish it I knew I was going to be left without purpose in life without him.

I know now that isn't love. I know now because I have someone who loves me properly, and even in the years before my husband, I had worked out that what I had with him wasn't anywhere near love. And I still . . . I found it hard to untangle that from my brain. He had done that. He had managed to get me so brainwashed that when I was an adult, when I was married and had children, I almost let my husband walk away because I was ashamed to talk about him and confess that despite everything I loved him. So that was what he was like.

'So that was what he was like. Poppy would probably tell it differently; he was different with her, I suppose, but it wasn't easy. He wasn't an easy man and even now I feel like I'm glossing over what he did to me. To make it more palatable for you, and also to make it easier to remember in my head.'

Jack Halnsley has bowed his head after listening to me speak. I saw him do it halfway through and even though I wasn't talking for very long, what I said is still working its way through his mind.

'Is he real enough for you now?' I ask. Probably unnecessary, but what is it he expected to hear? How did he think he would feel afterwards? I tried to warn him, but even what I said, without details, without a blow-by-blow account of what went on, it is still dreadful. 'Is that what you wanted to hear?'

He raises his gaze and our eyes meet. And for a moment I am looking at *him*. Marcus. *Marcus.* For this moment in time I am looking at the man who took my teenage years, who helped to create the Serena who lied to her family, who lied to doctors at various hospitals, who tried to tell the truth when it was too late. For a moment I am staring at the man I loved more than life itself and I'm tempted to step back there. To go back to being with him. Giving my whole being to this person I can't untangle myself from.

If this man leant forward and kissed me right now, I would not stop him, I would not resist; I would most likely kiss him back.

Because he is Marcus. Him. Sir.

And in this moment I am Serena, love-struck teenager.

The moment elongates itself, stretches and stretches the reality we're living in and brings me closer and closer to . . . one kiss wouldn't really hurt, would it? It wouldn't really mean anything so it wouldn't hurt anyone.

Anyone except *everyone*.

I break eye contact, stare over his shoulder at the bar. I watch someone come in off the street and march up to the large wood-brown bar and order a drink as though their life depends upon it.

Stop being silly, Serena, I tell myself.

Marcus isn't here, is he? And teenage Serena isn't here, is she?

Jack Halnsley, who I can see from my peripheral vision, is still staring at me. 'I'm not . . .' he begins. 'Look, what do I say to make it better? What do I do?'

'There's nothing you can do. And it's not for you to do. You weren't the one who did all those things. This is what I meant about wanting to climb into the past and reshape it. You can't do anything. And it all happened so long ago there's nothing you can do to help now. It's there. A fixed thing that happened.' A fixed thing that keeps bleeding out into my present – whether that present was ten years ago or today. I cannot change the past but the past is changing my future all the time.

'I'm glad I know, but then I'm not. I mean, there's no way to romanticise him in my head now. It's absolutely clear why my mother didn't want anything to do with him, but it's even more maddening that they've all been participating in making him out to be all right but a little flawed. He was nothing like that. He was nothing like they made out.'

'But you'd prefer it if I said those things, too, wouldn't you? You want everything they told you, all those lies, to be true, don't you?'

He says nothing.

'You thought I was going to tell you he had a bit of a temper, that he'd sometimes get a bit aggressive and shouty; you thought you'd hear his flaws and it would tack nice and neatly onto the things people don't talk about. You never suspected I'd have to tell you all that, did you? And now you don't know what to do, what to think. Cos he's not here for you to hate. Or for you to talk to and get the "real" story.'

'Please stop,' he begs softly. 'I'm really . . . this has floored me. I can't deal with hearing anything else or your version of "I told you so".'

'Sorry,' I reply, shamefaced. 'I'm so sorry.' That was exactly what I was doing. And while I was directing it at him, it was meant for Evan, too. For not believing me when I said this could end up with Verity properly behind bars. 'Look, I'll go. I'm sorry to drop all of this on you and not be able to make it better.'

He suddenly seems to see me again and holds me with his look.

How he – Marcus – used to. 'Actually, it's for the best. I am, weirdly, glad that I know. I thought everyone was keeping things from me and now I know. I just have to work out how to live with all of this information.'

Jack Halnsley stands when I stand. From his pocket he produces a business card that he holds out to me. 'I don't imagine you'll want to, but, I don't know, if you do want to talk some more, here is how to get in touch.'

I reach for the card, taking it more out of politeness than anything else. He doesn't relinquish it straight away, instead he hangs on to it a bit longer. 'You're very attractive, you know?' he says quietly.

'What?' I say.

'You're really quite beautiful. I've thought it both times I've talked to you.'

'What?' I repeat and he lets go of the card.

He immediately sticks his hands in his pockets again. 'Guess there's something else my father and I have in common.'

'What?' I reply.

'It looks like attraction is genetic.' He offers me a half-shrug and a shy smile. 'I might not see you again so I had to tell you what I've been thinking, feeling. I think you're pretty incredible and I'm really attracted to you.'

My eyes search his face, looking for it, trying to see where it is hiding. I can't spot it, can't unearth it in the time I have left. But that doesn't mean it's not there. 'That is a perfect example of what *he* would do. I've made myself vulnerable by opening up to you and in response you come on to me. Knowing that I'm married, too. See you later, Jack Halnsley. I really hope you have a good look at yourself and try to be a better person than your father.'

I place his business card on the table in front of us.

'I'm sorry, I shouldn't have said all that,' he replies.

'No, you shouldn't. I'll see you.'

I leave before I get any more sucked in, before I start to let what he said infect my mind. Because I know myself. I know that the chance to do it over, to get it right, will become far too overwhelming if I don't walk away now. Walk away and tell Evan everything.

Part 13

Part 13

serena

Now

This book stool is not working out how I expected it to. Usually by now, when I'm months into a project, I can see progress, I can see how the final item will look or how it's supposed to look. And every time I sit down in front of it, I know whatever I do next will be another necessary step to the final piece.

This book stool? Nope. I can't seem to get the books to tessellate, fit together in a way that will make it secure with smooth lines, while still showing off at least some of the books. I try and I try, I waste hours here, putting the books out, stacking them and then taking them down and reordering them again. And it comes to nothing. Nothing.

Verity has been gone ten days.

Ten days feels like a lifetime, and every day I wish she would let us come to see her. She won't entertain it, though. Not even Con is allowed to go down there. I was hoping that she'd change her mind about him, at least, but she has been intractable. I'm trying to respect her wishes even though it is slowly killing me. It's doing the same to Evan, but we don't talk about it because the heartbreak of speaking of it would be too much for both of us. I'm desperate to see if she is all right, as she instructs Mr Palmer to tell us she is. Or if she's just pretending. I want

443

to see if she has bruises, cuts, darker circles under her eyes, more lost weight.

At the back of my head, of course, is the worry of when the change will start. When she'll start to become like Poppy. The Poppy who came out of prison was nothing like the young woman who went in. The one who emerged after twenty years was hard. Properly hardened, granite-like in everything she did. Even now, ten years later, I can see that edge is still there, only slightly under the surface. If threatened, it will come out, as we saw when she came here to attack Verity. The Poppy who went into prison would never have done that; for the one who came out it was the first course of action.

It's only been ten days, but when did that start for Poppy? Was it something she needed straight away to make sure no one messed with her, or was it something that she put on to protect herself and it stuck? Or was it a slow, slow boil, like a frog in a pan of boiling water: put the frog in while it's hot and the frog will jump out; put the frog in cold water and slowly turn up the heat so it becomes acclimatised to each increase in temperature and you can keep going until the water is at boiling point and the frog will be boiled alive. Is that what happened to Poppy? Every day something needed her to put on a hard face, take a strong stance, exhibit a certain attitude; every day she had to be that person to survive until that moment when she was boiling and forgot who she was at the start. I worry every day that this is what will happen to Verity.

Slowly, slowly, slowly she'll have the heat turned up on her until she is like Poppy, she is boiling.

I toss down the book in my hands. I can't concentrate on this right now. I can't concentrate on much right now, but definitely not this.

Jack Halnsley keeps coming to mind, too. Evan hadn't been happy when I told him I'd met with him and that he'd started to come onto me. But he'd understood my desperation, my trying to help someone because I couldn't help Verity. It's not what Jack Halnsley said about being attracted to me that keeps coming to mind, it's what he said about his mother and their family. How they had all rewritten history to try to protect *his* name and reputation. All the schools *he* worked at had done that. And he must have screwed other pupils but they were too scared of the repercussions, I suppose.

I keep wondering what will happen to Jack Halnsley now he knows his mother lied about what his father was like. Will he go back and confront her with all these new truths? Will he leave it because he hinted that she was fragile?

I pull my scarf off my head and stand up. My eyes are tired. I'm tired. At night, though, there is nothing that will put me to sleep for more than a couple of hours.

During the day I walk around like a zombie seeking its Armageddon, too exhausted and ineffectual to actually feast on brains if I did find any.

I leave my shed, padlock it and head back to the house.

Maybe reading will help. Although the words jumble themselves in front of my eyes and whole passages are read without me deciphering or absorbing a single word; maybe if I switch books something will connect. Something will stick. I've decided to go back to work in a few days. I'll not want to be there, but I don't want to be at home without Vee either, so I may as well earn money while I don't want to be somewhere.

What I really want to do, of course, is have a drink. To open up that expensive bottle of fizz we got for Evan's birthday and crawl inside. I don't tend to drink that much, or that often, but these past few weeks

I've been battling with the urge to do just that. I've been fighting and fighting it because I'm not sure I'd ever be able to stop.

After I wash my hands in the downstairs loo, I'm heading for the kitchen when the doorbell sounds. From the outside you can probably see my outline coming to answer it, but the person on the other side still feels it necessary to press the doorbell again. 'Give us a blinking chance,' I mumble as I swing it open.

Her.

Obviously it's her.

'I'm not allowed to talk to you,' I say and step back ready to shut the door in her face.

'Please,' she says, pushing the palm of her hand flat against the door, holding it open. 'Please.'

'What do you want?' Instinctively, I fold my arms across my chest and stand up to my full height. I want her to know that she won't be able to threaten or intimidate me. Now that everyone knows everything, now that my daughter is in prison, there is nothing about Poppy Carlisle that scares me.

'To talk.'

'I'm not allowed to talk to you. I could be done for witness tampering. Or is that the point? They've got my daughter, now you want them to get me, too?'

'No. I just want to talk.'

'I don't want to talk to you, Poppy. Everything goes wrong whenever I'm around you. I just want to be left alone by you and your family until I have to see you in court.' I move to shut the door again.

'I'll tell you about prison,' she says quickly, loudly, before I can shut her out of my life. 'I'll tell you what it's like and how you can help your daughter.'

I halt the door in its path. 'And what do you want in return?'

'To talk.'

'Yeah, right.'

'I'm serious, I just want to talk.'

She doesn't look much like Poppy today. Her hair is swept back into a low, neat bun, her clothes are smart – she's wearing a grey skirt suit with a light-cream sweater top, under a light-brown leather jacket.

'All right. I'll meet you at the end of the road in five minutes.'

'You'll definitely come?'

'Yes.'

'OK, I'll meet you at the end of the road in five.'

Without any more ceremony, I shut the door in her face.

'It's slightly different because she hasn't been convicted yet,' is how Poppy begins.

We're walking down the huge hill at the end of my road towards Preston Park station. I didn't want Poppy in my house, but maybe I should have let her in. If anyone sees us, if she's playing me, I will have no defence. I know how the police twist things, how barristers reframe situations; this is innocent, something she came looking for, but I could end up damaged by it.

'She'll be able to wear her own clothes all the time, for one thing. She'll be allowed to keep a few more things, for another. Anything she's not allowed will be kept in the prison safe until she leaves. When she first got there, they'll have searched her and asked her if she needed any medical attention. She'll have then been assigned a personal officer before they showed her where she'd be sleeping. I don't know what the prisons are like around here, or even nowadays, so I don't know if she'll have to share a cell or if she'll have one to herself. There are advantages and disadvantages to both. She'll have then been allowed to have a shower or bath after arrival. And someone would have explained to her how things work.

'If she's lucky, one of the other prisoners will take it upon themselves to look out for her. I had someone called Tina who basically took me under her wing right from the off and she really helped me. Hopefully someone will do that for her.'

Poppy's footsteps quicken and she surges ahead of me so she can stop in my path and turn to look at me. 'You don't have to worry about her, you know. They'll assess her and if she's really upset or overly worried and anxious, they'll help her. But she's strong, she should be OK.'

'You know what, Poppy? I don't want my daughter to be "strong". I want her to be an ordinary young woman, with all the vulnerabilities and flaws and fuck-ups that other women have and do without having to act to the outside world as though she can handle anything. Actually, no, what I want is my daughter to come home. Barring that, I'd really like her to not have to be fucking "strong".'

Poppy dramatically sighs and looks, for a moment, like she understands. 'I had to get strong to survive in prison,' she says eventually, the bald truth of it. 'If you don't get strong you get beaten down and basically eaten alive. I tried the non-strong version. I know which one I preferred.'

I look beyond Poppy at the Brighton vista that is laid out in front of me. From here, the whole world looks like a mid-year picture on a calendar. One that's perfectly nice, with its hotchpotch of greens and reds and browns and creams; its composition of shapes and shades and moving parts, set against the backdrop of the blue, blue sky, but ultimately it's not the picture that will make it to the calendar cover; and it's not the picture they'll choose to show the year out. It's something that is ordinary enough to be chosen but to be effectively hidden away.

This vista is how I thought I had lived my life. Nice and ordinary enough to be stuck in the middle of the world, not bothering anyone, not showing up on anyone's radar, normal enough to be left alone.

I step around Poppy and carry on down the slope. 'What did you want to talk about?' I ask over my shoulder with a little turn of my head.

She catches me up and falls into step beside me. But she doesn't speak straight away and I chance a look at her, wonder what's holding her back.

'It's more of a request,' she says.

'A request? This should be interesting. What is it that you want that you think I can and would give you?'

'I want you to persuade your daughter to see me. I need to talk to her. I need to find out why she did it.'

449

poppy

Now

Serena looks like she is going to punch me. That she's going to raise her fist and smack me several times right in the kisser.

I totally get why. It wasn't what she was expecting to hear. And it's probably pushing all of her buttons. But I have to understand why, and she is the only person who can help me with that. And, you know, possibly, it will help her, too.

'Look, you have to help me,' I say quickly. I stand in front of her, my hands open so she can see I'm being as honest and clear as I can be. 'I just want to talk to her, to understand. Logan loved her so much. If you'd read his diary, listened to the way he talked about her before I knew who she was, he adored her. She was his whole world and she took advantage of that. She *abused* that love. I just want to find out why.'

I see Serena's jaw clamp down, a clear indication of how much she is grinding her teeth together. As well as punching me, she wants to shout at me. She wants to use all those nasty words none of us knows we know until moments like these arrive and suddenly they're unleashed into the world.

'Look, this is as much for you as it is for me. This is the first time we'll get to understand why they do it. We both loved Marcus. We both gave him everything he wanted and more. I adored him. More than life itself sometimes, and I just want to understand why that wasn't enough. Was it me? Was it Logan? Or was it something in *them* – in Marcus, in your daughter – that made them incapable of accepting that love and not using it against those who adored them? I've never had the chance to talk to an abuser before. Not like this. Not when I can see both sides of the story.' I'm frantic here. 'I mean, was he annoying? Too clingy? Did she just think he was too pathetic and couldn't help treating him like that to see how far she could push him? I just want to talk to her. Calmly. I won't go there to upset her, I just want to understand.' Because if I understand her, then maybe I'll understand Marcus. And what it was about me that kept me there.

I stop and wait for Serena to speak. I know she's going to tell me to fuck off. But I needed to try. I needed to keep asking until she understood why I needed to do this.

'If you go anywhere near my daughter, I will kill you,' she says quite simply.

When she walks away, back towards her house, I know without any shred of doubt that she means it.

verity

Now

This is one of those moments.

Mum and Dad used to tell me: 'Only let it be once.'

I've never had a reason to use that advice. Not ever. Not really. Even when I was fighting off Logan I knew I wouldn't be fighting him again.

This is one of those moments that our folks used to warn Con and me about: if someone hits you first, hit them straight back and then go and tell the teacher. Con never would, not even when there was a little shit who was messing with him and his hair. I never did because I never had to. No one messed with me. No one paid me much mind. Until now.

I have been here twelve days. Twelve days, and today seems to be the day when something is going to happen. I could taste it in the air of my cell, even before I opened my eyes. I could feel it in the attitudes of the others, the sly looks over breakfast, in the corridor, in the shower block, in the daily leg stretch. Something was going to happen and it was going to happen to me, today.

Right now.

She's bigger than me, of course. Better connected. Her hair should be a mass of grease, her skin should be an uneven mess of pimples and scars, her body should be doughy and lumpen. That's what the stereotypes demand, that's what I've been taught to fear in here. But this one is slick. She is pretty, her skin cleansed and toned and moisturised to the point where she glows. Her blonde hair is shiny and wavy and well cared for. I know how she does it – other people's rations. She accepts all sorts of payments in kind for all sorts of things. She is taller than me, but we're about the same build and she obviously has the home-field advantage – I don't know who will jump in to help her if I somehow get the upper hand.

She is used to doing this, that's clear. I don't know if she usually waits till the twelfth day, but she is well versed in this. The menace I felt earlier was probably ignited by her; the promise of it is about to be fulfilled.

We are on the lower floor, outside the cells, by the bigger area where a lot of people play cards. I am bracketed by a large semi-circle of other inmates, as is she. I don't know who I can trust, who won't jump me first, so I am keeping as close an eye as possible on who is around me.

'You all right, Vee-Vee?' she asks.

I nod, smile, but don't speak.

'Not too, erm, *basic* for you?'

I shake my head and smile.

She is edging nearer and I have folded my arms across my chest to protect myself.

'Aww, I thoug—'

She doesn't finish her word let alone sentence because I have laid her out. I folded my arms to give me more room to hide the sudden movement of my hand curling into a fist before I move it in a smooth, upper-cut arc.

She has a glass jaw and is knocked clean off her feet. 'Let it only be once' only really applies when you have the luxury of walking away and staying away from the person who hit you first. In this situation, I couldn't wait – I had to hit first to make sure I wasn't the one laid out on the floor. And I had to hope her friends and supporters wouldn't jump me.

The collective gasp of shock strengthens my spine. I'm hoping this buys me some kind of protection or, at the very least, enough 'cred' to make people think twice before they approach me. I plaster a certain expression on my face – not a hard-case look, that's just inviting all kinds of trouble from people who want to knock it off. No, I have a small smile teasing at my lips, a controlled wildness to my eyes. I want people to think I might possibly be a bit unstable so they should be wary of me.

I want people to leave me the hell alone so I can work out how to get Logan to tell the truth.

'Excuse me,' I say and walk past my would-be assailant, who is still spread out on the floor, and go towards the stairs for my cell on the next floor up.

Hopefully, *hopefully*, that is all the once that I need.

poppy

Now

'I'm sorry,' I say to Alain when he arrives home with Betina.

I've cleaned the flat, I've got dinner on the table.

'Wash hands, stuff in your room,' Alain tells Betina, who goes running off to do as she's told.

My sort-of ex comes into the kitchen, staring openly and approvingly at the feast I have prepared. All their favourites: lasagne, garlic bread, green salad, cupcakes for afterwards.

'I'm sorry I've checked out of life, our family. I'm sorry for not being here and leaving everything to you. And thank you for looking after Betina. For not turfing me out; for being here when I haven't been.'

Alain stands and listens to me talking, apologising, trying to reintegrate myself back into this life. I've abandoned them, tried to escape from my responsibilities because I couldn't cope. Not with any of it. I thought I'd feel better once Logan was awake, but I don't, not really. That's why I went to see Serena. I thought . . . I hoped being allowed to speak to Verity would give me some insight into why I feel so terrible. It would allow me to be all right with still loving Marcus. Obviously

Serena won't help me to talk to her daughter and I am left here, floating around in this nebulous sea of ignorance.

I don't know who I am or what I'm meant to do. How am I meant to carry on, knowing that I am still capable of loving Marcus but I don't know why? All the theories, all the things I've searched for to understand, don't fit. They don't chime with what I feel.

'I'm going to do better. Stop all this. The drinking. The cutting up.' The desperation to smoke. 'I'm going to check back into family life. Permanently. I'm sorry. I'm so sorry.'

Alain listens to me talk with an impassive look on his face. He stands in the doorway paying close attention to everything I am saying but gives nothing away. Betina comes racing back in, and I can hear her shedding clothes and chucking them behind her as she runs.

'I'm so hungry,' she says. 'Is it dinner time now?'

'Not quite,' Alain says.

He's still not giving anything away.

'Betina, go and pick up your stuff from the corridor and outside of the toilet,' Alain says without breaking eye contact with me.

Oh.

He wants her out of the way so he can say what he's going to say.

I inhale, hold it. Keep it in.

'Will you marry me, Poppy Carlisle?' he says.

What?

He comes closer. 'I love you. I have never loved anyone as much as I love you. I cannot imagine a life without you. Will you make me the happiest man alive and marry me, Poppy Carlisle?'

'*What?*'

He gets down on one knee. 'All right, hoping third time is the charm. Poppy Carlisle, will you marry me?'

He's serious. He means this. He really means this.

And so do I when I say, 'Yes. Absolutely yes.'

'What did I miss?' Betina cries when she returns and Alain has me in his arms, and the pair of us are kissing and laughing and kissing.

'WHAT DID I MISS?'

Part 14

Part 14

poppy

Now

'You're looking well, mate,' Alain says to Logan.

Even in Logan's current state, they manage a bros-type shake/hug before Alain takes the seat Mum usually sits in when she's here. It's odd how things have settled down into a routine, with people and their usual seats; me with my usual time to visit so I don't run into our parents. Bella comes with Mum and Dad to give me and Logan space and time, I think.

'I'm feeling better,' Logan replies. 'Can't wait to get home.'

Alain frowns and glances in my direction. 'Yes, Alain, Logan is pretending he didn't have a seizure the other day, and hasn't had several more since. He thinks if he pretends hard enough I'll join in. And that the doctors will join in and they'll forget they told him he was going to be here indefinitely for now.'

'It's not as bad as she's making out,' my brother replies, practically sticking his tongue out.

'No, not as bad,' I say. 'But they're not as keen to let him go home as they previously were. More tests needed.'

Alain settles his brown leather courier bag onto the floor in front of his feet. 'I think I'll stay out of this thing for now,' he says. 'I am not getting in between brother-and-sister stuff.'

461

We haven't told anyone our news yet. I want to keep it to ourselves for a little bit and Alain completely agrees. It does make me smile, though. It makes me so happy I can't help little grins escaping when I'm doing nothing in particular. I've gone back to work properly, I take our daughter to school, I play with her, feed her, get up with her. I run our house and clean it and make plans for it. Things are better. So much better. 'So, Logan, Poppy said that you gave some thought to my request to interview you for the paper?'

'Hmm,' my brother replies.

'We don't really get that many male victims of domestic abuse and I thought it'd be great to speak to someone who is, in many ways, still going through it. She said you'd at least think about it, so I've come today to see if you've got any questions that may be stopping you from saying yes.'

'Won't it prejudice the trial?' Logan asks.

'No, because this will all be published afterwards. What I want to do is start the interviews now, while it's still fresh, and then we can talk several times over the coming months so we get a long view of the crime – the immediate aftermath and then how you feel and experience life over the following weeks and months.'

My brother does that thing with his face that he does when he is visibly thinking about something, churning it over, working through the avenues and lanes and what each of them could lead to. Eventually he looks at Alain and says, 'All right. I'll do it. When do you want to start?'

'No time like the present,' Alain replies and reaches for his bag. He removes his notebook and tape recorder as well as a pen.

I've never seen Alain work like this before. It's always something he does elsewhere, or he shuts himself away to type. It's kind of odd. And attractive at the same time. Having said that, Alain breathing is attractive to me right now. I am totally in love with him at the moment. Despite all the rubbishness that is going on, I am feeling thoroughly loved up.

Before Logan starts talking, telling his story again, I decide to move to the other side of the room, out of his eyeline so he can forget I'm here and he can be as honest as possible with Alain.

'Can you tell me about the attack?' Alain asks. If I was a journalist, I wouldn't start there. I wonder why he does, especially when I can see what it does to Logan; his whole body becomes rigid with the upset of remembering.

I notice Alain make a couple of notes. That's why he started there – he wanted to get a visceral, real reaction, to note it down. He'll probably keep monitoring his reaction during the interview, see how he changes. It'll probably add to the background of his piece.

'From the beginning?'

'Yes. How did you end up at her flat?'

'I texted her,' Logan says. 'Too many times. I was annoying, I know. But I was desperate to go to her father's party so we could tell everyone we were together. When she arrived, she was angry. She hated the fact that I'd summoned her, she didn't like things like that. I guess, in her eyes, I was never her equal so me convincing her to come and meet me was something beneath her.

'I tried to talk to her, tried to get her to understand that she was it for me. She was the love of my life. She began to mock me, saying how pathetic I was for loving her. It'd been nothing that deep for her, and that she'd lost interest in me the moment I stopped being a real challenge.

'She told me that when I was ready to grow up or start acting like a man, she might listen to what I have to say. I don't know, maybe I'm remembering it wrong because of my head injuries, but it felt really vicious, like she didn't mean those things but felt she had to say them so she could hurt me.' He sits back, seeming uncomfortable against the pillows. While he talks he looks desperately wounded; so very hurt and damaged.

'We were in the living room, standing beside the fireplace at this point. The row was escalating, we were both saying not good things. I told her that she used me. That I was a convenient dick for all her sexual needs. She was really upset and tried to initiate sex. I said no, that I didn't want to. And she got really aggressive. She grabbed at my crotch, tried to kiss me. I pushed her away slightly so she tried even harder. I was going to let her, because I love her and thought if I did, it might make her come back to me. I closed my eyes, and waited for her to kiss me again and instead . . . instead she hit me around the head with this award that sits on her fireplace. I opened my eyes just in time to see her do it again. The second time it was really hard and I went down.

'I was still in shock lying there when she hit me two more times before I passed out. When I came round she was gone. I don't know, some kind of homing signal or something kicked in. I just wanted to be with her. Wanted to see her. So I started to go to where I knew she would be – on the seafront. I don't really remember much else. I mean, I know I was on the seafront, so I must have been able to find her, but the only thing I really remember after that was waking up here.'

'That wasn't an easy listen,' Alain says to me as we walk back towards where he's parked his car. We were all subdued after Logan had spoken. Quiet and contemplative. We left not long after that as it felt awkward and uncomfortable to be sitting there, chatting about anything else and we obviously weren't going to keep going over and over his attack.

'No, it wasn't,' I reply.

At Alain's car, we stand in the same awkward atmosphere we thought we'd left behind in Logan's room.

'Poppy,' Alain suddenly says. He has clearly come to a decision about something, wants to say something significant. Something that will change a lot of things.

I know what he is going to say and I'm not sure I want him to do it. To name it. I don't want anyone to name it, but I especially don't want him to say it.

'Yes, Al?'

'I . . . erm . . . well . . . do you want to go shopping for an engagement ring in the next few days?'

I beam at him. Grateful that he doesn't do it. If he had, it would have ruined everything between us. 'That would be brilliant. Let's take Betina with us, otherwise we'll be in big trouble.'

He grins at the consequences we'd face if we even thought about leaving our daughter out of something like buying an engagement ring. She'd carried on screaming 'What did I miss?' for a good few minutes before we'd explained that we were getting married and Daddy was coming to stay with us for ever.

'Are you coming home now?' he asks.

I shake my head. 'I have a couple of things to do. But I'll be back at a decent time. Certainly in time for bed.'

What I have to do won't take long, but it is important and necessary.

poppy

Now

She still parks in the same place as she did all those years ago.

She has a different car, but she parks it in the same place near her office. I know this because I started watching her again. Not lots, nothing like when I was stalking her back in the days after I left prison. It's just now, I need to talk to her. And I fear if I go to her house she won't open the door after last time.

So I checked and her car is different but her job is the same and her parking spot is the same. And here she is, leaving work, checking all around like she always does because she's used to someone following her. My legs don't want to move, don't want to approach her, but they have to. They have to go and do this.

'Hello, Serena,' I say, coming up behind her.

Her arm freezes mid-push of the button to open her car door. A beat or two later, she inhales deeply then turns towards me. 'Are you stalking me again?'

'Yes,' I reply. 'But only for a couple of days.'

She lowers her head in frustration. 'Why? What do you want? To ask me to get my daughter to admit she's an abuser again? To find out what you can get me locked up for?'

'No, nothing like that. Look, I need to talk to you.'

'Get lost, Poppy.'

'I am lost. But I still need to talk to you.'

She runs her hands over her face, and I watch her beautiful features contort in anger and frustration. 'About what?' she almost screeches. 'Why can't you just leave me alone?'

'Logan's . . . Logan's lying and I don't know what to do about it.'

We've come to Granny Morag's beach hut. Technically, it's mine, yes, but it doesn't feel like mine. It'll always be hers, even when I pass it on to Betina. This place was so much about Granny Morag and I like to think of it as hers because she was the one person whose belief in me never wavered, not for a moment. If I think of it as hers, then she's still here with me.

The locks open quite easily because Alain regularly brings Betina down here, especially now that we're officially into summer. They had quite a cool little routine going without me, where he would pick her up from school and bring her to the beach before getting something for dinner. Serena marches in and sits on the left-hand side of the bench at the back of the hut. We painted the bench seat a bubblegum-pink to match the door colour that Betina chose so it's like being inside a stick of rock in here.

Serena took a lot of convincing to not swear at me and drive away, and then even more to come here to talk to me. I don't blame her, not after the stunt I pulled the other week. She perches on the bubblegum-pink seat and waits for me to talk to her as promised.

'Do you still love him?' I ask her. I have to know. I have to know if it's just me who's defective, who has something wrong with her.

'No, Poppy, I don't.' She knows who I'm talking about without me having to name him. And she confirms what I knew: there *is* something wrong with me. 'And neither do you,' she adds. 'You just think you do.'

'That's just it, I don't *think* I do, I actually do. I can't tell anyone else, especially not Alain. I still have feelings for him even though he's been dead thirty years.'

'Evan asked me why I loved him a while ago. Not why did I stay with him, not why didn't I leave, but what was it about him that I loved. I thought it was my memory loss that had made me forget the specifics of what I loved about him. And then Evan said that maybe I didn't love him, not in the end. Maybe I had loved him at the start, but I just convinced myself I did as time went on because it was the only way to cope with the trauma. And afterwards, looking back, it was the only thing that could account for my staying for so long. No one believed us when we said what he was like. Much easier to believe we were slutty, murderous vixens than accept he found a way to terrify two people into staying with him no matter what. Better for your brain to believe you loved him than to accept you endured all that brutality for nothing.'

'Your husband said that?'

'More or less.'

'Dr Evan is really wise.'

'Stay away from him, Poppy. I'm not fifteen any more.'

'Didn't mean it like that.' I say that in a distracted manner because I'm trying assimilate what she's just said. If that's true, that would make so much sense. It would explain everything. *Everything.* Why I still feel this way. Why I have so much hate for him but always find it tempered with love. Or maybe just tempered by a need to find a way for my mind to cope with it all. Love erases all mistakes, after all. Love makes everything all right, doesn't it?

'Why am I here, Poppy?' she asks after more than a few minutes have passed.

'I think Logan is . . . I think Logan is lying. About what happened the day he was hurt. I've heard his story three times and each time it's different. And not just a little different or, you know, embellished. It's different, like he's forgotten what he said before and is making it up.'

'Right. Have you told the police?'

'No.' I hang my head. 'I can't. I keep trying to convince myself that it's because of his head injury. But there's something underneath everything he says. It's like he's hiding something. And he can't explain the blood splatter from Verity's friend because he can't remember. And it's making me doubt everything. It's making me wonder . . .'

'Wonder if she abused him at all?'

'He wouldn't have lied, though, surely? He didn't make it up, surely? I mean, he couldn't. He wrote about it so . . . I just can't believe that—'

'That he's an abuser.'

'I didn't say that,' I protest. 'I didn't say that.'

'Poppy, he forced Verity to have unprotected sex. Who does that remind you of?'

Rubber johnnies don't always work, Poppy, and they completely kill the pleasure for me. I want to experience what sex is really about. You do when you love someone.

'He drove a wedge between her and her friends. Does that sound familiar?'

Those girls are all sluts, you know, Poppy. You're better than them. Think about who you hang around with. Think about what they bring to your life. You can have friends, but just not girls like that. Not girls who are so loose.

'He distanced her from her brother, who she was so close to.'

Your siblings sound delightful, but they're a real drain on you. Looking after them all the time is making you look old before your time. And you know one of the reasons why I love you is for how you look. How free and young you are.

'He dripped poison into her ears about me for almost a year so she actually started to hate me. She thinks I don't know, but the way she used to speak to me, look at me . . . he did that.'

I really don't know how your mother can call herself that when she won't learn to cook. I mean, how hard is it? And the way she's so cold with you. Sometimes I just sit and think about how much she's damaged you and I'm glad you've got me. I'm the only one who'll show you what love should look like.

'He was moving on to making her hate her body, her looks, so he could start to control what she wore.'

It'll break my heart, girls, if you both got too big to look pretty any more. Poppy, sweetheart, you're on the edge, and Serena, my love, you know how you balloon at the drop of a hat. I'm only saying it because you both mean so much to me. I wouldn't bother, otherwise. And if I don't say it, who else will? But, hey, don't let me stop you. If you really want that ice cream you eat it, as long as you know what you're doing as you eat it.

'Does any of that sound familiar, Poppy?'

Logan can't be an abuser. He just can't. The way he spoke about her before I found out who she was . . . He can't. He just can't.

'But this is worse. Verity's solicitor told us that he had evidence of her abuse? A diary? That's beyond anything Marcus did.'

I need a drink. And I need a cigarette. I rub at my forearms, hidden and protected under my long-sleeved tops. I need something immediate and strong that will take me away from this . . . this horror.

'Being an Ice Cream Girl really is the nightmare that keeps on giving, isn't it?' I say to Serena.

A small smile ghosts across her lips. 'Yes, yes it is. And I should have told my kid about it. I blame myself for all of this. If I'd have told, if I'd warned her what men could be like . . . I mean, I lived the ultimate rotten man experience and I didn't think to warn her. She has a brilliant brother, a near-perfect dad so I let her go around thinking that's what all men are like. That she's going to have equal, loving relationships with all men. And now look. I hate myself for this. I really, really hate myself.'

'Yeah? Well, get in line. What am I going to do about this? I don't want to believe Logan is . . . I can't even say it. What am I going to do?'

We sit in silence for a long while, each of us spinning and self-hating in our own little worlds. 'I'm serious, Serena, what am I going to do?'

This is like the moment standing outside Marcus's house. As far as we were concerned, he was dead. He was dead and Serena was so lovely to me, she was kind and gentle and got me out onto the street. And I didn't know what to do. I asked her, asked Serena, and she shouted at me that she didn't know. Even though I would have done whatever she asked as long as she would keep being nice to me. This is like that moment because I don't know what to do.

'How the hell should I know? I'd be all for racing down to the police station and telling all about Logan. But who would believe me? Apart from being her mother, I'm an Ice Cream Girl, the one who "got

471

away with it". Who's going to be rushing to listen to me when I tell them my daughter is innocent and her victim is lying?'

'I'll tell them. I'll back you up.'

'OK, other Ice Cream Girl.'

'He's my brother; they'll know for me to be questioning him I must think he's lied.'

'Yes, and don't you remember how much time they spent trying to prove that we were lovers?'

'It was all so long ago, that must all be behind us now.'

'So no one has brought it up at all to you? Given you a funny look? Made some semi-off-key comment about you and me?'

'The only thing I can do is get Logan to tell the truth.'

She doesn't have to say 'OK, other Ice Cream Girl' out loud for me to hear it.

'Will you come with me?'

'Me? You want *me* to come with you?'

'I can't go alone and there's no one else. Everyone else will be devastated.'

'What about your husband?'

'Alain's a journalist writing a story on Logan and the long-term effects of his attack.'

'Seriously?'

'Seriously. There really is no one else.'

Serena appears haunted for a moment; she looks every one of her nearly fifty years – every line is accentuated, every crease scored deep into her skin, her hair seems to grey while I'm looking at her. 'Fine. I'll come with you to get your brother to confess. I mean, why wouldn't I want to come see the man who abused my daughter and has set her up to go to prison, where who knows what is happening to her right now?'

472

verity

Now

It wasn't going to go unanswered, of course it wasn't.

I had a good few days, though, of freedom. Of feeling that everyone was going to leave me alone. They were never going to leave me alone. Not after what I did. But those few days? They were golden.

Payback isn't a bitch.

Payback is doing what Howie said he did at times like this. Curl up into a ball, really tight. Really tight. Keep your arms around you to give your chest a frame, keep your head in to protect your face, close your eyes and find somewhere safe to hide in the dark.

And wait for it to be over.

Wait for the shouts, the kicks, the laughter to be over.

serena

Now

As ideas go, I've had better ones.

Coming here is probably up there with terrible ideas that will have dire consequences – for his sake more than mine. I'm not sure if I'll be able to stop myself harming him. This man who has done these evil things to my child.

I'm more than prepared to go to prison for hurting him, and he probably won't die from his injuries since we're already in a hospital, but I am here for one reason only.

If Poppy needs support to get him to confess, which will get Verity out, then I'll do it. I'll do pretty much anything.

I'll even find a way to not hurt him.

Poppy tells me to wait out of sight when we arrive at the hospital so she can check if her parents are around. The last thing any of us need is *that* meeting.

She has been shaking all the way over here. She thinks I haven't noticed, or maybe she does know I've noticed and doesn't care enough to hide it. I'm probably shaking, too. So many emotions are coursing through me right now, while others are firing in my brain so it'd be a miracle for them not to be exposed physically.

I am rapidly trying to erase the things Verity told me, the things he did to her, the way he manipulated her. Because I can only do this if I walk into that hospital with the equivalent of a blank mind.

Poppy enters first, holds the door open for me. The room is small because it is crammed with so much equipment. At the centre of the chaos of machines is a hospital bed with sides and a white man in blue pyjamas who is staring blankly at the television that hangs above his head on a hinged arm. I remember seeing him lying on the ground outside the Sea Maiden. I would not have recognised him as the man sitting here now.

His face lights up when he sees Poppy, and I suppose it says something about their relationship that he is genuinely happy to see her. Obviously the joy instantly evaporates when he sees me, probably for the first time since he began this thing with my daughter.

'Nice,' he says. 'Witness intimidation. I'll be sure to add that to the list of charges against your daughter.'

Why did I think I could do this? Because right now, in my fantasy, I have a pillow in my hands . . .

'She's not here to intimidate anyone,' Poppy says.

'Are you sure?' he replies. 'We all know how violent her daughter is; it's most likely she got it from her wayward mother.'

'Stop, Logan, all right? Just stop. We know, all right? We both know the truth.'

'What truth?'

'We know that your attack didn't happen the way you said it did. We know that she didn't abuse you. We want you to tell us the truth.'

Logan Carlisle styles it out for a few seconds, looking from her face to mine back to her. 'Lot of "we"s there, Poppy. Sounds very much like witness intimidation to me.'

'Just tell me why you did it, Logan. Or tell me what really happened. But stop pretending it was how you said it was.'

'I'm not saying a word with *her* in the room,' he eventually concedes.

He is handsome. Good-looking in that way that Poppy was pretty. I remember how awful I felt when Marcus first took up with Poppy. She was so pretty, voluptuous and perfect. I'll never forget how much it hurt. I used to watch him with her, how he'd touch her hair, smile at her, kiss her pink lips, and the jealousy would almost consume me. When he made me listen to him screwing her, it was a new kind of torment; there was nowhere to hang my feelings, no way for me to hide from it. And then he progressed to making me watch him fuck her. That was the type of suffering he was good at, that was the type of torture he loved to deploy.

This Logan Carlisle, he is handsome in the way that Poppy was pretty. I bet he is charming in the way Marcus was seductive. That is how he would have smarmed his way into Verity's life – first as a friend so she would have fallen for him without knowing what was happening. I didn't prepare Verity for such things: for good-looking people who were snakes. And I should have. I should have told her about me, I should have shown her my scars, I should have explained to her what the world could be like.

But I liked to pretend. Even when Poppy reappeared and upended everything, I liked to make-believe that I'd had a normal life as a teenager. That I hadn't got involved with someone as twisted as *him*. In my head the years from thirteen to eighteen didn't exist so there was no point talking about them.

And now look where I am. Where my daughter is.

And look who I have to rely on for help.

'I'll wait for you outside, Poppy,' I say, and firing a glare that holds every molecule of hate I feel for him at Logan, I leave the room.

My legs give way, depositing me on one of the black-grey chairs outside his room. *Good luck, Poppy*, I think. *Because I don't know how you're going to get to the truth without beating it out of him.*

poppy

Now

I'm still shaking.

Shaking and shivering; quivering and quaking, as I have been ever since I forced myself to talk to Serena. She was the only one who I knew would understand, who would listen without shutting me down. I couldn't imagine trying to tell Bella or Mum and Dad what I suspected. I couldn't imagine the pain merely saying those words would cause them. Alain suspected, after he spoke to Logan the other day, and I had willed him to stay silent, to not say what he thought because I would be forced to defend Logan rather than agree with Alain. Thankfully, *thankfully*, he had picked up on the damage it would do and had left it.

I want to stand as far away from Logan as possible, but I need to sit close, to hear every single one of his words even if he lowers his voice so no one else can overhear. After Serena leaves, we sit in silence for long, long minutes. I look at him, trying to work out when he changed, when he became like this. Capable of this. Although, I don't know what 'this' is, not yet. It might just be the fight he was lying about. It might not be everything.

'Now she's gone, you can call the police and tell them she's put pressure on you to come here to try to get me to change my story,' he says conspiratorially.

'I went to her,' I tell my brother. 'I realised you were lying and I went to her. She didn't want to come here. This is the last place she wants to be, but I begged her because I needed someone else to hear why you did it.'

'Why I did what?' His voice has frosted over now. He's not looking at me and I can feel him physically drawing away from me.

'Logan, just . . . just stop it. Just tell me why. Why you lied. Cos I know you did. I just don't know why and how much of it was lies.'

'It wasn't lies. It just wasn't my truth.'

'What do you mean?'

'I went to talk to that bitch—'

'Don't call her that.'

'I went to talk to *her*, *Serena*, like I said. I've watched you, Poppy, and I've watched our family and I just wanted her to know what it's been like. I went to see her and when I got there . . .'

logan

Now

I went to talk to *her*, *Serena*, like I said. I've watched you, Poppy, and I've watched our family and I just wanted her to know what it's been like. That it's been ten years and nothing has got any better. I went to see her and when I got to her house, she was coming out with her daughter. The pair of them were laughing and joking and were clearly the best of friends.

And I just thought: how does she get this? How does she get to laugh and joke when we get none of that? And I thought, no, this shouldn't be like this. I was going to tell her precious daughter all about her. All about how she should have been in prison, how she got away with killing a man.

I thought twice about it. I honestly did. And then I find out her name. That lying bitch had the temerity to call her daughter Verity. She named her daughter 'truth'! Fucking *truth*. That was it. That was when I knew the best way to get to her was through her daughter. And to do that, I had to show *Verity* what her mother was like.

So I went back when I knew her mother wasn't around and she was. Pretended that I'd come to see her mother, started the process of showing her who her mother really was. That was the best part, watching

480

her come to the same realisation that I had – that at the very least, she should have gone to prison as well as you.

I didn't actually mean for the rest of it to happen. But then I saw how she started to behave around me . . . How I started to feel around her . . . And I thought: how would her mother handle the truth of me fucking her precious child? Imagine the look on her face when she realised a Carlisle had screwed her offspring just like she'd screwed over a Carlisle.

It was only meant to be for a few weeks, love her up, get her to introduce me to the folks – get to see that look on *Serena*'s face – and then dump 'Verity' in the most brutal way possible.

But then . . . I don't know . . . You've seen her. As well as being a looker, she's so *likeable*. Sweet. Funny. Good to be around. When I was with her I felt better about myself. I kept . . . I kept having doubts about what I was doing. I kept wondering if it could work out between us. After a few weeks with her, I realised that I had to stop myself falling in love with her – I had to protect myself in case I got weak and chickened out.

I started my 'diary' as an insurance policy. In case she dumped me before I was ready to do it to her or before she introduced me to her parents. I had something up my sleeve that would really hurt her.

Sometimes I'd get so mad: why did it have to be her? Why did I have to fall for her? But then I'd see you or Bella or Mum and Dad and I'd be reminded of what that bitch did, why it was all her fault, and I'd be refocused. I'd go back to breaking *Verity* so I could hand the pieces back to her mother.

When she told me that her mother was planning a fiftieth-birthday party for her father, I knew that would be the perfect time. Perfect. I show up, and in front of everyone they know and love and respect I tell them who I am. I tell them who Serena is. I tell her I've been fucking her daughter for the best part of a year. Blow her world wide open.

But then Verity decides to dump me instead. Like that was allowed! How dare she. I got her to meet me on the day because I thought last minute I could change her mind. But no, she was adamant that if I did get introduced to them, it had to be another time. Another day.

No. She didn't get to decide that.

We got into a row. We were both shouting at each other and then she was trying to leave. I pulled her back. Told her she didn't get to decide when to walk away. I decided these things. And she started fighting harder to get away.

Next thing I had my hand around her . . . around her throat, and I was pulling at her clothes. I just wanted her to remember what we had. Who I was to her. How good it always felt when we fucked each other. I wasn't hurting her. I was trying to calm her down. I wanted us to go back to what it was like before. I knew once we started making love it'd be all right. She was making this noise and trying to get my hands off her when I would have let her go if she would just calm down, you know?

Then there was this pain in my head. She'd hit me with the stupid award thing she kept on her mantelpiece. I kind of staggered back but didn't let go of her so she hit me again.

That's when I went down, I guess.

I don't remember anything after that.

Not until I woke up and her stupid friend was standing over me, shaking me.

She was nowhere to be seen. I suppose she sent him to make sure I wasn't dead or something. He was going on and on about how worried Verity was and how he was going to patch me up so I could go home.

Home? *That* was my home. I'd been living there for months, where did he think I was going to go? And who was he to be standing there telling me I had to leave?

She was mine and *he* was telling me to go? No.

He took me into the kitchen because that's where Verity keeps her first-aid box. Yes, he knew that. How did he know that? He went straight to her drawer and got it out. Started to patch me up.

Which just *pissed me off.*

I asked him how come he knew where Verity kept stuff in her house and he wouldn't answer. He kept talking about letting her go. What the hell did he know about letting her go? Let her go so he could have her? No. *NO.*

The knife was just there. I didn't mean to hurt him.

I just wanted him to shut the hell up. I sort of waved it at him and then I wasn't waving at him any more. And then . . .

And then my head went again. I couldn't stand, I fell down and I couldn't move. It must have been a seizure. Except I didn't know about them, then.

When I woke up her stupid friend was gone. It was dark, I was on my own. And I knew what I had to do: get to the party. Tell Verity's parents and let them see how she'd left me. Let every single person at that party see how much like her bitch mother she was.

The next thing I remember was waking up here.

poppy

Now

'The next thing I remember was waking up here.'

Who is this psychopath and why is he wearing my brother's face? Why has he branded himself with my brother's name and wrapped himself up in my brother's body? Who is this psychopath and why aren't I allowed to run far, far away from him right now?

I curl my fingers inwards so I can dig my ragged nails into the palms of my hands. I want to drink, I want to smoke, I want to ribbon my arms until this pain goes away. What has he done? What. Has. He. Done?

'So it wasn't a semi-unprovoked attack? It was self-defence. The stuff with Verity at her flat, she was acting in self-defence?' I have to get that clear. I have to properly understand. 'She didn't attack you, it was self-defence because you had her by the throat and you were trying to r— You were trying to rip her clothes off so you could force yourself on her.'

'You make it sound bad. If she had just calmed down, I wouldn't have had to keep such a tight hold on her.'

'Just tell me, Logan, did she hit you in self-defence?'

'Yes, she hit me in self-defence.'

'And your diary? Was any of that true?'

'In a way,' he replies.

'What do you mean?'

'It happened, but not how I wrote it down.'

My nails are puncturing my skin, they are drawing blood, they are bringing me the pain I need to be able to hear this. 'I don't understand.'

'Everything happened that I wrote down, but not always from my perspective or not always in the way that I made out. Like the sex thing. She didn't want to do that. She said it messed with consent and she didn't want to do that. But I convinced her. I kept on and on at her until she would grudgingly do it. I enjoyed it, every second of it. But every time she gave in to me and did it, it gave me something to write down.'

'She was never violent?'

'Not in the way I made out.'

'And what about the sex without a condom thing? Did you force her to do that?'

'I wanted to move things along to sex without condoms. She didn't. Rather, she *said* she didn't. Said she wasn't ready. But she was ready. Of course she was ready. I just made it a non-issue, which showed her she was ready. Once we'd done it a few times I saw that she'd made an appointment to get the Pill. No more issue.'

Don't you want things to be nice for me, Poppy? Don't you think I deserve that?

'You have got to tell the police the truth.'

'Why do I have to?'

'Because she's in prison for no reason.'

'Like you were.'

'This isn't about me. You have to tell the police the truth. If you don't, I will.'

485

'Yeah, good luck with that. It'll literally be my word against yours. And I'm the victim. Why do you think I wanted that *bitch* to leave?'

'Don't call her that,' I say. He doesn't realise how it makes him sound when he says that; how much it sounds like he hates women. I uncurl my fingers from my hands and across each palm there is a chain of red crescents. I reach into my pocket and pull out my mobile phone. 'And it'll be your word against yours.' I press stop on the recording and start to name it when Logan lunges at me. I dart out of my seat, holding the phone out of reach. He can't get out of bed easily so I move even further back. Working quickly, I name the recording and I email it to myself at work. 'I've sent it to myself and the cloud,' I tell him as I watch him look for ways to unhook himself from the machine he's attached to. 'So, go ahead, come for my phone. There are copies out there that you can't destroy.'

Now he knows that he has been caught, Logan collapses back against his white pillows and glares at me with such contempt, such *hatred*.

'This is all your fault,' he accuses, his teeth bared like an animal preparing to attack. 'It is all on you. I wasn't going to use that diary. It was just back-up in case I needed it. No one was meant to see it. You're the one who gave it to the police and started this mess.'

'I can't believe you're blaming me. I thought you were like me. That you'd been hurt like I was but . . .' I resist the urge to dig my fingernails into my palms again. I resist the urge to claw at my flesh. 'Why did you do all this? Why?'

'I told you – why did she get to be happy when we didn't? It wasn't fair.'

'But I am happy. This is what I don't understand. I am happy. For the first time in thirty years I was happy and then you do this.'

'You weren't happy. Our family is a mess. Bella's been dating a guy for years and neither of us knew because she was keeping him hidden, secret. She doesn't let us in on anything about her life. I mean, when was the last time you went to her house?

'I am so angry all the time with Mum and Dad that it's going to drive me insane. And you, you are not happy. You pretend to be but you can't be with Mum and Dad and you can't settle in a relationship. You are not happy, no matter what you pretend.'

I sit myself down in Dad's seat again. 'Don't you get it, Logan. Me and Mum and Dad, we're never going to be the same. I told Bella this when you were in your coma. Even if I hadn't gone to prison, we would never be all right. I fucked a teacher and I got caught out. Everyone knew. That's what has messed up our relationship. Not prison. And that had nothing to do with Serena. She would have been a lot happier if I hadn't fucked him, to be honest.

'And Alain . . . We were on and off because he has truth issues. I told you we met in a pub but I didn't tell you he engineered those and other meetings because he was writing a story on The Ice Cream Girls. He started off lying to me and didn't really stop. I love him, I absolutely love him, but I can't trust him. And now, thanks to you, thanks to all of this, I've just been reminded that I can't trust anyone. Not anyone.' I push my hands over my eyes, try to stem the tears, push them back into my eyes. I do not need to be crying right now. I do not need to be anything but stern and disapproving and angry right now. 'I was so happy. So happy that I had you and Bella back, that I have Betina. Even Alain is back properly. You're my family. And now that's gone. *You* took it away from me.'

'Don't cry,' Logan begs. Suddenly he's back from wherever he has been these past few minutes, my brother has returned. This is what it was like with Marcus, sometimes. He would switch in a blink – one moment he would be romantic and adoring, the next – nasty, vicious, dangerous; then back to adoring, attentive, loving. It was disorientating, destabilising.

'I'm so tired,' I say to no one in particular. These past few weeks have been exhausting. They have dragged me to my past, held me hostage there. I've tried to exist in the present but my grasp on the here and now has been with numb fingers; tenuous at best. I've ignored my daughter, neglected my business, completely dismissed my friends. All because I thought my brother needed rescuing. All because I thought I could save the version of me that had been recreated in my brother.

'I'm sorry, it was never meant to get to this stage,' Logan says in his normal voice. But aren't they always normal after the fact? After the assault, in the aftermath, when you're hurt and broken and scared, when you're wondering if you're going to be able to hide this lot of injuries and bruises and damage, when you're scrabbling around thinking of how you're going to recover, the sweet voice comes out . . . gently dropped apologies, nicely delivered excuses, prettily murmured promises. This is how it goes. I've been away from it for years, but nothing has changed.

People don't change. Abusers don't change. They just get better at hiding it. At wearing different faces. At ingratiating themselves into different parts of your life. No one would look at Logan and think he has spent the better part of a year brutalising a woman he could have just as easily fallen in love with. That he quite clearly did fall in love with. No one would look at my brother and think him capable of such depravity in the name of revenge.

'I'm going to call the police,' I tell him. 'You're going to have to tell them you've finally remembered what happened. That she didn't attack you. And that the diary is part of a book you're writing or something. That it wasn't about her.'

'They'll never believe it,' he states.

'Well, you'd better make sure they do. Otherwise, I'll play them the recording and you can take your chances. You admit to all sorts on there, not least wasting police time and assault and sexual assault. And let's not forget you stabbed someone – not in self-defence.' I shake my head and stand up. 'Make them believe it or they hear all about it from your own mouth.'

'It wasn't meant to be like this,' he says as I walk away. 'It wasn't meant to be like this at all.'

serena

Now

'Where's Howie?' I ask Poppy when she has finished telling me as much as she can. We are standing beside my car in the hospital car-park, our faces hidden by the darkness in there.

She hasn't told me everything, because some of it she cannot say. I could see the words that were there, that would not form themselves in her mouth; I could hear how her voice skittered away from what it was meant to say. But I understood, overall, what he had done. I understood that he would hopefully now confess and get Verity out of prison.

But this was the question that has been on my mind, no doubt has been on Verity's mind – where is Howie? After Logan Carlisle stabbed him, where did he disappear to?

'I don't know. I don't think Logan knows. I'm pretty sure he was telling me the truth when he said Howie was gone when he came round after his seizure.'

'Do you want me to drive you home?' I eventually ask her. She cannot meet my eye. Her gaze flitters away from me, just like her words skittered away from telling me everything that had been done to my daughter.

'No, no. I have to stay here while he talks to the police, make sure he says enough to free your daughter. Talk to my parents about what sort of a person their son is.'

I'd offer to stay with her, but I can't. I simply cannot.

'Poppy,' I call as she starts to walk away.

Tiredly, she turns back to me. I feel exactly how she looks – exhausted, drained, hollowed out.

'I think about him, sometimes. I know I don't still love him, but sometimes I'll get the echo of a memory about a moment between us that was nice, or a ripple of a feeling I had towards him. And, I don't know, it seems like I'm back there and the world is perfect for that moment. What I had with him feels perfect for those seconds. It's only occasionally, and it's never for very long, but yeah, I think about him. Sometimes.'

I watch tears rush to Poppy's eyes; recognition that she's not alone. That someone out there understands what it's like. We don't love him, we remember him, we remember versions of us with him. 'Thank you,' she says.

I nod in response and get into my car before I allow myself to cry, too.

Part 15

Part 15

verity

Now

I don't think I've ever been so pleased to see them.

It's been hell, my twenty days in prison, but I am out now. I am standing in the Crown Court, while Nerissa Bawku explains that the Crown Prosecution Service are offering no evidence in relation to my charges. In other words, they don't have a case against me so I should be immediately released.

I'm not really listening, I'm just counting down the seconds till I'll be free. Properly free. Not out on licence, not waiting to be arrested again, just free to be Verity Gillmare again.

Although who she is, I have no idea.

From what Darryl told me, Logan has been setting me up for over a year. From the moment he met me he was using me to get at my mother. The thoughts that have been firing around my brain all night have made all my injuries from yesterday's beating seem insignificant. I'd wanted to ask Darryl question after question after question. I wanted to know when did Logan decide to do this thing? When did he decide to seduce me? How did he know it would work? And *why*? Why did he get to know me, behave as if he cared for me and *still* carry on with his sordid, grubby, devastating plan?

I am itching to get to my parents. To have them put their arms around me, hug away all of this mess. All that time I've wasted, all the hurt I've caused. I could weep when I think about it. Tears do form in my eyes when I remember how I was with my mother, how I treated her like dirt. All that resentment I was carrying, all that hurt that she didn't open up to me. That was put there and set alight by Logan. But I kept it going, I kept listening to him talk and, rather than challenge or ignore, I took it on board. I allowed it to become a part of my mindset. I would carry his hate inside me like a bomb and every time I saw my mother, I would detonate it in her vicinity.

I can't stand to think that Logan got me to do his revenge work for him.

Nerissa finishes speaking and the judge looks down, going over the paperwork. All the while, I stand and look forward. If I sneak even the smallest look at Mum and Dad I know I'll lose it. I'll make a run for it, start to sob.

After many more words, reassurances that the CPS really aren't offering evidence and won't be bringing this against me again, it's over. I am free to go.

Free.

I never knew so much could be piled onto, plied into, four little letters.

Mum reaches me first, her arms are the ones that encircle me and draw me towards her warm body. Everything hurts because everything is bruised, but I don't flinch, don't shy away. Every bit of pain is worth it to be in my mother's embrace and to have my father's arms slip around her, encompassing us both. Loving us both. Protecting us all.

verity

Now

'Do you think he ever had any feelings for me?'

I ask my mum this after a long shower followed by a long bath followed by another long shower. I would never normally do something so ecologically unsound, so wasteful, but this is a one-off. It's not every day you get out of prison. And I needed to wash and scrub every single trace of that place off my body. I had to reacquaint myself with seemingly decadent things like temperature control and water pressure; privacy and calm, too.

'I don't know for sure. But from what he told Poppy months ago before she found out who you were and also while he was confessing, yes, yes he did. That's the main reason for it going on so long – he had proper, genuine feelings of love and adoration for you and he didn't want to end things. And also, in his mind, that was why he had to behave so badly. He didn't want to be in love with you but he was. I mean, you could ask him, but that would be difficult since it's him who is now under arrest at the hospital.'

'And he really has no idea what happened to Howie?'

'Poppy says not. I've tried driving around the area near your flat to see if I can spot anything and . . . nothing. It's like he's disappeared off

497

the face of the Earth. But from what your father told me, I'm not surprised Howie's gone into hiding – with his record of violence, he must have been terrified of getting blamed for what happened to Logan.'

'I'm really worried, Mum. It's not like him to not contact Beccie at least. What if he's dying and can't get help? What if he's dead? That'd be my fault. I wish I had some clue where he is.'

'Me, too. I'll go out again with your dad, see if we can spot something. In the meantime, I'm trying to do that thing your dad does and stay positive, hope for the best. You should, too.'

I reach out and put my hands on hers, which are wrapped around a large mug of tea. She's made it weak, no milk, half a teaspoon of sugar. I don't know when my mother started drinking tea. I've spent the last year or so actively avoiding knowing her so I don't know a lot about her, to be honest. I hate myself for that.

'I'm sorry,' I say to her. 'I should have spoken to you. I shouldn't have treated you the way I did. I should have trusted you. I don't even know why I got so mad – you were hideously abused, you were let down by your lawyers and the courts and all I could seem to focus on was why you didn't leave and the fact you should have gone to prison like Poppy did. There was such a disconnect, and I couldn't make myself understand what it was like. I know some of it was Logan's doing, but a lot of it was me. I feel horrible about it. Truly. And through it all, you've been consistently behind me.'

Mum doesn't say anything. She watches me speak and I can't see what's going on behind her eyes, what thoughts are whirring through her head. She's supported me, but does she hate me? Cos when I think about it, I started resenting her for a lot less than I have done to her.

'I'm really sad, Vee,' Mum eventually says. 'I'm really sad that something I did more than thirty years ago has resulted in all of this. Just so sad.'

'You weren't to know.'

'No, I wasn't. Doesn't stop me feeling . . .'

'Sad?'

'Yes, sad.' She takes my hands in hers. Holds them tight. 'I'm sorry for all of this, Vee. I can't tell you how terrible I feel. That you were targeted like this . . .'

'No, Mum, don't apologise. You didn't do it. Any of it. And you know what, I'm going to focus on the good times I had with him. He can't have been faking it all that time. And he did make me feel loved. Especially before he started to change. I mean, I can't pinpoint a moment when he did change, but he did love me. I know he did.'

I'm not going to let anyone take away the good bits. The bits he didn't scrawl down in his 'diary' to set me up. The times when we were just lying on the bed, laughing about nothing in particular. The moments when we'd simply look at each other and share a brief kiss. The parts when he'd stroke a loving hand over my hip and press a kiss onto my temple. Those weren't the actions of a man who hated me. Who was all out for revenge. They weren't planned or orchestrated. Those were times when he must have had doubts, when he probably forgot what his mission was.

I can't believe he was that completely evil and calculating all the time. What he's done has been horrific, but I can't believe all of it was fake, that all of it was done as payback for the slights against his family.

Mum hugs me close, kisses my head. 'I love you,' she says. 'I want to protect you from everything bad in the world. I'm sorry I didn't manage it this time. I'm so sorry.'

I let Mum hug me. I'm still aching, my muscles and flesh tender after being pulverised by my prison pals. How Poppy Carlisle coped with being inside for all that time, I don't know. And to come out and be confronted by parents who don't want to know you . . .

I understand why Logan is so angry, why he would want someone to pay for that happening to someone he loved. I just wish he hadn't used me.

'He's asked to see me,' Mum says. 'Logan Carlisle has asked to see me. I don't know why me and not you. And I wasn't going to go but . . . if you want me to, I will. I will tell you what he says. If you don't want me to go, I won't. It's up to you.'

If she goes, she can tell me what he says. She can ask him if he cared for me. She can find out if he feels bad about what he did. What he feels now. But then, what if he says he doesn't feel bad? What if all he feels is justified and satisfied because he got the result he wanted – Mum to be devastated. And you only have to look at my mother to see she is devastated. This has brought her pretty close to breaking point.

'I don't know, Mum. Part of me wants you to go but most of me just wants to protect you from someone who clearly means you harm.'

She smiles her Mum smile, and she looks for a moment like she's going to fall over. Collapse under the weight of her troubles. 'You don't have to protect me any more, Verity. If you want me to go, I will go. It really is up to you.'

I contemplate my mother. Think about what is on offer.

There really is only one answer.

Part 16

Part 16

serena

Now

This is like the night we left Marcus, the night he died.

We stood near each other, looking at a man who had done terrible things, ready to tell him that his supremacy of fear had ended.

Logan's reign of quiet, hidden terror is over and, like any abusive person who is about to be left, he can't let his victim go without trying one last time to destroy them.

'What do you want?' I ask Logan Carlisle when he has spent several minutes contemplating me in silence.

I'm here for Verity, of course. She wanted me to come and see him. She still has feelings for him and she wants to know if everything was fake. He wouldn't tell me it wasn't, but I have to give Verity hope.

'To see your face now you know what I did to your precious bean,' he says. As I suspected, as I thought: Logan Carlisle wants to torture me. He wants to see me suffer.

'OK, now you've seen me, does it make you feel any better?'

'Yes.'

From the corner of my eye, I see Poppy close her eyes as if in pain, and shake her head slightly. 'Logan . . .' she begins and then her words fail her.

'Yes, Poppy?' he asks nastily.

'Stop, just stop this. This isn't you.'

'You have no idea who I am,' he replies, the nasty edge creeping further into his voice.

'For ten years I've known you. You have been by my side through so, so much. Even a few weeks ago, you were the one who told Betina's school to move her up, when I was just sitting there stressing. And it's worked amazingly. She's thriving. I can't believe you're the same person who is facing all these charges. Grievous Bodily Harm with Intent – and that's only *if* they find Howie Scarber alive – coercive control, rape and sexual assault.'

'At least I'll be going to prison for something I did do instead of something someone else did,' he spits in response.

Poppy shakes her head. 'You said you did this for me. How? How can you even pretend it was for me? You planned to emotionally and sexually abuse a young woman to get at someone else.'

'She never said no.' He stares at me when he says that.

'I never said no to Marcus,' Poppy replies, which makes him re-focus on her. 'After the first time he coerced me into sleeping with him, even though I wanted to wait, I never – not one time – said no, even when I didn't want to. That poor girl.' Poppy shakes her head, bites her lower lip and battles tears that threaten to spill over. 'How could you? That poor girl.'

'Poppy, she isn't a girl.' He turns his attentions to me again. 'And she wasn't whenever I was sticking it in her. Sometimes every night.'

He hates me. That is clear. But he also hates Poppy. He speaks words that pretend he did this for her, but everything about him says he hates her. That he has spent a lot of time planning how to get back at her just as much as he got at me. He knew that he couldn't hurt me. Not directly. Confronting the me he thinks I am – the hard-faced bitch who let his sister go to prison – wouldn't have worked. But to come to my child, fill her mind with poison about me to the point she started to resent me, and then to damage her . . . that is the pain he wanted to inflict. That is the pain he has inflicted.

I'll never forget that Verity has been hurt because of the choices I made when I was a teenager. I'll never forgive myself, either. In that respect, Logan has won.

And he resents his sister, her part in it, too. His hatred throbs through every word he says to her, every sly look he shoots her – he resents her for not being there, for being in prison, for being so passive about their relationship after her release. But I'm guessing it might also be the shame of having a sibling go to jail, or it could be a general hatred of women that manifests itself like this. It could be a multitude of things.

But, in the same way I decided not to let Marcus win by letting his legacy destroy my marriage, I'm not going to allow this man to win by letting him obliterate my daughter or my peace of mind.

'I feel really sorry for you, Logan. This must have been so awful for you. Doing all those things and then, at the end of it, I'm not destroyed but you *have* fallen in love with your target,' I say to him.

'HA!' he replies. 'HA! HA! HA!'

'Deny it all you want. If you had truly got revenge on me like you wanted, I wouldn't be standing here right now – I'd be broken and crying somewhere. You would have obliterated me. And you would be talking to Verity right now. You would have asked to see her so you could say all of this hideous stuff to her. But no, you wanted me because you wanted to be near someone who is like her. I mean, she's basically going to look like me so you wanted me to be the proxy – I'd have to listen to your bile and you could say it without feeling the guilt of it being to the woman you love. I bet you thought: "just a little bit more pain for Serena – have her deliver these words to her daughter. Something I could never do because I love her too much."' I smile at him, force myself to grin in the most natural, relaxed way possible. 'Don't worry, Logan. I will tell her about this meeting. I'm going to make sure she knows how much you love her. I'm going to make sure that, every day, she knows the reason you confessed in the end was because you couldn't bear to do that to her any longer. I've already said this to her, I've already told her that you must have had feelings for her. And now I am here with you, so whatever I go back and tell her, she will believe came directly from you.'

I move closer to his bed. 'I'm going to get her counselling to make sure she's OK, and every day between now and the trial, I'm going to tell her that you adored her. Which is why it took you so long to follow through. That you had many, many second thoughts because you were so completely head-over-heels in love with her. And that you're a coward. That you weren't brave enough to just allow yourself to be loved, so instead you carried on with your ridiculous plan.

'By the time it gets to the trial, she is going to know that none of this was her fault, she is going to know how much she is loved. And how I am fine. That what you tried to do didn't work because I don't blame myself. I only blame you.' I look at Poppy. I am not going to let his hate ruin Poppy, either. I didn't let Marcus kill her, and I didn't go through all of that so some other guy could do it instead. I don't care who he is. 'And I'm going to get to know Poppy. I'm going to stop telling myself I hate her and I am going to spend time with her so she has more friends. She has more people in her life.' I move even closer to Logan Carlisle. 'Basically, you are going to fail. You tried to destroy me to get revenge for something you think I did, and you've failed. The fact I'm standing here, talking to you, able to see the future and how I'm going to carry on, just shows how your plan didn't work. I feel sorry for you because all the stuff I'm going to tell people may well seem like a lie but it's all true.'

I manage a smile at him. He is not going to win. I am not going to let this define my daughter. I am not going to let this damage me. And any damage that is there, I will bury deep. I will hide so that he can never even begin to crow about what he has done.

'Goodbye, Logan Carlisle, enjoy knowing that we're getting on with our lives out there, while you're stuck in here looking at prison for a plan that you failed to execute.'

His face has lost its arrogant nasty sneer while I've been speaking. The powerlessness of his situation, how I am now in control and how I can redefine all he has done to make it all right for everyone involved is dawning on him in the most blatant way.

By the time I have made it to the corridor outside his room, my legs are like rubber, shaky and unstable, and I just about make it to the chairs before they give way. Poppy is horrified and rushes to help me.

I brush her away, the last thing I want is help from a Carlisle.

'Are you all right?' she asks.

'No, I'm not,' I reply, gulping huge breaths. I can feel the panic racing to overtake me, shortening my breath, thundering my heart, trembling my body.

'What can I do to help?' she asks.

Nothing, Poppy, I want to scream. *There's nothing anyone can do.*

I sit back in my seat, grind the base of my thumbs into my closed eyes, try to count the breaths as they're going in and out, try to hook into the rhythm of my heart banging in my ears. I need to not run from this, I need to go into it. I need to make this a part of me so it doesn't take over me. I have to focus on doing whatever I can to get to the other side.

'I thought you were going to pass out again,' Poppy says when I can sit upright and open my eyes.

The policeman who had been, I presume, in the toilet instead of standing outside Logan Carlisle's room, looks us over as though he recognises me, knows I shouldn't have been in Logan's room and knows he should one hundred per cent do something about it. He peers at me . . . then he looks away. It's almost as though he doesn't want to deal with the hassle and trouble (for him more than anything) challenging me will bring to him.

'I thought you were going to pass out,' Poppy states again, 'like last time' She doesn't look at me while she speaks. 'I'm sure your husband would have loved to get another call from the hospital and find me here with you.'

'It was just a panic attack,' I say quietly.

'You sounded so strong and confident in there, I had no idea this was what you were feeling inside,' Poppy says. 'I actually believed all that you said.'

'I meant every single word. I'm not going to let him destroy my daughter or me.'

'I'm sorry.'

'It's not your fault, Poppy. I'm just trying to get myself back together.'

'Did you mean what you said about getting to know me?'

I stare at the wall opposite. Did I mean that? Or was it something to say to needle Logan Carlisle? 'I don't know,' is the answer I give Poppy. 'I mean, what are we going to talk about? How many times

Marcus broke our ribs? What it was like to find out my daughter had been lying to me because of your brother?' I run my hands over my head. 'But then, it'll drive that man in there crazy. And because of that, it's tempting.'

We sit in silence for long, long minutes. I am trying to re-centre myself. Get myself back together. When my legs stop shaking and I feel strong enough, I stand up. I need to go home. Find somewhere to be alone for a bit. I was perfectly serious about what I planned to do. I just need to gather myself together first.

'I'll see you, Poppy,' I say. Hoping against hope that I don't.

'I'll see you, Serena.'

Tap, tap, tap.

I nearly jump out of my skin when Poppy taps on the passenger-side window of my car. I wasn't steady enough to drive – I was still shaking – so I sat in the multi-storey hospital car park racking up pounds in parking charges. I wasn't sure how she found me and I probably didn't want to know. I lean over, pop open the car door.

She gets in and shuts the door behind her. 'I'm not stalking you,' she immediately says. 'That's my car, there.' She points to the silver family car parked in the bay directly in front of me. Of course that's where she'd park and I would park. Of course Poppy and I keep being connected in so many seemingly insignificant ways.

'We wouldn't have to talk about us, you know, if you did want to be friends,' Poppy says. 'We could talk about the easy subjects – you know, politics, religion, etc . . .'

That does raise a small smile.

'I have to go and see my sister,' Poppy says. 'I haven't heard from her since . . . since I had to tell them all about Logan. I'm a bit worried about her now. This came at a bad time. It sounded like she was split-ting with her boyfriend. They've been together for ages and ages.'

'And you're telling me all this because?'

She doesn't reply so I turn to look at her. She's looking at me with the same expression she had in her beach hut when she asked me to come to see Logan with her. The exact same.

'You're joking, right?'

'I just need someone else there.'

'Get your husband. I'm sure he's not writing an article on her, is he?'

'It kinda has to be you because I think she'd benefit from talking to you.'

'And how would I benefit from talking to her?'

'You'll see that we're not all psychopaths? She's the normal one in the family.'

'Where does she live?'

'Portslade/Southwick.'

'If I do this one last thing for you, will you leave me and my family alone after that?' I turn to her again. 'Please?'

'Thing is, I can't promise you that. I'll try, is probably the best I can do.'

'I suppose that's the best I can hope for,' I reply sourly. 'What's her address?'

poppy

Now

Logan was right about one thing – none of us ever came to Bella's house.

The last time was when the three of us ended up drinking the afternoon away. Logan and I didn't even go in, just waited outside for her to finish getting ready. Apart from that, nothing. She met us in town, she met us at Mum and Dad's and she rarely came to my place. Bella is removed from us, I realise, and I need that to stop. Now that Logan has shown who he is, and that person is a monster, I need to keep Bella close. I need to make sure she doesn't go off at the deep end, too.

More than anything, I'm horrified that Logan was doing all this and still being a supportive, loving brother to Bella and me, and a fun, devoted uncle to Betina. *The snake has the prettiest smile*, Tina had once told me. And when I found out about Alain, I'd agreed with her. Not knowing that, all along, my brother was the biggest snake with the prettiest of all the pretty smiles.

Like Mum and Dad's, Bella's road is quite narrow when there are cars parked on both sides, but Serena easily manages to slot us into a space outside Bella's place that I wouldn't have dreamed of going near.

We knock and ring the doorbell several times and despite that,

Bella doesn't answer. I know she's in there. Her car is outside and I can feel that the place isn't empty. In between each ring and knock, I text her and call her. Still no reply, no hint of answering the door.

'She obviously doesn't want to talk to you,' Serena says. 'Maybe you should come back tomorrow.'

'No, I need to speak to her. The longer I leave it, the worse it'll get until it'll be impossible to connect. She might not want to talk to me right now but . . . I'M NOT GOING AWAY, BELLA CARLISLE,' I bellow suddenly. 'I'M GOING TO STAY RIGHT HERE UNTIL YOU TALK TO ME. AND IF THAT MEANS ME SHOUTING LIKE THIS IN THE STREET UNTIL YOU OPEN THE DOOR, THEN THAT'S JUST—'

The door opens a fraction and Bella's pale face appears in the gap. 'I don't want to talk to you,' she says in a shaky voice. When her eyes alight on Serena, she double-takes and, if possible, even more colour drains from her face. 'Who else have you brought?' she asks me.

'No one. Look, can we come in?'

She sighs with her whole body. And then she steps back and opens the door wider to allow us to enter. Once we are in the corridor, I notice Serena's discomfort levels shoot up. She didn't want to be there in the first place and now she looks like she's about to cut and run. I stay behind the door to stop her legging it before she can talk to Bella and see that not all Carlisles are bad.

'Are you sure you didn't bring anyone else?' Bella asks.

'Who would I bring?' I reply. She's trembling ever so slightly. She looks genuinely shaken. Something has clearly happened to her, although I have no idea what.

'The police.'

'Why would I bring the police?'

She sighs dramatically, chews her lip, and then sighs again. 'He didn't tell you, did he? I *told* Logan to tell you.'

'Tell me what? What's going on?' My patience is running out – I came here to reconnect with my sister and show my rival/ friend/ nemesis/co-conspirator that we aren't all crazy. And she isn't helping on either front.

'Of course he didn't, he didn't tell you.' She shakes her head. 'Still trying to protect me. Even though I don't need him to, he's still trying to . . . It was me!' she almost shouts. 'I did it! I put Logan into a coma by hitting him over the head. It wasn't Verity. She didn't give him those blows to his head, I did.'

'Pardon?' I reply.

Serena doesn't say a word, she just stares at my sister.

'And you might as well come upstairs,' she adds, her voice proud and defiant, like she's ready to fight us both if we look at her sideways. She doesn't give us a chance to ask any more questions or argue, nor does she wait for us to decide if we want to go upstairs, she simply takes the stairs two at a time so we're forced to follow.

Her large spare bedroom at the back of her house is dark because the blinds are down and there are no other lights on. It takes a few seconds for my eyes to adjust, but once they do, I can make out the figure of a man propped up in the bed. He looks vaguely familiar, like I've seen his face in passing on television or something.

'He wouldn't let me call a doctor or anything,' Bella says. 'I've been looking after him as much as I can, but he's still really ill.'

'Howie?' Serena says as she enters the room. She goes straight to him. 'Howie!' Even in this low light he looks dreadful; I can see his skin seems to be drained of life and he appears weak and barely able to hold his head up against the pillows. Serena drops to her knees beside him, she puts her hand on his forehead, then moves her fingers to his neck in the same way I learnt to check Betina's temperature. 'He hasn't got a temperature so he probably hasn't got an infection, but he is not in a good way.' She pulls her mobile out of her bag. 'I'm calling an ambulance.' She is already dialling 999.

'*Please don't*!' Bella screeches, her hand outstretched to stop her. Howie tries to shake his head but he is so weak he has to move his whole body to do that. 'No,' he manages to whisper. 'No, please.'

'He doesn't want that,' Bella says. 'He really doesn't.'

Serena looks so frustrated, scared. 'All right, I'll call Evan instead.'

'What is going on?' I ask again, while Serena leaves the room to call her husband. 'I'm so confused. What did you mean you put Logan into the coma? How did this man get to your house?'

Bella leaves Howie's side and comes to me. Her shaking is more pronounced. 'I walked into Verity's kitchen and found Logan stabbing him. He wouldn't stop. He just wouldn't bloody stop.'

bella

Now

That day, I was here when Logan called and texted me.

He told me he was at his girlfriend's house and they'd properly split up this time and could I come and pick him up. He said he'd been calling her to talk to him but she wouldn't. He was pissed off about that. Really pissed – even in texts you could tell how angry he was. Eventually he told me he was packing up his stuff and hadn't taken his car so could I bring mine in a couple of hours when he'd finished getting his belongings together. Well, I'd had that argument with Myron so I'd come back early from London and I wasn't in the best mood. Actually, I was just pissed off with everything and everyone. The very last thing I wanted to do was walk in and witness the end of someone else's stupid relationship, but how can I say no to Logan? He told me where he'd put a spare key in case he got locked out. I don't think Verity knew about that, that he'd had a spare key made, but I don't suppose that's important right now.

When I arrived and let myself in, I wasn't being especially quiet, but I could hear voices from one end of the flat. I followed them and there they were, in the kitchen. The first-aid kit was on the table and it looked like Howie, as I found out later was his name, was patching up Logan.

I was about to say hello when Logan grabbed the knife from the side and just stuck it in Howie. Just like that! He didn't even hesitate or think twice, just . . . I couldn't believe what I was seeing! I was frozen for a moment or two, but then Logan went to do it again

I shouted at him to stop it, ran over and grabbed his shoulder to pull him back, but he just turned around and pushed me away so he could do it again. Howie was just, like, frozen there, shocked. Logan went to do it again and again. I knew I couldn't stop him by shouting or pulling at him . . . I saw this small cast-iron-pan thing on the table so I grabbed it and swung it at him. He sort of turned to me when I hit him.

'Stop!' I told him and he got this awful smile on his face and stuck it in Howie again.

I had to hit him two more times before he would stop. Then, he looked at me and went 'Bella?' just before he collapsed. He was lying when he said he'd had a seizure because he was protecting me. *I* hit him over the head.

I just completely panicked then. I mean, I have this weapon in my hand and a man bleeding to death in the kitchen. It wasn't even my flat! I dropped to my knees to check on the bleeding man. I asked his name and he told me it was Howie. 'I'm going to get you an ambulance,' I told him.

He shook his head. And was kind of whispering, 'No, no,' as I got my phone out. 'Trouble. Logan, no trouble. Me, trouble.'

I didn't know what to do. I couldn't just leave him there, and I had to help my brother. In the end I told Howie I was going to take him back to my place for a few hours. He agreed to that, so I used Verity's tea towels to stem the blood and I took him to my car. I'm surprised no one saw us. I brought him back here and I managed to stop the bleeding. It took ages. I tried to dress the wounds and then

I had to get myself cleaned up because I couldn't go back looking how I did.

I stood in the shower, water pouring down on me, crying. I couldn't believe what had happened. What I'd seen Logan do, what I'd had to do. My mind kept going to Howie, too. He was lying in that bed, and I was sure he was going to die. I was so scared. Terrified. Of literally everything and I didn't know what to do.

After the shower, I checked Howie was still alive. I sat with him, holding his hand, watching him breathing. I kept thinking I should call the police. Call an ambulance. Call someone who would help me. It was like all the strength had left my body. I just sat there, holding this stranger's hand and praying for a miracle.

Calm came to me while I was sitting there. It was the moment of stillness I needed to be able to do what I had to do. I left Howie sleeping; he looked really peaceful . . . I actually thought as I was leaving that he would probably die while I was out.

When I got back to Verity's flat, the door was slightly open and there were bloody handprints on the door and doorframe. I went in, found the flat empty. I just panicked. I grabbed the pan because it had my fingerprints on it and tore out of the flat, trying to work out where he'd gone. He mentioned Verity's father's birthday party but he hadn't told me where it was.

I kind of went into a daze. I couldn't really think what to do except go home and wait for that call. I did drive around a bit, trying to see if I could spot him, but he'd disappeared. By the time I got back Howie was awake.

He was weak and I knew he was basically dying and he needed proper medical help. But every time I tried to call an ambulance, he kept saying no.

Then I got the call I'd been dreading. I'd been waiting for it, but I wasn't prepared. It was like I didn't actually know who had done it to him. That was why I was able to be so shocked and upset. It wasn't an act, I hadn't stopped feeling like that from earlier on.

When Logan woke up, I thought he was going to tell them what I'd done. When he was dithering, I told him. I told him not to protect her, to tell the truth. I wanted him to do it because every time I tried to speak the words would not come. And as Howie grew stronger he explained to me how he'd been arrested before and how he knew he'd get blamed.

So I was stuck. No one really asked me questions about anything, so I didn't really have to lie. I've hardly slept, hardly eaten. I want to drink all the time.

When Logan confessed to all that stuff he'd been doing . . . I couldn't quite believe what I was hearing. I mean, how could he? I knew he was going to tell the whole truth then. I told him to. I just decided to keep trying to get Howie better and then make him go to a hospital once the police came for me.

poppy

Now

I take it back, I think.

No one in our family is normal. We're all 'out there'.

Howie has been nodding while Bella talks, and I have been staring wide-eyed at her. How did it get to this? My sister nearly killed my brother to stop him from killing the friend of my 'rival'.

'You should have just told me the truth,' I say to Bella. 'I would have helped you and Howie.'

'I couldn't risk it. I just couldn't. More for Howie than me.'

'But he's not a suspect any more.'

'I told him that. He didn't believe me. He still doesn't believe me. I just . . . I don't want to go to prison. I don't want to face Mum and Dad. I want to hide from the world and what I've done.'

'What you did was defend someone while they were being attacked,' I tell her. 'No one is locking you up for that. Logan will tell them the truth, too.'

While we are speaking, Dr Evan arrives. Serena lets him and Verity in, and he is upstairs in seconds, crossing the room quickly and without ceremony. We all stop to watch him work as he pulls back the covers, begins the process of checking Howie's wounds.

We stand there, waiting to hear what he has to say; if he thinks Howie will be all right. I'm not sure about anyone else, but I am holding my breath, desperate for him not to say it's too late.

Verity hangs around in the doorway, wringing her hands and moving from foot to foot in a dance born of pure fear and anxiety.

'He'll be OK if we get him to hospital now. And I mean *now*. I'm not quite sure how he's survived nearly six weeks like this,' Dr Evan says and leaves the room to call an ambulance.

Verity rushes in to take her father's place. She grabs Howie's hand and he lights up at the sight of her. 'I'm so sorry,' she says to him. 'So very, very sorry. I had no idea he would do that to you.'

'Not. Your. Fault,' he falteringly replies.

'I'm still really sorry, though.' She shakes her head, bites her lower lip, I think, to stop from crying. 'This is his fault, Logan's fault. But it's also hers.'

My fault? Does she mean me?

'If it wasn't for you protecting Beccie when she hurts you, you would have been able to tell everyone your side of the story. You have to leave her.'

'Vee . . .'

'I said she was going to kill you and she almost did,' Verity says sternly. 'I will come with you, but you have to report her. You have to report everything she's done to you. You have to get them your hospital records and everything. You have to make them see that she's the abusive one, not you. That's the only way.'

Howie just reclines against the bank of pillows and says nothing.

'You have to do this, Howie. I will stay with you. For as long as you need, but you have to do this to save your own life.'

He doesn't react for a long time and then slowly he nods. 'OK,' he says. 'OK.'

Dr Evan returns and takes Howie's pulse and we all stand around in silence again. No one knows what to say, but I know we're all hoping and praying he lives.

Part 17

serena

Now

I've been sitting here on this road for a lifetime.

I honestly don't want to do this, but I have to. I should have left it, but I couldn't. Once I had hold of it, I honestly couldn't do anything other than this.

Before I change my mind again, before I turn on the car engine and drive away from here as fast as is legally allowed, I open the car door and get out. This is a nice area, lots of privet hedges and net curtains. The neighbours pay attention to what is going on, so I won't be surprised if someone already has my car registration noted down somewhere, just in case, you know, something dodgy happens.

This road I am crossing seems to be huge and I'm sure it's getting wider as I walk, trying to keep me away from my destination. I have to keep going, I have to avoid all the mental tricks my mind is playing to stop me doing this. I have to. No matter how much I don't want to do it, I need to.

The shadow that appears behind the door after I knock is oddly familiar and completely alien at the same time.

'Hello,' I say when he opens the door.

'Serena? What are you doing here? How did you find me?'

'Finding you wasn't hard.'

'Well, what are you doing here?'

'I need your help, Jack.'

Jack Halnsley, Marcus's son, frowns at me. If he has any idea what I need him for he doesn't let on. Instead, he lets me into his home and then he just stands in his living room and listens as I tell him exactly what I need and how he can give it to me.

poppy

Now

Serena asked to meet me at the hospital.

I told her Logan was being discharged – to prison – tomorrow and could she wait until that was all sorted since it was bound to be traumatic for everyone.

'No,' she replied. 'It has to be at the hospital with him and all your family. I need to tell you all what happened the night . . . the night *he* died. I know it's difficult with your family right now, but do everything you can to get them all there, please.'

And here we are, crammed into his tiny room awaiting her arrival. The nurses have given up trying to 'two at a time' us because Logan is handcuffed to his bed most of the time and a police officer permanently stands outside.

We don't speak as we sit in this room of machines; we can hear each other breathing, we can feel the heat of our bodies rising up together and creating an almost stifling warmth, but we're all here because Serena is finally going to confess.

She must feel guilty, must have seen the devastation that keeping quiet has caused and has decided to come clean. Or maybe the memory loss that she told me about is improving. Maybe more has come back to her and, now everything is back, she needs to tell the truth. Enough of those lies; only truth now.

A little later than the three p.m. she suggested, the door to Logan's room opens and a man steps over the threshold.

My heart stops when I see him.

Marcus.

Marcus.

I shoot out of my seat and rapidly back away until I can go no further and my back is literally against the wall.

Marcus is back. He's come to finish what he started that night – to kill me. Behind him comes Serena. She is dressed all in black, something I've never seen her do before. Her hair is pulled back into a tight, slicked-down bun and her face is set in a harrowed, harrowing expression.

My eyes dart from her to him, from him to her. I think the others recognise him as well because I'm sure Mum and Bella gasp, but I can't really take much in because of the apparition in front of me. I'm not sure if they're gasping about Marcus or they're gasping about Serena. But I am not able to get any further away from it, this thing that has come here to haunt me.

'Thank you for meeting me here,' Serena says, going straight into it. No hello or small talk. 'I don't know where to start, really, so I'm going to ask Jack to tell you what we talked about two days ago. Jack?'

Jack inhales and exhales very loudly. He stares at the ground for so long none of us expect him to actually speak by the time he raises his head. He looks sad, if anything. Not like Marcus at all now. The only time I recall Marcus looking sad was when he would talk about his son . . . *Jack.* My eyes widen in sudden understanding just as he says, 'My name is Jack Halnsley. I'm Marcus Halnsley's son. I know I look like him – enough people have told me so over the years.

'I, erm . . . there's no easy way to say this.'

My gaze goes to Serena, who is staring directly at me.

'I'm going to tell you who killed my father, but it's complicated. I made a bargain with Serena. I tell the truth, she agrees to spend some time with me, telling me about my father.'

He shifts his focus to Serena briefly, and I can see this has cost her. It's cost her dearly. 'I'm only telling you that because I don't want to lie about the truth.'

I keep staring at Serena as Jack Halnsley explains it all. Who did it. Why. How he found out who did it. What he's wanted to do about it.

As he speaks, as he explains, tears waterfall down my face, tears tsunami down Serena's face.

We stare at each other, we wipe away tears and accept that this is how the story and the legacy of The Ice Cream Girls ends.

serena

Two days ago

'What do you need my help with?' Jack Halnsley asked me.

I lowered myself onto his sofa, trying to avoid taking in anything about his house. I didn't want this to last for any longer than necessary. 'I want . . . no, I need you to tell Poppy, *the* Poppy, that your mother did it.'

He did not speak for long seconds and in that time I noted the tea towel over his shoulder, the water stains on his clothes from where he'd been standing at the sink washing up. I wondered for a moment if he had a girlfriend, wife, kids. We hadn't talked about any of that.

'Did what?' he asked. He knew very well what, but he wanted me to say it out loud so I could hear how appalling a thing it was to be asking of him.

'That your mother killed your father. And she didn't come forward and confess because she was scared of what would happen to you if you didn't have him or her.'

Jack took a couple of steps backwards while keeping me in his eyeline. 'Why would I do that?'

'I need . . . Poppy saved my daughter. At the expense of her family. I just need a way to help her to move on. She still half thinks it was me. I need her to have someone else as the perpetrator so she can let it all go.'

'And what if she goes to the police?'

'And says what? There's no proof. She won't go to the police without proof. And you can just say that you'll deny it if she goes to the police. That you've tried to get your mum to confess and she won't.'

'Is that what you think happened? That my mum did it?'

I shrugged. 'I don't know. But it's a possibility. At various points over the years I've been convinced it's everyone from my sisters to your mum to one of the other girls he abused to Poppy's father.'

'But not Poppy?'

'Yes, Poppy. Everyone with the slightest connection to him. Even myself because I have memory loss from around that time and I sometimes wonder if I did it and blocked it out.'

'So why my mum?'

'Poppy will believe you if you tell her it was your mother. It will make sense to her because she will have felt like hurting Marcus to get away from him. I know I did. I'm sure most people in a relationship like ours would. And Marlene had years of him. It wouldn't surprise anyone – especially not someone who experienced it – that she would eventually snap.'

'Why would she have told me of all people?'

'Just say that after you met me you started to have your doubts about me or Poppy having done it. And that when you talked it over with your mother, she broke down and confessed. That you're still trying to work out what to do about it, but at the moment she won't talk about it again and you're not sure what you can do because she'll deny it if you go to the police and there's no evidence.'

He shook his head and paced a little across the cream rug. 'You make it sound so easy, Serena. Like it's a simple thing. Accusing my mother of murder to relieve the suffering of the person who probably *did* kill him. Why would I? And why would you think it was OK to ask me to do this. She's my mother.'

'Please. *Please*. She would never have to know. I can pretty much guarantee that Poppy won't do anything with the knowledge. It'll just be a relief for her to know for definite. And like I say, there's no evidence for anyone else to do anything else. I wouldn't ask you if it wasn't at least plausible that she'd done it. If it wasn't a real possibility.'

More silence.

'If I do this, what would I get out of it?' He followed up this question with a stare that was direct and unwavering.

I inhaled deeply before I replied. 'What do you want?'

We both knew what Jack Halnsley wanted – it was clear in the way his desire shaded his father's face.

'What do you want, Jack?' I repeated.

'I want you . . . to . . . to tell me about him. Properly. Just spend some time with me, talking to me about him. Not just the stuff you told me last time. The good things as well. Just more about him.'

'As I just told you, I have memory loss,' I replied. 'My husband, who's a doctor, thinks it's post-traumatic stress. I think it's cos I got hit in the head a few too many times. Either way, I have memory loss, especially from that time.'

'I'm sure you can remember enough to tell me what I want to know. It won't be for long. I just want to know about him from someone who will actually tell me things, not twist it to be whatever they think I want to hear.'

I pressed my hands on my lips.

'It won't be for ever. And . . . and if you want me to do this for you, then I want you . . . to do this for me.'

'Fine,' I stated. 'Fine.' It wasn't fine. But what could I do? Poppy helped to free my daughter from hell. This was a small thing for me to do in exchange.

Part 18

Part 18

poppy

Now

'Grandma! Grandpa!' Betina screams.

Outside Granny Morag's beach hut we've set out the white fold-down table and have put out four chairs. We're having supper here tonight and the table is covered in various Tupperware boxes with copious amounts of food. The large water pitcher has blackcurrant squash and the smaller water jug has rhubarb gin and pink soda. Alain has been reading a newspaper and I've been reading a book with my right flip-flop off so I can tease Alain under the table. A more perfect summer evening we could not have envisaged, planned or executed.

We both look up at our daughter as she hurtles like a bowling ball along the promenade towards her grandparents and almost knocks them over when she connects with them.

My reality is completely different now. I don't feel the need to hide away from the world any more. I have a new sense of freedom that was given to me when Jack Halnsley told me the truth about who killed his father. Part of me, the tiniest little part of me, wants it made official. I want to look 'the Law' in the eye while they tell me they're sorry and that they'll compensate me for my lost years. But that is the tiniest part of me.

Most of me is free now, properly free, and I do not need anything else.

Mum and Dad tried to talk to me at the hospital but I couldn't, I just couldn't. I couldn't engage with anyone; I just went home and got straight into bed and began to cry.

Properly, properly cry.

I didn't even want to drink or to smoke or to cut up. Those things were distractions, ways to mitigate my feelings, transmute uncomfortable feelings. With this knowledge, this truth, I didn't want to veer away from a moment of feeling this. It was like it was finally, *finally*, over. And because of that, I could finally weep. Properly sob. What happened to me was awful and wrong and I could finally acknowledge that by being sad, being hurt, being properly broken.

Alain took Betina to stay with his parents for a few days so she wouldn't witness my breakdown and to allow me the space to do what I needed.

On the third day, after two whole days of non-stop lamenting, I woke up without crying. I spent the day zombie-like but without tears. And I went to sleep without tears. On the fourth day I managed to do something different. To go to work. And Betina and Alain came home.

And it was like a new beginning. Catharsis had finished and I entered the stillness of afterwards. Everything felt like Day One. Like I had finally, finally, been let out of prison and I was allowed to enjoy life.

My mind didn't have to keep flitting away to wondering who did it, whether Serena would come clean, whether I should try again to make her confess. I was finally, conclusively, whole again. And that meant my life was whole again. It was fabulous. And terrifying. And what I had needed ten years ago when I left prison.

Now everything is new and shiny and fun and scary and complete.

And I can do things like sit at the beach hut sipping gin, discreetly sexually teasing my fiancé with my toes and listening to our daughter chat as she draws. I can do all that and not feel as if I should be doing something better with my time. And I can watch my parents walk towards us, Betina between them, chatting and chatting as she leads them to our table.

'Hello, Poppy love,' Mum says.

'Hello, Pepper,' Dad says.

'Hi,' I reply simply because I'm still getting used to this. To them acting as though I am here in 2020 and not like I died back in 1989 and have been reanimated to haunt them. We have a long way to go, my parents and I, but we are getting there. We are at the start of this path called the future and I know, as I walk along it, they'll be somewhere along it with me.

'Aunty Bella is coming later,' Betina informs me. 'And she's bringing her special friend Myron.'

'That'll be nice.'

'Can we go and see Uncle Logan again soon?' she asks, in case anyone felt at ease or comfortable or anything.

'Yes,' I say. 'I've told you yes.'

Mum and Dad have been on a journey. They are trying to balance the absolute horror of what Logan has done with wondering how complicit they were because of the way they handled my imprisonment. I don't envy them their journey and I've mostly kept out of it as it's their problem to solve.

I love my brother, I will visit him in prison, but I will never tell him he was right to do what he did. I thought hearing Jack Halnsley's story would have changed Logan, but no. He still feels justified in what he did because he hadn't known. Mum and Dad need to work out how they deal with that. I've made it clear that I am not going to help them with anything, and I am not going to go running around after them any more.

Bella is on an even keel. She and Logan have worked out what happened and in all of this, she's the only one who he has 'forgiven' or has real compassion for. He would never have told about her hitting him, he's said. He would have protected her till the end of time.

Logan and I have a complicated relationship now because he thinks I am friends with Serena. He hates her, will always hate her. He thinks she should have gone to prison with me and have had her family's life implode, too. He sees me, especially since I bring Betina, and we talk and joke until he remembers how much he dislikes me for my newly brokered friendship with Serena. There is nothing of the sort, of course – if we see each other in the street we say hello, but other than that, nothing.

Serena was right – what would we honestly have to talk about?

Alain gets up and grabs a couple more seats from inside the beach hut.

Mum has a large plastic bowl of food wrapped very tightly with cling film, the condensation from being covered while hot sits on the underside of the temporary lid.

'How are the wedding plans coming along?' Mum asks, while Dad grabs a section from the newspaper in Alain's hands and sits down next to him. They often just sit and read together in companionable silence.

'Oh fine,' I say as Mum hands me the bowl of food. I daren't look down, can't face seeing what she's decided to bring to our little beach gathering. 'I've got some magazines over there if you want to have a look. Everything in them is too over the top for me, but it's fun to pretend I might go for it.'

She goes to my seat and starts to flick through the magazine pile.

'Mum,' Betina whispers so loudly she may as well have shouted at me. '*Mummmm!* Grandma's been "cooking" again.' My bright, bright daughter even does me proud by using her fingers to air quote the appropriate word.

'I know,' I reply, plastering a smile on my face. 'Isn't that nice?'

'Chuck it out for the birds, Pepper love,' Dad says without looking up from his paper. 'It's what we had for dinner last night. And she boiled the pasta for twenty minutes and it was still like chewing rocks. And don't get me started on the salad cream and tuna she put on top. Do us all a favour and chuck it out for the birds. Might cull the seagull numbers a bit.'

'Did you mean to say all that out loud, Dad?' I ask.

'Say what?' Dad looks up innocently.

'Grandpa, you just told Mum to throw Grandma's food away and that it might kill a few birds.'

'Ahh.' Dad returns to his paper. 'It was bound to happen one day. I've had fifty years of defending her cooking, it was inevitable that I would break.'

'Everyone has their limits, love,' Mum says without looking up from her magazine. 'Who knew it'd be tuna pasta that would break your father?'

Alain looks up at me with a smile. Just six months ago this type of conversation would not have been possible. 'Well, I think it's great this is all out in the open,' Alain says.

'Are we allowed to tell Grandma the truth about her food now?' Betina asks with glee.

'NO!' Alain, Dad and I exclaim. There is admitting you don't enjoy something and then there are Betina's character assassinations that start on one subject and then very rapidly segue into various things that you did when she could barely talk that she has been hanging on to for many, many years. Very few people recover from those.

'All right, calm down. I was only asking.'

'I know you were, sweetheart.' I can't help but get down and give my daughter a hug. That is the best part of this new reality. I give her more hugs, more time, more of the me who has been hidden under layers of worry, and the past and not feeling like I deserved to be out there in the world. Over her shoulder I see Tina sitting on the sea wall, her face turned up to the sun, her body relaxed and unburdened. That's how it should have been, and whether she's here for real or not, this is how I'm going to think of her from now on. Chilled, calm and free.

I'm free now, too.

Truly free.

And I get to spend all that freedom with the people I love.

serena

Now

'Surprise!' everyone cries when Evan and Conrad enter the living room.

Conrad, who knew all about it and who had taken his dad out to give us a chance to set the party up, actually jumps and looks genuinely 'surprised' while clutching his chest. 'Cool, everybody, thank you,' he says, looking around at our various gathered family and friends. 'Thank you.'

'Think the party's for me, son,' Evan says with a grin. He seeks me out in the crush of people I've managed to cram into our house. 'There's a fifty banner right above your head there.'

'Ahhh, right,' Conrad says, looking genuinely upset.

I go to my husband, slip my arms around him. 'I know you don't like surprise parties, but since you didn't get to celebrate properly last time, I thought we'd do it "our style" this time.'

'Thank you,' he replies, dropping a kiss on my lips. 'And thank you, everyone for coming here today. My apologies, first of all, for how Serena will have been in the run-up to today. I know what she will have been like and I can only say I appreciate each and every one of you for putting up with it.'

'Oi,' I say, needling his side.

'I'd like to say thank you to my family for being there for me, always. Conrad, Verity and Serena, I love you all. I'll come and talk to you all individually, but thank you for now, this feels so special.' He raises his glass and everyone in the room does the same. 'To special times with special people.'

Everyone cheers and drinks and begins to break up into smaller groups.

'My speech would have been well better than that,' Conrad says, giving his dad some serious side-eye.

Within minutes, Evan's favourite music pumps out through the house and the place is filled with happy energy and relaxed, loving vibes. After the last few months with police raids and dramatic revelations and arguments, I think the whole place needs this, it deserves this. I'm also happy that Medina and Faye and their partners and families could make it, as could my mum, who is upstairs having a lie-down. Evan's parents will be arriving later, no doubt to smile their disapproval at me, which they've been doing since we had that very brief split ten years ago.

'Come with me, young lady,' Evan says when the party is in full swing. We navigate our way around the people on the stairs, and make it to the upper floor without too much trouble. In the bathroom, Evan shuts and locks the door behind us. It's a moment of calm. Our lives have calmed down. Logan Carlisle is where he needs to be, although still unrepentant from everything I hear. Verity seems more fine than I could have anticipated. She accepted what I said about Logan actually loving her. She's said more than once that she can look back over their relationship and see where he was loving and kind and focused on her. She can believe he loved her and I think that is helping her to cope with the other times.

Jack Halnsley is on my mind a lot. I have only met him twice so far and he has been professional, if that's the word, about it. It's not completely unpleasant drinking coffee and chatting with him, but he makes it clear he's emotionally and sexually attracted to me and that's the only reason why he helped me, so I – and Evan – will be glad when it's all over.

When it's over, the reason why he is constantly on my mind might go away, too. What Jack Halnsley told Poppy . . . He didn't say it how we talked about. He said that his mother had made various slip-ups over the years that gave him the impression that she knew more about Marcus's death than she told anyone at the time. She'd been particularly unsettled and nervy when Poppy was released from prison, but he'd convinced himself it was nothing. Eventually, a couple of years ago, after a particularly bad bout of depression from his mother, she had started to confess something. He asked her outright and she broke down and told him everything. He said that Marlene had felt trapped at the time because she was scared of what would happen to her son if she went to prison, and now she is too scared of going to prison at her age because she won't leave alive.

The way he said those things . . . The detail and nuance, the easy way the words fitted together to make his explanation. I'd expected a little doubt, hesitancy on his part, but no. Everything he said sounded so *honest*. And I can't stop thinking about it. I can't stop thinking that maybe that is what actually happened. She did do it. That Jack's lie is true.

Evan pulls me towards him, jolting me out of my thoughts of Jack Halnsley and I slip my arms around his body

'Did I ever tell you how much you love me?' he says. Evan and I are back to being us. And I love that.

'No, I don't believe you ever did.'

'Oh, how remiss of me. Serena Gillmare, you love me so much, you can't imagine life without me.'

'That sounds about right.'

'And even though you love me so much, you are especially loving how hot I look right now. In fact, you're finding me so irresistibly hot, you're seriously contemplating taking off a couple of items of clothing and engaging in an extra-exciting, extra-fast quickie.' He pulls me closer so I can feel what he is thinking, even with a house full of people.

'Dream on, buddy.' I point to the right-hand wall. 'My mother is just there, on the other side of that wall, and of all her senses that have dulled over time, her hearing is not one of them.'

Evan's excitement wilts right there and then. He continues: 'But do you know you love me more than life itself? And you feel so lucky to have loved me for so long?'

'You know me so well, Evan.'

'Yes, I do. And I need you to know you've done the best you can to make sure everyone is all right.' He cups my face. 'And you can take the time to look after you now. Everything will be all right.'

He may or may not be correct about things working out all right, only time will tell. I have to try to accept that, I have to try to relax into life because there is nothing else I can do to control how things will turn out.

'Thank you, love of my life,' I reply. And I kiss him. Knowing that this kiss, this perfect kiss, will feel like it will last for ever.

verity

Now

'Knew you'd be up here,' Conrad says to me.

In recent years, our parents converted the loft to be a chill-out space with storage. There are sofas, a large screen projector, an old-fashioned record player, as well as a CD player. The best part of the space, though, is the roof. They have put in large windows that allow you to look straight up and stare at the sky. You can skate along the clouds and plunge yourself into the sea of stars. I'm reclined on the sofa staring up at the darkening sky, listening to the party as it plays around the house, waiting to get lost in the cosmos.

'Bit too much party for me right now,' I tell him.

My brother settles himself on the other sofa. 'Are you OK, though?' he asks. 'After your stint as a jailbird. Are you all right?'

'I am more than all right. I am great,' I tell him. That is a lie, but it is also true. I feel all right, fine, but at the same time, I don't feel fine. He doesn't need to know about the not-fine bit because that is manageable, that is what I am exploring and laying to rest in therapy.

'Me and the Brain's Trust are glad you're out.' Conrad nods sagely. 'We were plotting how to get you out. You don't want to know what some of them came up with. Just that they were thinking of you.'

'I'm not sure which I love more – the fact you lot like me enough to think about breaking me out of prison, or the fact you've just called yourselves the Brain's Trust. It's like I have finally, *finally*, been vindicated.'

'Why fight it?' he says. 'How's your mate, Howie?'

'I saw him earlier,' I reply. Almost every day Conrad asks about 'my mate, Howie'. I think it upsets him that my friend, a man like him, almost died because he was too ashamed to come forward about his abuse. 'He's almost completely healed. And he is proceeding with charges against Beccie, and the police are taking him seriously. I thought for a bit that he wouldn't do it, that he'd let her get away with it, but no. He's done it, he's doing it.'

'That's good. That's really good. But are you really all right, Vee? Some heavy stuff has gone down. You know you can tell me if you're not OK, right?'

'Yes, I know that, bruv.'

Conrad rapidly shakes his head. 'Nah, Vee, nah. That word ain't for you. You've crossed over to the old side recently. It'd be like Mum or Aunt Fez or Aunt Mez saying it. That word is not for you.'

'The brother giveth and then he taketh away,' I say. He completely ignores me cutting my eyes at him and shooting him a Grandma glower.

'When are you moving back to your flat?' he asks.

'I have no idea. I'm actually thinking of selling it. Not sure I can live there again.'

'Ahhh, no, don't do that. I'll move in instead.'

'Yeah right, and how are you affording that rent?'

'Man, you'd charge me rent?'

'Yes, sweetheart, if I can't use "bruv" you don't get rent-free living.'

'Right, let me get you another drink and we can start the negotiations for real.'

'Yeah, good luck with that one.'

Once I'm alone, shut up here by myself, I go back to staring out at the now almost-here night sky. The pinpricks of stars could be other universes, as far as I know. Each one of them could be the moment where a decision I've made has caused a quantum split, and created another universe. I have a theory that we all see the stars differently because they are our other universes, the other ways in which we exist in here and out there.

I close my eyes, try to get lost in the darkness behind my eyes. I keep trying to get lost out there, lost in here. And nothing works. Not really. I can't hide from my reality. I can't push myself into those multiverses when I live in this universe.

I think again about how fine I am, how sometimes not fine I am, but how I feel most days that things will work out. Now I have my mum back, truly back, and we talk and share and treat each other with the kindness and love we always had before Logan, I know, deep down, that I will be more than all right.

I run my hand over my stomach with my eyes still closed, thinking about consequences. Thinking about what I have to do.

And I have to do it soon. I have to tell Mum and Dad and Conrad that I'm pregnant.

THE END

Acknowledgements

One of the loveliest bits of the book writing process is this bit.
Thank you to . . .

My amazing family

My agents, Ant and James

My brilliant publishers (who are fully credited at the back)

Graham Bartlett and Victoria Schroter for the research help

My wonderful friends

My incredible MK2

You, the reader. Thank you for taking the time to buy my book.
I hope you enjoy it.

And, to splendid E & G always and forever.

Credits

Dorothy Koomson would like to thank everyone involved in the production of All My Lies Are True *(There are loads of fabulous people as you can see!)*

Editorial
Jennifer Doyle
Katie Sunley

Copy editor
Gillian Holmes

Proof reading
Sarah Coward

Audio
Hannah Cawse

Design
Yeti Lambregts

Production
Tina Paul

Marketing
Vicky Abbott
Jo Liddiard

Publicity
Emma Draude
Annabelle Wright

Sales
Becky Bader
Frances Doyle
Izzy Smith

Agents
Antony Harwood
James MacDonald Lockhart

Read on to find out more about

DOROTHY
KOOMSON

and her inspiration for the book

About The Book

All My Lies Are True is the sequel to my bestselling sixth novel, *The Ice Cream Girls*, that I didn't know I needed to write. Anyone who has followed me, read my books or been to any of my events will know that I have always said: 'I don't do sequels'. My reasoning was that I've already put my characters through too much, they do not need to go on another journey, down the path filled with thorns and rocks and boulders.

I meant it, too. I meant it right up until early 2019. I was preparing for *Tell Me Your Secret* to come out, I was thinking of the next book to write and I was thinking a lot about Serena and Poppy and what happened next. That's nothing unusual – a lot of my time is spent thinking about my characters and where they are now and how they would cope with the various things that are going on in the world.

However, what Serena and Poppy went through seemed to be popping up all around me: laws about coercive control were coming into force, and everyone seemed to be talking openly about the emotional and psychological elements to domestic abuse.

But I had to wonder if anything had really changed. While we all talked, exposed and examined the things that had previously dwelled and grown in whispered spaces, was anything really different? Were there actions to go with the words? Were we calling out the abuse when we saw it and creating safe spaces so those being abused could leave?

Not really, is the short answer. When I started exploring the idea of what life was like for those in abusive situations, I found that despite all the talking, very little had changed. And that, in part, was to do with the fact that those of us outside these relationships hadn't changed – we might be aware as bystanders, but we were still bystanders all the same. While disheartening, it wasn't that which tipped me over the edge into writing the continuation of Serena and Poppy's story.

What did was getting on an intercity train and sitting near a couple who were clearly having an argument.

The row was quiet and kept mostly private, but it was quite horrific to witness. The man very carefully and precisely took her apart with nothing more than calmly delivered words. He didn't swear, didn't call her names . . . he just spoke at her – she had no real chance to reply – and spoke at her, until she broke down and began to silently cry. On top of the triumphant look on his face as he sat there, pleased he'd got the reaction he wanted, the jolly way he handed the ticket inspector his ticket while his partner sat there trying to hide her tears was really quite chilling.

And all of us close enough to be witnesses did *nothing*.

We sat and listened and watched it all play out until they got off at their stop.

The thing is, while he'd been going on, I realised that I didn't know what I could do about this type of abuse. If he was physically hurting her, any one of us could have stepped in; if he was loud and sweary, we could have stepped in, but he wasn't. He was calmly violent and I had no tools to deal with that.

I offered the woman a look of solidarity as she left the train and she looked away, embarrassed that we'd all heard. And anyway, what would I have done if she'd mouthed 'help me'? How would I have helped? That was when I realised what *The Ice Cream Girls* sequel should be about: what it means to be a bystander in a loved one's abusive relationship.

Yes, we are all talking about the mechanics of abuse and coercive control nowadays, but what do we *do* about it? How *do* we handle the charmers and the manipulators? How do we know when it's time to step in and stop enabling the abuse?

All of those things and more are explored in this book. Poppy and Serena are out of their abusive relationship with Marcus, but the echoes of what happened still reverberate around them. Then there is Verity, Serena's daughter, and Logan, Poppy's brother. And there is the relationship between them where we are not sure if there is abuse, and if there is, which one is the abuser? Is it always as obvious as we seem to assume? Is it always the man who is the abuser and the woman who is the victim? When do we have to accept that a loved one is in an abusive relationship and try to help? When we tell our truths about our relationships and lives, do we also inadvertently lie as well?

I hope you enjoyed *All My Lies Are True*. I hope it helped to inspire you to maybe talk to your friend who is in a relationship you've got a nagging doubt about. I hope it encourages you to find out from the many professional support organisations out there how to talk to a loved one and what you can do to help. The information is out there and you can find it if you want to be more than a bystander.

Let me end this by saying that writing a sequel was hard. Much harder than I expected. I had so many worries: being authentic to the original story and the stories of the people I spoke to that time around; honouring the tales of the people whose stories helped shape this book; and being accurate when it comes to timelines and character narratives and plausibility. My goodness it was difficult. And wonderful. Because you should know by now that I love what I do. I love writing and telling stories and opening up new worlds.

That is my truth, no lies.

Dorothy Koomson

2020

Reading Group Questions

These reading group questions can be used to spark conversation and debate about the book.
WARNING: They may contain spoilers so don't read on from here if you haven't finished the book.

1. *'And I love you, Logan Carlisle.'*

   What was going through your mind when you found out Serena's daughter, Verity, was involved with Poppy's brother, Logan? Were you surprised?

2. *We stand staring at each other and wait for the sands of time to smother us.*

   'Hello, Poppy,' she eventually says.

   'Hello, Serena,' I reply.

   How shocked do you think Serena and Poppy were when they were brought back together? Did the author manage to convey the horror they both felt when they discovered Logan and Verity's homework?

3. *I don't want to whisk her out of here. She does belong in 1988, because, after all, she put herself there when she started sleeping with Poppy Carlisle's brother. My eyes continue to bore into her, glaring and staring until it's too much for her. She has to give in and turn to face me.*

Do you think Serena is unnecessarily harsh on Verity when the police arrive to search their house? Why?

4. *I march towards them. I want to swear at them. I want to unleash the full Prison Poppy on them so we will all know that I'm done now. I'm not going to play this game anymore. I'm not going to pander to their sensibilities.*

Why do you think Poppy tolerates being treated so badly by her parents for so long?

5. *'Add to that the fact that your mother is notorious, and you haven't a cat in hell's chance of this not going to trial.'*

When Verity was first arrested, were you surprised at how much her mother's reputation as an Ice Cream Girl was going to influence how she was treated?

6. *'This is so complex. So confusing. What do I do? What do I do?'*

When you were given both accounts of the months leading up to Logan being hurt, who did you instinctively believe – Verity or Logan? Why? How did you feel when you found out the truth?

7. *'I had to get strong to survive in prison,' she says eventually. 'If you don't get strong you get beaten down and basically eaten alive.'*

Serena hears from Poppy what life was like in prison and it scares her. What were you thinking at this point of the novel? Did you have any theories as to what might happen given the author often doesn't go for the 'Hollywood' ending?

8. *I nod in response and get into my car before I allow myself to cry, too.*

   Both Poppy and Serena are at breaking point towards the end of the novel. How has the author showed us the journey to this moment when they're both about to fall apart?

9. *We stare at each other, we wipe away tears and accept this is how the story and the legacy of The Ice Cream Girls ends.*

   Serena makes a huge sacrifice for Poppy at the end. Why do you think she does this? Was she right to? Would you make the same sacrifice?

10. *I can't hide from my reality. I can't push myself into those multiverses when I live in this universe.*

    Verity isn't where she thought she would end up at the beginning of the novel. Do you think the legacy of the Ice Cream Girls is really over, or will it continue with her?

Read your heart out...

Have you read them all?

THE CUPID EFFECT

Ceri D'Altroy has an extraordinary talent for making people
follow their heart, with occasionally outrageous
consequences! But will it ever be Ceri's turn to find love?

'Colourful characters and witty writing' *Heat*

THE CHOCOLATE RUN

When Amber Salpone has a one-night stand with
her friend Greg Walterson, neither of them are prepared
for the trouble it will cause in both their lives.

**'A fantastic blend of love, friendship and
laughs'** *Company*

MY BEST FRIEND'S GIRL

Best friends Kamryn and Adele thought nothing could come between them – until Adele did the unthinkable. Years later Adele needs Kamryn's help. Will Kamryn be able to forgive her before it's too late?

'Both funny and moving, this will have you reaching for the tissues . . . A heart-breaking tale' *Closer*

MARSHMALLOWS FOR BREAKFAST

Kendra Tamale has a painful secret, one she swore she had put behind her. But can she build a future without confessing the mistakes of her past?

'So darn good that we had to read it all in one evening – ★★★★★' *Heat*

GOODNIGHT, BEAUTIFUL

Eight years ago, when Nova agreed to be a surrogate for her best friend and his wife, she had no idea things would go so drastically wrong. Now, faced with tragedy, can they reconnect before it's too late?

'Irresistibly complicated' *Red*

THE
ICE CREAM GIRLS

As teenagers Poppy and Serena were known as the Ice Cream Girls and thought to have committed murder. After twenty years leading separate lives, they are about to be forced together once again. Will they both survive?

'Incredibly gripping' *Now*

THE WOMAN
HE LOVED BEFORE

How Jack's first wife died has always been a mystery to Libby, but when she almost dies in an 'accident', Libby starts to worry that she will end up like the first woman Jack loved . . .

'It had us all gripped from start to finish' *Woman*

THE
ROSE PETAL BEACH

When Tamia's husband is accused of something terrible, she doesn't think things can get any worse — until she finds out who has accused him. Someone is lying — but who?

'Pacy and compelling, the twists and turns come thick and fast' *Heat*

THAT DAY
YOU LEFT

The murder of her husband leaves Saffron grieving and alone. But no one knows what she did to protect her family. Now, as secrets threaten to reveal themselves, is she prepared to do it again?

'Combines romance with dark themes, and has a surprising twist' *Sunday Mirror*

TELL ME YOUR SECRET

Ten years ago, Pieta was kidnapped by a man calling himself The Blindfolder and she was too afraid to tell anyone. But when he starts hunting down his past victims, Pieta realises she may be forced to tell her deepest secrets to stay alive . . .

'A totally addictive, can't put down, rollercoaster ride of a story' Araminta Hall

Available now in paperback, ebook and audio

REVIEW

The brand new novel from

DOROTHY
KOOMSON

I KNOW WHAT YOU'VE DONE

Are your neighbours spying
on you?

Coming July 2021

REVIEW

All About

DOROTHY
KOOMSON

Dorothy Koomson is still trying to come up with something interesting for this bit of the book. In case you didn't know: she wrote her first, unpublished novel when she was thirteen and she's been making up stories ever since. Her third novel, *My Best Friend's Girl*, was chosen for the Richard & Judy Book Club Summer Reads of 2006, and reached number two on the *Sunday Times* Bestseller List.

Her books *The Ice Cream Girls* and *The Rose Petal Beach* were shortlisted for the National Book Awards and a TV adaptation loosely based on *The Ice Cream Girls* appeared on ITV in 2013.

Dorothy has won awards, had most of her books on the *Sunday Times* Bestseller List and is currently working on her seventeenth book. *All My Lies Are True* is the long-awaited sequel to *The Ice Cream Girls* that Dorothy never thought she'd write.

Dorothy has lived and worked in Leeds, London and Sydney, Australia, and is currently residing in Brighton on the South Coast.

Get in Touch

To find out more about me and my books,
as well as writing tips and more,
take a look at my website here:

www.dorothykoomson.co.uk

You can also sign up to my newsletter to
make sure you're the first to hear about what
I'm up to next.

You can also keep in touch by following me on:

@DorothyKoomson

@DorothyKoomsonWriter

and

@dorothykoomson_author

I'd love to hear from you!